MARCH THE NINTH

In high summer the Adriatic reflects the sun so fiercely that to live on its shores is like living in t
lamps.
of the
longer
such a
defines
parade ...., for eyes accustomed to a soberer sky, the scene has a constant theatricality: that monument, that balcony, cannot be wholly real if it shows so solidly when you know it is a minute's walk away.

I was sitting by myself in the Piazza dell' Unita when I heard the sound of shots from somewhere in the direction of the Cathedral. The first report might have been a tyre bursting, but you do not expect three tyres to burst in quick succession. I imagined, too, that through the noise of traffic I heard excited shouting. Almost at once a toylike armoured car ran across the far side of the square and an ambulance followed shortly after.

Nothing in this concerned me: it simply took its place in the spectacle which occupied my hours of idleness every day. Here, in 1947, the flutterings of an underlying restlessness were a part of normality . . .

MARCH THE NINTH

NINTH

R.C. Hutchinson

A Zenith Book

Published by Arrow Books Limited
17–21 Conway Street, London W1P 6JD

An imprint of the Hutchinson Publishing Group

London Melbourne Sydney Auckland
Johannesburg and agencies throughout
the world

First published in Great Britain 1957 by Geoffrey Bles
This paperback edition 1984

Reproduced, printed and bound in Great Britain by
Hazell Watson & Viney Limited,
Member of the BPCC Group,
Aylesbury, Bucks

ISBN 0 09 933760 6

For
M.J.R.H.

Chapter 1

THERE WAS A short period in my life which I remember as a piece taken out of it. Though I had friends then, and enough occupation to amuse me, there was no one to fill for me that central part of the mind which, in a human creature, the largest egotism leaves unfurnished.

At the farther end of that gap is the recollection of my mother, in her small bed in the apartment I rented at New Haven, lying with her exquisite hands crossed outside the bedclothes, awaiting the embrace of death with perfect composure. Dying, I had almost said, radiantly; so unembittered by the earlier indignities and suffering, so much a mistress of this as of every other situation; the set of her weakened eyes still revealing that refinement of intellect which I always credited to her small portion of Jewish blood, the courage of her delicate mouth manifesting to the last the Catholic soldier. That picture is as vivid and exact as a Rembrandt engraving. It is fixed in time. At the other end there is no such easy landmark, for the image which came to take possession of me seems to emerge stealthily from a confusion of experience. One may say, 'On such a day I heard for the first time Mozart's *G Minor Symphony*.' But I cannot point exactly to the time when Franziska's beauty had so worked in me that I saw my own existence as meaningless apart from hers.

Childishly, I have often imagined that it was an influence mysteriously deriving from her which brought me back to Europe. The more prosaic truth is that after my mother's death I found myself forlorn and restless in New Haven, much as I liked my work there at the School of Medicine. I felt like travelling again, and when I saw the chance of travelling at others' expense I seized it with both hands.

Chapter 2

I

IN HIGH SUMMER the Adriatic reflects the sun so fiercely that to live on its shores is like living in the glare of arc-lamps. By mid-September the quality of the light has altered, you are no longer bemused by its violence; but in such a city as Trieste its brilliance still defines so sharply the detail of the high, paraded houses that, for eyes accustomed to a soberer sky, the scene has a constant theatricality: that monument, that balcony, cannot be wholly real if it shows so solidly when you know it is a minute's walk away.

I was sitting by myself in the Piazza dell' Unita when I heard the sound of shots from somewhere in the direction of the Cathedral. The first report might have been a tyre bursting, but you do not expect three tyres to burst in quick succession. I imagined, too, that through the noise of traffic I heard excited shouting. Almost at once a toylike armoured car ran across the far side of the square and an ambulance followed shortly after.

Nothing in this concerned me: it simply took its place in the spectacle which occupied my hours of idleness every day. Here, in 1947, the flutterings of an underlying restlessness were a part of normality. No one was gratified by the settlement at Paris, for while justice demanded that the Italians, who had largely made Trieste, should now possess it, the common sense of geography insisted that it was part of Tito's Republic; so, with the prize withdrawn from competition, it was natural that patriots of one complexion or another should still gather at street corners, that a flag or two should be torn from the roofs of municipal buildings, that now and then a home-made bomb should explode, wounding some minor bureaucrat and engendering a scurry of policemen. I should scarcely have remembered this particular disturbance of my siesta if a man sitting at a table close to mine had not, at the second shot, put down his newspaper and walked off rather quickly in the direction of the harbour. I caught sight of this man's face as he passed me and I recognized it instantly, though I had not seen him for some fifteen years.

I thought he recognized me as well; and had I been a genuine American—such as Dollis Andersen, the head of my Section—I should have called out "Kurt!" and plunged into a boisterous reunion. But experience alters a man's intuitive behaviour. Once you have lived for even a short time where any former acquaintance may betray you— once you have learnt to watch your words, to disguise your voice on the telephone—you will scarcely recover the confident habits of freedom. I hesitated. Probably the instinct which restrained me had restrained Kurt as well. With a faint amusement I watched him moving with the gait I so well remembered, a woman's walk, short-paced and sinuous, until he was lost in a stream of people moving towards the quays.

The picture has stayed in my mind impressionistically— the slight, round-shouldered figure, a black homburg and a swinging brief-case, against the shuttling polychrome of pavement traffic, a file of tired, urban trees, the high bluff of Venetian houses transfixed in the flooding sun. The significance I attach to that incident must be purely retrospective: I cannot have thought it likely, then, that I should meet the man again, much less have foreseen the double life I should be involved in by a second meeting. And yet I believe that this glimpse of an old friend brought nearer to the surface a current of sentiments which I had previously been able to suppress. I had tried, since the early forties, to persuade myself that the European in me was dying, was dead. Arriving here, catching once more the smell of Europe, the feel of its age and untidiness, I had seemed to see it with transformed and alien eyes. But that, in the end, was self-deception. One sight of Kurt's face, recalling in an instant the music of summer evenings in the Wiener Wald, the laughter and bustling freedom of Franzensring, was enough to puncture my pretences: this continent had nursed me, and the bonds of its maternity were not yet broken.

2

'The double life': that term, belonging to the *feuilletons*, has moral overtones which disturb me. But why? Is there a single life for anyone to lead? You, in your relations with other people—with your own family—do you not consistently disguise yourself? Could you, if you would, present to the world the delicate and infinitely ramified complex of memory and emotion in which you find your own identity?

Be that as it may, I had slipped already into a dual existence some time before Kurt Wenzel's appearance. And for this I was hardly to blame. The fortunate live long lives in corners which history does not discover. We others, caught when history is in spate, can do no better than keep afloat and land where the current takes us. In Trieste, in working hours, I was—as nearly as I could make myself— a pattern of American good sense and science, American decorum. I spoke to those who came to the office with the best imitation I could achieve of that pleasant, regulated informality which to my colleagues was first nature and the essence of their charm. I dressed with exact attention to appropriate carelessness, I treated files of useless data as Holy Writ. Was it my fault if heart and intellect remained aloof from such scrupulous performance?

If Dollis Andersen had had his way, I should have spent my evenings in a pattern of similar virtue. He wished our Section to live together in the Mess which occupied the first floor of the Isonzo Hotel: by that means we should get to know each other better, we should 'share ideas and maybe fix a lot of problems' in an easy, sociable way. Poor Dollis—I think there was a morbid element in his nostalgia: he needed men of his own tongue about him, for fear some foreigner should offer to cut his throat and he should make the wrong reply. At least he believed, with a mysticism that may have come from his Anglo-Saxon strain, that some excellent result must always emerge from the herding of good men together. It grieved me to disoblige him, for he had my deep respect. In his natural state he taught political economy at some university in Wisconsin: I never knew a more serious or honest man. But I could not spend all my waking hours in the odour of good-fellowship and coca-cola. I found in an inland suburb an unpretentious family of Serbs who knew the meaning of *cuisine*, and I lived with them.

It was agreeable to be among the privileged. From my office window high above the Via del Campanile I used to look down at the crowded pavements, at the men loading barges on the Grand Canal, and contemplate my own good fortune. While those people swarmed and laboured as ants do for a bare livelihood, in equal anonymity, I, high and lifted up, threatened neither by police nor by hunger, had only to read some dreary letters, to dictate memoranda, and all my bodily needs were amply provided. Perversely, I was not quite satisfied. One needs, among other things, reality. The voices that sometimes reached me through the uproar of motor horns and engines, a burst of argument, the flutter of a girl's gay dress, these would suddenly remind me with a curious poignancy of a time when I had shared existence with creatures of my own kind.

With the summer's passing we became very slack.

Earlier, when people thought we were laden with the corn of Egypt and could work any miracle to order, they had besieged us all day long. Now there were few who believed us capable of any service. The flood of paper never abated, but it seemed to have less and less significance. Our voices sounded along the corridors like those of ushers in a concert hall when the last of the audience is departing.

On a Friday—the last, I think, in September—I was moved by idleness and *accidie* to ask, "Mr. Andersen, would it matter if I didn't come in tomorrow?"

"Why, no, Doctor, surely!" he said. And then, because his official conscience never gave him a moment's peace, he added, "Your work's up to date, I guess?"

I answered, foolishly, that there wasn't any. Nothing, at least, that mattered.

"You've done the consolidation of the August nutritional reports?"

"No, I'm waiting for Derocque's. That's not likely to be to be in before Tuesday."

"That French guy's an idle bastard!" Dollis said.

He was sitting on my table, swinging his fine, ball-player's legs and frowning anxiously through his high-powered spectacles. Privately, I think, he saw us all as idle bastards. And I realized acutely just then how much it troubled him to have a subordinate who had been born eight years before himself, and nowhere near Wisconsin.

"Of course," I said, "if you'd rather I came in——"

"Hell, no! You can do with a vacation—set you up for next week. Things will be warming up next week, I guess."

That was sheer hallucination. He must have known at least as well as I that we were virtually a rear party engaged in winding up the organization. But perhaps he believed what he said, for he had great faith in the world's essential excellence, and a good world, for him, was one in which virtuous men produce more memoranda every day. At least he had found an ethical formula to solve the immediate problem: I needed building up, therefore it was right that I should spend a salaried day idling elsewhere than at my desk.

"But, Eugen, what are you going to do?" he persisted, still eyeing me with maternal solicitude. "You can't go out of the Free Territory unless we get you special documentation, and there's no place much to go in this dump."

No place to go? Nothing to see in the Revoltella? Nothing to wonder at in San Giusto?

"I might do some fishing," I said, "or else I shall just eat and drink." Leaving him, dear fellow, to imagine that I should spend the week-end in a gloomy perambulation from one disorderly house to the next.

In truth, I had made no plans. But these, in the event, were made for me. For as, on my way home, I dawdled along the Corso, I had the sensation (familiar to me from the memory of 1938) of being followed; and further on, when I stopped to look at a shop window, I found that Kurt Wenzel was beside me again.

3

It was his reflection in the window glass that I saw, while he glanced at mine. Again we both went through a moment of indecision. Then, without speaking, he walked on towards the Old Town.

Now it was my turn to follow, and this was easy, for he kept loitering as a child does who has coaxed a grown-up into the game of pursuit. He led me in that way into one of the narrow streets which wind steeply towards the Castle, and presently, mounting a short flight of steps, entered a shabby delicatessen store. I waited for a while, then followed him again. The shop was empty, but the door at the other end had *Ristorante* chalked on it, and passing through I found myself in a room with several tables. Kurt was already seated in the far corner, with a copy of *Praznik* spread before him.

In this room most of the space was taken by a single party of Italians, four or five young working men and as many girls, all firing their voices like light machine-guns, kissing, slapping and gesticulating in the manner of their kind. It was safe to presume that their interests were not political. The slightly superior couple in the corner opposite Kurt's had the look and manner of Slovenes: that was immaterial —they were stupefied with love. I realized as I made my way to the table next the one Kurt had chosen that a greater privacy could scarcely have been found in all Trieste.

There seemed, then, to be no need for further caution. But I kept my voice low as I asked, leaning over to light my cigarette from his,

"Do we know each other nowadays?"

He smiled, gazing at the Italians.

"That's for you to say, my dear Eugen. It appears to me that you've gone up in the world, you look highly respectable. I should have thought you'd do much better to keep away from people like myself."

His voice had scarcely changed: it was the finished voice of Vienna, soft, liquid, a delicate pattern of shadow and light.

"Then why did you follow me all along the Corso?" I demanded.

"Why—because I have an incurable love of beauty. When I see a man whose classic features reveal a rare nobility of mind and spirit, I find myself drawn towards him as if by polar attraction."

"Exactly," I said, "—but at the moment I'm rather short of money."

"Money?" He turned his expressive hands outwards. "Money is out of fashion, I lost all interest in it years ago."

"Including the hundred schillings you borrowed from me in the Marburger-Konditorei in 1931?"

"Those I have never touched—I treasure them as a souvenir. Tell me about yourself, dear friend."

"Me? I am now an American. *Heil Truman!*"

"*Sieg heil!* Excellent! Let me congratulate you! Yes yes, I can see that you are splendidly dressed, and your manners improved beyond measure. An American? Fabulous! I shall ask you presently for a job on one of your newspapers."

"My newspapers?"

"You don't tell me that you are not the owner of several newspapers! Or do you specialize in oil-wells? Don't say you have not even a railroad!"

"I'm working," I told him, "at an extremely moderate salary, for one of the least important branches of the World Universities Relief Organization. Health and Nutritional Co-ordination, to be exact."

"As a surgeon?"

"Certainly not—I am no longer a tradesman! I consider questions of Policy, I correlate statistical data, I seek for Broad Solutions."

"I apologize . . . Yes, I always wondered what had become of you. I heard—when was it?—I heard you were no longer in Vienna. You—you got bored with Vienna?'

"A little—when the Decorator came. My father—you may remember—had befriended Engelbert Dollfuss in his early days. I felt that that might be held against me. And then my mother's ancestry was not wholly Nordic."

He nodded sadly. "Indeed? I confess that I attach the greatest importance to racial purity, though nowadays it is hard to come by. I am myself a rarity, perhaps—I am of pure German stock, going back for nine generations."

It would have needed some research to dispose of that statement as it deserved. Undoubtedly some part of his

16

ancestry was Jewish—how much I did not know. He came from Zemplen, he may have been Polish as well as Hungarian on one side—certainly the cast of his features was predominantly Slav. Probably he had some Turkish, possibly some Spanish blood. If there had been a single undiluted Teuton among his forebears the incidence was casual and remote.

"So you were *persona grata* with the new régime?" I said.

"Well, a lawyer is always useful."

"Even when law has ceased to operate?"

"But of course! Law is a codification of morality, and when existing laws are abrogated men need to be supplied with new ones as they go along. The Germans are a passion-ately moral people, they are always looking for some ethical justification of whatever they have it in mind to do. They feel the need for a sympathetic lawyer just as other men, when they have overeaten, feel the need for a kindly doctor."

"So all these years your real concern has been with morality?"

"Not in the particular sense that you would give to that word. Morality, as you understand it, is one of the graces of life, like art. And like art, it is a luxury to be forsworn in times of crisis—men have more important things to think of then. Still, there are always little helpful actions open to people of goodwill and intelligence. One may tell Herr Hauptmann X, in a friendly and confidential way, that his superior officers have been talking disapprovingly of some private enterprise in commandeering he has been engaged in. This may not be the strict truth, but it exercises a restraining influence on Herr Hauptmann X, and at the same time wins his gratitude. In a hundred little affairs like that a legalistic conscience would be nothing but a hindrance."

"And now?" I asked. "You have some appointment in Trieste?"

"Appointment? Not exactly." He frowned with concentration, and then, finding the desirable word, smiled again. "You might call me a general agent. I try to perform small services for all kinds of people."

"At twenty-two-and-a-half per cent?"

"I have many friends in all walks of life," he continued, ignoring my vulgarity. "Often I can bring them in touch with each other and sometimes such contacts prove extremely helpful."

I should have known by then, if it had not occurred to me before, that he had not taken so much trouble to promote this meeting for the sake of my *beaux yeux*. Unobtrusively he had now become my host: an old man in slippers had arrived, apparently unbidden, with a bottle of Asti Spumante, somehow I had before me the confection of eggs, shellfish and spiced spaghetti which is a classic of Venetian cooking. It was clear that I should presently be put to use.

But already I was under a familiar spell. Now, as in our earlier days, Kurt Wenzel was far from handsome. His skin had always looked unhealthy, his head was much too large for his chestless body—one could imagine that in childhood he had been fed without intelligence, so that all the nourishment had gone to his face and neck. Even his eyes, to speak aesthetically, were poorly made—the thick root of his nose kept them too far apart, the whites were flecked and dull. Yet to these eyes his ranging intellect had given a vitality which no one could resist. As a student he had charmed me with his lawless wit—one hunted for him in the cafés, certain of delight from the dulcet Viennese ridicule which he poured incessantly on Vienna's solemnities; and now it seemed to me that the years had only subtilized the flavours of his mind, ripening its humanism without the smallest injury to its independence. Here was a European, a connoisseur of the human comedy; one who took you, as it were, to a point of vantage, whispering, 'Yes, life is a bewildering and grievous thing to be involved in, but let us for the present examine it from the outside. Is it not a curious and amusing exhibition!' In this he had no virtue to show. But virtue was available elsewhere. At New Haven it had been in generous supply.

Strangely, it was the moral weapon which he presently used to get his way with me.

We had been together for perhaps an hour, talking of old adventures, recalling half-forgotten friends, and my hold on reality was weakening. Wine does not much affect me, but the atmosphere of the room was close, and the raucous chatter of the Italians, seeming to advance like a barrage, numbed my faculties. As I listened with a slackened sense of time and place to the allegro music of Kurt's voice, I forgot I was a man of some position and obligations: the fears and darkness in which my life in Vienna had ended, these took the semblance of illusion, while the richness of those earlier days, their zest, their irresponsibility, returned with almost the persuasion of actuality. That was my mood—I can only guess how deliberately he induced it—when Kurt said, on a note of melancholy,

"Ah, but they have all gone, those people! Some of them are dead, and the rest, if we met them now, we should hardly know them. At twenty a man is an individual, he is ready to fight the world single-handed with his own ideas, his own beliefs. At thirty his individuality has vanished—by then he has become a banker, or the adjutant in some tedious regiment, a churchgoing man, worst of all, a husband. The world has caught him, he is part of its machinery, his cogs must be reshaped to fit the other cogs exactly. In a word, the original man is dead."

"And me?" I inevitably asked. "I am still unmarried— but I am thirty-five . . ."

"Alas, my dear Eugen, you also are a good deal changed."

"What—am I starting a double chin? I should say my belly has kept its shape better than yours."

19

"Indeed, yes, and if that is the shape you admire you have every reason to be satisfied." He raised his eyes to my face, smiling wickedly. "Shall I be most unkind if I give you a portrait of yourself as a young man? When you were young you were charming—as of course you are now. You were gay, you talked a great deal, you pursued young women, you were indefatigable in exploring all the thousand delicious ways which Vienna provided for students to waste their time. But you had your serious side. You used to say, 'No, Kurt, tonight I shall not go out with you, tonight I must work, a man who fails his examinations has no right to the pleasures of this place—he is nothing but a parasite!' And then when you were just a little drunk you used to talk about the nobility of your chosen profession. You had dedicated yourself to a life of healing. You were going to perform miraculous operations on the wealthy, money would flow into your pocket and you would then exercise your gifts upon the poor of Vienna for nothing. 'I shall consider myself,' you said, 'a servant of humanity'."

"Really, was I such a prig! Had I so little originality!"

"A prig? No, not really. You were simply saying what was in your heart. In those days you were in love with all your fellow-men, you genuinely wished to serve them."

"Perhaps!" I said. "But history intervened."

"Not only history! The law of growth, the gradual decay of a man's pristine idealism, these things have intervened as well. What are you today? A person of extreme respectability. You've told me yourself—you sit in an office, you attend committees, you draw a comfortable salary. If you were asked to perform an operation this evening you'd be frightened out of your wits. You wouldn't remember how to begin."

Here I was able to contradict him: "As it happens, I've taken pains to keep my hand in. Although my principal work was teaching, I was operating right up till the time I left the States—that was in April. If you happened to be

20

suffering from diverticulitis I could perform a colostomy straight away, with a bandage round my eyes."

He blinked benignly. "Well, that is a most courteous offer! It would give me the greatest pleasure to witness such a demonstration of your skill. But since your tools, I suppose, are still in America, I am denied that fascinating opportunity. Or did you think of cutting me up with this knife and fork here?"

"No, that might antagonize the proprietor. No—believe it or not—I carry my tools about with me, like a hairdresser doing his military service."

"What, your pockets are full of scalpels?"

"Again, no! But I have a case of surgical instruments and other necessaries at my lodgings."

"Then let me tell you, with the keenest disappointment, that I have never been so free from diverticulitis in all my life."

For a short space I thought, in my innocence, that the subject was closed; and I felt a modest satisfaction in having scored a winning point in debate. He continued, however, to mock me for the loss of my ideals—amiably, but not without effect. And before long he was attacking from a new position.

"Tell me, dear friend—if you wanted to do some work as a surgeon, here in Trieste, you would need to get permission from your excellent employers?"

"Theoretically," I answered, "yes. But in fact I shouldn't dream of asking anyone."

"So if someone offered you a very large fee——"

"I shouldn't take it! I'm not here to enrich myself."

"Then—what would persuade you?"

"Necessity," I said. "If I heard of an operation that needed urgently to be performed—and supposing no other competent surgeon were free to do it—then I should certainly offer my services."

That was the utterance of a fool.

With instinctive artistry, Kurt waited for a little before closing the trap. He talked for a while of surgery in general, obliquely flattering me, before he said,

"I forget if you knew the Schwarzenbergs—the ones who used to live in Maximilianstrasse? No? I thought you might—they kept open house for nearly everyone, even for young men like myself. Enchanting people, so unpretentious. Of course they came from a cadet branch, there was nothing political or military about them."

"Why do you ask?"

"Only because I've been having some dealings with Ludwig Schwarzenberg—he's a cousin of theirs, I thought you might have met him. Your kind of man—you would like him very much."

I tried to get one jump ahead by asking, "And is he in need of an operation?"

"Ludwig? Great God, no—I never knew a man in such robust health. But it's curious that you should ask that, because he has a friend staying with him who seems to be in a bad way. A Swiss, I think he said."

"Indeed. And is the Schwarzenberg living in Trieste?"

"A little way outside."

"Then no doubt his friend is getting treatment from one of the admirable doctors who practise hereabouts. If not, my own advice would be to have him moved to the Carmelite hospital in Via Coroneo, where the nursing is excellent."

Kurt shook his head. "Unfortunately, no—the man's in too serious a condition to be moved."

"What's wrong with him?"

"A chest wound, a bad one. He was out shooting, and he had some accident with his gun. I believe a cartridge exploded before the breech was closed—but I don't understand these technicalities."

"Well, no doubt your friend's regular doctor is doing what is necessary."

"There are certain difficulties," Kurt said.

Difficulties—I was not surprised to hear—of a legal nature. The Swiss was travelling without proper papers. Why? Because he had left Switzerland rather hurriedly. Again, why? Well, he was a director of several companies in Basel, an incompetent accountant had led him into transactions which proved to be technically illegal—it was something that might happen to anyone . . . I almost accepted this. I almost believed—such was Kurt Wenzel's urbanity, his power of persuasion—that only business men of pitiful conservatism and gross timidity avoided a periodical prosecution for fraud.

"In other words," I said, "the man's a rogue and is in hiding."

"In a sense, he is, as you say, in hiding."

"And you think the first doctor who sees him will send a report to the local police?"

"Do you think any ordinary citizen could afford *not* to, in these days? Have you forgotten what our world in Europe is like?"

I had not. Neither had I forgotten that I carried an American passport, that I was immeasurably beholden to American kindness, that I had signed a specific undertaking not to meddle with anything which might possibly have a political complexion. I said, rising,

"Kurt, I am truly sorry that I can't help you in this matter. And now I must thank you for a delicious dinner—it has been delightful to meet you again."

He rose as well, smiling.

"Well, yes, to tell the truth I knew all along that that would be your answer. I saw—well, I've told you—I saw that you had changed."

"You may be right."

"Surely there's no doubt about it! The Eugen Reichenbach I once knew would have said, 'If a man is dying, if I have a chance to save his life, then no other circumstances

23

are worth a moment's consideration.' Well, there it is—it would be something outside nature if I'd found you with all your old knight-errantry. . . . But I've enjoyed it so much, this meeting—in some ways it has been like old times."

He stood holding my hand affectionately in both of his, and I thought I saw tears in his eyes. I remember noticing how shabby his black coat was and now, suddenly, he looked tired and old and defeated. In that moment my own feeling for the rascal was something not far from affection.

"I shall stay here a few minutes more," he said. "It might be not too good for you, to be seen in the street with me. But look—here's my telephone number. At some time I might be of use to you—one can never tell. You would have to ask for Dragutin—in Trieste, as you know, it's the fashion to vary one's name a little. . . . What? Oh, non-sense, my dear fellow—why, you came here practically at my invitation, and all the pleasure has been mine!"

4

No, I was never in reality a selfless doctor, if such a thing there be. I enjoyed my profession at least partly for its own sake, as any other craftsman does. Since my appointment at Yale was awarded me on my merits, it is not perhaps too boastful to say that I have been a surgeon of some skill. My mother was a 'cellist of distinction, and I claim most fortunately to have inherited her hands. Then, again, my father had infinite powers of concentration upon any subject which captured his interest. That capacity I believe may also have descended to me.

So when, back in my lodging, I opened my surgical case and handled the instruments, my thoughts were not as altruistic as they should have been. I was—let me confess—like a musician who has been kept for some time away from his pianoforte or his violin. My hands, so to say, cried out against me for leaving them so long in idleness.

But Wenzel's words, contrived and sentimental as they were, had not been without their effect on me. The disreputable foundation of his story I could only conjecture, but its centre-piece was outside the realm of argument: a man deprived of medical aid was sick and likely to die. I thought how my mother, on the very eve of our escape from Vienna, had risked arrest and the horrors that would follow by going to visit an acquaintance who was dying; and if that was her conception of duty—she who had nothing to give the sick except her tenderness—could I, who had solemnly dedicated my life to healing, turn my back on such an appeal as this! It was easy to argue that my fixed obligations exempted me from doing what Kurt had asked; but that respectable thesis stood only limply beside the picture which my mind was insistently conjuring, of a human creature in the pain and weakness of which I knew the lineaments so well, cut off in his extremity from the allies on which civilized man has learnt to depend. As I stood at the window of my attic bedroom, looking across the city's roofs to the lights that were appearing out at sea, I became convinced that if I took refuge in a legal scruple from the deeper responsibility the memory of this cowardice would haunt me always.

I walked very slowly to a café at the end of the street where one could telephone, and there I called the number Kurt had given me. He himself answered.

"Kurt, I've changed my mind!" I said. "I'm willing to have a look at your Swiss friend and see if there's anything I can do for him. But if it's a case of operating I shall probably need an anæsthetist."

"I've thought of that," he said at once. "That can be managed."

"Very well then! Tell me where your friend lives."

"It's a house you wouldn't very easily find. But listen—that's no problem, I'll arrange everything. If you will kindly go to Via Giolitti—you know it? behind the old fish market, it's only a little street—there's an office I use there, next door to the Farmacia Antitche. I'll have a car for you there."

"Yes, but there are one or two things I want to get straight. .... Kurt—are you there?"

No. Silence. I went back to my lodgings and checked over my portable equipment: morphia, tubes, syringe ...

Chapter 3

I

I NEVER DOUBTED that every action in Kurt's life had money as its ultimate objective. But I think such men have in them a poetic vein which makes the circuitous means no less enjoyable than the financial end. That was in my mind when the taxi put me down in Via Giolitti, for Kurt's description of the rendezvous proved now to have the vagueness of romantic poetry. The Farmacia Antitche was an easy landmark, but the tidy door with the name of some firm or partnership which I expected to find beside it did not exist. On one side was the long rear wall of some workshop, on the other the entrance to what looked like a builder's yard. The shop itself was closed, there was no car standing in the street.

A square of light, however, guided me across the yard to a timber shed, and after some hesitation I looked inside. This, indeed, might have been called an office, for the trestle-table at one end was littered with papers, and a typewriter stood on the floor beside it. On a bench opposite the door three or four people of the labouring class were sitting in the attitude of despondent apathy which one associates with the out-patients' department of a hospital.

I asked at large, "Is this Dragutin's office, please?" and the woman who sat nearest the door nodded.

That was done with only one swift upward glance, but it gave me a glimpse of her face which, even in the poor light from a dim bulb hanging over the table, caught my attention. Although she wore a black cotton shawl over her head, as any peasant woman might, she was certainly not of

27

peasant standing. This face, of a woman in early middle age, was one of physical refinement, the white skin free of blemishes, the features nobly cut—the sexless face, I thought for an instant, of a prioress, with the eyes' intensity, the decision of the small mouth and chin. But even the severity one may see in the features of a true Religious will suggest a latent charity, and I could imagine no charity here. Politeness forbade me to take a second look. But as I stood—since there was no space left on the bench—with my back against one wall and my eyes drearily exploring the other, I could feel that I myself was being covertly scrutinized.

In this situation the quixotic impulse which had brought me rapidly faded. The air was insufferably close, I sweated, I was wretchedly conscious of my bourgeois clothes. In five minutes I might well have retreated. But I did not have to wait so long. A car stopped out in the street, a young, too-smartly dressed Italian came in with two other men behind him. He said, "Dr. Reichenbach? . . . Ricotti!" and enthusiastically shook my hand.

"This is Dr. Babitch," he continued, and then, switching effortlessly into Serbo-Croat, "Dr. Babitch, it is a great privilege for me to present you to Dr. Reichenbach—his name, of course, you must know very well, he is one of the half-dozen leading surgeons in New York and his reputation in Europe is also unequalled."

"Indeed, yes!" Dr. Babitch answered. "I consider, sir, that I am very greatly privileged. I have been associated, in my time, with many distinguished surgeons, but this is the opportunity to which, throughout the whole of my life, I have been most keenly looking forward."

In this courteous avowal I detected some imprecision: at a rough estimation the man must have been living for forty years before I was conceived. But since fame is agreeable to nonentities I did not contradict him. A fine man he was, a Serb, something over six feet in height even with the slightly bent shoulders; athletically thin, his skin burnt to leather by sun and wind. His grey hair was as thick as a boy's, and to his remarkably handsome face the grey down on the cheek-bones gave a further dignity, while in his very light blue eyes I saw such a bravery and kindness as are not found often in the eyes of men or women.

"For myself," he told me, "I make no claim of any kind, except that I am adaptable. Yes, sir—and that is perhaps a rarer quality today than in times gone by. What does your young doctor say nowadays? He says, 'Build me a surgery, build me a theatre, build me a hospital costing half a million lire, then I will treat the case.' Now I myself, on the other hand——"

"Exactly!" said Ricotti. "Everything Dr. Babitch says is true—you couldn't ask, Dr. Reichenbach, for a finer assistant." He laid one hand on Babitch's shoulder, one on mine. "It is an event for me, a famous event, to have introduced two remarkable doctors to each other." And then, turning to the other man, "Vlado! Go and get my case out of the car . . . This is an occasion, gentlemen, which we ought to celebrate. We shall drink to the success of your united mission, and Fräulein Kern, I hope, will join us."

He smiled towards the woman on the bench, but her only return was a little bow.

"Ah, forgive me!" he said, "I forgot that I had not presented Dr. Reichenbach to you. I have the honour, Doctor, to present you to Fräulein Kern of Basel."

Again the little bow, such as a woman in the extremity of illness might give to visitors brought to her bedside. No smile, no meeting of the eyes. But Ricotti was in no wise disconcerted—he was a master of ceremonies whose assurance no coolness could disturb. I should not have trusted the man for an instant, but at least, I thought, he was a happy one—a creature who responded to each new circumstance with such fullness, such simplicity, that the drama of living totally absorbed him.

"Ah, Vlado, excellent!"

The brief-case which Vlado had brought contained two bottles of Chianti Mazzoni, in the drawer of a filing cabinet there were glasses for everyone. Like a prima ballerina, like a nobleman famed for hospitality, like Ceres, Ricotti moved about his guests, no less attentive to the humbler folk than to the principals.

"These gentlemen, my friends, these highly skilled and very famous gentlemen, they are setting out on a mission of the highest importance, an errand of mercy which does the highest credit to their spirit of philanthropy. Let us wish them the aid of Almighty Providence ... Vlado, see if there is another bottle in the car."

"I have campaigned with five armies," said Dr. Babitch. "Ah, that is where a surgeon learns his trade! A tent already torn to bits by shrapnel, an old hurricane lamp, flies swarming, a line of stretchers waiting outside."

Ricotti smiled at him paternally. "Yes yes, Dr. Babitch is a man of remarkable experience."

"I too," said a man like a whiskered baby, "I was in the earlier War, perhaps on the other side—but what does it all come to! In the field it's like the doctor says, if the medicals are busy the orderlies will take your leg off with a bayonet—a mug of brandy and away they go. Still, there is much good fellowship in the field of war."

"Indeed, yes, war is the only real test of a man's personal resource! Let me tell you, gentlemen, what happened to me at the battle of the Morava. I was entirely alone, walking through the woods—I had dysentery, you see, I needed solitude—and I came upon a man strung from a beech tree. Not quite gone—some soldiers had tried to hang him, so I gathered afterwards—they'd made a mess of the job. Amateurs—drunk, most likely. An officer of some kind, I could see that, someone fairly high up. In rank, I mean—his feet were only just off the ground. I said, 'Good morning, General!' and saluted. It was an awkward situation——"

"Yes, yes," said Ricotti, "in war-time the greatest presence

of mind is always necessary. Fill the doctor's glass, Vlado!
… For you, once again, gnädiges Fräulein?"

But Fräulein Kern had not touched her glass. She sat
quite motionless, sometimes with her eyes closed, sometimes
fixing them on us, the eyes of a rebellious boy kept back
in school.

"Signor Ricotti," I said, as soon as I could get a splinter of
his attention—it was like trying to photograph a kingfisher
in flight—"I should like to know, please, if my friend
Dragutin is coming. I understood he was going to meet me
here. If not——"

"Dragutin? Yes yes, he must be coming some time, all
these people are waiting for him, they want his advice on
their little legal problems. A wonderful man, a friend to
everyone—there's nothing he doesn't know about getting
round legal difficulties. Vlado, fill the doctor's glass!"

"But listen!" I persisted. "If I am to attend a case of
serious illness, the sooner I get there the better. All this delay
may have serious consequences."

"Indeed, yes, I see that point of view entirely! Signor
Dragutin must have been held up somewhere—he is a very
busy man, you understand. But if he's not here before long
I shall make all arrangements myself—perhaps I may say that
Signor Dragutin has been good enough to place a great deal
of confidence in me. Excuse me one moment, please——"

He was lost again, engrossed in the troubles of one of
Dragutin's patients, and I found myself once more in the
verbal clutches of Babitch; Babitch was back, now, in the
Bulgarian War of '85, of which he seemed to have some
boyhood memory, and the husky music of his voice was
flowing like one of his own mountain streams. The
Austrians, he was saying in parenthesis, were booted hyenas,
every whore's son of them. But he meant no impoliteness—
if he had ever grasped my original nationality he had long
forgotten it. It was now supremely clear that the world he
lived in had only the flimsiest connection with his physical

31

surroundings. And I, as I stood in the misted sunlight of his gaze, my ears submerging in the waves of his Slavonic eloquence, was almost as far removed from actuality. From time to time I asked myself, *Que fais-tu dans cette galère?* But the shroud of chatter and smoke possessed me as a dream does—a dream one knows to be a dream but which offers no escape.

"What time do the new men come on duty?" "Nine o'clock?" That question in Ricotti's voice, the answer in Vlado's, reached my ears by chance. It was only later that I saw their significance.

There is sometimes a curious power in taciturnity. Though Fräulein Kern had neither moved nor spoken, I never ceased to be conscious of her presence, and increasingly it made me feel as boys do when their playground is visible from the professor's window. No one was less to be blamed than I for the monstrous delay in a business which—I assumed—she was deeply concerned with. Yet I felt that she included me with those who were turning duty into a social occasion, and her anger, which never touched the others, was like a flame against my cheek. I believe it was her will rather than my own which at last roused me to action.

Babitch had paused for a moment, to light one of his strange, home-made cigarettes. Ricotti was talking earnestly to the child-like man in the corner. I suddenly put my hand on his arm.

"Excuse me—I have certain other engagements which cannot wait indefinitely. Tell Dragutin, will you please, that I am sorry our arrangement has failed."

"But, Dr. Reichenbach——!"

Quick as Ricotti's reaction was, I had picked up my instrument-case and slipped outside before he could move to stop me. I had not gone four yards, however, when he caught me up.

"But Doctor, you should have told me—I had no idea! I understood you had the evening at your disposal!"

"I am sorry," I said, "that you were mistaken."

In the feeble light of a distant street lamp I now had my first sight of the vehicle Ricotti had arrived in: a small, tilted motor-wagon of a kind I had seen in the 'thirties on Styrian farms. It did not at once occur to me that this relic had been intended for my own transport. Such a design, however, was now disclosed. Before I was out in the street the man Vlado, darting ahead, had dropped the tail-board, and he stood there bowing with peasant obsequiousness while Ricotti, holding my arm in a grip of ferocious comradeship, guided me firmly towards him. I could feel Fräulein Kern close behind me, and Babitch was rumbling in the rear.

"Starting this instant—*immediatamente*!" Of the several tongues in which Ricotti was proficient Italian still served him best of all, and his speech came now as if played back from a recording at the highest possible speed. "A complete misunderstanding—you must please forgive me, Doctor, I had no idea you had other engagements. . . . Vlado, start your motor at once. . . . The car, I'm afraid, is rather old-fashioned—there has been a little accident to Signor Dragutin's regular car, it's being repaired at this moment, but this one runs like a deer. There are sacks to sit on, they're not at all dirty, you'll be surprised how comfortably you travel. . . ."

Alone, those whirlwind tactics would not have sufficed. As I hesitated, I found Fräulein Kern close to me on my other side.

"Dr. Reichenbach, I hope you will fulfil the duty you have undertaken!"

That was spoken politely, but it was something more than a polite request—it had the urgency of a queen's command. She did not wait for my reply, but with the dignity such women achieve in every circumstance climbed quickly into the truck. I could only follow. I sat beside her, my back against the wall of the driving compartment; and a moment afterwards Babitch, lifted and propelled from behind like a sheep at the dipping trough, landed sprawling on our legs.

"I go in front to guide the driver," Ricotti called, fastening the tail-board and letting the rear screens fall together.

Before there was time to sort ourselves the truck was moving. I was too much occupied with getting Babitch settled to collect my thoughts, and we must have travelled a mile or more before a particular discrepancy began to engage my reason. Fräulein Kern had uttered only a single sentence, but one sentence was enough to tell me that her German had not been learnt in Switzerland. On this evidence she was no more a citizen of Basel than I of Königsberg; and it needed no special powers of deduction to infer that I was involved in a business less innocuous than I had previously imagined. I knocked angrily on the partition, but the squeak and rattle of the truck were so clamorous that Ricotti was unable—or did not choose—to hear.

2

There was a chance to escape. I neglected it through what can only be called irresolution.

We had travelled for some miles—I had no idea in which direction, since I could not see out at all and the road, in any case, would not have been one I knew—when the car halted and Ricotti came round to the back. I asked, peremptorily,

"Are we there? Is this the place?"

"Two minutes!" was his answer. "You won't be kept more than two minutes—please stay where you are!"

With that he left us, and I heard him walking forward along the road. When the footsteps stopped there were voices, loud against the surrounding silence but not near enough for me to distinguish anything that was said. In my

34

memory of those moments there occurs, as well, the sound of notes being handled, but that obviously derives from retroactive imagination—so frail a sound could not possibly have travelled a hundred paces. Presently Ricotti returned.

"All is in perfect order," he said complacently, "and from this point Vlado knows the route. Perhaps you would just remain silent for a little way—there are people living by the road who don't like being disturbed at night."

He spoke in German, and I noticed that he had lowered the pitch of his normally penetrating voice.

"I hope everything will go famously," he said. "I'm sure it will!"

What? So he was leaving us?

I started, "Signor Ricotti——" but the truck was already moving again.

"*Auf wiedersehen!*" he gently called.

Till then, Babitch had hardly uttered a word. From the childlike composure of his face which I saw now and then in the glow of his cigarette I had supposed that he was browsing upon delicious memories. Now, without warning or palpable reason, he began to sing. It was an old marching song of the Serbian army, one where comrades boast in turn of the number of Bulgarians, Croats or Macedonians they have slain, leading triumphantly to the disembowelling of a thousand Austrians. He sang in a very low, husky voice, but intuition told me that the theme was inappropriate to this time and place, and Ricotti's warning had waked in me the old mentality of the fugitive.

"Dr. Babitch," I implored, "quiet, if you please!"

"I beg your pardon? That is a capital song!" he responded loudly. "It has carried men with raw and bleeding feet over mile after mile of the worst roads in Europe. Up to the mountain heights, across the scorching plains——'

"Yes—later on I should like to hear you sing it."

He fell into silence, contemplating my odd procrastination, just as the truck stopped again.

This was but a momentary halt; I heard, "*Sta bene!*" and the creak of a hinge, then we moved on. But only for a few yards. Now there were voices speaking rather sleepily in Serbo-Croat, "The certificate's out of date. . . . You will have to sign the goods manifest!" and Vlado's laconic answers, "Nothing but empties. . . . Yes, from the Barbia Market . . . Well, they told me it was all arranged." And simultaneously I realized, from instinct or from a preparatory flexing of Babitch's vocal cords, that he was about to continue his song.

It was not a moment for pondering the situation. Intensely scared, I whipped out my cigarette-case, felt for his face and pushed a cigarette between his lips. To strike a match would have been to betray our presence; I could only whisper, "I'll give you a light in a moment—just be quiet, will you, *keep quiet*!" And even as I said those words someone was coming round to the back of the truck.

"There is an even finer song," said Babitch, removing the cigarette, "but one that goes best with high voices. I will try——"

I put my hand firmly over his mouth.

Standing at the tail-board, a man parted the screens and leant inside the truck, searching with his hands—I felt him actually touching the toe of my shoe. From what I saw of his shape in the opening I judged that he was a large and powerful youth, but I believe—now—that he was frightened, and perhaps with reason; for Vlado had come quickly up behind him and was saying with a dangerous edge to his voice that he had no time to waste. Otherwise the fellow could hardly have failed—unless he was stone deaf—to detect our presence even at so cursory an inspection. True, Fräulein Kern sat like a graven image, and I, remaining almost as still as she, was keeping my hand tightly on Babitch's mouth. But from that imprisonment, which appeared in no wise to distress him, the voice of Babitch came as the voices of the unquiet dead are said to come from their graves at night—a smothered but triumphant bellowing: "*We shall come again, we shall come again, the remnant of Black George's men!*"

"You say you've nothing but empty cases in here?"

"I've told you three times!" Vlado said.

"*And that is the way to glory!*" sang Babitch beneath my hand. "*To glory, to glory!*"

"There's one box here—is that all you've got?"

"I don't do the loading—I'm a driver. You've got the signatures—I can't wait here all night!"

I felt a sudden impulse to call out, 'Look, I'm a passenger —and I don't mean to be involved in anything illegal.' But a swift prognosis of infinite complications intervened. Two or three seconds passed in which I seemed to feel the inspector struggling with an indecision as fearful as my own. Then, standing clear, he said with brittle severity, "Next time, you'll please come in regulation hours—we people want some sleep occasionally!"

Without answering, Vlado returned to the driver's seat. The truck jolted forward. Before we had covered twenty yards Babitch had pushed my hand away, and his liberated voice boomed out exultantly to flood the sleeping countryside, "*Again, again, and not in vain, the remnant of Black George's men!*"

I no longer tried to subdue him. That he should advertise our trespass to all the world, that the frontier guards might rectify their negligence with a burst of machine-gun fire, these aspects appeared trivial beside the central fact of my situation: that I, a person of quasi-diplomatic status and corresponding obligations, accredited to the Free Territory of Trieste, had violated its boundary to enter a country where I had no legal status or commission. In those moments of sombre appreciation I had a vision of Dollis Andersen, his face crimped with civic virtue, and I could almost hear his soft, judicial voice requesting me to explain my conduct. This sibylline image was to visit me too frequently in days to come.

3

Yes, for Babitch the journey was a social occasion. He talked for half an hour at a stretch, he sang, as far as he remembered them, the peasant songs he had learnt in his childhood in Novi Pazar. We were not a responsive audience, Fräulein Kern and I, but our coolness never discouraged him, since he lived within a cocoon of contentment spun from his own words and reflections. Occasionally he seemed to fall asleep, but after two or three minutes the need to relight his cigarette always waked him, and he would continue his narrative as a speaker does who has only paused to clear his throat.

Those cigarettes of his gave a slightly nauseous smell, which I afterwards identified as belonging to a confection of *Cannabis Indica*, and which, on a later occasion, was to recall to me the composite sensation of that drive into the Slovene Karst. On myself the fumes must have had a faintly soporific effect, for though the discomfort of the ill-sprung truck increased as we came on to rougher roads I dozed repeatedly and at least once may have slept for more than an hour. But there was no clear contrast that night between sleep and wakefulness. The grinding of the engine, the merciless jolting of the boards against my spine, these were woven into my dreams, and the dreams pursued me into sensibility. Sometimes I woke with my head on Babitch's thighs, sometimes with his on mine; always in bewilderment and profound depression, believing I had lost for ever the life of dignity and freedom I had so hardly gained. Even now I could have jumped from the truck—it was never going fast—and have trusted my intelligence with a little luck to get me home. But the power of will was lacking:

38

in sleepy misery I felt that destiny had cast me for the part of outlaw, that the years of liberty had only been a fortuitous intermission.

Or was it a species of cowardice which restrained me? From Vlado I had little to fear—he was only an hireling—while Babitch was as likely as an unweaned child to interfere with any plans of mine. There remained the prodigious presence of Fräulein Kern.

She, as far as I could tell, did not once fall asleep: certainly the sound of her breathing never altered, and each time a lurch of the truck threw me against her I felt her body as stiff as a soldier's on parade. At first encounter she had appeared a formidable person, but hardly more so than certain Ward Sisters I had known who, with the same austerity of face and bearing, had proved on better acquaintance to be simple, self-distrusting women harshly veneered by their responsibilities. Fräulein Kern, in the darkness, was not reduced to the common stature; and if Vlado was technically in charge of the expedition, I never doubted that the figure beside me, taciturn and motionless, was really in command.

"Do you know where we're going?" I asked her, shortly after we had passed the frontier.

"Yes."

"Is it some distance?"

"Not too far."

Later, I ventured to say that I had understood I was to attend a case in the neighbourhood of Trieste. To which her only answer was that my extra expenses would be paid.

"It is—a friend of yours I have to see?"

"My brother."

"And he—he comes from Basel?"

No reply.

Instinctively I kept my body as much as I could away from hers, but towards the end of that seemingly interminable ride I must have fallen, in sleep, with my shoulders on her lap instead of Babitch's. This chanced to be a position of comparative comfort, and for a few minutes I experienced the contentment which comes from a tired body surrendered to repose. Soon, however, the violent shaking of the truck and an angrier note of the engine pierced my drowsiness, and by degrees the increasing coldness roused me. We were climbing in bottom gear, the road had become a chain of pot-holes and the constant shift of weight told me that it was twisting sharply as it ascended. When my eyes opened there was light just showing through the canvas, and above my head the face of Fräulein Kern was now faintly visible: a mask cut in marble, the bitter mouth tightly fastened, the eyes of a Savonarola so fixed on some scene invisible to me that I felt their dreadful compulsion even while they passed me by.

I had just pulled myself together and recovered a position of less indignity when the truck turned at right angles and stopped. Babitch, whose boots were at that time planted on my stomach, said vaguely, "Ah, this would be our billet!" It was, in fact, our destination—or as near to it as the truck was to go.

4

It is possible that my parents took me in early childhood for a holiday in the Vischak district; otherwise, I had never been in that part of Slovenia before, and I can only suppose it was some oblique memory of the lower Julian Alps, where I had often walked and climbed in boyhood, which made me seem to recognize my surroundings the moment I got out of the truck.

This vague sense of homecoming brought me a curious content. I must have been stiff and sore after the hours of boisterous confinement, but I remember only the delight of physical liberty, the magic that lies in the quiet and freshness of early morning. The rough lane had brought us to a cleft in the limestone hills where boulders up to a man's height lay haphazardly on the shelving turf among holm oaks and thorny scrub. Behind us the ground fell away steeply—I marvelled that the truck should have climbed it—and if there were greater heights ahead they were hidden, in the still feeble light, by a mist which hung like folded silk between the outcrop and the crouching trees. I felt as if I had been lifted to a secret country, remote from earth yet gently familiar, washed with brackish mountain air and alive with the music of trickling water.

In this exaltation I no longer troubled about the rationale of the expedition, and I bore without complaint the physical effort of its final stage, which was by no means trivial. What Babitch called 'my good old doings' was contained in a seaman's chest, rope-handled, weighing some fifteen kilos, and by reason of a former hernia Babitch himself preferred to take no part in carrying it; so it fell to Vlado and me to do so, while he panted behind. Now openly in charge, Fräulein Kern led us without compunction on a steep bridle-path, not lately used, where awkward footholds of slimy rock were often hidden by barriers of tangled thorn and bracken; when we fell, or when we stopped to get our breath, she turned to survey us as one whom experience had taught to be long-suffering with shiftless men. And still my spirits sang. In the livening daylight the mist grew opalescent, on a thousand spikes and webs the beads of moisture scarcely visible themselves flashed gold and blue. The world of smallest creatures was already awake, grey moths which our passage disturbed rose to flutter sleepily and sink again, a bird scarcely larger than they darted and hung above us, crying alarm, on furiously vibrating wings. Capriciously, I thought of my office desk, of pavements baking in imprisoned sunlight, and it seemed as if yesterday was part of the nightmare from which I had emerged to the reality of morning. I was a little bemused, perhaps, by hunger and sleeplessness; for in this eccentric hour I believed that the life appropriate to a man of my kind was to follow a sexless woman on Sisyphean paths, linked by a sea-chest to a blasphemous churl and with a lunatic as rearguard—so long as the living soil was below my feet, its smell in my nose and the morning wind in my lungs.

In half an hour the path began to descend, and now, on a southerly, more sheltered slope, the aspect of the land was dramatically changed: here the bush was of a tamer kind, whitethorn and bramble, the gorse had given place to tiny conifers, to rank grass and sorrel crowding upon luxuriant fern, and as the ground became less steeply pitched dwarf beeches gathered to hide the forward view. This had the look of habitable country; but I had fallen into the explorer's mind, where some point of desolation is the last objective, and the appearance of a partly ruinous rubble-and-plaster wall took me by surprise. Beyond, as the trees parted, I saw shuttered windows and an Alpine roof. Forgetting for an instant that a house may have a back and front, I thought, 'Does someone, then, live as remotely as this? Can this wretched path be somebody's connection with the outer world?'

Once more I stopped and put down the chest—my arm felt as if the muscles had been permanently displaced.

"What is this place?" I asked.

But at that point Fräulein Kern was betraying a faint excitement, she became at once impatient and slightly furtive.

"Vischak," she answered curtly; and added, "You can rest indoors! Will you walk quietly, please—there will be people asleep.'

We followed her, then, as swiftly as our burden allowed, across a fenced paddock and a stable yard.

In this first, fleeting sight of the place I had an impression of incongruity. The farmstead was a near copy of many I had seen in the valleys of Tirol—I recognized at once its air of protracted senescence, of neither getting nor needing through the centuries a builder's attention. But as if a mad and military spirit had lighted upon it, there were signboards lately painted on almost every rotted door: '*Agricultural Coöperative, F. District.*' '*Secretary of Council, No. 18 Station.*' '*Office of Technologist*': and across a corner of the stable yard, hanging rather limply from a knotted line, was a faded streamer which proclaimed that '*The Worker's Liberty is dug from the Worker's Soil.*' This overlay of earnestness disturbed my pleasure in the scene. In earlier life I could have enjoyed such innocent theatricality, but I had learnt in the 'thirties to regard ecstatic verbiage as one regards the indications of sepsis in an injured limb.

The infection stopped at the back door. Within, where a wide passage led to a flagged hall, the house showed an almost barbarian simplicity, and so obtrusive were the signs of neglect—the faded paintwork, the vast stains of damp—that I should have guessed it to be empty, but for the domestic smell, primarily of turned milk, which prevailed a little over the odour of decay. In the hall there was no furniture except for a row of kerosene drums and the rusty tines of a dismantled harrow.

There Fräulein Kern paused, as if she had come to an end of her instructions; and then, with an impulsive movement, she opened a door.

"If you will wait in there, please, Dr. Reichenbach, we will bring you something to eat."

For the first time she produced a smile, like sunlight on a field of ice. I moved as I was bidden, and the door was immediately closed behind me.

Once more I needed to adjust myself to sudden contrast, and again I had the sensation of travelling back through time. It is a common illusion that as the locale of one's life changes the scenery folds up behind; and I am enough a realist to have supposed, when I fled from Europe in '38, that the Austria of my childhood was as likely to return as

Homer's Greece. Now, in the long and pleasantly propor-
tioned room where Fräulein Kern had adroitly stowed me,
that Austria was recalled to life. The two eighteenth-
century portraits on the wall facing the windows might have
been of my own ancestors. The sparse and rather shabby
furniture, of a kind that in any age would look old-fashioned
rather than antique, could have come from my grand-
mother's house in Salzburg. Even the worn Ghiordes rugs
resembled those which I remembered in my father's study at
home. I wandered up and down, examining the books and
ornaments. The pictures on the shorter walls were copies
of Italian and Flemish masters, some wooden figures decor-
ating the writing-desk were most likely local work; but
these, equally, had been chosen with an Austrian taste—you
would not have found just such ornaments in any Slovene
farmer's house. It may seem absurd that I was so much
affected by the simple furnishings of a rural landowner's
sitting-room, but here was a flavour which for years had
been denied me; here was the homeliness of my own Austria,
her unaffected pleasure in the varied fruits of men's genius,
her tacit belief that the good life was to be had without
extravagant expense. In the two or three minutes in which
I was left alone I forgot the means by which I had reached
this place, and the object of my coming. I enjoyed for that
time what might have been the feelings of the Prodigal Son,
a glowing gratitude, a curious return of innocence.

The experience was incomplete. A kindred creature was
needed to perfect it.

5

And this, I thought, had been supplied when the door
behind me opened and I turned to see an elderly man standing there with a loaded tray. 'A stage servant!' was my
first impression in spite of his singular dress; and almost as a

stage servant would, he said, "Good morning, Herr Doktor. I've brought you some breakfast." But when he had put down the tray he faced me with a smile which immediately transformed him. "Schwarzenberg!" he announced, shyly, as if forced by an attack of honesty to reveal a discreditable detail.

Rising quickly, I said, "Reichenbach. . . . This is most kind of you!"

To which he answered, "Ah, but my dear sir, all the kindness is on your side! To be willing to make so long a journey, for the sake of total strangers!"

But now he did not seem a stranger: the vanished civilization which had produced him was for me the last that was natural to man. In style—rather than precise appearance—he resembled the youngest of my father's brothers; and so I saw him in the first few moments of our meeting, as one who needed naked soil to walk on, who would rather trim the household lamps himself than submit to electricity, and who yet would neither look nor feel out of place in a Vienna drawing-room. He was wearing a shooting coat much too short for him—his height was well over six feet—and above the rubber boots which contained his lower legs and knees there was visible a length of pyjama trousers of a pale lemon colour patched with irregular strips of mauve and green. In this costume his figure and instincts both appeared to be at ease—his shyness was from another source. He was wholly patrician, his brow grave, his nose Augustan; but the eyes were young, the mouth tender and supple—one felt, from moment to moment, that he was a tall schoolboy to whose face the lineaments of age had been applied extrinsically.

"I shall not pretend," he said, frowning, "that this deserves the name of coffee." And then he smiled again, as if he had found some secret absurdity for him and me to enjoy together. "One finds the resolution to drink it, and it passes into the draught, they tell me, with little harm."

He sat to watch me as I ate, and his manner was that of one charmed to receive an unexpected visitor. Ignoring my errand, he talked of the Enns valley, where I had spent my childhood and where relatives of his own had lived before the War; of Vienna as he had known it in his own early days; frequently falling into the present tense, as if he had escaped the bondage of history.

". . . I expect you know the Restaurant Halasinski in Annagasse? The head-waiter in the round room there is a great friend of mine—he started as a footman in my cousin's house—a very shrewd fellow, I always get his opinion on political questions. Oh, but possibly he has gone now. I don't get to Vienna very often nowadays—well, hardly at all. There are these frontier restrictions."

It transpired that he had spent the greater part of his life in this farm, which he had inherited with a considerable estate.

"My friends always say it is lonely—they could never live so far from what they call amusements. But I like it—you can do what you like in a place like this, where everyone knows you.'

"Even now?"

"Now? Oh, things have changed, of course. I'm not the owner any longer, I am here on sufferance. They call me a technical adviser, a co-ordinator—I never quite remember what I'm called. No, nothing belongs to me now. That chair you're sitting in, it's the property of the Agricultural Co-operative, but my former bailiff very kindly allows me to use it. Yes, sometimes it's hard to remember. I see one of my men harnessing a horse which quite obviously needs shoeing, I shout to him, 'Franjo, you nincompoop, you'll have that horse lame!' Then I recollect myself, I apologize to the great gawk, I suggest to him that we submit a joint report on the horse to the Advisory Council. It comes to the same thing in the end. Mercifully my people are quite well-disposed to me—the Slovenes, you know, I

46

regard as the best of all Europeans. The older ones still call me 'Baron', the young fellows regard me as just a curiosity, an interesting survival. So we get on tolerably well."

That was easy to believe—no one could have been hostile to so honest a creature. For myself, listening to his gently humorous voice, I surrendered wholly to the pleasure of his company. If he regarded my visit as purely social, why should not I!

But I think—or I like to think—that I did not mistake the nature of his simplicity. He was not a stupid nam. Although he appeared to guide the conversation with no other object than to entertain me, I realized that he was learning something of myself and my history as he went along. His eyes were on my face all the time; not inquisitorially, only with a courteous attention; but in those mild and friendly eyes I detected both an acute perception and a lingering anxiety. If I had been hiding some secret they would have disturbed me. It was not, however, I who had anything to hide.

When the cigarette which concluded my breakfast had burnt to its end, I thought it was time to return to reality. I found an opening in which to say, with some awkwardness,

"Herr Schwarzenberg, I am worried about Herr Kern. I think—"

"Herr Kern?"

"Your friend from Switzerland."

"Oh, yes—yes, of course!"

"I imagined I was to see him as soon as I got here. From what I've been told, his condition is very serious."

"Indeed, yes!" he answered, a little distractedly. "His sister is getting things ready. She said—she said she would let me know when everything was in order."

I might have told him that when I was at work my aesthetic sensibilities were not dominant. But I could not bring myself to be professional with one as unhappy as I saw him now, playing a part for which he was quite unfitted.

There was no guile in the man, no gift for evasion. He read my questioning look; we spent a few moments in grotesque embarrassment, and then he broke the silence by saying,

"I think you ought to know that my friend is in rather a complicated position."

Wishing to help him, I said at once, "Wenzel has told me already—I gather that Herr Kern had to leave Switzerland in a hurry because of some financial embroilment."

But he would not be helped. "Financial embroilment?" he repeated.

"In any case it makes no difference to me. As a doctor I'm only concerned with people's bodies—their legal standing doesn't come into my view at all."

He nodded, as if this text-book answer was worth his grave attention. "I wish," he said reflectively, "that we could all keep our thoughts and feelings in compartments like that. I had a man working for me once, he was the most expert woodman in the district, and also the most notorious adulterer. He treated his wife and family with a callousness that was beyond all bearing. Well now, I tried to pretend that the man's iniquities were nothing to do with me. A first-class woodman is not so easy to find . . . However, that's all over, the man's been dead for many years—a jealous husband stabbed him."

He had slipped into the kind of digression where a mind like his moves most naturally, and I wondered how long it would take me to recall him to business. But his eyes, which had wandered away, suddenly returned to mine, and he said with a painful humility,

"Look, Doctor, I have simply no title to ask you for any favour—I can only ask it of your goodness of heart. I want you to do what you can for this poor fellow, and then to forget that you've done it—to forget you ever came here. I beg you to do that! It sounds unreasonable, I know. But the happiness of more than one person depends on that. I—I hope you may feel it as a kind of compliment, if that's worth anything. I mean, I am putting the most complete trust in you."

I had, as it chanced, no time to consider the implications of this appeal. A boy of nine years or so, thin and peaked, but with a precocious dignity of features and bearing, had come in very quietly. Schwarzenberg, catching sight of him, said,

"Ah, this is my grandson. Johannes, come and wish good morning to Dr. Reichenbach!"

The child bowed to me, "I hope you are well, sir!" and then turned to his grandfather. "My aunt would like to know if the Doctor is ready."

From the way that Schwarzenberg answered I guessed that the form of that question had been agreed beforehand. He said deliberately, "Yes, I have seen to it that the doctor is perfectly ready. I think, Johannes, you had better show him the way."

6

With an assurance which much impressed me, the child picked up my case and led me to the door by which I had entered the house. Then he turned to look gravely up at my face.

"Perhaps you will have the goodness to wait here, while I see if the way is clear. There are people about who we don't quite trust."

He said that without any of the theatricality I should have looked for in a small boy; and with the calm of an old body-servant he nodded to me and went out to the yard, closing the door carefully behind him.

There was sense in his precautions. He had not gone far when I heard a man call out to him in a local variety of German:

"Hi, what are you doing at this time of morning?"

"I like the fresh air," Johannes answered sedately.

"Well, that's no robbery!" The voice was jocular but I did not care for it: I had heard one like it used by men with a grudge. "Whose food are you eating, though?"

"I'm staying with my grandfather."

"You're here to keep an eye on things, eh?"

"It's just a holiday," Johannes said patiently.

"Yes, kids of your sort get plenty of that!"

The crude teasing went on a little longer, giving me some discomfort. Then I heard the man moving away, and Johannes came back to me, still soberly collected, as if he had only executed some trivial routine.

"It's all clear now," he said, "but we have to go rather quickly."

I followed him across the yard and through an opening between two of the outhouses, to a stone-built barn where several carts and a tractor were standing. Without his direction, I should probably not have noticed the broad-stepped ladder which went up at one end.

"You will find my aunt up there," he whispered, handing me my case, "I am not allowed to go up myself. If you please——!"

He gave me once more his absurd, small, courtly bow, and almost magically disappeared.

By now I had become infected with the boy's sense of caution, and I waited for a few seconds, looking every way, before ascending the ladder and raising the heavy trap which, when I had made my landing, I lowered again as quietly as I could. The loft in which I found myself seemed as dark as a coal cellar—all the outward openings had been stuffed with sacking—and I had the impression that it was piled from end to end with bales of straw. I appeared, then, to be quite alone. It was first alarming, then a relief, to hear in the darkness not far off a wheezy laugh which I recognized as Babitch's.

"This way!"

That was the low voice of Fräulein Kern. And now as my eyes became adjusted to the twilight, I saw there was a gap in the wall of bales and an open space beyond. There, by degrees, I discerned the covered shape of a man on a folding bed.

I said with authority, "I shall want some light!"

Obediently, Fräulein Kern went to where the slope of the roof brought it within her reach, and shifted a piece of board. The window thus discovered was coated outside with leaves and grime, but the dull light it admitted was enough to show me the patient as a man in early middle age whose condition was serious: a bandage encircling the forehead partly hid his eyes, and his mouth was also half-concealed by a plaster that went from cheek to chin, but no one could have failed to recognize the shade of cyanosis in the part of his face which remained visible, and the laboured, painful breathing told the same tale unambiguously.

"Are there head wounds as well?" I asked.

'No no—only scratches!" Fräulein Kern said quickly. "I put on those dressings to avoid infection." And she added, in a tone of polite admonition, "We have to be very quiet here."

Babitch had come up beside me.

"He's in a mess, poor fellow!" he remarked agreeably.

Ignoring him, I turned to Fräulein Kern again. "How long ago was the accident?"

"Oh—two or three days. A week perhaps. I can't quite remember. His friend was re-loading his gun——"

"You mean, a sporting rifle?"

"I suppose so. Of course it was criminally careless——"

"Never mind about that!" I said.

She was betraying a new nervousness, but she answered my further questions with a clinical precision that argued some training as a nurse. Meanwhile the patient himself said nothing, though he cannot have been unconscious at that time. More than once I made some remark like "We'll get you more comfortable soon," but there was never the smallest response, and I had the feeling that he was not only suspicious of me but also hostile. He was plainly of North German stock, physically a powerful man, and from the little I could see of his face I guessed that normally he might be extremely handsome, as the Junkers can be in their own fashion. That was a transient speculation: the effective part of my mind was occupied by more important ones.

At the start of my examination, which I made with my own small electric torch, I found that his heartbeat was displaced towards the centre of the chest. With the stethoscope I heard no air entering the left lung, and the whole of that side of the chest was dull to percussion. There was no exit wound. He had been shot from the back (at what range I could not tell, since I had not the evidence of the punctured clothing) and evidently the force of the bullet had been broken in shattering a rib. It became clear to me that he had lost a considerable amount of blood into the left pleural cavity and that some additional reactionary fluid had probably set up still further pressure on the left lung, which was no longer functioning. As a result of this and the displacement of the mediastenum, there was now a developing pressure on the right lung, causing severe respiratory embarrassment.

Normally such a case would have given me no problems, but nothing was normal here.

To remove the bullet was clearly impossible: to leave it was to incur the risk of a lung abscess, but that risk had to be accepted. The central question was that of time. A draining operation would require experienced supervision for several days, and I had fewer than forty-eight hours at my disposal. Was there any hope that Babitch could safely be left in charge?

"Dr. Babitch," I said, "are you able to stay here for a week or so?"

"A week? Why, for the rest of my life!" he answered

52

buoyantly. "In all my life I have never left a case until I was fully satisfied that my humble powers were no longer needed. Let my tell you of a case I once attended when I was a young house-surgeon in Beograd."

"Yes, but later, not now! . . . Fräulein, there are various things I shall require besides what I've brought with me. First of all I want you to prepare an antiseptic solution. And then I shall need a number of small towels——"

"Will these do? They have been sterilized."

She showed me a pile of linen strips, the product of a torn-up sheet, which I saw would serve me perfectly. Indeed, she had everything ready. Her nervousness had disappeared, and as she knelt with her face not far from mine, following my movements with concentrated attention, I saw her afresh as a woman of intelligence as well as will-power. If, with these qualities, she appeared to be devoid of human feeling, that characteristic also was of value to me now.

"Can you get hot water?" I asked her. "I shall want plenty."

"Yes, we've got a spirit stove." Turning her head, she said, "Franziska, will you re-light the stove, and put on the second kettle."

Behind me, where the light did not reach, someone instantly moved, and a match was struck. I was thus informed for the first time that a fifth person was in the loft; but the fact scarcely registered, since any attention I had to spare from the patient was devoted to Babitch. He was being good (as they say of children)—standing quietly at the correct distance, watching me with a slightly histrionic smile of approval. Yet I felt no confidence in this virtue: it resembled that of a dog which will walk to heel for miles but forgets all obedience the moment a rabbit darts across the road.

I had given a preliminary injection of morphia and atropine. As soon as the water was ready I removed

Fräulein Kern's bandages and started to wash the wound and the minor abrasions with soap, talking to Babitch in Serbo-Croat at the same time. I had decided, I told him, to remove part of the eighth rib, so that I could drain out the fluid and blood-clot: I should attend to the drainage myself as long as I could stay, and after that he would have to maintain it, following my directions exactly.

Yes yes, of course, he would do that, it would be child's play—he had carried out such treatments a thousand times.

But I had only a fraction of his attention. He was kneeling now beside the chest which we had dragged over the hill. From it he had taken, together with two or three cylinders of the field-ambulance type, what appeared to be a modification of Guthjahr's apparatus; and this archaic contraption he was handling with the besotted care that a boy gives to his first bicycle. It was callous to say, as I did then,

"I think a local analgesic will serve me best for this. About half-per-cent procaine, don't you think?"

He got to his feet.

"Madness!" he exclaimed. And then, "Forgive me, sir—I speak with the greatest possible respect. I only mean to say that I myself have always been strongly opposed to local analgesia in such a case as this. I venture to tell you, sir, that in more than fifty years of extremely varied practice——"

"Please, Doctor," Fräulein Kern put in sharply, "if you would avoid raising your voice!"

"You have to consider," he said, "the psychological effects!"

This, of course, was nonsense: if anyone could survive the mental disturbance of feeling his chest being opened it was—as I saw him—the virile and insensitive creature who lay between us. Plainly the real danger was that during the induction of gaseous anaesthetic the respiration would

54

become still more difficult, perhaps fatally. I had finished the washing and was about to apply iodine. In the few moments I had to spare I looked at Babitch afresh and saw that he was on the verge of childish tears. I saw also, in his face and in his hands, which were feeling the connections of the Guthjahr even while he spoke to me, something one comes to recognize: the born anaesthetist. The anaesthetist's gift is not to be explained. There are people of high scientific attainment and manual dexterity who prove to lack it hopelessly; and there are large, ham-fisted, seldom-sober men in whose use of anaesthetics one's confidence is justified again and again. In the shambling veteran before me I seemed to detect instinctively one of the latter breed.

"You've used this apparatus before?" I asked.

"A million times, dear sir. It has been with me in a score of campaigns. In the little cart I used to have, drawn by mules over the mountain roads——".

"Very well—but I shall ask you, please, to pay the most strict attention to any special directions I give you."

That was a quick decision and at this distance I think it was formally a wrong one. But what, in the conditions of that operation, was formally correct? Where everything is makeshift, rapid thinking may count for more than scientific deliberation, and at this stage my mind was much occupied with a problem of equal importance—that of a working light.

"Can we get any more light in here?" I asked Fräulein Kern. "This torch of mine isn't good enough."

"I could unblock the window at the end," she said uneasily. "But that might be seen from outside."

"Well, we must take that risk. I'm taking plenty in any case."

Still she hesitated. "I think there may be another torch here."

"Where?"

She produced it: a Swedish electric stable-lamp which threw a strong, white beam. I could scarcely have asked for anything better.

"I wish you'd told me about this before!" I said curtly.

She did not answer. But I knew afterwards—I think I almost realized at the time—what the reason was. She did not in the least trust me, and with the childish cunning one can find even in women of high intelligence she had hoped to prevent my getting a clear view of her brother's face. As if his identity concerned me, when I was wholly occupied in keeping him alive!

While I was telling her exactly how she should hold the torch, and what other assistance I should need, she interrupted sharply:

"Quiet, please! There's someone down below."

I broke off in the middle of a sentence, and the force of her whispered injunction was such that even Babitch stopped humming and kept his body still while he fiddled with his valves.

Myself, I had heard nothing. But now, directly beneath me, a man called "What's the hurry, lad, what's the hurry!" and simultaneously the sound of shod hooves rang from the yard. I realized presently that a horse was being harnessed to one of the carts, and from the procession of noises—the jingle of chain traces, the stamping and oaths, the ritual badinage—I could follow as if visually the whole leisurely performance. It was nerves, I suppose, which made me imagine that the patient's respiration had suddenly worsened. 'He will die on me,' I thought fleetingly, 'before I'm allowed to begin.'

I looked at Fräulein Kern's face, which betrayed neither impatience nor any other emotion, and then, attentively, at the patient's own. The eyes, slightly filmed by the morphia, were now wide open; and although his whole body was racked by the struggle to breathe, those eyes, looking directly at mine, revealed no conscious distress.

In this indifference to pain I recognized—even if the morphia helped it—an uncommon fortitude. Yet it did not move me as one is moved by the martyr's acceptance of suffering. Until this interval of galling inactivity I had been too much occupied by practical questions to consider Kern as an individual. Now, with leisure to think more humanly, I found myself still curiously void of compassion. As a rule a few moments at the bedside are enough to establish some kind of understanding—to make the patient feel that he and I are partners in the work to be done. With this man I could not have achieved such sympathy. He had given no sign of desiring help, human or divine. Reading this loveless and bitterly disdainful face, I could only think that he saw himself as possessing a kind of deity, which excluded him from the need or possibility of men's affection. I had never before undertaken a work which so refused to engage my spirit.

The incentive of pride remained. I waited till the peasants' voices were at last subdued by the rattle of wheels across the yard, and then—in accordance with practice—I said gently but distinctly,

"Herr Kern, it is vitally necessary for me to perform a small operation on your chest. I am assuming that you consent to it?"

He made a slight, impatient movement of the head which—after glancing at his sister—I took for a signal of agreement.

I continued: "The critical part will be over in quite a short time. I have every hope that it will lead on to an entirely successful conclusion. But I think I ought to tell you that I have come much later than I should have wished ... I can wait for two or three minutes more if you would like, for instance, to have a few words privately with your sister before I begin."

With renewed impatience he merely shook his head. Turning again to Fräulein Kern, I said, "I shall want the light held absolutely still—for an hour, it may be. You feel equal to that?"

This, too, was a superfluous question. The woman had no physical nerves, no weakness. I wasted no more time.

"Are you ready, Dr. Babitch, to start the anaesthetic?"

With a flourish, the old man lit a fresh cigarette.

"Dr. Babitch," he replied, "is always ready! Wherever there is a call to arms, Babitch will be found in full accoutrement, his loins girded, his staff in his hand. When the trumpet sounds, my honoured friend, Babitch is already on parade!"

7

Up to a point, my instinctive confidence in this man's professional ability was justified. True, he was somewhat happier in his work than I should have wished: he babbled and sang, and however often I told him to put out his cigarette he automatically lit it again. But from a dozen indications—the comparative constancy of the patient's respiration, the appearance of the skin—I saw that he was controlling the induction with uncommon skill. This was as well; for although Fraülein Kern, kneeling close beside me, held the torch with admirable steadiness, the light it gave was far removed from the almost shadowless illumination which is achieved in American theatres. I felt rather as a musician might feel if he had to play a composition not lately rehearsed with a sheet of grubby glass covering the score.

Yet as soon as the body before me lost its identity with a sentient creature, becoming only the damaged vessel I had to care for, there was pleasure in the work: partly the satisfaction of doing a difficult thing—never before, for instance, had I operated kneeling—and partly that which comes when a familiar occupation of the hands allows the undercurrents of the mind to flow as they will. It pleased me that I made the cut over the eighth rib as certainly and easily as if I had been in my own theatre; and as I bared the bone from the covering periosteum, with the meticulous care in which Vorbich had trained me, I felt once more the kind of contentment that a good wheelwright finds in perfecting the shape of a felloe. The rugine I was using was of French manufacture; I had bought it in a tiny shop at the corner of Werdertorgasse, just before my intermediate examination in orthopaedics, and the memory of that drizzling afternoon set me on a train of faintly mournful reflections. A city whose monuments proclaimed the unity of past and future, whose tram-cars with their load of factory girls and elegants and down-at-heel professors appeared as symbols of the world's compatability—how solid a framework this had given to my years of hope and confidence! The morning when old Katz the porter had come limping down the passage to post a blue sheet in the students' vestibule, '*Passed, with special commendation . . . REICHENBACH, EUGEN F.*'—how simple and superb the prospect then! I had dined that evening in a party of twelve—where? most likely Mareginski's—and late at night had delivered myself of an oration: we, men of great inheritance and of peculiar gifts, had but to marry our ambitions with the altruism which nature had sown in us, and under our leadership the archaic miseries of Europe, her senseless poverties, her stultifying confusions, would yield to a new authority of charity and reason. . . . And now——?

"Very nice!" cried Babitch, leaning over to view my handiwork. "Neat as a pork-butcher!"

"Please, Dr. Babitch—someone may hear you!" Fräulein Kern protested.

But he did not seem to notice her. "A useful heart you've got there!" he said robustly. "It's giving me quite a steady intake—shouldn't have thought it. Not that I'd bet a dinar on its lasting now!"

"Yes—well, please attend very closely to your controls!" I said.

To sentimentalize the past, to lament the ideals of adolescence, was ingenuous and idle. But we, surely, had suffered something outside the common scale of disillusion. You discover by degrees your own limitations; but you do not expect that the structure in which you labour and have your being will fall apart while that discovery is still going on. We had assumed that certain fundamentals of our state were inviolable—the historic conception of law and common justice, the sanctity of confidence given to friends. And that had proved a false assumption. It was as if, from the known and seemly mechanism on which I was working now, the brain or liver had been wantonly stolen. Again I found my resentment warming into fury. It was not a Mongol horde which had ravished our virtue, but men of our own tongue, the heirs of Kant and Schiller, some who could even have claimed to be Mozart's countrymen. One's bitterest hatred is kept, I suppose, for those who manifest the evil latent in one's own blood; and in those moments when my physical faculties were concentrated on a tiny area of light I had a Dantesque vision of the legion which had poisoned our estate: soft-cheeked, ingratiating faces I remembered from the schoolroom; youths who had realized early that physical prowess would absolve them from the fatigues of cerebration; men with marble lips and vulpine eyes whose callousness was counted for virility by women: this was the kind which had opened the postern doors to its more ruthless cousins—these, the bubonic fleas of our polity, had found in the invaders' arrogance a culture they could understand and feed on. For though the face of cruelty may be ferocious or only mean, sly and lecherous or merely puritan, it is recognized—I thought—and hallowed by all her children.

The voice of Babitch, singing huskily a tedious ballad about the navels of Bulgarian maids, had begun to waver. "I could tell you blindfold," he said with a yawn, "that this is a German cadaver. They all smell the same. An acquired taste, sir, an acquired taste!"

I said, "Quiet now, if you please!"

His childishness had recalled me from useless brooding, but my nervousness, which I ascribed chiefly to the paucity of working light, was increasing. With the portion of rib removed, I should only have to incise the pleura over the chest wall to expose the underlying blood-filled cavity, and this was the critical stage at which I most depended on Babitch's skill. I said, as I was completing my work on the rib,

"Dr. Babitch, I am about to open the pleural cavity. If the patient's breathing gets worse I want you, if you please, to aid him with artificial respiration."

The fact that he made no reply did not at once disturb me: he was not a man who wasted on professional courtesies breath which might be used for more lively communication. But to be sure that I had his attention, I added,

"You know what you've got to do? Depress the bag in time with the patient's own inspiration."

It was fortunate that as soon as I could relax from concentration on my own work I turned to glance at him. From kneeling on the floor he had fallen gently on to his shoulder and was fast asleep.

The situation was not one which could be calmly reviewed.

"Fräulein Kern," I ordered, "will you please rouse Dr. Babitch and keep him awake! I'll manage the lamp myself. You must tickle him or pinch him or do anything else you can think of—he *must* be kept at his work."

With that, I took the torch from her. But of course it was absurd to suppose that I could hold it and work one-handed. I tried. I tried to grasp it under my chin. And the thought which came to me then was, 'Well, I have done my best for this fellow, but the odds were too great!'

In a corner of my mind was the knowledge that someone else was available for service if I needed it; but the child or woman whom Fräulein Kern had addressed as Franziska had kept herself so much in the darkness, engaged with the stove and kettles, that she had counted for no more than one of the stolid ward maids who furnish odd corners of the scene in every hospital. In the emergency I did not waste time with politeness, but called like a foreman,

"Here, you, come and hold this! . . . No, come closer—I want the light right on what I'm doing."

By then, Fräulein Kern's operations on Babitch had achieved some success. "I beg your pardon, madam!" he was saying, "I'm afraid we have had a small collision. . . . Indeed, there is not the smallest chance of my falling asleep, I never sleep at night—it is a great affliction. You see, I learnt in my campaigns to live without sleep for ten days and nights at a time. You were saying, Doctor——?"

I repeated my former instruction, in a voice whetted to penetrate the crust of his somnolence. And since further delay would waste the last, faint chance of success I got ready to make the incision, directing Fräulein Kern at the same time:

"There's a length of rubber tube on top of my case there. I want it re-sterilized—as soon as you've got a moment——"

But now the light was wobbling.

"You must keep that torch steady!" I said sharply, and then glanced at my new assistant's face. She was a girl perhaps in her twenties, perhaps younger. Even in this feeble light I saw that all the blood had gone from her cheeks, and her eyes were tightly screwed.

The recognized treatment—to slap her face and shake her—might well have been effective. But my anger took another form. For I had reached the stage of desperation at which—they say—a stupid and cowardly soldier will sometimes fight prodigiously. I was saying to myself, 'I will save this man's life (which means nothing to me) just because these people are all in league to prevent me!' Aloud, I spoke with a quick, hard pedantry:

"Listen, Fräulein, you and I are dealing with a beautiful piece of mechanism. At the moment it looks rather ugly because it's under repair. There has to be a certain wastage of chemicals—blood is just a chemical compound—but only a very small wastage, because I am an expert at this kind of job. Now—you will hold the torch like this, and you will keep it *absolutely fixed*. So long as you do that, I shall allow you to keep your eyes shut if you want to. Do you understand!"

From that point the light remained relatively steady; and I could spare no more attention to the nervous creature. The exact performance of a number of small works in swift succession—the incising of the pleura and the swabbing which this immediately involved, the insertion of the tube and then the suturing of the wound about it to make as nearly as possible a watertight closure—this was occupation enough for all my faculties, and I had other cares besides. The opening of the pleura put a strain on the patient—as I had feared—which he was scarcely in a condition to tolerate. His breathing slumped like an engine running out of fuel; once, for a moment or two, it appeared to have stopped altogether, and I heard myself muttering with impotent anger, "Babitch, for God's sake keep it going! ... You—woman—make him do it, *make him!*" I think that Fräulein Kern whispered some reply, and I seem faintly to remember the noise of Babitch giggling, but those sounds were remote from the small, vibrating pool of light where, for the time, all that mattered to me was comprehended. The faltering life which had returned to this intricacy of veins and cells would not wait patiently while I sealed the channels of escape: time was being measured out to me in seconds, and in the hampering shadow of my own hands

63

the tube must enter to a calculated depth, the suture be made close and even, the tissue saved from tearing. In that space of anxious struggle, in the joy of utter absorption, I was oblivious of the other lives surrounding mine in the semi-darkness. Only when the work was done, when—by God's grace—the heart and lungs were returning by degrees to the rhythm of their labour as the sails of a mill start slowly moving in a fresh wind, only then could I emerge like a miner from his work far below the ground.

"For a moment," Babitch was grunting, as he coughed from the smoke of a fresh cigarette, "I thought I'd lost the bastard!"

But while I was wiping the sweat away from my eyes my head had turned in the other direction. I had so far forgotten the girl holding the torch that I was startled to find her face close to mine, unnaturally large, as if I were viewing it with an opera-glass; and even now I saw it only in the way that I had seen the patient's opened chest—as a pattern of light and shade, a display of exquisite workmanship. But I noticed, as my vision cleared, that the eyes were open, staring along the torch's beam, and the mouth tightly fastened with resolution.

"You can rest now," I said, but she did not seem to hear me.

She was not, after all, a girl: the youthful cut of her hair—like a black helmet shaped to her head and neck—and the childish moulding of her cheeks had given me a false impression. The lines of tension which I saw now told me that this was not the face of immaturity. Nor was it commonplace. No doubt my recollection of that first encounter has been furbished by later memories. I only know that the picture has remained as vivid and authentic as one of Caravaggio's paintings: the superbly fashioned head in grey, reflected light against the dark design of sacks and queen-posts, the appearance of immutability which came from its solitude and stillness. I was tired then—the effect of a practically sleepless night had abruptly overtaken me—and even in that second appraisal I saw nothing in the portrait except its physical beauty: at the time, I was unconscious of any heroic quality in this image of conquest, by one so young and so womanly, over disgust and fear. With no more than courtesy I said,

"I must thank you, Fräulein—you have done very well."

For a few moments she still made no response: it appeared that the exercise of will which had fastened her attention on the patient's body could not be reversed. And when she did speak she turned her head only a little way towards me.

"Is it finished?" she asked.

It was not. I had still to complete the apparatus for syphonage, to strap the final dressings, to attend to a dozen details which a professional nurse would have done at my direction; and it was more than desirable that these adjustments should be complete before the patient returned to consciousness. I said, however, taking the torch again,

"As far as you're concerned—yes, it's done now. But I should like you, if you please, to get some more water boiling. I shall need it before long."

8

As I waited in the village—very early on the Monday morning—for the baker's van which was to take me to the main line station, I thought the episode was finished. It had lasted less than forty-eight hours.

In those hours I had experienced the inflated sense of actuality which comes with certain dreams; and as the logic of dreams brooks no interruption from reason, so I accepted my surroundings as a child accepts his first school, finding in the small and darkened world I had come to an organism independent of other existence. With the rest of its inhabitants I shared a single business, that of restoring Kern's body to his use. So occupied, I had little leisure to speculate about the man himself and I avoided doing so. In this there was cowardice of a shapeless kind: I felt that I could not be implicated in the man's illegalities so long as I did not precisely know them.

He was a good patient. As soon as the effects of the anaesthetic had cleared he showed himself a person of practical intelligence, perfectly disciplined; and however little he liked or respected me, he followed every direction I gave him as if it were a legal obligation—keeping his arms in the position I advised, following carefully what I taught him about the management of his breathing. There are many who at that stage of illness become fretfully self-conscious, ashamed of their bodies' weaknesses and indignities. He, on the contrary, seemed to view his case as objectively as I did—to regard the work of repair as one of sober importance in which he had a vital share. To be sure that Babitch made no mistakes when I had gone, I gave him my instructions about the drainage several times over; and I could tell that Kern was taking in at least the gist of what I said—that if necessary he could almost have supervised the treatment himself.

Was I—were we all—a little frightened of him? Else, how did he so command our service? The sick have their own authority, deriving from our emotions: their helplessness demands our ministry, we are always prisoners of their gratitude. But I could still neither see nor imagine gratitude in this man's eyes, which reflected nothing of his physical infirmity, nothing that asked compassion. Between him and his sister there was, I supposed, some sort of affection, but of the many kinds of love this one was outside my knowledge: perhaps it resembled most the attitude of hardened servants towards an imperious master, an admiring loyalty informed by understanding. In the wretched light we lived by, the sexual difference of his face from hers was partly eclipsed; sometimes in those close, fatiguing hours I imagined that what I saw was two aspects of the same cold face, each equally contemptuous of pain and of others' opinions. And if Paula Kern was in service to her brother, I—however watchfully I maintained my professional status—was servant to them both.

On the fringe of that picture, Franziska's face remains so much in shadow that it is scarcely visible. She, too, seemed to exist merely as a minor part of the sick man's retinue. Yet for me her presence had a particular value, for it served to remind me of a more natural world: whenever I asked her for some small assistance she responded as if it was agreeable as well as normal for one being to help another. I imagined that instinctively she feared Kern no less than I did, but I saw in her fear a quality of tenderness which played no part in mine. Sometimes she was clumsy in her movements, but her approach to him was always gentle, and when he groaned in his sleep she showed an acute distress. It is easy to say that the sick-room is no place for sentimentalists: to me, shut up for hours in one small space with nothing visible except the panoply of illness, hardly a word spoken save those of clinical routine, the strain would have been intolerable without the feeling that at least one of my companions could breathe this cankerous air and retain a common sensibility.

I had started by vaguely assuming that she was some kind of servant to the Kerns—perhaps an impecunious cousin whom they had taken into their employ, since she used with them the familiar form of address. I must call myself slow-witted for having rested so long in that assumption, but I remember nothing in Kern's behaviour at that time—or in his sister's—which should have contradicted it.

It was from Schwarzenberg that I learnt the true relationship.

For the first night I stayed in the loft, for fear that the patient's condition might deteriorate. On the second, it seemed safe to leave him, and a little after dark I went across to the house, where a bed had been made up for me in what had once been Schwarzenberg's dressing-room. It was the competent Johannes who led me there. But Ludwig Schwarzenberg himself brought a supper tray to my bedside.

"You must be worn out!" he said paternally. "Cooped up like that for all those hours! In other days I shouldn't have submitted my beasts to such treatment!"

I reassured him: there was plenty of straw in the loft to sleep on, and the food Johannes brought over during the hours of darkness had more than sufficed us.

"Food?" He smiled despondently. "Yes, that's about all one can do for a guest nowadays—one must be content if they don't actually starve to death! Well now, I shan't keep you talking—you must eat those scraps and then get some rest!"

But that was a mere embroidery of manners—he was firmly seated at my bedside. And for my part, I found his company even more desirable than sleep: he made me feel as if I had moved not a few yards only but a hundred miles from the cheerless, alien stage on which I had been performing. This bedroom had no luxuries. But my return to the farm was almost like homecoming; here I felt myself a friend of the house, here I could talk, if I wished, unguardedly, certain that no words would be misinterpreted and none betrayed. The window behind me was open, letting in the sweetness of upland air and the endearing complaint of tawny owls. In the velvet light of a Nissa lamp the seasoned face of Ludwig Schwarzenberg was a country over which the clouds passed swiftly, yielding his eyes and supple mouth to flashes of sunlight, and his voice as he spoke of his own countryside and his former neighbours was instinct with all the pleasantness which had encompassed my childhood.

". . . But nowadays one hasn't so much social life, I don't think our Josef Broz approves of it. Well, he's right,

I expect. His mother, you know, was a Slovene, so he should be a good and sensible person . . . On the whole I find it satisfactory to have no possessions. My wife—God rest her—she wouldn't have felt the same. A certain style was necessary for her, she would have found the present situation dreadfully lacking in style . . ."

Yes, he had long been starved of conversation with men of his own species, and I saw that he would rather have continued to use me as a friend than as a visitor on business. I had almost a feeling of tactlessness when I took the first chance that came to speak of my patient.

"I can give you a fairly good account of your friend," I told him. "He has come through a small operation remarkably well."

"Oh. . . . Oh, yes!" he said.

When you give news—good or bad—to an invalid's closest friends they are often tongue-tied. That is natural —their thoughts are moving in country where language has no foothold. Yet it astonished me that a man of Ludwig's maturity should be so affected by my sober report; for in an instant all his humour had gone, all the shyness of our first meeting had returned.

I said, giving him time, "I don't want to raise your hopes too far. The next few days will still be fairly critical, and even after that there may be complications. But I think we can call ourselves fortunate—really the operation should have been performed much earlier."

And still he looked down at the bed, in a troubled and foolish way, like a timorous child who is offered a pony ride.

"Yes, I must take that as good news," he said slowly. "It's different from what I expected."

"You mean—you hoped that all the danger would be over by now?"

He shook his head. "I'm not sure what I hoped. But Paula—his sister—Paula thought he had very little chance.

So little, it seemed to me madness that she should make that journey to Trieste."

"Well, I'm glad I've been able to do something to justify it."

"Indeed, yes! I know that Paula will be grateful. And my daughter Franziska more grateful still."

"Your daughter? You mean to say she——"

But I did not need to finish the question: tired and slow-minded as I was, I could only marvel at my previous density. As if to relieve my embarrassment, Ludwig had already turned towards the door.

"I'll show you something," he said over his shoulder. "It may perhaps be of interest to you."

He came back presently with what seemed to be the minor archives of his family—bundles of letters and news-paper cuttings in a sandalwood box. Turning these over on the bed, he picked out a photograph and brought it to the light.

"There you are!" he said.

It showed in half-profile a man of perhaps thirty years, in the uniform of an officer of the Armoured Corps. As a portrait it was crudely conventional: the stiff, martial pose, the highlighting of forehead and cheek-bone, belonged to the furniture of half the drawing-rooms in Germany. But the virile sculpture of this face had needed no photographer's tricks to display it.

"You recognize him?" Ludwig asked.

"Yes, I can see it's Herr Kern. Taken, I suppose, about ten years ago?"

"A little more. Siegfried was just twenty-eight then. Good looking, do you think?"

Yes, he was singularly handsome, and if the face was one I did not care for I had to allow for private prejudice. Besides, the boldness amounting to insolence which I saw in these eyes, the faintly contemptuous set of the lips, might well have derived from the nervous irritation which most men suffer in the studio.

70

"At least," said Ludwig, "you can understand the appeal that such a man makes to a young girl?"

"In a way, yes. I mean, I know that people are supposed to look for their opposites—that very often a particularly gentle woman somehow wants hardness in men. At least, that is the rule, they say."

"Hardness?" he repeated, weighing the word in the palm of his mind.

He rummaged again and produced another photograph, this time an amateur snapshot.

"That was at Salzburg, shortly before they were married. It was at Salzburg that they first met—he was spending his leave there."

I knew the exact spot on the Mönschsberg where the picture had been taken—it was one where all the lovers of Europe are wont to be photographed—and it started a small spring of memories. The vulgarities of tourism had never killed, for me, the magic of that place—that citadel of fantasy, nursed by sunlight and Alpine winds, where in a September evening you imagine it is Mozart himself who slips past you in a shadowed street. So for me the artless picture had a kind of immediacy, as if it were a page from my own history; and at the first glance I saw this pair as one of a score who had served to decorate amusingly the pleasure of my Salzburg holidays—the man so consciously relaxed in his flannels that you still saw the uniform, the woman playing her part as the tired warrior's recreation. That first impression, however, was superficial. No one looking a second time would have called the face of this girl conventional, or her demeanour vapid. She was seated on a roadside bench, her eyes turned to look at Kern's: not with the smiling complacency of an accepted lover, but with an expression of wonder and of self-distrust, as if (I thought) the splendour of masculinity had been revealed to her for the first time—as if she could not believe that a man like this had troubled to take her into his possession.

Here I recognized the reality of love in one of its complexions, refusing utterly the oversight of reason. For an instant, only one, remembering the phase of hero-worship in my childhood, I saw the patterned officer of the photograph as the young Franziska had seen him.

Ludwig was looking over my shoulder.

"It's hard to understand!" he said. "You educate your children to recognize what's good and bad in other people. And we have to believe, surely, that when love comes to the young and innocent it comes from God." He made a curious face—one that peasants make when the weather turns against their plans. "It was useless for me to talk to her—it only made her sorrowful. There was nothing, nothing I could do!"

I could neither pursue the old man with questions, nor try to lead him back to easier topics. We spoke disjointedly of arrangements for my departure; and then, with a reluctance which I found greatly moving, he wished me good night.

Before it was light I returned to the loft for an hour to attend the patient for the last time. Throughout that visit Babitch was snoring, and Franziska was also asleep—I caught sight of her head among the grain sacks. But Paula as usual was awake and attentive, and I had no misgivings about entrusting her with my final directions. Thereafter, if our leave-taking was somewhat embarrassed—I naturally refused the fee she proffered—she and I could at least express a sincere respect for each other's ability. By five o'clock I was on my way to the village.

9

There, standing at the roadside in a drizzling rain, I spent a fallow ten minutes freshly wondering what would happen when the pass-control officers came aboard the train and

72

how the ultimate consequences would be shaped. Was it legally possible for the Department of Justice to abrogate my American citizenship? If so, should I become a stateless person? Was prison a possibility? At that hour a man who is cold and short of sleep has neither sense nor courage. With bitter pessimism I saw my 'vacation' ending in a pageant of disgrace and finally in destitution.

In this mood I was impatient to get clear of everyone connected with Siegfried Kern, and the sight of a woman hurrying down the lane I had come by made me draw farther into the shelter of a cottage doorway. She saw me, however, and came towards me. It was Franziska, wearing a man's grubby coat, still tousled from the loft and very wet. She was sweating and out of breath.

I said rather stupidly, "Good morning, Frau Kern! Have I—did I leave something behind?"

"What?—Oh no, Doctor, no!"

I had then to wait while she recovered her wind, and because she made a joke of this, smiling as she panted, I was able to face her as manners would else have forbidden. In those few moments I caught for the first time her likeness to Ludwig, which was in the eyes and brow. I could see, too, something of the girl in the photograph, but strangely little of the one who had held the lamp for the critical phase of the operation. In the prosaic light of a rainy morning the Greek perfection of this face had given place to the tiredness, the signs of self-neglect, which belong to every mother of young children; and I remember how I reflected, with a momentary disappointment, that one saw a score of women like this in the shopping hours in any Vienna tram.

"I didn't know—I didn't realize you'd be off so early," she said. "I can't think why Paula didn't wake me."

I answered, "But why should she! You need all the sleep you can get."

"But I hadn't thanked you—I hadn't said a word."

73

At five in the morning no man is capable of social graces, and I could only assure her rather stiffly that what I had done was, for a surgeon of experience, mere routine. I added the usual words of caution: she would do well not to suppose that her husband was already out of danger.

All that seemed to pass her by. Her next words were, "I don't really know why you came."

I said, "I was asked to by an old friend."

"And you agreed to come without knowing anything about my husband?"

"Only that he needed medical attention. Oh—and I was told that he was in some sort of legal difficulty. But that was irrelevant."

"You mean, it didn't concern you as a doctor?"

"Exactly."

She seemed to ponder this view, then she said gravely, "I should have thought it needn't concern anybody, in any way. When someone's dying, I mean—surely they haven't got to be hounded then, whatever they've done."

To this I could only answer lamely, "No, I shouldn't have thought so, not when they're dying."

The remark was careless: I think she realized its corollary, for I saw with consternation that she was suddenly at the verge of tears. It was a great relief when the van which Ludwig had arranged arrived a few moments later to take me away.

Even then my embarrassment was not quite over. She got her voice sufficiently under control to ask for my address, which—from official prudence—I politely withheld from her: and when I was seated in the car she made another effort to thank me, putting her hand over the lowered window to take hold of mine as a troubled child would do. Only the impatience of the driver, who let in his clutch with a jerk, put an end to this display of absurd and tongue-tied gratitude. When I looked back I saw her standing motionless in the empty village street, an odd, dishevelled image, gazing vacantly at the opposite wall as a rustic might in a strange city.

And that vision accused me of insensibility; for, although obsessed by my own anxieties, I was all at once aware that this creature now removed from my life had hoped for something less cavalier than my professional responses—some word of encouragement which I had not even tried to give her.

Chapter 4

I

How RIDICULOUS, IN retrospect, my dire forebodings!
Providence favoured me with a ram caught in a thicket.
The small, respectable and transparently harmless Croat
who sat beside me in the train had his papers in magnificent
disorder; it took two officials on the Jugoslav side of the
boundary, three on the Trieste side, to expose to this man
the complex illegalities involved in his travelling or even
drawing breath. With so rich a seam of depravity to
excavate, these people had no time to waste on me. I
lazily displayed the W.U.R.O. stamp in my American
passport, they murmured apologies for having intruded
upon my excellency. A little before ten I was back at my
office desk.

This was unpunctual, and provided fun for the boys.
Was the girl so beautiful? How was my head this morning?
Had there, in fact, been several lovely girls? If I found their
wit a little hackneyed, I could share their lightness of heart,
for I was pleased with myself. Responding to a call on
my good nature, I had taken undoubted risks—indeed,
I had placed my whole future in jeopardy. From all that
danger I had made a clean escape; and now, back in the
corridors of public virtue, I could look on the closed
adventure with something more than a sense of deliverance—with a boy's triumphant self-conceit.

But I was heavy-eyed.

"Poor Reichen!" my colleagues said. "He's all washed
up from his vacation."

"They took you a boat-ride, brother?"

76

I explained that I had spent the week-end studying local monuments.

"Yeh, he's taken in a big load of art appreciation'! Why, culture, surely, that's what gets a guy all washed up," they said.

The morning was delicious, the sky clear, the constant hubbub from the street a hymn of reassurance; and I loved these men as never before. Insensible to any world but theirs, they lived in a daylight of their own so broad and uniform that one's private shadows were paled in its reflection. Theirs was the company I needed to exorcise the sense of outlawry which had returned to terrify me in the besieged hours at Vischak. Accepting me as one of themselves, they almost made me share their assumption that freedom and safety were the perquisites of all mankind.

Then Dollis called me on the internal telephone: would I, please, come to his office at once.

I found him standing by his window, hands clasped behind his back, eyes locked, as if his mind were advanced in labour.

"Shut the door, will you, Doctor!"

This alone was disquieting. Only a revolution, or the tactical necessities of love-making, will normally cause Americans to shut their office doors; and I saw here no other symptoms of love.

"Doctor, I've had bad news."

"Oh—I'm sorry!"

"From Ljubljana."

So—as quickly as this! But how? With the sense of guilt flooding back I found myself calculating the distance between Ljubljana and Vischak, deciding that someone on Ludwig's farm had seen me, recognized me as an official out of bounds, telephoned to our nearest headquarters. . . . Everything was known.

"It's a signal from Pete Adcock." He paused significantly. "You may or may not like Pete, but I'll say he's a straight kid. And I'll say he was a hundred-per-cent right to tell me what he has told me. It was a tough decision for the kid to make—nobody wants to squeal on a colleague who's higher up in the organization. He could darned easily have kept the whole thing under his thatch."

This preamble might have continued all morning— Dollis was one who liked to delineate a moral situation with scrupulous care. But my nerves were not equal to giving him his head.

"What," I asked cautiously, "was it about?"

"Vanderholst, I'm afraid."

Vanderholst was our No. 1 in the Ljubljana office.

"Yes?"

Dollis lowered his voice. "He's been drinking."

The shock of relief almost overwhelmed me. I said, fighting hysteria,

"Drinking what?"

"Hell, how should I know! What do they drink in a place like Ljubljana? All I know, he's been cock-eyed the last three weeks—I thought a long time back his reports were screwy. Now he's been talking to the Mayor, or whatever they have, telling him the Town Hall's full of pink-eyed conies. And, brother, that kind of vaudeville doesn't help our organization any."

He was much in earnest, and I felt myself a miserably inadequate audience.

"Why, no, surely!" I said.

"Well, it's darned lucky I put a smart kid under him," he went on lugubriously. "Pete's done fine, taken care of the whole situation—he's pulled in a local doc, had him chase Vanderholst into a drunks' clinic and hold him there for the duration."

This sounded like a happy ending, but I saw that Dollis felt otherwise. It now appeared that Adcock, however adept in handling a bibulous superior, had not the experience or qualities required for running the Ljubljana office

78

by himself. Someone older—and one who at least spoke German fluently—would have to be sent in Vanderholst's place.

"God knows, Eugen, it's not an assignment I feel like handing out to any friend of mine. This place Ljubljana— I've not been there—I'd say most likely it's the kind of hick town you get up north in Montana. Maybe if a guy doesn't get himself pie-eyed in Ljubljana he just goes plain nuts."

I did not trouble to disabuse him.

"But I've got to send someone," he continued. "And it won't be for more than three weeks, I guess."

He was watching me now with an anxious kindness, and once more I was touched by his consideration. He could so easily have ordered me to do this job—which, after all, involved no sort of hardship. But because I was his senior in years, and a foreigner, he was granting me the dignity of making my own choice.

And how much I should have preferred a positive command!

Ljubljana: I had once spent a night there with cousins of my mother's: a city of peculiar culture, one whose flavours would not quickly bore me. The question came again—how near to Vischak? In physical terms, not much nearer, perhaps, than where I stood; but they lay on the same side of the border I had crossed so thankfully this morning. What harm in that? The border was a political invention, a paper rampart to be pierced with appropriate papers—this time my documents would be in order. Only, for me it had become the final boundary between my past and present lives. These last two days had shown me the magnetism of the past as something stronger than I had previously imagined, and in this the farm at Vischak had its part. A dangerous curiosity could lead me there again.

What brought me—in a matter of seconds only—to my decision? Was it merely discipline, the wish to oblige a

79

considerate chief? Did I sensibly tell myself that at Ljubljana I should still be miles away from the small area of danger? Or was I influenced by that profounder part of my understanding which would not recognize my concern with Vischak as a casual one?

I said to Dollis, "I'm afraid it will mean unloading my work here on to other people. . . . Can I have a day or two to get my things together?"

2

The fear that Vischak would exert a magnetic influence upon me seemed—during my first fortnight at Ljubljana—to have been fanciful and childish. In moving eighty kilometres along the railroad from one office to another I had not ceased to be a rational adult, and in the new responsibilities there was sufficient occupation for my mind. In retrospect, however, I see that this confidence was flimsy. I should have been warned, not so much by the curiosity which continued to plague me as by the pains I took to resist it. For if (as I told myself) my connection with the Kerns was finished for ever, what harm could have come from my knowing all about them!

To discover the facts should not have been impossible. Though there was at that time a great number of people all over Europe hiding from authority because of various peccadilloes—or merely for lack of political status—I could not think of Siegfried Kern as one of those: his was not the face of a dealer in smuggled currency or gasoline. If, then, he was a fugitive of greater importance, there would surely be some record of his career in the files of any newspaper; and further, unless the shot which wounded him had in truth been accidental—which I never believed—the incident was most likely to have been reported in the Press at the time. Now the local office of *Praznak* was not a hundred paces from my own, and a dozen men at the Press Club, where I had honorary membership, might have led me quickly to the information I wanted. Several times, indeed, I was on the point of starting an inquiry, but on each occasion something forbade me: possibly the spirit of discretion which falls on even amateur officials; or perhaps an echo of the words which had come to me with such simplicity—'Surely when someone's dying they haven't got to be hounded, whatever they may have done?'

In this duality of mind I was thankful for the Augean stable which Vanderholst had bequeathed to me—drawers full of unanswered letters and cables, an appointments book where every page looked like a Dadaist exercise. These, I thought, would allow me little time to amuse myself with private investigations.

He had left me Adcock as well, and for this bequest I was only moderately grateful. Adcock was British, a winsome youth, fresh-faced, delicately moustached, and anxious—as he said—to 'pull his weight'. Had I become an alcoholic he would doubtless have tidied me away as nimbly as he had tidied Vanderholst—that practice, I have heard, is part of the curriculum at English universities—but in other departments of staff work he was less at ease. To draft a simple letter took him half the morning. Often I found him sitting at his desk in a Byronic abstraction so profound that it seemed a sacrilege to interrupt him, and at times I had the feeling that he had been snatched too early from someone whose personality had sheltered his—a sister, perhaps, or a football captain. He had not acquired one sentence of Slovenian or Serbo-Croat, and his German was unique. Our two Slovene stenographers were timid girls, and a dozen times a day one or other would appear before me in giggling embarrassment, trying to imitate the sounds which Adcock had dictated and requiring me to tell her what he had said.

It follows that I had little opportunity for sightseeing in Ljubljana. On most evenings I returned to the office after dinner and worked till ten or eleven o'clock. When I got back to the Koroshets Hotel—where to save myself trouble I had taken over Vanderholst's room—I was fit for nothing but my bed.

Kept late in harness, the brain will not yield comfortably to sleep. Those nights, the state into which I passed immediately on turning out the light was not unconsciousness but a gross resemblance of waking life, where the images I saw were solid, the voices I heard close and distinct. More than once or twice I was back in the loft at Vischak, staring again into Kern's opened chest. There the wavering light confused me, no instrument I needed was to hand, and Kern himself, watching me with a gelid smile, would say, 'You'll have to answer for this, you know—it counts as homicide if you don't put me right!' While sometimes it was Paula who addressed me with bitter impatience, her lean face growing to fantastic size as it drew towards mine. With a terror I have seldom known in waking hours I would struggle against the force which held me pinioned, until a cry breaking from my own throat returned me to consciousness. Then for some moments I would lie trembling, scarcely able to believe in my escape, and still so subdued by fear that I could not stretch to put on the light.

Franziska's face was never a part of that experience. Yet I knew that she was just outside the narrow arc of my vision, waiting for me to turn and speak to her. Once, indeed, I caught sight of her figure in the shabby, masculine coat, but it was distant and receding. And once, quite close to me, I heard her in tears. Strangely, that sense of her distressful presence followed me into daylight, persisting like a mournful tune beneath my mind's serried engagements, when the monstrous phantasms of the night before were drowned in the flood of actuality.

It was in the nature of things that the intimation I was trying to avoid should come to me from a casual and unexpected source.

At odd moments I was amusing myself with a stack of *Life*s and *New Yorker*s which Vanderholst had left in his room. One night, afraid of sleep, I was turning over the pile in search of an issue I hadn't read when I came across a newspaper published in Altus, Oklahoma (which I suppose was Vanderholst's home town). A vociferous headline caught my attention; I consumed the tame article attached to it, then my eye slipped over to a column headed *Round the World* and to a line of heavy type half-way down: *Nuremberg Escapee Winged?*

The report was from a Zurich agency: at Hochfilzen, in Tirol, French soldiers had encountered a man they believed to be Col. Siegfried Zempelmarck, and when they tried to question him he had bolted. They had fired, and thought they had wounded him, but he had got away. A codicil for forgetful readers explained that in December '45 Zempelmarck had escaped from the military police who were conveying him to his trial at Nuremberg.

I glanced at the date of the paper. It was September 25th.

There was no photograph, nothing to establish a connection between that item of news and the invalid at Vischak. A swift calculation of time and space told me that the connection was possible, but that was all: the common operation of coincidence could well account for the wounding of two fugitives in the same broad region at approximately the same time. That, at least, was how I argued, as I tore the paper into small fragments and threw it away.

I was lunching with Adcock next day, and on an impulse I asked him if he knew anything about a man called Zempelmarck.

"Zempelmarck? No, Sir, I don't think so. I mean, should I, Sir?"

"No—I just thought you might."

"Well, you know, now I come to think of it, I may have heard that name somewhere. Only, these German names, if you know what I mean, they're all rather the same."

"Well, possibly!" I said.

"If there's something you want to know about this chap I could beetle round to the local library. They'd help, I should think. They're madly intelligent, these people round here, Sir."

I thanked him but refused his offer.

You cannot deceive yourself—that is a contradiction in terms. But you can put a turbid screen between yourself and the truths you do not want to accept. As I see things now with more honest eyes—looking back at the rather Spartan bedroom in the Koroshets Hotel, the bamboo table, the shutters that refused to fold into their recesses; recalling the loneliness and boredom which were the medium of those days' experience—I realize that I had already determined to pay one more visit to Vischak. There was professional pride, at least professional curiosity, to be satisfied; and then my shapeless leave-taking from Ludwig Schwarzenberg had left me with the sense of a ragged edge that needed to be repaired. But that was not all. With the wisdom that only follows events I see how the memory of my last encounter with Kern's wife—when I had received her thanks with such meagre grace, refused her even the little warmth which her isolation demanded—had become a chronic abscess on my mind. I wanted, I needed, to see her again: to excuse my cold behaviour, to say at least some word of gentleness. And where should I see her except at Vischak? And if I were compelled to visit Vischak again, I must go in the innocence of knowing nothing.

4

Perhaps the folly of going at all would have been avoided if I had never had business at the Town Hall. In the entrance lobby of that rather forbidding edifice one met, sooner or later, the whole small world of Carniola; and since I was working in close contact with the provincial department for resettlement and rehabilitation I had to be there almost every day.

One afternoon I was in the office of a man called Pishade— a minor functionary of outstanding charm and intelligence— when I heard, from the other side of a plaster partition, a familiar voice raised as if to rally troops under murderous bombardment:

"You besotted virgins, *I tell you I will not sign any more of your accursed forms!* I have fought and bled in nine campaigns, I have spilt more blood for my fatherland than you have got in both your bellies, and you are trying to prove to me that I was never born. What kind of proof do you want? My mother, God rest her, has been dead for fifty years. Do you want me to dig up her bones? Do you think I'm going to hunt out the midwife for you—*she* went off with a venereal bugler! *Don't goggle at me, you brainless little cows!*"

I raised my eyebrows towards Pishade, and he smiled.

"They have a difficult client in there," he explained. "He comes every few days, demanding a ration permit— a man who calls himself Surgeon-Captain Babitch."

"What—has he no papers?"

"On the contrary, he's got enough to fill the city archives. He has documentary evidence to prove that he was honourably acquitted by no fewer than four Courts Martial. Unhappily, according to our records he should be domiciled in Trieste."

I knew Pishade well enough to say lightly, "I thought when people were in that sort of difficulty you found room for them in the city gaol?"

He smiled again, a little wearily—he had always too many problems on his hands. "We did, for one night. Then the Lieutenant of Police had to decide between letting him go and facing a mutiny of gaolers—the Surgeon-Captain is a man who likes to sing."

All this time the altercation in the next room was continuing in the manner of a tuba concerto, the voice of Babitch rolling in like ocean breakers to crash upon the prim, unceasing twitter of female clerks, and the performance showed no sign of abating when my business with Pishade was concluded. Leaving him, I went across to the Dravska Café and waited there at an inconspicuous table for Babitch to emerge.

When he appeared I had no need to chase him, for he passed, swinging his Magyar gloves as if they were the handles of a skipping-rope, within a few feet of where I sat. I hailed him and he came at once and shook my hand with great enthusiasm.

"Good God, General," he said, "I never thought to see you again, not after Monastir! Why, I remember saying to Tsiganovitch, 'I've done what I can for the General, I've hacked out half a shell-case from his lower bowel, now I'm off to find some scrounging priest who'll say a Mass for the old bastard's soul.'"

At the first break in these friendly reminiscences I bade him sit for a glass of slivovika.

"What I really wanted," I said softly, "was to ask you about our patient."

"Our patient?"

"At Vischak."

86

For a moment, staring at me closely, he seemed to be faintly troubled. "Those flat-papped creatures over there," he said, pointing a sardonic eyebrow at the Town Hall, "those virgin cockadoodles, they put a man out of his memory. All this talk about Slovenian education—two whole hours it's taken me to teach that pair of petticoated constables they don't know their own regulations!' Why, of course, I remember you well, Sir! You are perfectly right—if I may say so. Our last meeting was at Vischak."

"And you're still living there?"

"Where? Vischak? Yes, of course. I assure you, Dr. Rittershausen, I never leave a case till I can hand it over to the coffin-maker. I shall not pretend to you that the living conditions are good—I've done better in a komitadzi encampment. Still, a man like myself, I can exist on nothing, like a desert eagle."

But not, I thought, without the cigarettes for which he was hunting now in the sack-like pockets of his long coat. As soon as he had found them and got one alight his eyes became steadier, encouraging me to persevere.

"So our friend Kern is making progress?"

"Friend? I can't stand the bastard! (Let me offer you one of these cigarettes, they do miracles with my asthma.) A Swiss, they tell me. Someone—I can't remember—someone said they'd chased him out of Switzerland for spatchcocking the local imprest. Well, I suppose they all do that! Switzerland—it's just a herd of dismal Protestants cooped up in the mountains, they've got to rob each other to occupy the winter months."

"Tell me, did you have any trouble with the syphon-age?"

"What? Trouble? Why, no, Sir—I've done jobs like that at the bottom of a shell-hole, water freezing all round my genitals. Finished that part of the business days ago."

"It was the lack of light," I reminded him, "which made things awkward for me."

"Ah, yes, I couldn't put up with such nonsense—keeping the body in that coal-black dovecote just because the police were after it! I've had him moved to the house. That sister of his—God's claws, what a pikeshaft!—I took that chalk-faced bitch between my teeth. 'Either I get proper conditions to work in,' I said, 'or else I report back to my regiment tomorrow morning.'"

He was now in his sunniest mood, and as the cigarette began to calm his mental processes I drew from him by degrees the news I wanted. In his judgement, Kern was making satisfactory progress. It was to Ludwig's room that they had moved him, Babitch himself was sleeping in the small room which I had occupied, Fräulein Kern next door. It sounded as if their existence was hardly less cramped than it had been in the loft—none of them ever went outside the house except Babitch himself.

"That sister," he said caustically, "she thought she'd confine me to barracks too. Never heard such rubbish! I go about as I please, I talk to the helotry man-to-man—they think I'm a horse-doctor from Beograd. And I take my own leave to come down here when I feel inclined. Not that there's anything for a man to do in this forsaken town. But a labourer, I say, is worthy of his hire."

"Is it easy to get here?"

"Why, yes, for a man who doesn't care how he rides. Tuesdays and Fridays—this rattle-trap they call an omnibus —they wedge you in between the ploughboys and the dairymaids and you pray the Blessed Anthony it gets you to the railway station before you suffocate."

I asked about Ludwig, to which he replied that Herr Schwarzenburg was in better health than any Austrian had a right to be. The man was most civil in behaviour, he conceded—God, perhaps, had first intended him for a

Serb. "And why he lets these Swiss bodies clutter up his house is more than I can conceive!"

"And Frau Kern?"

"Who? Oh, the young female—she's never in my way at all! Yes, of course, she's Kern's wife—I'd forgotten. Well, that man's in no state to have anyone in his bed, not yet, so the girl's on the surplus stores list."

"But is she well?"

"Oh, I should think so! She hasn't reported sick to me."

By this time I was getting nervous, reflecting that if Pishade or someone else who knew us both were to see Babitch and me together our association would not be easy to explain. And now that I had won from him all the information he was capable of imparting I was meanly impatient to get him out of my way. At the first appropriate opening I said,

"You will give my regards to Herr Schwarzenberg?—I take it you're returning to Vischak tonight?"

"I expect so, yes. There's nothing for a man to do in this place."

"Then you have a train to catch? What time does it go?"

"Ah, that I never know! I put myself in the hands of Almighty God and the Stationmaster and wait to see what either will provide."

"Well, I myself have an appointment——"

"Then I shall give myself the pleasure of accompanying you some part of the way to the lady's house."

In the end I walked with him as far as the capacious Romanesque lavatory in Kosmajska and there made my escape. I doubt if he remembered for more than a few seconds that I had been with him.

Next day I looked up the trains to Osrovek, where the Vischak bus connected and where, failing the bus, I should probably find a drosky to take me on. For, after a night of little sleep, I had made up my mind: I would visit Ludwig once again. The prospect affected me with the nervous excitement which schoolboys feel in planning an escapade. But I told myself that this was nonsensical: what could be wrong, or even illegal, in a short excursion into the country to visit an Austrian friend!

Chapter 5

I

Yᴇs, ᴀɴᴅ ꜱᴜᴘᴇʀꜰɪᴄɪᴀʟʟʏ the first of my voluntary visits to
Vischak had something of the feel of a social call: it was
strangely informed with the shyness that attends polite
engagements. I remember how, standing by the back door
by which I had first entered the farm, I suffered exactly
the sensation I had known as a young man waiting, gloved
and expensively barbered, at the imposing entrance to a
house in the Josefstadt district where I was required to
present myself to some political acquaintance of my father's.
It amuses me a little to think that on this later occasion—
when a voice calling 'What are you doing there?' out of the
darkness might have put me in at least a grave predicament
—I was sheepishly fingering the knot of my tie.

My first timid knock was unanswered. My second
brought the sound of a distant door opening, of light
footsteps on the flags within and then the small voice of
Johannes:

"Who is that, please? Is it Mr. Gubets?"

I answered, "No, it's Dr. Reichenbach."

"Oh ... Are you by yourself, please?"

"Yes."

It took the child a little time to slide the heavy bolt by
which the door was held. Then he opened it just far enough
to admit me, and as soon as I was inside closed and bolted
it again.

"You wish to see my grandfather?" he asked.

"Well, if it's convenient——"

91

"I'll go and see. Perhaps you will kindly wait here for a minute."

He had started to go down the passage when he remembered that he had neglected the first detail of civility. He returned, said, "I hope you are well, Sir!" shook my hand and departed again.

The only light in the passage came from one small lamp which smoked and fluttered on a bracket at the farther end. As, in the semi-darkness, I breathed the particular odour of the house, the time behind me seemed to fall out of scale: although I had previously spent but a few hours within these walls, and those mostly in sleep, I found myself looking back at the intervening days as if they had been no more than a brief interruption in the settled experience which the present hour resumed. This sense of continuity was heightened when Ludwig, after greeting me warmly, led me into his sitting-room; for if at my first approach the aspect of the room had seemed familiar, that illusion was now turned to reality. In all its reflections upon Vischak my mind had carried faithfully the tones of the pictures here, some stains of damp below the ceiling, the rococo moulding crowning the bookcase; so that these, as if time had worked with them intensively, were already woven as durably as the strands of earlier sensation—the smell of Plachte's Balsam in my first bedroom, voices of forgotten nurserymaids, the cold of gaslit evenings at the School of Anatomy—in the stuff of my permanent possessions. In feeling, I belonged here a little, as I should never have belonged to the Koroshets Hotel.

I did not behave, though, as if I had household rights: the presence of Paula Kern was enough to forbid such assumption. She was at work at a table near the stove, patching the shoulder of a man's shirt, and when Ludwig presented me—"Paula, we have an old friend to see us!"—she only looked up for an instant, murmuring, "Oh—Herr Doktor—good evening!"

I was not content with this. She and I had worked together; we did not love each other, but there was no personal quarrel between us. I approached her and offered my hand, saying,

"I wondered if I might see Herr Kern again? I've been so anxious to know how he's getting on."

Again she only met my eyes for an instant, and then went on with her sewing. "Oh—yes," she answered uncertainly. "Yes, I'm sure you can see him. My sister-in-law is with him at present, I expect she'll be down before long."

"Sit down, do please sit down!" Ludwig repeated, embarrassed by Paula's coldness. "It's so good of you even to think of us! You—you've come a long way?"

"Only from Ljubljana—I'm working there at present."

"You've come on the bus from Osrovek?"

"There's no bus on Friday," Paula told him.

"No," I said, "I got a car from Osrovek. It's waiting for me in the village."

"But you told the driver you were coming here?" she asked quickly.

"Yes, but I said it was on farming business. I made him think I belonged to the District Co-operative."

In the shrewd glance she gave me I read a deep suspicion. But then she had never trusted me, and I saw no reason why she should do so now.

"Dr. Babitch is still with you?" I asked.

"Yes. At least, he's out tonight—we never know where he gets to."

"You find him all right as a doctor?"

She rolled her lower lip. "I think he knows more about medicine than most people would think."

"An unusual person!" Ludwig said, passing me his cigarettes. "I sometimes wish he could forget my nationality."

And at that, for a fraction of a second, I caught sight of Paula smiling.

I had not before seen her in so feminine an occupation. That, and the mellowing light of the Nissa lamp, may have done something to alter her aspect, for she appeared physically smaller than the impression she had formerly left upon my mind—I had remembered her as a tall woman—and a good deal more frail. It would be inexact to say that she seemed more human now: this was still the face of loveless virtue, narrow in intelligence, forbidding in its very refinement. But the labour of nursing and the prolonged strain of living in concealment (one that I intimately understood) had not been without their effect. The colour of her skin was morbid, she was pitiably tired. And I thought for the first time, 'Once—perhaps in childhood—there may have been some gentleness within this creature, some pliancy of the spirit which would have made an understanding with her possible.'

On the impulse of that reflection I might have tried, if she and I had been alone, to get on better terms with her: at least to persuade her that I still had no concern with her brother's legal position. But the climate of this meeting was not one for confidence. With Paula, Ludwig was almost as reserved as I—an onlooker might have supposed that he and I were both her visitors—and the fact that Johannes was in the room put us all under further constraint. Not that Johannes would ever have interrupted us. In the way of children of old-fashioned breeding he sat cross-ankled on a tall chair a little way from his grandfather's, ostensibly reading a nursery annual, but I could see that he was listening to every word as if we were hatching some plot which deeply concerned him. In profile, his thin face was not only serious but disturbingly unchildish—it affected me a little as the faces of midgets do. But I did not blame him for his curiosity. In this house everyone was always nervously listening.

For a time we went on talking of Babitch, making the subject last like tactful guests for whom too little food has been provided. Then Paula, with a sudden impatience, put down her work.

"I'll see what Franziska is doing!" she said, as if speaking of a child who habitually dawdles.

She went in her quick, forceful way to the door—one imagined her in low heels and trousers—but there she stood for a moment irresolute, recollecting perhaps that Franziska's rights in the sick-room were superior to hers, or perhaps imagining some danger in leaving Ludwig and me together.

"You did bolt the back door again?" she asked Johannes.

"Oh yes, Aunt Paula!"

"Oh—all right!"

The tension she had imposed stayed behind her. It was still in the manner of a polite visitor that I asked, when she had gone,

"I hope Frau Kern is well?"

The question seemed only just to penetrate Ludwig's intelligence. He murmured absently, "Franziska? Oh, yes—I expect you'll see her. . . . I'm afraid Paula is very tired."

"Yes, naturally!"

"Johannes," he said abruptly, "be a good boy and go to the medicine cupboard in my room—you'll find a bottle on the bottom shelf with a label which says 'Pantermahl'. Bring it here very carefully, will you please, with two glasses if you can find them—or coffee cups would do."

Even when the boy had gone he was not at once the easy host I had known before—he made me think of a man lately released from long imprisonment. His eyes were not on me, but on the place where Paula had been sitting, when he said,

"You know, Reichenbach, I find it hard to believe that you are with me. I never expected to see you again. Since you left us I haven't seen a soul—anyone, I mean, except Franziska—that I could really talk to."

Those words made me conscious of my own inadequacy. "The Kerns cannot be easy to know well," I cautiously suggested.

And that at least brought a mournful smile.

"Yes, I'm afraid that woman is on my nerves a little. It's something you may understand—only a fellow-country-man could understand it. But I keep telling myself that I must get rid of these stupid prejudices—it's absurd, at my age, to go on thinking that everyone who comes from the north must be nothing more than a soulless militarist. This poor woman, I keep trying to admire her courage and loyalty, I have to remind myself over and over again that her life has never been easy."

He was silent for a time, his eyes clouded. I could see that he wanted to confide in me, but it was difficult for a man of his nature to speak frankly of those closely connected with him. Trying to help him, I said,

"There are people who don't invite an easy life, for themselves or others."

"Yes, but she belongs to a fated generation," he answered. "The father was killed at Tomaszow—as my own brother was. Then the mother was evidently a feeble creature—from Potsdam, I think, some minor courtier's child. When she found herself a widow she could only throw herself on the charity of her relatives. They lived with a brother of hers, a Pastor—a man who looked like a hungry civet—I once had the misfortune to meet him. What little money there was had all to go to Siegfried, to support his military career—and you can see what that meant for the girl, when the time came for her to want pretty dresses."

I agreed: "It could have made her loathe her brother."

"Yes, and one should admire her for turning exactly the other way. Of course she was four or five years older than he, that makes a difference in such relationship. But, as I say, one ought to admire her."

Again I could only make a conventional comment: "It's

96

sometimes easier to admire people when one hasn't to live with them!"

Johannes had failed to make the door fast, and in a bout of nervousness Ludwig went to shut it. He came, then, and stood close to me, looking at my face as a foreign tourist puzzles over a street plan. He said, with a bitter deliberation,

"At least it is sometimes easier to love people—as we are commanded to do—when we don't have to live with them. Reichenbach, I wish you would tell me what is right and what is wrong! Listen! Before this couple came here—arriving in the middle of the night to beg for refuge—I was at one with my own people, my peasants here. Things had changed, yes—there are busybodies sent from Beograd who say that the old landowners like myself are nothing but carrion, we have no place in the world any more. Well, I accept that, I accept all the changes, so long as I can look my people in the face. But can I do that now—now, when they actually ask me in their kindly way if there is any news of my son-in-law, pretending that they've heard nothing against him!" His voice had started trembling. "That is the kind of thing a creature like this Paula could never understand. And may God forgive me—that's why I hate the sight of her! I cannot stand her Junker speech and I loathe her cold-blooded Prussian face!"

It had a curious effect on me, this outburst from one who had seemed the gentlest of men: it brought into operation that trick of the brain which delivers to the tongue the very word that has been assiduously suppressed. I needed to say something quickly, to relieve the embarrassment which follows impassioned utterance; and the words which came to me were:

"At any rate I hope that Zempelmarck will be well enough to be moved in quite a short time."

The name had scarcely passed my lips when I realized my *lapsus linguae*. I had been looking away from Ludwig, and my eyes turned quickly to see—as I hoped—an expression of bewilderment or perhaps of outrage. There was no such expression. He found nothing odd in my remark. All that he said, in a voice now subdued and disconsolate, was,

"Yes, but how can I turn out the husband of my own Franziska! How can I, when all Europe is hunting him! Where is he to go?"

It was a troubled Johannes who returned, a few moments later, with the bottle and glasses. He begged for forgiveness—he had been careless, he had stumbled and broken a glass . . . Oh, and Aunt Paula had said that if the Doctor would like to see Papa now, he was ready.

2

It was Paula—inevitably—who met me at the top of the stairs. I said as she was leading me to the sick-room, "Strictly speaking, it's a breach of etiquette for me to see your brother without first speaking to Dr. Babitch. Perhaps you will make my apologies to Dr. Babitch when he returns?"

She agreed. "Though I do not think," she said bleakly, "that Dr. Babitch vexes himself unduly over matters of decorum."

That might be; but when I came to examine the patient —whom I found sitting, skilfully supported with cushions, in an arm-chair—I could discover nothing to criticize in the fresh evidence of Babitch's professional ability. True, I should have known from the moment I started my examination that the man at work here had not been trained in Vienna: there were subtle differences in the signature. But I could guess at once that my directions for the completion of the drainage had been carried out precisely, for the final suture showed astonishingly neat workmanship, and the patient's whole condition was a tribute to excellent management—the respiration was better established than I had dared to expect, the tone of the flesh more than satisfactory. I had, indeed, an intuitive feeling that the indications were a little too good: they faintly suggested to me that the pace of recovery had been more rapid than what nature ultimately approves of. Moreover, certain of the patient's minor movements appeared to set up reflexes which by now should have ceased to operate. But when I asked him if such movements caused him any pain he answered coolly that, though he felt unequal to riding in a steeplechase, he had never been so free from pain in his life.

"Then I think we must congratulate Dr. Babitch," I said shortly. "There is every sign that his treatment has been remarkably skilful."

He nodded. "I suppose that even for Serbs Almighty Providence has some use!"

"I venture also to congratulate you and Frau Kern on your nursing," I said to Paula. And I wished her brother good night.

He called me back, however.

"Dr. Reichenbach! From what my sister has told me, I think I have to thank you for saving my life."

I replied that I had done no more than perform the comparatively simple operation dictated by the nature of his wound.

"Yes," he said, "that's the way doctors are apt to put things! All the same, you must allow me to say that I am extremely grateful." He held out his hand; and then, with a smile which came quite unexpectedly, he said, "Whether it was worth saving is not a question for me to answer!"

I took refuge in the obvious courtesy: "I am sure Fräulein Kern would have no difficulty in deciding that question!"

"Ah, but women are sentimentalists!" he said.

He glanced provocatively at his sister, and I turned to see how she would take this pleasantry, but she was looking towards the door. There, standing ungracefully with her weight on one foot, and reminding me of a schoolgirl summoned to the Principal's room, Franziska had appeared.

That scene has remained in my mind as a line cartoon. Both women were politely smiling, the one as if to say, 'I hope I'm not interrupting!' the other, 'I was just about to go!' while both, for a second or two, kept resolutely still; so that I saw this comedy of camouflaged warfare as something permanent, like the frieze of the Parthenon, or—more nearly—those periods in a wrestling bout where each man has so shrewd a hold upon the other that they appear to be locked for ever. If either woman was to triumph it would, I thought be Paula, to whose inflexibility was added the authority of her extra years. But perhaps those years were telling her which battles were worth losing; for it was she, at the end of the long moment, who nodded and went away.

Left in command, Franziska with scarcely a glance at me went to sit at Siegfried's side, fingering his hand. But he, in turn, seemed to notice her no more than the rich notice a servant's small attentions: his eyes had remained on me, and he went on speaking as if there had been no interruption.

"Well, Doctor, if you feel any regret about prolonging my life you can always put the action into reverse." His voice was quiet and humorous, a little mannered. "I think you know that quite a number of people are looking for me—Russians, Americans, God-knows-who. Really, you've only got to stop the first man you meet in Ljubljana and tell him where I am, then they'll come and hang me with the most genteel ceremony."

I answered briefly that I was not accustomed to meddling with what was not my business; and for the second time I prepared to leave him. Was it curiosity that detained me? I prefer to believe so—I dislike the notion that Siegfried Zempelmarck ever exerted the smallest magnetism on me.

But I will admit that I found something more than a doctor's interest in the surging assurance of a man who had escaped death so lately and so narrowly. He knew I was Austrian. He must have realized that men of his breed were anathema to those of mine. And yet, from a desperate position, he was virtually challenging me to destroy him. Nor was this in truth a sick man's appeal to my chivalry, or a madman's bravado. Released from the extremity of illness, the lean face before me now was one of robust intelligence, the mouth suggested an individual humour, the blue and finely modelled eyes were lit by a steady flame. In a sense, I saw them as religious eyes. He believed in himself, I thought—in his right to live, in the primacy of his own virtue—with a perfect singleness of mind; and just as the glowing faith of priests will kindle faith in others, so the heat of this man's conviction—as I saw it now in the stringent command he had of his body, in the brilliance of his gaze—could have lit in feebler spirits an answering devotion.

"Dr. Reichenbach," Franziska said, "won't you sit down!"

Siegfried was still watching me intently. He said, as if he were picking up the trail of my thoughts, "I admit that I myself have an irrational desire to go on living. It's just a habit, I suppose."

"It's one on which doctors rather depend," I said.

"But I specially want to at the present time. I can't expect you to understand this—for one thing, it's considered old-fashioned and romantic to love one's country nowadays. But there it is! At least you'll agree with me that we Germans have never been in so desperate a condition as we are now—we're a stricken body that the wolves are tearing to pieces. Well, some would say that that's the end of the matter—*res finita est, nunc dimittis!* Only I happen to think otherwise—I am that much a philosopher—I just don't believe that Germany's wounds are mortal. We're in a period of ordeal, it has lasted now for thirty years, and that's only a moment of time in the scale of history. Our country's in ruins, yes—but those ruins are the hardcore that patriots build on: we're not at the end, we're at the beginning. That's why I want to live—it's because I'm going to be needed."

This was said quietly, with a dignity to which few would have been impassive; and one cannot ask more of a man than to express the deepest thought of which he is capable. For myself, I saw the love of country that he spoke of from a different station: I saw the triple file of armoured cars sweeping apocalyptically through Franzensring with its retinue of prostituted children, I remembered the nights of lying awake and listening for a knock on the street door, the face of my mother's aged cousin Margarete after a day's interrogation. But since this man was my patient, and we were not alone, I kept those thoughts in restraint—a prosaic answer seemed to be all that was needed:

"I should say there are limits to what any one man can do in the public service. It's better, I think, to face that fact."

This brought from Franziska an anxious, questioning look, but it had no such effect on her husband. He surveyed me as if I were a youth of promising but limited intelligence.

"Yes," he said, smiling, "but perhaps you will allow me to calculate the limits in my own case. Up to now—to tell you the truth—I've done almost nothing. I was bred as a soldier—I was almost born one. You could say that my whole existence began to be justified on the day we moved to clear up the shameful situation with Poland. And then what happened? In just one week I was a cripple. Not from bullets—not from a shellburst—that would have been at least respectable. No, just a bloody fool of a motor-cyclist— on the Torun road—a half-baked reservist who couldn't be bothered to look where he was going. And that's where my soldiering finished. Static commands for the rest of the War—in fact, I was a glorified policeman."

"That was a disappointment for you—I see that——"

"Yes, and I was trained never to accept defeats and disappointments. There's one thing that I've gained—I'm still alive. You may think me superstitious, but I believe that Providence has spared me from one task to use me for something greater. In the years which are coming, my country is going to look to people like me. Well, I shall be ready."

I was watching Franziska's face, but it told me nothing: it was the face of every loyal wife, self-trained to suffer her man's grandiloquence with apparent content. To me it had always been distasteful to encounter men of her husband's breed in their moods of self-pity or exaltation, and I turned to meet his eyes again with discomfort, as one approaches the insane. But these eyes were neither fanatical nor lachrymose; he was, as he had said, entirely a soldier, he had portrayed himself and his vision of life with nothing but sincerity. A moment later he gave me a smile of simple good-fellowship which showed me for an instant the man his male friends would have known—the austerely dedicated officer who could yet be genial company in his hours off duty.

"But that's of no interest to you!" he said courteously. "Why should I be anything to you but a medical case! . . . And really I shouldn't be keeping you—my sister told me you have a car waiting."

I did not see Paula again that evening, though I fancied she might be watching from somewhere along the passage when Franziska was leading me downstairs. Her presence in that house was curiously pervasive. While we were talking in the sitting-room—Franziska, Ludwig and I—I had the feeling that we were all uneasy, expecting at every moment that she would come, chilly and estranged, to join us.

Of course, my own presence may have come between Franziska and her father. Yet it seemed to me that they would have been still less at ease alone. Though no one, watching them as Franziska gently fussed over the old man's comforts, would have doubted their devotion, I saw their love for each other as a plant trained to grow away from sunlight. Most likely there had never been a spoken difference about Franziska's marriage, a hint or gesture of reproof; and if so—if the father's distress, the daughter's self-reproach, had never been exposed to the cleansing of speech or of tears—how much less soluble the shadow which overhung them now! For them, I thought, the intrusion of Paula might well be no more than a symptom of the malady which had fallen long before on their affection.

"You must go very carefully!" Ludwig warned me when I rose to leave them. "I used to keep up the road to the village at my own expense. Now, of course, it's a public charge, so nothing's ever done about it—there are pot-holes every few yards. You've got a torch?"

This I had stupidly forgotten.

"I'll go with him as far as Gubets's cottage," Franziska said. "I'll take the stable torch."

I protested that I could make the passage of less than a mile with reasonable safety—I had done so on the outward journey.

"And Paula thinks you should be out of the house as little as possible," Ludwig reminded her.

"Sometimes," she answered quietly, "I feel like deciding things for myself."

I ceased to argue, suspecting that she wanted a word with me alone. And in this I was right. Setting off together, we were hardly out of the house when she said—as if we had both been acting parts hitherto——

"Now, I'd like you to tell me, please—is Siegfried out of danger? Medically, I mean."

I answered, "No. But his progress has been remarkably rapid. If everything goes equally well for another two or three weeks I think my reply will then be 'Yes'."

Scarcely waiting to take this in, she asked impatiently, "Then how soon can he be moved?"

"You mean—in an ambulance?"

"Well, yes—or a vehicle of some sort, I suppose."

I considered this. "Again, I should say at least another fortnight. You see, there are several kinds of risk. For one thing, I should never willingly subject a case like this to a succession of changes of air—changes in temperature and humidity."

But women do not listen to technicalities, and she broke in, "Is that really the very earliest?"

"In my opinion, yes. Actually, I'd rather leave it somewhat longer."

"You wouldn't," she retorted, "if you were living in a sort of siege like us!"

She spoke in the tone, lightly impertinent, that one schoolboy will use with another; and this familiarity did not strike me as unnatural. Indoors, she was a component of the household, the rural landowner's child who had grown to be the self-effacing wife of an officer. Of those uniforms the darkness in the lane had divested her, and the person who walked beside me took shape invisibly as another of the students I had once gone about with, girls we met on equal terms, who charmed us as much by their likeness to ourselves in humour and intelligence as by their difference. Released from my own uniform, I answered her as easily as I should have answered one of them:

"Frankly, if I were in your shoes I'd have gone mad or committed suicide long ago!"

"Then what would have happened to Johannes?"

"I suppose your sister-in-law would take charge of him."

"Paula? My God!"

"A most capable woman, I should have thought——"

"Yes, insufferably . . . Oh, I know she's been marvellous!"

"Tell me," I said, "where is your husband to go to when he can be moved? Or perhaps I ought not to ask you that."

She hesitated, but only for an instant. "There's a family he knows in Ciudad Real. They would shelter us for a time, anyway."

"Spain—that's not an easy journey."

"I know. But Paula thinks it's possible—by sea. I think she's got most of it planned, only she doesn't tell me much. I suppose she thinks I'd babble about it to Papa, and he'd go and tell somebody. She never trusts him. Well, she doesn't trust me either."

I said, "Surely that's foolish of her!"

As if she had conducted me far enough, Franziska halted. Her hand which held the torch fell slack, and the pool of light we had followed dropped behind like a dog brought to heel.

"Is it?" she said. "Sometimes I'm not sure if I trust myself."

In the vault of stillness left by the cessation of our footsteps, those words, falling in a whisper, came as if printed in the centre of an empty sheet of paper. They were scarcely addressed to me: she would not, I think, have so bared her mind but for the darkness which enclosed us. But for me, in the moment when I heard them, the world of physical sensation lost significance, yielding to one where spirits move in freedom. I had known almost nothing of the creature beside me: suddenly I seemed to know everything. If I saw her again in the common light we should be back in our former places, a man and a woman bound to separate conditions and engagements. But a barrier had once fallen.

For one brief space I had lived incredibly within another's being; and as if there were magic in that simple phrase, *Manchmal traue ich mir selbst nicht,* I should preserve the voice which had uttered it—the depth of its humility, the load it bore of man's experience. Later, I was to search for her particular meaning. But not at that time. We went on slowly, and I waited till the flow of silence had quieted my thoughts—as perhaps it quieted hers—before I spoke again. Then, with constraint, I asked,

"If your husband goes abroad, you're definitely going with him?"

"Why, yes!" she answered simply. "What am I his wife for!"

"I was only thinking of your other obligations. Johannes, for instance."

"Those are different. But in any case, Johannes will come as well. That's to say, if we go at all."

"You mean, the difficulties may prove insuperable?"

"No, I mean that in the end Siegfried might decide to do something else."

"Such as——?"

"He could give himself up—he could let those people try him."

This took me by surprise; and in the moment of confusion I gave words to the question which for my own sake I had meant to suppress:

"I don't actually know what he's being accused of——"

She seemed to be in no way discomposed by this intrusion. "It's something that happened in Bosnia," she said calmly, but with a feminine vagueness, "—he was commanding a district there. Some people were shot, some civil prisoners, they were saboteurs, I think—I think they were trying to escape. They say the soldiers fired under his orders—I mean, that's what it said in an Occupation newspaper. But in any case they would make him responsible, in the position he had."

In the weariness which had come into her voice I seemed to recognize an aspect of the realism of women. For her, I thought, all which had to do with legal process was a masculine artifice that had little relation to right and wrong. But this, I realized presently, was a specious judgement.

"But he won't do it—he won't let them try him," she continued tonelessly, "as long as Paula's there to say 'No'."

I asked, with caution, "You haven't attempted to influence him yourself—one way or the other?"

"What I want," she answered firmly, "is for Siegfried to make his own decision. I don't see that it would count, otherwise."

'Count'? I did not understand that. I said,

"But you—you're inclined to hope that he'll decide to stand his trial?"

We had stopped again. She did not answer at once, and I was afraid I had pressed her further than our slender acquaintance warranted. Then she spoke with a control which I knew was far from costless.

"Sometimes I think it's just my cowardice—I sometimes feel I can't stand it any longer, living all shut up, using my father the way we are. Wondering all the time when the hunt's going to close in."

"Yes, I——"

"But it isn't just that. It's wanting to be innocent again. These war trials, I don't know if they're just political arrangements—Paula says so. But all the same, I don't see how we can say we're innocent unless we're ready to go through one."

Just then I forgot that there must be fewer than ten years between us. I said, as if to a slow-thinking child, "My dear Franziska, no one in the world could suggest that you yourself are guilty of anything! Whatever happened must have been hundreds of miles from where you were."

"That isn't the question!" she retorted with a gentle authority. "When you marry someone you accept the whole of him. You become the same person. If he does something wrong you can't say its nothing to do with you."

My mind was not asleep. Yet I heard that preposterous statement with no more sense of outrage than if she had uttered a commonplace of human wisdom. That is the power of one person's conviction over another's reason. She had not been speaking for effect. She had not expressed an esoteric piety which someone else had taught her. Her belief that one being could be guilty of another's crime was so simple, so patently a part of her nature, that I had to accept it as one which for her was valid and final.

I said aloud, fumbling with my words, "I couldn't feel like that. Not for myself. I'm a much more ordinary person. I can only respect what you feel."

To which she gravely answered—as if she were entering her particulars on some inquiry form—"I am ordinary as well."

However far from truth, that assertion increased the sense of peace which her companionship had brought me. Although we were walking perhaps a yard apart—I know that all the way we never touched each other—I felt that we were held together now not only by the patch of light we followed but by a unity in understanding which had ceased to depend on what was spoken. We had almost reached the cottage where she was to leave me; from here lights in the village were visible, the night air which had tasted only of rank herbs and rotted leaf became tinged with the smells of habitation, wood smoke and burning oil. Here reality returned. But it was thin and insignificant against my fresh experience, which would not be ended with our parting. For in a room as small as mine, as poorly furnished and untidy, I had come upon a radiance by which all other experience would be exalted. If I went back to an existence which seemed narrow and purposeless, the recollection that I had once been trusted with another's solitude would still illumine and transmute my own.

"You must turn back now," I said. "Your father will be getting worried."

"Papa? Yes, I suppose he will . . . But Paula will be worried too!" And now she surprised me again by laughing—she had the laughter of Vienna, delicately derisive, which breaks like the notes of a clarinet upon a day of mourning. "Poor Paula!" she said.

"What—she'll think you're telling me her plans?"

"Oh, worse than that! She'll think it's wrong of me to have gone with you at all. You can't imagine what their minds are like, these Lutheran spinsters—they imagine that married women are always on the brink of infidelity!"

I said we must not allow her sister-in-law to die of moral anxiety; and I thanked her once more for coming to light the way.

"Oh, but it's I who am grateful!" she protested, now serious again. "You don't know what it means to me, to talk to someone who hasn't anything to do with us—someone who's right outside our trouble . . . I suppose you won't be coming any more?"

"Well, it's doubtful."

"Yes, of course, this is a fearful place to get to from Ljubljana."

"And I may not be at Ljubljana for long."

We separated with no more than the conventional phrases; so that I thought again of the student girls I had once gone about with, who looked for nothing from their male counterparts beyond a kaffee-kognak and an hour's amusement. Nor, at the time, did I regret this casual parting. To grasp at the small comforts of sentiment would have been to hazard the rarer enrichment which the protection of darkness had brought us; and I felt a fresh gratitude to Franziska for the Viennese perception that kept her from asking more of this hour than any will afford. We are both, I thought, fully grown. We knew that life yields only to limited demands.

Again there came a sense of relief. I reasoned, as I turned to watch the fleck of light leading her home, 'We have given each other what we can. She herself has said that I am not involved in her predicament. Elsewhere I have a valuable calling, and I have earned the right to follow it in freedom, having long since had my share of our time's fear and distress. For me there is no place in her Gethsemane.'

4

As if it were possible to plan the architecture of one's inner and outward lives: to say, 'These will be my friends, the others mere acquaintances; here will rest my faith and sentiments, elsewhere the motives on which I shall act'!

My days continued to be full. A camp for Hungarian refugees that we were concerned with had to be moved, and this was involving us in political complications. At the same time my social life tended to broaden, for Pishade was a hospitable man and people I met at his house wanted me to visit theirs. These occupations were grateful and often amusing: no one can be long insensitive to the charm of Slovenes, the wistful modesty which thinly covers a sturdy, racial pride, their startling and almost unconscious wit. But now my sense of being merely a performer in an alien theatre took firmer shape. We travel, most of us, with the thought of going back to where we started; what we see and accomplish has no meaning unless some part of it can at last be gathered to the room, the desk, the listening face to which we shall return. For me this point of reference had once been a sprawling homestead which looked across the valley of the Enns; and now the genius of that place, which I had thought was long since dead, seemed strangely to have overtaken me, settling where I should least have sought it. At Vischak there was little that the word 'home' embraces; least of all, security. Yet it was this cold and disordered house which I thought of now as fishermen think of their cottages on shore. In the noisy restaurant of my hotel, in conference rooms where I listened for whole mornings to unfeasible projects being argued from a dubious Marxian exegesis, my inward eyes and ears were turned to the flaking walls of the farm-house passage and the worn treads of the stairs, to Ludwig's troubled smile, to a bodiless voice which had come to sound as if it were my own: 'Sometimes I'm not sure if I trust *myself*.'

Of course I went again. What you have done once with impunity comes to feel innocent and safe. In the newspapers which I regularly scanned there was never a reference to the missing Zempelmarck, and it seemed at least possible that the authorities concerned had lost their interest in him as well. From the narrow embrasure through which I surveyed the larger scene I could imagine that the wind of sentiment in Europe was veering: men had begun to see the future as something more than mere survival, and in minds that were looking forward the question of one individual's past offences against the rules of international slaughter was perhaps assuming an academic flavour.

I had, besides, an excuse for going. In casual conversation with Pishade I learnt that Babitch's truculence had become too much for the Slovenian tolerance of eccentricity. The police of Ljubljana were by no means ignorant of the principle whereby one bureaucracy transfers its problems to another, and the person of Babitch had been returned with appropriate courtesies to the police of Trieste. So the Zempelmarcks were again in need of a medical adviser.

They accepted me as such; and as my evening visits became regular I attained to something like an inmate's status. Johannes came to recognize my knock, he would run to the door, unbolt it almost before he had heard my voice and greet me as if I were an amiable uncle. There was no longer any fuss about taking me upstairs—I went to Siegfried's room, or lingered talking to Ludwig in his separate world, just as I pleased. It especially flattered me to feel that I had reached a certain understanding with Paula. At least her suspicion of me seemed to have expired; and by degrees she appeared to welcome me not only as a doctor in whom she had confidence but almost as a family friend. No doubt her life had been short of friendships, certainly of those with men; for although, in a narrow light and in repose, her features might have won a Holbein's admiration, I could imagine no man's emotion being stirred by them. That would have explained the vein of shyness which was sometimes visible beneath her self-sufficiency. If, when I was talking of some clinical matter, I turned suddenly to face her, I would see her watching me as young women of an earlier age were said to watch their music-masters, and then she would avert her eyes in quick confusion. Once or twice I let fall a compliment (which she fully deserved) on her skill in nursing, and this brought a smile of such embarrassment, such artless pleasure, that it was almost pitiful to witness: as though an actress in her failing years had slipped for a horrifying instant into one of her early parts, that of a timidly expectant girl.

Yes, to have overcome this woman's distrust was agreeable to my vanity, and such conceit may have dulled my natural antipathy to her brother. For my relations with him took on at least an appearance of easy neutrality. Deprived of other masculine associations, he may have been in some way glad of my visits; and the situation between us appealed, I think, to his particular humour. He was a creature born to dominate. His empire had been much reduced; and now, to the two devoted women left under his command, there was added a man of the kind from which he had least right to expect either friendship or service. In his mind my rating was probably the same as Babitch's—I may have come somewhat lower, since Babitch had at least his military pretensions—and he must have felt for me, a reactionary Austrian, the contempt of a Jacob for an Esau. From this distance I can see how it amused him to have brought such a creature under his control at the cost of no more than a specious amiability.

Had I any reward for accommodating myself to such people as those? Could the tolerance they disguised as friendship have answered in any way my need for a place, a circle, to belong to? The truth, I think, is that I accepted them in loyalty to Ludwig, much as one accepts a tiresome child out of fondness for its parents. The house, for ever breathing the Austria I had loved, was his; and despite the distance at which he kept them, the Zempelmarcks, no less than Franziska, were included in his protection. I could not be at once his friend and at open enmity with them.

With Franziska herself I had little to do at that time: she was much engaged in the kitchen, and elsewhere I saw her merely in her accustomed roles—as Paula's humble colleague in the sick-room, as devoted mother and daughter down-stairs. Only once or twice, when we happened to meet in the hall, did she give me fleetingly her serious, private smile, as if I were the faithful guardian of some object which she had secretly placed in my care.

5

But if I came to suppose there was no risk in my adher-ence to Ludwig's household, it was not for lack of warning.

The frequent journeys by car from Osrovek were expen-sive, and one evening when the bus was running it seemed a rational economy to use it. Like all such buses it was a social centre: the women returning from their marketing chat-tered like poultry, stretching across each other to shout at neighbours or to point censoriously at an old man who had fallen into liquorous sleep on the floor. And in this tumul-tuous hive, lurching on broken springs through the dark countryside, I was peculiarly a foreigner. In Serbo-Croat I am reasonably at ease; Slovenian I can manage *tête-à-tête*. These people, talking all together, so blunted the Slovenian consonants that at times I could almost imagine I was hearing the speech of an African tribe.

Not that I had any need to understand them—I had thoughts to last the journey. But when the word 'Schwarzenberg' came to my ears it set me listening more attentively.

It came from one of two country girls who sat together —I was leaning on the back of their seat. "You'd better go ask Old Man Schwarzenberg"—something like that.

"Oh, I wouldn't dare!" the other girl said.

A young labourer with a face of remarkable intelligence leaned towards them from the seat opposite theirs. He spoke more clearly than they did—he had been schooled, perhaps, in Ljubljana.

"Schwarzenberg's nothing!" he said. "He doesn't own the place any more."

"Who does, then?"

"Nobody. We do. It belongs to the Republic."

"But he lives there."

"We let him, that's all."

"And his daughter does."

"She's only visiting," the other girl said.

The topic seemed to be of general interest. A youth who had constantly turned to ogle the girls from the seat in front of theirs now knelt upon it and hung over to join in their conversation, and as their voices rose in argument friends farther up the bus shouted their own replies. I lost the greater part of what they said, but I could trace the general course of discussion from phrases which now and then reached me distinctly:

"That's his daughter."

"Another woman, I tell you!"

"It must be a spectre—Draga is always seeing them."

"Who pays—that's what I want to know—who pays for feeding those people?"

Standing close to me was an elderly man whose dark, respectable clothes were incongruous with his labourer's hands and weather-hardened face. His mouth was of the kind which looks as if it were not made to open; and I was surprised when he suddenly addressed the girls in a voice of vexed authority:

"You maids, what do you know! A farm's got to be supervised, you need a scholar for that."

The young, intelligent man half turned his head towards the speaker and then winked at the youth on the other side. He said something which I did not catch, but his friend's answer just reached me:

"Put up with them? How long?"

Already I was suffering some discomfort. I had fancied that in a place like Vischak, away from the highroads and torpid under the weight of custom, the effects of the new economy would be superficial—an overlay of comic opera on a machinery which could no more change than the pitch of fields or the faces of the cattle. But these, the simple countrymen of an earlier day, had altered. They had seen the latest face of war, some had travelled and heard the voice of cities. One could scarcely look for manorial sentiment in men who had discovered a larger allegiance. And now I became aware of a man standing in the central gangway who, previously buried in his newspaper, had started listening to the talk around him with a faint, disquieting smile. Very small, but neat and powerful in body, he looked more like a miner than a farmhand, with a white skin tightly shrunk to the cranium and the eyes deeply recessed. Scarcely parting his lips, this miniature Samson said suddenly,

"They're all the same, those people. That Schwarzenberg, if I had my way I'd no more keep him on the place than I would a bog-rat."

That was spoken without the smallest emphasis; but

because of a faintly alien inflexion his voice seemed to cut more acutely than the others through the hubbub of the bus.

Someone said, "Schwarzenberg? Why, he's harmless."

"You think so? And his daughter too?"

"I knew her when she was toddling," a woman said. "She was a sweetie."

"Yes, and who did she decide to marry?"

This question, delivered as with the point of a stiletto, set up a ripple of embarrassment. Perhaps, after all, some part of the *zadruga* mentality had remained in Vischak, some reluctance to exhibit a domestic scandal to comparative strangers. But presently, from a fresh crossing of voices, I caught the name I had been in dread of hearing.

"Zempelmarck? He's never been here."

"They shot him at the end of the War—that's what I heard.... All right then, he escaped—what of it? ... Well, whatever he did, his wife can't have known. She was here most of the time. When a man's away at the War you don't blame his wife for what he does ... Now? One of those divorces, I shouldn't wonder. You can get them if you're high up. *He* wasn't Catholic."

The miner (as I think of him) had returned to his newspaper, as a father would when his children are chattering nonsensically. But in a moment when the other voices dwindled, his broke out again.

"You people, you forget everything! You forget that you were ever hungry, you've forgotten the War already. Perhaps they left you out of it. They didn't leave me!"

He made no gestures, he never raised his voice. But he spoke with the anger and conviction of the Hebrew prophets, and everyone in the bus was listening.

"This Frau Zempelmarck, she belongs to the Lord of the Manor, so nothing can possibly be brought against her! And Zempelmarck himself? Oh, he's forgotten, what he did was in the War, years ago! Yes, my friends, you don't even remember what he did do! But *I* remember—I have comrades of my own who were there. You, I suppose, if you heard where that man had got to, you'd keep it under your hair. 'Why, he married Schwarzenberg's daughter, it would hurt the lady's feelings if anything was done to him!'"

Pricked by this sarcasm, the most alert of the young men was bold enough to interrupt, "Well, what would you do?" and he was slyly answered by another: "He'd go and ask for the reward."

"Reward?" the miner flashed. "Do you think I'd let the Americans have that bastard! Do you think I'd give *them* the job of hanging him! No, my friends, that's a piece of work I'd do myself, and I'd make it last all day. Yes, and if anyone got in the light I'd string them up beside him."

Had it come from a youngster, that ugly boast could have been dismissed as cheap bravado. But the man before me was one of mature intelligence, whose afflatus—as I read his face—came from a life's experience of cruelty and privation. In a narrow sense he was a righteous man, who would not flinch from the logic of his virtue. Every searing phrase had come from his heart.

He had not once looked in my direction, and the other passengers were plainly too intent upon his eloquence to notice me. But with every sentence he uttered my self-consciousness had increased, till I felt it must be visible to everyone aboard; and those last words of dreadful sincerity made me feel as if I wore a label: 'This fellow is one of them. He belongs to the Schwarzenbergs and is a friend of Zempelmarck himself.' It needed all my self-control to stay on the bus till it reached Vischak.

I was to dream of that man's face. And although the incident appears so tame an overture to the experience which divides me from it now, my recollection of his voice is curiously exact and painful. So may the voice of Jeremiah have come to sound in the memory of those who rejected his prevision.

There was snow falling when I left the bus, but the coldness which set me shivering was mental—I was despicably frightened. Had any vehicle been at hand to take me straight back to Osrovek I should have given in to this cowardice (calling it a righteous discretion); as it was, I walked to the farm as slowly as if I still had to find my way, and several times I stopped in irresolution.

But even if I had turned back the retreat would not have been final. For, as I see now, I was already and finally committed. Not by reason or conscience: I had ceased to argue that I was tied to these visits by professional obligation. In truth, I believe that such decisions are to be traced to a region of the spirit where the voices of self-interest and morality alike are silent. I had made no promise to Franziska; but my constant return to Vischak surely implied that I was bound to her cause, and I had almost ceased to ask myself what elements of right or wrong that cause might embrace. Enough that it was hers. We do not, I think, select our loyalties. We march behind men's flags because of their power and confidence: I followed a woman's, finding in her powerlessness, as well as in her goodness, a compulsion against which I myself was powerless.

Chapter 6

I

IT MUST HAVE been four or five days later that I attended an afternoon Reception in the old Windischgrätz Palace, a civic affair put on, as far as I remember, to welcome one of those international groups of subsidized tourists which even then were perambulating Europe as mites parade on a sheep's carcass. In the way of such parties it was borne on its own inertia well into the evening. I drank a little more than usual, in reaction to the peculiar dullness of the company: the men were mostly bureaucrats of crushing earnestness; their wives, dressed like art students, kept pinning me against the wall to talk with the ingenuous pedantry of sophomores about Vodnik and Freud.

I was manœuvring to get away when a man I knew called Gregolnitch materialized to block my path—he was a staff officer of police, a young giant in whom the face of a debauched cupid concealed a lively intelligence. He was bellowing,

"Well well, here he is! Here's the man who ought to be under lock and key!"

It was apparent that his drinking had drawn ahead of mine. Even so, the words faintly alarmed me.

"Me? What have I done?"

"Done? You're an American, aren't you! What do any of you Americans do but spy on our country!"

"Well, yes," I said, "I must admit the charge. Only yesterday I broke into the Ministry of War at Beograd and stole the plans of a spherical balloon."

"Balloon? What the hell do we want balloons for?"

"Why, to carry off some of the hot air from Ljubljana."

"You, you're a neo-Trotskist, you're a counter-revolutionary!" he roared, shaking me by the shoulders. I saw now that he had drunk even more than I had supposed—he was famously happy. "And you're a liar as well! No one who gets into the Ministry of War comes out alive."

"Yes, I noticed that everyone in there was moribund. Well, I'll hand over the plans any time you care to come round to my hotel."

"My friend, I am far too busy."

"You look it!" I said.

I was beginning to enjoy the man. In the huge surface which his face presented there was room for a great variety of nervous exhibition, and as he hunted for a shattering retort I seemed to be watching several comedies played simultaneously on a panoramic stage. I baited him on.

"Everyone knows," I said, "that in a place like this, soaked with democratic virtue, the function of the police is purely decorative——"

"But how dainty a decoration!" said a young woman passing behind me.

Gregolnitch's voice, suddenly released, went up two octaves. "You obfuscated alien!" he squealed, quivering with joyous indignation. "What do you know about police work! Not only do I toil from morn till night, keeping track of undesirable elements like yourself, but I'm expected to do the work of foreign parties as well. This gentleman here, for example."

Beside Gregolnitch's bulk I had scarcely noticed the slim, dark man in military uniform who stood patiently at his shoulder and who now, faintly smiling, bowed.

"Let me present you"—Gregolnitch said abruptly —"M. le Capitaine Sautreuil. My very good friend. Regimental Police—something of that kind."

"Section of Security," the Captain modestly corrected.

"Like yourself," Gregolnitch continued, "the Captain

thinks we civil policemen have nothing to do. So he comes here in a most charitable spirit to invite us to share in his own labours."

Sautreuil had already lost the thread. I offered him a rough translation and he smiled again.

"Only," he said, "if M. Gregolnitch can do so without the smallest inconvenience!"

"I have not one word to say against our French friends," Gregolnitch went on contentedly. "It is just unfortunate that they do not know how to hold their prisoners."

"I would venture to point out," Sautreuil replied, when I had given him a slightly softer version of this sally, "that the man in question was never a prisoner of ours. It was the Americans—with the greatest respect to you, sir—that he got away from."

I put this, for Gregolnitch, into Serbo-Croat, and with the glistening guile of a schoolboy he gathered himself for a flank assault.

"Why, yes, I remember all the details perfectly—I have them in your admirable report. The Americans, yes, a careless tribe—with every possible apology to our friend here. You Frenchmen, you are altogether different, you are known to be the cleverest people in the world."

"What is he saying now?"

"He says he greatly admires the French."

"Indeed? What kindness! For our part, we hold the Slovenes in very high respect."

"I remember now," Gregolnitch pursued, "all the French soldiers did was to encounter the man at a later stage. 'How do you do!' they said. 'You haven't by any chance escaped from the Americans?' Yes, the French intuition is something to marvel at."

This was beyond my powers as interpreter. I let it go. Gregolnitch was sailing before the wind.

"The German—I gather from the report—asked them to excuse him. He said he was in a great hurry—he wished to write a love-poem or to observe the forthcoming eclipse of the moon—I forget exactly what the poor fellow's business was. But the French soldiers were still suspicious. They waited very courteously till he had run three kilometres and then fired their rifles at him. A pity, perhaps, that their marksmanship was not a little better. Still, you can't have everything. Every French soldier, they tell me, can quote the works of Aristotle with the greatest fluency. Naturally there's no time to teach them to shoot as well!"

By now I was more interested in this conversation than I should have wished. But I had drunk enough to give me a feeling of agreeable detachment and, for the rest, I was fully occupied as a linguistic shuttle between my two companions.

"I must allow," said the Captain smoothly, "that the personnel concerned were inadequate as riflemen. One was a Divisional Veterinarian in his early sixties, and the other his Orderly. The Orderly was some ten years older than the Veterinarian. Men of that class are often a little negligent about their musketry."

Gregolnitch nodded. "As a fighting machine," he suggested delicately, "the French Army would perhaps do better with fewer Staff Officers and more soldiers. Or perhaps the Veterinarian would have had more success if he'd flung his brief-case at the fellow."

"Indeed, yes! A Slovenian soldier would probably have pounded him to bits with a copy of *Das Kapital*. The fact remains, my countrymen showed great prudence in driving the fugitive towards the Slovenian border. They were evidently well informed about the excellence of your police service."

To my surprise, Gregolnitch suddenly stopped laughing. "But did they actually drive him across? That's what we want to know!"

Sautreuil, serious in his turn, said, "All our investigations go to show that he came this way. If he hadn't, we'd have traced the car by now. I've spent weeks on the case myself."

"So! And you expect me to find him in about three days, I suppose?"

"Ah, but I haven't the privilege of knowing your methods."

"Already," said Gregolnitch, with a touch of theatre, "I have made up a dossier."

"A dossier? But that is miraculous! I had no idea that such science could be brought to the aid of police work."

Gregolnitch got hold of that remark without my translating it; and, light as the sarcasm was, it seemed to graze him. The smile of avuncular benevolence remained, but I detected a trace of acid in his voice when he said,

"No doubt there are better techniques! In more advanced countries I suppose they plot the course of escaping criminals with radar apparatus. Here, I'm afraid, we're very backward in our ideas. We merely ask ourselves, 'Where is this man likely to go, whom does he know, who is likely to shelter him?' Strangely enough, these old-fashioned methods have been known to succeed."

"Then we may hope," said Sautreuil gently, "that you will be handing our man back to us in—a month or so?"

I translated, and the smears of blond hair which served as Gregolnitch's eyebrows went up a little.

"*His* man?"

The party had livened. Currents of chattering women, of men forcing a passage with plates of food, had swept us by degrees towards the inner hall. Gregolnitch stood now with his great quarters perched on the plinth of a statue, one of those misbegotten works which the Italians have always so shrewdly peddled to Balkan notables; and I retain a striking picture of his elephantine presence, the immense burlesque of dignity in the juvenile countenance gazing censoriously down upon us while, from above the rampart of her luxurious breasts, the vapid goddess in her turn looked down with an imbecile maternity at him. That was how I saw him when he said the words which—though I was more than half prepared for them—went through me like a shaft of ice:

"Tell the Captain, will you please, that I intend to have my hands on Zempelmarck in *less* than a month. Possibly within a week." And with that, the last trace of frivolity suddenly left his voice. "But listen! Whether we hand him over to the French or any other cockadoodle foreigners, that can be settled higher up. This morning I've been refreshing my memory from the dossier I spoke of. We, here, in Jugoslavia, *we* have matters to settle with Zempelmarck ourselves!"

My face might easily have betrayed me. But Gregolnitch's vehemence had drawn a pair of idle girls towards us —"Oh look," one was twittering, "Gregolnitch is making a speech!" while the other, staring upwards, said demurely, "I think his Mummy's waiting to give him his din-dins"— and few men, even sober, can hold their course against the frivolity of women. Sautreuil, in the way of his kind, had already transferred his attention to these damsels: a hundred tiny movements of his lips and brows were signalling astonishment and curiosity, a solution of outrage in worldly tolerance, a diffident demand to be acquainted. Another voice, that of a young man like a pugilist, shouted, "Gregolnitch—he's *always* orating!" and from Gregolnitch himself the mood of combat started sliding like snow from a sunlit roof.

"Well, here, Captain, we've something more worth our time than your war criminals! Sophie here is a decadent, but at least of post-war vintage——"

Already the younger element, eddying and squealing, had wedged me apart from Sautreuil, and in commerce with the feminine he was unlikely to need help from me. Convulsed with laughter at some fresh witticism of his own, Gregolnitch ceased to be aware of my existence. I had only to let myself be carried in the swirl and I arrived like sea-wrack in the vestibule and thence in the street.

The snow which had fallen the night before had been thawing all day, but the wind was again intensely cold and my brain could not at once respond to so fierce a stimulant. I fancied, as I walked through the freezing slush towards my hotel, that I had been the spectator at a performance too bizarre to have any meaning for me. The communal sense of exhibition in social gatherings gives them the falsity of theatre. A bailiff had been boasting in his cups to impress a brace of foreigners; by morning the braggadocio would be forgotten, and if the Zempelmarck file were placed on Gregolnitch's desk he would say correctly that he had more important things to attend to. . . .

But when I turned away from the river and gained the shelter of the printing houses my mind steadied: I knew by then that I was concerned with something more than a costume parade. 'We here, we have matters to settle with Zempelmarck!'—no utterance could have sounded less histrionic than that. And how long would it take, in an office devoted to exhaustive records, to find that the daughter of Ludwig Schwarzenberg had married a man of that name!

I knew at the same time that the course of events was one I could do nothing to interfere with. I had to give Franziska warning; but that, the smallest service my feelings demanded, was also the largest in my power.

The clock on the Lutica building told me that the train for Osrovek had gone. I should have to be driven the whole distance. There arose the question of security. A drosky driver, summoned from the rank to take a foreigner far into the countryside, would surely be inquisitive; if, alternatively, I sent to one of the large hiring concerns for a car my journey would be scrupulously logged, and it was not unlikely that the police made a periodic inspection of such records.

The problem was still unsolved when I reached the Koroshets. There I remembered that Adcock, to mitigate the tedium of exile, had bought himself a car.

I called his hotel and was told by the clerk that he was out; some English friends had taken him to dine at the Carniola Ski-club. There, after an exasperating delay, he was brought to the telephone.

I said, "Peter, I have a favour to ask you. I have to get out to see a man I'm treating privately—out Osrovek way—his case has taken an awkward turn. Could you possibly lend me your car?"

"Why, yes," he answered, "I'll nip back as quick as I can and take you."

"But I can drive myself!"

"Well, yes ... Only—I expect you know, sir—there are fearful regulations about foreigners driving. One's got to register with the police—all sorts of red tape and nonsense."

I told him not to worry over the legal aspect, adding—not quite untruthfully—that I had been in touch with the police less than an hour before. He then gave me the address of the garage where the car was kept, and his blessing on my voyage.

The garage was in the charge of a benign Hungarian who appeared to find it normal for strangers to drive away his customers' property. The car, a Chrysler which had seen better days, back-fired when I started it, but once under way it performed with a coltish eagerness which reassured me.

Two or three times in the first few kilometres I made wrong turnings, and even when I had found the trunk road the going was not easy. At higher levels the thaw had been incomplete, and between wide furrows carved by wagon wheels the wedged snow had frozen hard enough to act as rails, putting the car into violent swerves and once lifting it right off the road. But my memory of that long drive is detached and impersonal, as if it had been some other man who strained to see the road ahead, mechanically reacting to the alternations of ice and mud, while I was wholly absorbed in my objective. With small intelligence. A refracted portrait of the afternoon, a whiff of undigested food and wine which followed me into those lunar hills, relaxed my hold on reality. Franziska ceased to be the woman I knew, mother and wife with patient feet upon the ground; she became the virgin of a romantic student's vision, for ever young, in need of my protection; and from that soft image I evolved heroic fantasy. I saw myself contriving her escape, Siegfried yielding her gratefully to my care; I pictured our flight together to the safety of some sun-washed country, the Sicilian coast, the highlands of Africa, where in a life-time of my devotion the last of her memories of Siegfried would lose their harm: while, as the car cavorted on the snow rucks and the field of light before me shuddered and swung, the voice of Gregolnitch echoing in the vault of my brain turned to a trickle of fear that dripped incessantly towards my loins.

A village passed, of mean and straggling houses. The next, some twenty minutes on, could have been the same one over again. By then the hope of reaching my destination had come to appear illusory. Only a chance deflection which turned my headlamps on a familiar gable-end informed me that I was at Vischak.

I had retained sense enough not to stop in the village but to drive another kilometre or so and leave the car in a side-track, which a belt of spruce had shielded from the heaviest snow. From there I plodded back to the village, knowing no shorter way, and thence by my usual road to the farm. It must have been past midnight by then, but my watch had stopped and I had lost appreciation of time. The place was in such silence and darkness that for some moments I thought —with a relief which was curiously hollow—that the household must have had some earlier warning and taken flight.

It was Franziska who came at last to answer my repeated knocking and who, with hardly a word, took me to the kitchen. There she put the candle on the table and pulled out the dampers to reanimate the fire.

She said—as my mother would have done—"Eugen, you must sit down. Here, where it's warm! And you'd better take off your shoes."

I could only obey her; for at that moment, when I most wanted to have myself in perfect command, I suddenly felt faint and sick. I had eaten nothing—except the toy fare of the Reception—for some twelve hours; my feet and face were frozen; and the strain of the difficult drive, which I had not felt before, must have affected me in retard. Franziska behaved as if she knew all that—no doubt my deranged appearance told her a good deal. "I'll heat some broth for you," she said equably; and having made sure that the window shutters were fast she set about this business as if I were simply a boy late home from school.

I had time then to pull myself together. But it was hard to think about my errand—the ideas of enmity and violence would not connect with this quiet place. The cooking vessels crowding the heavy shelves, aged utensils hanging on grease-stained walls, these, vignetted by the modesty of light, were of that European visage which the marching and victories leave untouched. Franziska was part of this tranquillity. Her face showed her heavy with sleep, and yet there was neither fumbling nor impatience in the way she moved, collecting her materials and tools, finding me a pair of Ludwig's slippers to wear while my shoes were drying: as if the complexities of living were all subordinate to her philosophy, that a cold and shaken creature had to be warmed and fed. She looked her worst (another woman would have said), hair draggling on her forehead, her skin like faded linen in the candlelight. Nothing was left of her aristocracy. For me, had I been seeking beauty then, the play of her young back and shoulders as she stooped and stretched in the grey dressing-gown would have been enough. But her body's poetry was only an aspect of the comfort she gave me in that hour of desperate insecurity. Living within myself I had forgotten how, when you sit in a small room with one person of your own understanding, all experience is brought to stillness and perfection. We were, as it seemed, at the end of the short length where our roads coincided. And yet for a little while I had the feeling that the rest of our separate journeys could not matter, since in the last account we had reached our destination.

She asked, when she had given me the broth and sat down in a chair opposite mine, "I suppose it's bad news?"

I told her what I knew, and she said—rather as if she were discussing something in which she was not immediately concerned—"Yes, they were bound to start searching this country in time—I can't think why they've taken so long. You think they'll be coming for him any time now?"

There was nothing to be gained by equivocation.

"Within a day or two," I answered. "It depends how much work Gregolnitch has on his hands. He's the sort of man who might not hurry over things which aren't his main concern—his business is internal security."

"I see," she said.

The least fanciful of the speeches I had prepared on my way—'We must hope for an acquittal. . . . Whatever happens, I shall see to it that you and Johannes are looked after' —were as useless to me now as the condolences one frames for the bereaved. In this extremity she seemed to be older than I; and I could only wait to see where she would lead me.

Presently she said, "I'm glad in a way that it's coming

quickly. I don't think I could have gone on much longer, waiting for what's bound to come." And then, "If it wasn't for Johannes it would all be much easier."

I showed that I did not understand this.

"If it wasn't for him," she said calmly, "I'd try to make them take me as well. At least I could go to wherever they took Siegfried, I could stay somewhere near him."

I asked gently, "Would that be any use?"

"I mean, they might let me see him—even if it was only once a week, something like that. That would make all the difference. To Siegfried, I mean. Of course, you don't know him the way I do. You wouldn't think that a man like him—a soldier—you wouldn't think he needed any help from a woman. Only, he does. There's just a part of him that isn't sure of himself. I think it's because he was poor when he was young. I don't know. I only know there are times when he needs someone to reassure him—someone he's used to."

I remained helpless. In spite of her distress she spoke so quietly that I still felt young beside her wisdom. There was within me a voice which protested fiercely: that she should owe anything to such a man as the Siegfried I knew! But there was also the voice of my own selfish vanity: 'She is speaking to one she trusts perfectly, she would not so confide in anyone but me.' I said timidly,

"I think you're right to consider Johannes first of all. For the sake of Siegfried himself, for one thing."

"Yes," she answered, as if to a teacher of some reputation, "Yes, I suppose so. . . . But then, nobody's trying to do anything to Johannes. Johannes hasn't got half the world pursuing him."

Saying that, she smiled, but there was only pain in the smile. She seemed to have overdrawn upon her courage, and now she spoke unsteadily:

"I needn't tell him till the morning, surely! Or do you think I ought to tell him now? I suppose—I suppose I couldn't ask you to tell him yourself? In a way it would come better from a man."

"If you think so, yes," I said. "I've come to do just whatever you want."

"But perhaps you ought to be starting back now? I don't even know how you've come—it's selfish of me, I didn't think of asking you."

I told her that I had an automobile handy; that if I were not back in my office by eight o'clock in the morning I should merely have to find somewhere to telephone.

"No, I think you ought to start back now," she said. "I mean, as soon as your shoes and things are dry."

The authority with which she spoke was superficial. She had taken the empty bowl from my knees and now she stood regarding me abstractedly, as if she had forgotten what was our business together.

"I am glad," she said slowly, "that it's you who's brought the news. It makes it easier, when one's got to have that sort of news, hearing it in a voice one knows."

Stiff-tongued, I could only say, "It was a very small thing—it was the least I could do."

And she, losing equally the sinews of speech, answered in a whisper, "I know that God will bless you."

Had I obeyed my readiest impulse, stretched out and taken hold of her hands, that gesture would only have set us apart: she would no longer have accepted my service or affection if she had seen in it the pattern which is recognized as love. Looking at each other's faces, as small children do who meet for the first time a creature of their own kind, we were joint possessors of a country of unimagined serenity. We knew, I think, both equally, that we were there by peculiar licence; that a trick of circumstance had freed us from our separate selves, that only stillness would protect our private truth from what passes as reality. We remained, then, motionless, as if time might not observe us; while the creak of the house in troubled sleep, the noise of particles of ice blowing against the windows, brought me the illusion of being in a ship at sea.

The resurgence of the commonplace, the life of relations and decisions we were assigned to, came leniently. A light grew at the passage door like an artificial dawn. It belonged to a candle which Ludwig was carrying. In the anomalous dress in which I had first met him he stood, sleepy and old, smiling at us with his accustomed gentleness, with a courteous perplexity.

4

In my recollection of that curious night, here clouded and confused, here overlit, like a film faultily projected, the face of Ludwig is one of the components which remain solid and distinct. It was a face more pitiful because it would not yield supinely to his distress, as the faces of simpler people will. I knew what he was feeling: that the misery and shame inflicted on him over a long period were now being tightened into outrage. A man of firmer and younger mind might have said, 'This is no longer my affair. I have given your husband refuge, I cannot fight for him against the police of Europe.' But firmness goes hardly with such charity as his. He had but one desire, to be of comfort to Franziska. And where was comfort to be found for her!

At least it was he who determined, after a shapeless conference, that Siegfried must be told at once what was afoot. There may have been an old man's weakness in this—a wish to unload his own responsibility. Or he may have faintly hoped that Siegfried, at this eleventh hour, would be ready with some solution.

"I shall tell him myself," he said, as if that were an important decision. "But I shall want you with me, Eugen, to answer his questions."

Yes, let me admit that he and I were equally in fear; not

of our predicament but of Siegfried himself. As if I were facing an interview with some superior I was suddenly conscious of my own appearance—my tousled hair and bristling chin surmounting the egregious respectability of the dark suit I had put on for the Reception. But I could not ask for time to repair myself. We went upstairs in silence, like conspirators; Franziska and I together, Ludwig behind us with a candle which threw our shadows grotesquely on the risers ahead. I remember thinking, in that solemn progress with the worm-eaten treads bending beneath us, 'In a few hours from now, when I sit in my office dictating prosaic letters, I shall look on this as on a dream.'

Most dreamlike of all was the appearance, as we turned into the upper passage, of another candle borne by someone I had never seen—a tiny, oldish woman in a quilted satin kimono with her white hair immaculately dressed beneath a net. What she was doing in the house I never learnt: I can only suppose she was one of those survivals from a different age who never allowed the accidents of history to interfere with their social migrations. I do not even know precisely who she was—the widow, I fancy, of some Hungarian nobleman. Her face I remember clearly; it was that of a Dresden shepherdess. Encountering our strange procession, she did not appear startled or discomposed.

We halted. Franziska, dragging herself from her thoughts, said in a whisper, "Oh—this is my cousin Elfriede."

"This is my friend Dr. Reichenbach," Ludwig whispered. "He has come—most kindly—he has come to attend Franziska's husband."

The old lady accepted my bow with a smile I could have taken for pleasure as well as graciousness.

"But how good of you," she said, "when the roads are so bad!" She made no attempt to modulate her clear, Vienna voice. "My friends all say this is not the time of year for the country—but where else can one escape one's friends? I expect we shall meet at breakfast!"

She smiled radiantly again, dismissing me. We went on to Siegfried's room.

5

Possibly he had been listening for some time to our movements downstairs; he must certainly have heard Elfriede's voice. Could he have guessed, or known intuitively, the kind of news I was to give him? I had the impression that he had been bracing himself to receive it. He was sitting up in bed, a copy of *Jenseits von Gut und Böse* on his knees, a lamp at his side. Wide awake, slightly tensed like a hawk about to fly, he contrived to smile at me with a ducal amiability.

"Good evening, Doctor! Or should I say 'Good morning'? What may I do for you?"

A part of my mind, active independently, noted a certain deterioration in his physical condition. The pupils and the skin were less healthy than I had seen them a few days before, there was evidence of some renewed pain in breathing, which he might have disguised successfully from a less experienced observer. Had this been a normal visit I should at once have made a fresh and thorough examination: there were other things to think of now.

Ludwig, standing just behind me, said, "I'm afraid Dr. Reichenbach has brought bad news."

"Indeed?"

"The French have asked the Slovene police to start an intensive search."

His son-in-law nodded as a commander would on receiving the report of an expected reverse. He said deliberately, "I wonder if the Slovene police are very clever. I imagine they're mostly peasants in uniform. My sister bluffed them quite easily on our way here."

To this I answered—since Ludwig was silent—that I myself should not rely on the Slovenes for stupidity in any field.

135

He seemed to accept my opinion. "Then I suppose I must take up residence in that hayloft again," he said tersely. "Really I should never have allowed that madman Babitch to move me.'"

"Surely," I said, "the loft is the very first place they will search."

He nodded again. "Yes, Doctor, I must confess you're a more practical man than I am. Or perhaps you read more adventure stories."

For a moment he shut his eyes. Then, with a movement that cost him a little pain, he turned to fumble under his pillow and produced a P.38 pistol, which he rested on the bedclothes between his knees.

"That being so," he said stiffly, "I can only stay where I am, and do what I can with this thing. I used to consider myself something of an expert. I think I might still account for the first two or three arrivals."

I heard Franziska catch her breath—she was just inside the room—but she did not speak. For myself, the shooting-match he proposed was so far from my notion of reality that I was inclined to let it pass, as one ignores the bragging of a child. But Ludwig said incisively,

"There will not be any gun-play in my house! You will please understand that immediately."

"And what on earth would be the point of it!" I said.

Seldom, I imagine, had Zempelmarck been addressed with so little ceremony by an Austrian or a civilian; it surprised me that he did not lose his temper. He only said, subacidly,

"Then perhaps you will tell me why you've put yourself to the trouble of bringing me this information? What action do you expect me to take?"

I was ready for this, for I had not devoted the journey from Ljubljana entirely to romantic reverie. I said soberly: "If I were in your position, Colonel, I should concentrate on preparing my legal defence. I might possibly be of assistance to you in that. I have at least one lawyer—an American, a man of the highest standing—among my colleagues at Trieste."

"And what do you suppose an American could do for me?"

"There's very little," I told him "that an American will not do when he has set himself a task. He would at least hunt Heaven and earth for witnesses."

Siegfried slightly raised his eyebrows. "I think," he said shortly, "that Heaven might as well be excluded." And then he added, with the kind of simplicity which is found in soldiers, "In any case, I cannot see myself taking part in a tournament of foreign lawyers."

There was no trace of sarcasm in that last utterance; he was only stating a situation, as a woman of royal birth might say, 'I am afraid I do not know how potatoes are peeled.' His gaze was moving rather wearily from one to the other of us, as if we were pieces of furniture of which he had forgotten the use. In a special sense I thought he was lonely. Around him he saw people incapable of understanding his position; who, when a life which he held to be of infinitely greater value than theirs was threatened by a scum of aliens, could speak as if the wrangling of attorneys had an actual significance. Lonely, but not pitiful. To me, at least, it was impossible to find compassion for one who could never desire it, would have seen it only as an offence.

But Franziska—could she still penetrate the carapace he had grown to defend himself from pity? 'There is a part of him that isn't sure of himself'—was that what she was thinking now? She had moved to the head of the bed to occupy herself as women are fortunately able—order and comfort seemed to flow from the scarcely meditated movements of her hands. I watched her face, but she too was armoured, so that I saw only the dutiful wife of a soldier. Her father was observing her as well. He was shivering a little—the room was very cold—and the thought came to me, 'It is he who is most to be pitied. He is not old enough to withdraw himself from the agonies of affection, only too old to put affection to any use.'

So, when he spoke, I was surprised to hear his voice at once vigorous and perfectly controlled—that of a man who knew the world and was accustomed to be heard:

"In my opinion, this is not a time to be thinking about lawyers." His eyes were fixed on Siegfried now. "What you have to think of is acting with a sense of honour. You must surely know what I mean by that."

Siegfried, at a loss, said, "In this connection—no, I'm afraid I don't."

"Doesn't it occur to you that you have some duty to your wife? I should have thought—in your present position—it was the only duty worth considering."

Franziska stood still. I thought she was going to make some protest, but the words dissolved in silence. Siegfried said wearily,

"Perhaps you could be a little more precise?"

Ludwig's answer was patient and resolute:

"If you're going to be rearrested—and that seems inevitable now—your first concern should be to see that Franziska is no more involved than she has to be. It's not too late—not at this moment—to send the police a message. I could take it myself. I should say that my son-in-law was brought to my house to undergo a vital operation, that he is now ready to submit himself to rearrest and trial."

Siegfried had shut his eyes. "Listen——" he began.

"No, I must ask you to listen to me! I have told you how an honourable man would behave——"

"Thank you—but I am not in need of instruction on the subject of honour! I have been a soldier all my life. I am perfectly capable of deciding for myself what is and what is not my duty."

"By which you mean," Ludwig persisted, "that your sense of honour does not include that of having a duty towards your wife! Well, you and I shall never understand each other—we come from different worlds. I should have said that any man would have some consideration for the woman he once married, whether he still loves her or not."

"Father," said Franziska, whispering, "you are not to say that!"

"It was necessary," he answered, "for someone to say it."

For a moment I lacked the boldness to look at Siegfried's face. When I did so I saw no anger there, only bewilderment and incredulity. Remotely, I could trace his feelings, having known men of his school long before. To them 'honour' and 'duty' were the moral passwords of their profession, signifying personal courage, allegiance to fatherland and corps: in such observance a man's wife was identified with him, and the notion that 'honour' could connote a regard for her separate interest was to Siegfried a mere confusion of terms. He stared at Ludwig, and at me, as if he were face to face with naked insanity; then turned, searching for enlightenment, to Franziska herself.

"Franziska, surely it's for me to decide what is right—for you as well as for me?"

She was silent for a space, standing with her knuckles on the frame of the bed, her brows puckered as if she could not quite get his face into focus. Watching them in the bow of lamplight, motionless figures against a reredos of stacked pillows and rococo bedhead, I had the feeling that they were quite alone; and I was conscious, as perhaps never before, of the bridge that time by itself can fabricate between man and wife, the gravitation of days and nights possessed in common, the web of shared familiarities. She said,

"I don't want you to think about me."

"But I am asking you," he insisted, "to give me some direction."

That was spoken quietly, almost with gentleness, as if at the moment he saw himself as the Good Fellow, indulgent to the whims of eccentric friends. Perhaps he was even stirred by his wife's humility, perhaps he realized with regret—if only in the turning of a leaf—that there were harmonies to which he was deaf for ever. I believe that within the framework of his own nature he loved her; that he was hurt and mystified, finding one he loved so unresponsive to his need for independence and esteem. He had not moved: for him it would have been affection to stretch and touch her hand. He only waited patiently for her reply.

It came almost inaudibly: "I want you to be free. I mean, free of being accused of things. I don't see how you can really live till that's been cleared away, once and for all.'

"You mean," he said, still patiently, "till the people on the other side have made up their minds whether to treat me as a criminal for defending my own soldiers?"

She answered, with simplicity, "They couldn't do that."

"You think not?" He made an odd grimace, as one teaching himself to smile from a diagram. "Then I am just to wait here till they come for me?"

Again it was a struggle for Franziska to speak. "I think it would be more dignified," she said, "to do what Father says. To tell those people where you are. I think its the only dignified thing we can do."

Without calculation she had used the effective word. *Würdevoll*: that at least he understood. It was curious to see how, in an instant, his disquiet and lethargy both seemed to fall away. He pulled himself up a little in the bed and spoke to me.

"You've got some sort of vehicle here?"

I told him, "Not far away."

"Good! Then I shall ask you to have the kindness to drive me—I don't know where—Ljubljana, I suppose. Wherever I can report in person to the local police department."

"But not tonight!" I protested. "It's not as urgent as that. I should be strongly against it on medical grounds."

I looked towards Franziska, but she had turned to lean against the chest of drawers, stiff and white in the suppression of tears. Her support would have made no difference: Siegfried had passed the stage of attending to others' opinions.

"Medical grounds?" he said. "How on earth can that matter now! I see no argument at all for holding up this business, now I've made my decision. I shall want to say good-bye to Johannes—but that can wait. Will you please, Franziska, get me my shaving things. And then, Doctor, I shall ask you to help me put on some clothes."

6

This hour—when the whole weight of the past day bore down on my eyelids, when events seemed to move not forward but in a closed circle, returning with the movement of the candles up and down the stairs and along the denuded yellow passages—was the hardest in all that night in which to keep awake. With voices hushed, Franziska sealed in misery, the urge to nervous laughter licking about me like a flame, I had the sense of those gatherings which precede a funeral: only, this was a funeral with its centre-piece not coffined but upright and alive, surveying its own obsequies with reserved, discriminating eyes.

It was not an easy thing to get Siegfried down. He was a tallish man, heavy-boned. God knows what fool of an army surgeon had attended his earlier injury: the leg, even now, would not give so much as momentary support: and if the trunk had fallen forward I might well have had an actual corpse on my hands. Would that have mattered? Vaguely, at the time, I supposed it would. Someone had got the stove going well in the sitting-room and there we placed him on a long chair. The sense of urgency seemed to have left him now, he sat and looked about him with a faintly supercilious tolerance; pleased, I think, by our confusion, and interested to see how long civilians would take to organize the next, simple move.

"But *of course* you can't go till you've had something to eat and drink!"

Like an image left on the retina the face of Elfriede, risen again from the shadows, exquisite and convivial, was never to be escaped. On her darting voice the solemnity of the occasion had made no impression at all.

"I shall have the coffee ready in five minutes. And then I'm going to make *pirozhkis*—a kind of my own—you won't believe it, but I was once the best amateur cook in Szeged. What nonsense, though, to set off at this time of night! Ludwig, darling, come here and persuade this young man that his heroism is quite out of fashion!"

I was impatient to set out and fetch the Chrysler, I wanted the whole thing finished. But I longed still more to get Franziska to myself again, to tell her how closely my spirit marched with hers in every moment of her ordeal. (When should I see her again? What excuse should I have for returning here, with my professional duties at an end?) She came and went, a ghost harnessed to domesticity, now with a valise she had packed for Siegfried, now with a coat and rug, a hunting flask. I did not see her bring Johannes: I first heard the boy's voice, and turning caught sight of him, tidy and partly dressed, standing by his father. He did not look like a child roused from sleep, he was as ever grave and collected, listening with intelligent eyes, with a masculine constriction of the lips and jaw. I heard him say, "If I was older I wouldn't let them!" So far from offering to help his mother, as he normally did, he was totally ignoring her; and it passed through my mind that he could never have been in reality a motherable child.

"Perhaps, Eugen, you would fetch your car now.... But no—my cousin will be cross if you go out in the cold before she has fed you. You must wait, you must wait a little!"

More than once Ludwig repeated such words as those, his

voice shuttered and his head close to mine. Belonging no-where, finding no means to be helpful to anyone, he constantly returned to me as a nervous swimmer to shallow water.

"In the end it will surely be better for Franziska. When this is over. . . ."

Whispering, he searched my face for reassurance. But in his own, beneath the wretchedness, the creeping embarrass-ment, I thought I saw relief and triumph: not only in the prospect of deliverance from a private incubus, but in the resolution of a conflict within himself. He had been too long a prisoner of his own tenderness. These eyes were gentle, but not from feebleness of understanding; the lips could be softened by compassion, but it was not the more lenient virtues, it was no physical or moral cowardice, which had cast this mouth and chin, as I saw them freshly defined by the languid, horizontal light from the lamp at the far side of the room. And what had it cost in pride for a man like this to watch and help the evasion of justice, what must he have suffered from an anger which could only be left to blaze inside him!

"It may help him a little, the fact of his surrendering—it could possibly influence the verdict. For Franziska's sake one has to hope so. . . . At least it will be better for her when tonight is over. God does not let us stay on the peaks of suffering."

"You'll have to be patient!" Elfriede called, surging towards us with a bottle and glasses in her hands. "The *pirozhkis* are taking longer than I thought—I'm not used to that sort of stove. But look, this will comfort you—genuine kognak—smuggled. . . . So you live in Ljubljana, Doctor? All among those *savants*! I'm told they've proved by the latest scientific methods that the earth is flat, and about ten kilometres in diameter. . . . I think our friend over there should have a glass too—but not the boy, it's wicked to give vintage Delamain to children."

Yes, the room might have been divided by a screen of

glass, and on the other side father and son, heads close together, appeared content with their isolation: when I took the drink to Siegfried he murmured "I thank you heartily" without even turning his eyes and went on talking to Johannes—I caught scarcely a word, but the sound of his voice was lazy and amused. Next time I looked that way the boy was smiling. His face just then was a draft of his father's—whose smile was never more than a flag of self-assertion—and I thought I discerned a relationship more stable than mere admiration and response: it was rather as if two men were conversing on equal terms, perhaps finding in each other their refuge from a common immaturity. At the time that picture was printed only on the surface of my mind, for I was wondering what had happened to Franziska —she had been out of the room for some minutes—and trying to think of an excuse to go and find her. Half asleep, I had lost belief in the mission so abruptly assigned to me, for the man who had required it seemed to have forgotten his intention, and though Ludwig may inwardly have been tortured with impatience no one showed any will to hurry. The ceaseless thrust of wind against the outer wall accented the calm which the temperance of light gave to the warming room: one ceased to see reason in adventuring from the stillness which was falling on us as though a pendulum were coming to rest.

7

But I must have realized, however dimly, the particular risk involved in dawdling. For when the door suddenly opened it was not Franziska I expected to see.

"What is happening?"

With that voice of Paula's, still and small as the voice of God, came the chill which a professor's tongue brings upon guilty children. White faced, with her hair drawn tightly from her forehead, thin as a stove-pipe in her linsey dressing-gown, she was a figure more frightening than any man I have encountered. I had the feeling that her question was rhetorical—that she knew already what we had planned and why no one had welcomed her.

"Siegfried, why are you down here?"

He smiled as a boy would who, alone in the class, had finished his exercise.

"It's quite all right—I have my medical adviser with me! My father-in-law has a plan for me, and Franziska has given it her approval."

Ludwig damped his lips. "Fräulein Zempelmarck, we have news that the police are likely to be here in a matter of days or hours. Your brother has to choose between waiting for them here or going to them. In my opinion he's made the more honourable decision."

"Honourable? You mean, to give himself up?"

Ludwig nodded. "Dr. Reichenbach," he said, "has kindly agreed to drive your brother to Ljubljana. Now—immediately."

His voice was resolute, but firmness counted for nothing here. I myself was moving a chair for Paula to sit down but I stopped: as well might I have offered a seat to the tower of St. Stephen. No man, I think, could have kept his whole body as still as she kept hers, or spoken, as she did now, without appearing to use lip or breath.

"And this is what I spent two years for, two years doing nothing but planning his escape? Is that all we Germans have to do now—offer ourselves to the international hangmen? Have we spent our lives for that?"

In another glance at Siegfried I saw him still complacent, wholly detached. Then my eyes went to the door again: Franziska had come in.

Paula did not turn her head. She waited, still motionless, till Franziska was in front of her, and then she said,

"Franziska! Is it your idea—this lunacy?"

Franziska answered, "Yes."

I tried to break in: "If I may say——"

"No, you may not! Franziska, is this what you think a wife is for—to throw her husband away when he's become an inconvenience? Is that what you married him for—was it just to get a child and nothing else?"

I thought—with my superficial knowledge of women— that Franziska would be brought to tears. She was not. She stood almost as still as Paula herself, surveying her gravely. She said,

"Paula, it's no use—you could never understand. You're incapable of seeing what other people are like. I don't think of Siegfried as you do, I think of him as a child of God. I want him to be free in a different way from you. I want him to be innocent. That's why I've asked him to submit himself to justice."

"To justice?" There was no rise in Paula's voice, it only lost its substance as if a tumour had grown suddenly to press against her laryngeal nerves. "To be catechized by a crew of Russians—is that what 'justice' means to you! A squad of bolsheviks with a sprinkling of international attorneys to give them a look of respectability—with their own rules and witnesses, their own gaolers and executioners!"

"There is no other tribunal," Ludwig said succinctly. "There is nothing else we can do."

"Great God, there is everything else! Siegfried, you're not telling me you've given in completely to the childishness of these cowardly Viennese?"

We turned, all of us, to look at him as if he were a witness newly brought into court, and I expected to see him in some confusion. But he did not appear in any way disturbed. Haggard, yes, but only from illness; and in this mellow light the pallor and emaciation of his face had curiously increased its handsomeness. In bronze, it would have been a work of splendid power. He smiled; not weakly but with a masculine good humour.

146

"My dear Paula, I am at everyone's service! Do please decide among yourselves whether you want me to be finished off at Nürnberg or somewhere else."

"Siegfried, you know that is nonsense! It's for you and no one else to decide whether you're going to throw yourself away."

"Naturally!"—It was Franziska who answered her, with a perfect dignity. "No one has suggested otherwise."

But in truth it was not for Siegfried to decide. We all knew that.

I asked myself again, why were we helpless against this woman? It was, I think, that there was no common ground between her and us where reason could be brought to bear. What use, indeed, was any argument against a mind so single, a conviction so passionate as hers! To us she appeared —with her white, constricted face, the glasslike anger in her eyes—a creature of the theatre: to deal with her on equal terms would have been to cross into unreality. But to herself (as I believe) her blazing righteousness, her contempt for any view but hers, were no more extravagant than the walls about her, the floor on which she stood; for if ever she had surveyed herself from the outside she was incapable of doing so now. She lectured us, never pausing, never altering the pitch of her voice, and it was like enduring a day of bitter wind. Ludwig presently turned away to fiddle with something on his writing-desk. Franziska stood still, expressionless. I stared at the orator, no doubt with a face of hircine foolishness; while, in their corner, Siegfried and Johannes sat composedly, Johannes strangely smiling, his father listening as if to a piece of music so familiar that it no longer enlists the mind.

So stringent was the spell she laid on us that the rattle of a loaded tray and the flying open of the door did not disturb it. But it failed to fasten on Elfriede. Triumphant in her handiwork, Elfriede stood, a lifelong débutante, awaiting our applause.

"It's a shame to interrupt you, Fräulein Zempelmarck," she said, "but these have got to be eaten while they're hot, otherwise they're vile. Afterwards we will all sit down and listen. Doctor, you must be first, as you've got to hurry away."

"Dr. Reichenbach is not in a hurry," Paula said curtly. "My brother is not going on with that nonsense."

"What? Dear me—well, it's a woman's privilege to change her menfolk's mind. There should be a sauce of olives with these things, but I don't really know my way about my cousin's larder."

"And may I ask," Ludwig demanded, coming to life again and regarding Paula as a humanitarian would look at a dog with rabies, "what is your alternative plan?"

"'Alternative'? I should say I'm the only one with any plan at all!" Impulsively Paula turned to me. "Doctor, will you please wait here—I have something to give you."

She hurried out of the room. But the constraint she had imposed on us stayed behind her, and disregarding Elfriede's bustle the rest of us hardly moved. With a calculated wisdom Siegfried said to Franziska,

"My dear, if Paula has some sensible plan it seems wasteful not to try it—don't you agree?"

Hesitating, Franziska glanced at me for counsel. And I failed her: I sent her only a signal of despair.

She whispered, "Very well!"

Then Paula was back.

She was holding a small parcel. Ignoring everyone else, she took me over to Ludwig's desk as if I were her confidential clerk.

"Now, Doctor," she said quietly and swiftly, "you know the man who calls himself Dragutin—I want you to see him. He knows exactly what he has to do—I've had letters taken to him, but of course he can't send anything to me, not till the last moment. What you have to do is to make him understand that he must act at once, whatever the risks."

"But Dragutin—as far as I know—is in Trieste."

"I know—but you can get there, you're free to go where you like. *I* got there! Now listen, I want you to give him what's in this parcel. It's some things he is to sell for expenses —I shall have to trust him about the prices. Tell him the crucifix is Polish—an expert told me it's fifteenth-century work."

"Surely," said Elfriede, inserting herself between us, "the Doctor may be allowed to eat something now."

I turned, profiting by the interruption, and saw that Franziska had come close behind me. I said, in the voice that comes to me when I speak to patients' friends,

"Frau Zempelmarck, I had not realized that your sister-in-law's plans were so far advanced. It seems there is just a chance—I should say an extremely small one—of getting your husband away."

She answered, to herself rather than to me, "Yes. Yes, I suppose there is a chance."

"I am ready," I said, "to do what Fräulein Zempelmarck has asked me, if that is your wish."

"*I* do not wish it!" Ludwig interposed, coming to Franziska's side. "There are limits to what one may ask of one's friends."

I felt bound to ignore him. To Franziska I said, "I am perfectly willing."

Of that I was afterwards ashamed. It was cowardly to evade my own responsibility, cruel to shift it on to one torn as she was. She, however, seemed not to observe my pusillanimity: she had never, I think, been percipient of masculine feebleness. For a few moments she was locked in the struggle for decision; then she answered,

"Yes, if you please, Doctor Reichenbach, I shall be very grateful if you will help us in that way."

At that, I took the parcel from Paula and said, with the firmness of voice in which cowardice hides itself, "Very well, Fräulein Zempelmarck, I will make the journey to

149

Trieste as quickly as I can arrange it. I shall see Dragutin and do my best to make him understand the situation. That is all I can do."

"But first," Elfriede said with seraphic patience, "you must have another cup of coffee. I have only once been to Trieste, but I remember the coffee there was quite undrinkable. Really I feel we've entertained you very badly—it's a pity we couldn't have had some music. If I'd known——"

"Quiet!" said Ludwig suddenly.

He had hardly raised his voice, but it brought a stillness like that which follows an explosion. We listened intently, and the stretching silence was torn by a trident of sound, the soft, deliberate rapping of a bare knuckle on the outer door.

Elfriede beamed. "Another visitor!"

"Quiet!" Ludwig repeated. "Wait, I'll go myself."

In an instant Paula had moved to the lamp and put it out. I followed Ludwig to the passage door and closed it after him. Standing there in total darkness I heard him moving slowly down the passage, stopping to strike a match, calling in a steady voice, "Who is that?" A new silence fell and dragged like an empty day; then came the sound of the bolts being drawn.

8

I knew, as I did not hear the jerk of the door on its dropped hinge, that it was opened only a little way; and a second later the bolts were slid home again. Now there were voices in the passage, Ludwig's and another, an antiphonal murmur which went on and on like the talk of women at cottage doors. There were sounds within the room as well, Elfriede faintly giggling and Paula furiously quieting her. But in those frightening minutes I was wholly self-centred, imagining my situation when the police found me in this company —I pictured myself being brought before Gregolnitch and trying to bluff him with some flimsy story, I even forecast the witticisms of my colleagues when the news reached Trieste.

At last I heard Ludwig returning—whether alone my ears would not tell. The door opened, and he said with a nervous impatience,

"Will someone please give us some light!"

I felt my way across the room and re-lit the lamp. As I did so I heard him say, as if to himself,

"It was not the police."

Either the others did not hear or they did not believe him. Except for Elfriede no one had moved: they seemed to be frozen by the winds of fear and despondency, and as the flame of the lamp steadied I felt as one does on a voyage where, night after night, one finds the same four silent people nursing their cards in the same corner of the saloon.

"Who was it?" I asked.

For answer, Ludwig turned and called, "Mosha, I should like you to come in, please," and a small, grey man came and stood in some embarrassment just inside the room. At the second glance I recognized him: it was he who had reproved the girls on the bus.

He was recognized by Elfriede as well: "Oh, Mr. Gubets, how nice to see you again—we met when I was here before!"

"Mr. Gubets," said Ludwig with compacted ceremony, "is my former steward, and always my very good friend."

"But what," Paula asked liplessly, "is he doing here?"

"He has come at the greatest inconvenience and risk to give us a warning—the situation is worse than Dr. Reichenbach has told us already. The house is to be searched tomorrow morning."

"Searched by whom?"

With a gesture, Ludwig passed the question to Gubets himself, who said, in a laborious but dignified German, "There are young men in the village, gnädiges Fräulein, who take in any sort of talk. I said to them, 'People have a right to live where they always have!' but they won't listen to sense, these men back from the War. 'That house, it would take three families'—that's the way they talk. I said to them, 'There's not a lot of room in that house, when you come to look into it.' 'Well,' he said—this man Simovitch, he's the one who does all the talking—'Is there any special reason why we can't look into it for ourselves?'"

"It's reasonable!" Ludwig said.

"They'd have come straight on tonight—they've all been drinking in the club-house, Simovitch and his friends—but I told them there were wolf-traps set by the lane down there."

I saw that Siegfried was listening with sober attention. He suddenly broke in, in a voice which was reasonable and friendly:

"But by tomorrow they may have forgotten all about it, if they're all drunk tonight?"

"Sir," said Gubets, with his eyes averted from Siegfried's, "Simovitch won't have forgotten! They'll be here when it's light, Sir, if you'll kindly take my word."

That was not difficult—only a fool would have doubted it. Roused by the shock of Gubets's arrival, my sluggish wits were returning to my service, and they gave me a cold cartoon of what would happen. Men who had worked most of their lives on this farm would know their way to every corner. I saw them trapesing about the house in twos and threes, at once sheepish and insolent like schoolboys in revolt, their peasant eyes missing nothing—a scene, colourless in the indoor light of winter, where the last excitement would be submerged in a drab and sickening indignity. And Franziska was to witness this! I dared not look at her now. Instead, I turned to Siegfried himself, and in a tone which surprised me by its fibre, I said,

"Evidently there is not much time to spare. I've undertaken to drive you to Ljubljana. My offer is still open."

A movement from Paula, the sound a child makes recovering from tears, made me glance in her direction expecting a fresh tirade. What I saw was an exhausted woman, pitifully slight in stature, stupefied by defeat. In that instant I remembered her fortitude on our first journey together, her perfect self-command in helping me with the operation, her tireless devotion as sick-nurse. And I said impulsively,

"Fräulein Zempelmarck, I am so very sorry—I'm afraid it's too late now to get the help you hoped for from Trieste. But I do believe the other course is for the best—whatever happens, it can only redound to your brother's credit."

She may have been transiently grateful for my stilted sympathy: perhaps I imagined too much, but I thought from a clouding of her eyes that she was on the point of yielding to some gentleness latent in her nature. Almost at once, however, that look had passed. Deliberately, she turned away from me and spoke to Gubets:

"Mr. Gubets, I think it's most kind of you to have come to warn us. You say that a party will be coming to search the house—at what time?"

"It might be nine o'clock," he answered hesitantly, "or it might be before."

"Then tell me, if you please—is there any empty house you know of, any cottage, I could make use of for a few days? Not one that's close to other houses."

The old man pondered. "There's nothing I know of, only the sheds the men used to sleep in over at Tustar, at the old quarry there."

"And there's a road that goes to it?"

He looked at her narrowly—he was not a stupid man.

"A road of sorts," he said. "But if you were to drive a motor from there to here it would leave its tracks—the ground being covered like it is."

"Mosha," said Ludwig abruptly, "I am not going to have you mixed up in this affair! You have done enough for us. You must get home now, and not let anyone know you have been here. From now on you've got to pretend that your friendship with me and my family is over—that you see me only on business matters."

I thought the steward would submit at once to the authority in that advice. But there came to his face a curious obstinacy.

"Sir," he said, "my father was your father's servant. When he was old and useless—sixteen years—your father let him have his house and wage the same as before. We do not forget such things."

Of all this Paula was seemingly oblivious. She was questioning me in an undertone about where I had left the car. " ... You mean it's the other side of the hill behind us there—the hill we came over on foot when I first brought you here? ... That can't be far from the quarries this man talks about—I know that Tustar is over that way."

It was time to put an end to her fantasy. I said, loudly enough to get everyone's attention, "I see what you have in mind. So I must tell you that to carry our patient in his present condition over the hill is from every point of view an absolute impossibility."

And with that utterance, ruthless and final, I felt a plenary relief. Not for myself alone.

There had come to the soundings of my mind the memory of a tender-hearted family I had known in my youth, possessors of a wolf-hound which the children had always doted on, a creature now blind and crippled with age. No one could bring himself to destroy the animal, and its sufferings became a shadow by which all the life of the household was darkened; until a friend, a humane and sensible man, saying he knew a veterinarian who could relieve the hound's infirmities, took it away in his pony-cart and privily shot it in the woods. I saw myself as such a friend. There are those, I thought, who drift to disaster because they have forsaken the power and reason of resistance: they cling despairingly to the wreckage of perverse loyalties, imagining that the stream of life in all its breadth moves with the vicious current they are caught in—they have lost the will to swim. . . . Whether Siegfried gave himself up or waited here to be taken had come to seem immaterial. Whatever happened would bring anguish to those who cared for him, but from that distress they would emerge in time to unimagined liberty. His day had ended: I was in some way glad it had fallen to me to make that clear.

It appeared, though, that Paula had not listened. With the old, absorbed expression she was observing her brother, whose eyes had closed, and then Johannes. She said objectively, as one who has long finished with a problem on which the rest are labouring,

"Johannes, it looks as if you and I must do the work by ourselves. You, I know, will help me to get your father away from here before these rats from the village start to infest the house."

At which Franziska, with a violence that amazed me, said, "If anyone is to move my husband it will be myself! . . . No, Dr. Reichenbach, you are not to be mixed up in this, you've already put yourself in too much danger on our behalf. . . ."

9

Impossible? I still say it would have been so, but for Gubets. It was he—imperturbably, as if on a daily round—who found the poles we used for making a stretcher with coats and blankets as soldiers do; he who with native intelligence guided us across the central yard and through a range of sheds so that our tracks should be confused with those of the farm's normal traffic. Without him, thereafter, we could not have found a superable passage through the trees and scrub which covered most of the hill.

But the darkness too, though it recruited every obstacle, helped us in a fashion. Could we have surveyed the whole task we should not, I think, have embarked on it. As it was, we could imagine that every advance of a few feet was the main accomplishment—that at the next the gradient would be gentler, the undergrowth less vicious in its hold on clothes and limbs.

Yes, so intense was the blackness in that wood that, carrying the after end of the stretcher (with Ludwig doing what he could to support me from behind), I never saw the bearers at the forward end except as a bundling shape which occasionally reared between me and the sky. At that end Gubets, with a strap over his shoulders, sustained the greatest weight, with the women taking a hand where they could. It was he whose voice gave me direction as he repeated hoarsely, "Ready, Sir? On!" And at each of these calls I fought what felt like a solitary battle—lifted my end and shoved, pawed for a fresh foothold, shoved again, slipping on moss and slime, often collapsing on my knees, when twigs of thorn would whip against my face or from someone's boot in front I would get a mouthful of mud and ice. Inwardly I was weeping. Though most of my body dripped with sweat my hands stayed frozen, and the air in my lungs was like frozen flame. But the will-power I should have lacked to keep me struggling was lent by those ahead: through the crackle of snapping branches I could hear Gubets's determined breathing and the little grunts like a labourer's which escaped from Paula, while intermittently a stifled cry from Franziska reminded me that the weight of this ordeal was falling more cruelly on her than on me. Again and again their valiance overcame my reason, which would have had me surrender and slip away; so that I went on driving my muscles with reckless brutality, heaving and thrusting, responding like an automaton to Gubets's relentless word of command.

I do not know how Siegfried remained on the stretcher. We had fastened him with strips of cloth as well as we could, and Johannes, made responsible for steadying him as we moved, must have brought no small intelligence as well as nimbleness to the task. Even so, it seemed at the time a miracle that the whole contraption was never overturned. What the man suffered ı can hardly conceive—I should not willingly have subjected one in good health to such treatment. While we who carried him had the pumping of our blood to fortify us against the cold, he was exposed to it with no defence. To lie helpless on so precarious a litter would alone be a tax on courage, and when every jolt must have brought some pain to his chest or legs he was not only jolted but thrown violently in every direction. I do not pretend, however, to have spared much thought for his sufferings. There was no means to relieve them. The business assigned me was to get his body to the other side of the hill, and that could be done only by regarding it as lifeless cargo. He must have realized this, for he made no complaint. I was sometimes aware that he was doing what he could to check the slide of his body towards my end, and at intervals he said quietly, "*Vorsichtig! Vorsichtig!*" That was all.

Only when the ground had almost levelled was I given respite. There at last Gubets whispered, "I should like to rest," and Paula answered, "Very well—but not too long!"

The trees at this height had thinned, and what light the sky gave was reflected by an almost even drape of snow. We stood, gasping, with the stretcher on the ground as our centre, a blurred group in ebony that Meunier might have carved, bowed and voiceless like watchers at a tomb.

In such a theatre of sky and wind I could not think of the monoliths beside me as people I had talked to in light and shelter an hour or two before; and it was strange presently to hear Franziska speaking in a voice only a little changed by shortage of breath:

"Johannes, put this round you. . . . Siegfried! Siegfried, are you all right?"

From the motionless shape on the ground came Siegfried's ordinary voice:

'Why, yes! I've travelled more luxuriously—but never mind!'

I thought we had lost Ludwig—some distance back I had ceased to feel his hands beneath my shoulder-blades. But now from the darkness below us I caught the sound of breaking twigs, then the painful wheeze of his breathing, and presently he was beside me again, murmuring, "Such madness! . . . I'm afraid I'm not much use." I heard Franziska begging him to go back, and his whispered answer, "What for? What is there to go back to?" That contention died at birth, the inertia of utter weariness settled on us again. When Paula muttered angrily, "I see no point in waiting about!" there was still no movement, no response.

Afraid of getting too stiff to go on, I walked a little way along the shelf we had reached, chafing my hands and ears, to where through a gap in the trees I could just distinguish the roofs of the farm. Beyond them I saw a fleck of light which must have come from some window in the village, and for a moment I fancied that I heard distinctly, from that direction, the sounds of laughter and singing. But this I took to be a trick of the senses—the village was most of a mile away.

A new voice had started in the group behind me: "I've brought some things I found in the kitchen—I thought you'd want something more to eat when you got to wherever you're going." So Elfriede had managed to follow us! She sounded only a little short of breath, and pleased to be once again in company. "Yes, Ludwig dear, I think it's all rather foolish, but young people always do want to rush about at night."

In a stupid way I stood stamping my feet and still gazing towards the village; and now instead of a single light I saw two or three. Again I doubted if my senses were to be trusted—I could feel that my eyes were inflamed with the cold and my powers of co-ordination working slackly. But as the lights multiplied, and appeared to move towards me, I quietly called Gubets to my side.

"Tell me, do you see anything down there?"

"There are lights," he answered.

"Are they moving this way?"

He waited a little before replying: "Yes, Sir, they're coming this way." And then he said dispassionately, "They can't have believed me, what I told them about the traps. They're coming to search the farm now."

I went back and gave the news in an undertone to Ludwig. It would be best, I said, for him to return to the house as quickly as he could—otherwise Simovitch and his friends would draw an obvious conclusion and begin to spread their search more widely. He did not appear to understand me. Paula may have overheard what I said, for she moved a little way towards Gubets, who was still where I had left him. That was needless. From where I stood I could see now, through the entanglement of branches, the firefly dance of tiny lights which vanished and reappeared, parted and coalesced, drawing very slowly in our direction. Johannes saw them too; and losing for the first time his self-command he called out wildly,

"They're coming! They'll find us here!"

It must have been Elfriede who took Ludwig under control. In the confusion which followed Johannes's outburst I heard her say briskly, "I think if people are coming to the house there should be someone at home to welcome them," and a little afterwards a few words of Ludwig's reached me, a fluttering "God bless you. . . . I'll come to you when I can." But the boy's momentary hysteria had infected me, I ceased for a time to think of anything but getting farther away from the creeping lights, and the others were evidently caught in the same current of alarm. In a matter of seconds we were back in our places, had lifted the stretcher and were stumbling forward. I vaguely imagined then that Ludwig was still with us—we had covered some distance before I realized that he and Elfriede had gone.

It lasted, that unreasoning fear, to drive us like a galley-master. Without it we might never have completed the carry, for even when we started to descend our labour was not much lightened. In some places the fall was steep, in some the hillside treacherously pitted; and here, where a sweeping wind had borne the snow without interference, there were drifts which wholly falsified the contours of the ground. But we dreaded pursuit the more when it ceased to be visible, imagining that the lights would reappear, close upon us, at the crest behind, and the whip of terror was an antidote to all other sensation. Given the chance, I should have fled alone. But in the monstrous quilting of this country I no longer had even a sense of direction. The stretcher, now, was guide as well as burden, I felt its weight only as a convict would feel the irons he has worn for a life-time. And now it was the craft a shipwrecked sailor clings to as it climbs and falls between gigantic seas—it rose, as I dropped in a hidden crevice, to the height of my chin, when I stumbled on harder ground it dragged away, so that time and again I lost my hold and had to scrabble for it like a dog in a burrow. Yet it kept us together, this unwieldy thing, Sometimes I found my shoulder pressing on Paula's thighs. once I sprawled on the passive body of Siegfried himself, once caught at a small boulder to steady myself and found it was Franziska's head—till I felt that I was part of a single creature of several legs and arms, several gasping, whimpering mouths, which fought and floundered hopelessly in a nightmare landscape of dune and hollow.

Once more we owed much to Johannes. With recovered intelligence he had found a new service which fitted his capacities—he was moving some yards ahead of us, feeling about for relatively firm and easy ground, and at this stage it was his repeated cry of "Here! This way!" which kept us in something like a constant direction. For hours—or so it seemed—this slogan and occasionally Siegfried's "Careful, now!" were the only words I heard, and those with no more than a brutish understanding; for in the long downward haul something akin to sleep overcame me, and I laboured like a blindfold pump-horse, strangely detached from the agony of my arms and knees, remembering only that Franziska was near me and that at some distant time I had undertaken for her sake to suffer in this fashion. From this comatose condition I was hardly roused even by a change in Johannes's tone, his excited call—"It's a track here, I think! I think we've got to a cart-road." Remotely, I supposed the boy had gone off his head.

A road of sorts it was. We were not at the end of our struggles—there was more than half a mile, as I recall it, still to be endured. But at some time when the darkness had begun to thin I saw incredulously that a square and solid object stood in front of us: it was the car I had left some hours before. We summoned, after a space, the strength to get our load aboard. As one returning to an earlier incarnation I put myself in the driving seat; and at the first touch on the starter—a thing to marvel at—the engine came alive.

10

It must have been full morning when I left them, and the shed, with half its roof missing, cannot much have hindered the light. But the scene which memory presents to me is a drawing in graphite, empty of colour and of detail—a scribble to show where Siegfried lies cocooned in blankets among a litter of quarrymen's tools, like them a thing discarded; a few thin strokes for Johannes, a hazy line for Paula trying to screen the windows facing the road. Franziska alone, in that picture, is distinct and real, and the portrait is one I should rather not see too long. She stands by the wall with one arm stretched back for support, her bloodless face the face of a suicide rescued from the Wiener Kanal, the eyes open but appearing to see nothing.

I tried, with the little sense that was left in me, to make her lie down and sleep. This was useless—the will for action would not relax in her, it only worked without purpose or direction. "Sleep? How can I sleep!" she mumbled, as if to a stranger. Never had she so much needed to be cared for. And what could I do for this distorted effigy of the creature I knew—how break in to revive her inward warmth when my own had to be kept so harshly under guard!

It was all my mind contained as I drove somnambulistically back to Ljubljana, that image of Franziska in exile from her reason. My eyes photographed an endless lattice of ridge and gulley engraved in the rusted snow, a train of wagons passing, a man in uniform who stopped and questioned me on some matter I have forgotten. But a child's picture book would have been more real to me, since experience is meaningless where no goodness lights it, and all the goodness I could conceive of then was embodied in one person, left more and more distantly behind me, in whose life I should have no further part.

Chapter 7

I

I WAS THANKFUL for the extreme Englishness of Adcock's
mental complexion. To show surprise at my appearance—
when I reached the office nearly three hours late, half asleep,
with a face like speckled curd and hands covered with deep
scratches—would have been inconsonant with his breeding.
But in truth I doubt if he was hiding his curiosity—he simply
had none to hide. If, as my looks suggested, I had devoted
the night to some kind of saturnalia in a gorse-bush,
such deviations were only to be expected in a foreigner. "I
hope the car went all right, sir?" he said, and nothing
more.

This gave me confidence. Not troubling to work out a
detailed excuse for my next move, I merely told him that I
had a good deal of business to discuss with Dollis Andersen
and was going to run down to Trieste immediately.

"If he wants for any reason to keep me," I added, "you
can take care of things here for two or three days, can't
you?"

"Oh, I should think so! Only—I thought Andersen was
over at Zurich for the Headquarters Conference?"

That was so—I had forgotten.

"Well, I can talk to Ed Browning," I said. "It will come
to the same thing."

"Shall I put a call through to say you're coming?"

"No, don't bother. The shock won't kill them."

Yes, Adcock was easy to deal with. But I found no
pleasure in deceiving him. Earlier, it had faintly amused me
to be something different from the pattern of respectability

I had shown to that simple, honest creature. But now I was no longer involved in a merely passive illegality: even in the flaccid state of my mind that afternoon I knew quite well that I had passed to where no law—no argument of right and wrong—could defend me.

2

I slept in the train as if under morphia. My papers must have been examined as usual at the border, but the event left no impression, and the train had evidently been standing in the station at Trieste for some time when I was wakened by a porter. It was then towards evening, or so I thought, since all the station lights were on, the city overcast by heavy clouds and drenched with rain. I was very cold. And for some moments I could not think how I came to be in this surrealist world of ant-like movement and of ponderous, hollow noise.

The Italian porter was fatherly, he steered me into a cab and I drove to the home of the Obrenovitch family, who had put me up before. My old room, happily, was empty. They seemed glad to have me as their guest again, and began at once to spoil me with food and comfort, as they had always done.

Directly supper was over I went to the nearest telephone kiosk, called the number which Kurt Wenzel had once given me and asked, as before, for Dragutin. The woman who answered in Serbo-Croat said that he was not available.

I said that my business was of great importance. At what time should I ring again?

She was sorry, she could not tell me. Dragutin was away.

"You mean, out of Trieste?"

"Yes."

"For how long?"

164

Again she could not say.

It was a moment of despair. I was looking down the line of street lamps at people hurrying through the rain, but the picture on my mind's screen was all of Franziska, Franziska hungry and frozen in the shed on a bare hillside, waiting and waiting for the relief I was to send. How could I send it, how do anything at all without Kurt to help me?

"I wanted to speak to him," I said feverishly, "on a matter of the greatest urgency. A large sum of money is involved."

No answer—I thought she had rung off.

"If you can't give me any information now," I added, "I shall call you again every few minutes."

"Wait a minute!" the woman said.

It was not one minute but five that I waited, shivering and stamping my feet, listening to the faint charivari of twenty conversations, to the mutter of a distant typewriter and the drub of rain on the roof of the kiosk. Then,

"What name, please?"

I was wary of disclosing it. "My name is Eugen," I told her, "I am a very old friend of Dragutin's."

"Wait a minute, please."

Another silence, but this did not last so long. And now a man's voice came:

"Your present address, please?"

I gave it.

"All right—a car will be sent for you."

It came in half an hour, a once luxurious vehicle where the kapok leaking from dove-grey upholstery gave off a faint, pre-war aroma of cigars and eau-de-Cologne. Ensconced in this relic I was again attacked by drowsiness, so that I ceased to feel myself related to the world of blurred and wheeling lights which drifted past the windows. For a short while I may actually have slept; at least I yielded so far to somnolence that I became confused again about my purpose, and remembering only that I had some work to do for

Franziska's sake I was frightened and dismayed to find my brain as useless as a limb where the motor nerves are atrophied.

In this condition I allowed the driver, when he had stopped the car in a wide, residential street, to lead me as one leads the feeble minded. He was a very little creature with the big, affectionate eyes of Italian children. "This way! This way!" he kept calling, smiling at me over his shoulder, coaxing me along. We went through the sparsely lighted vestibule of what must once have been a fashionable house and up the broad, bare staircase to an entresol where children were playing and where an old, abstracted man wandered past us in his dressing-gown. The house was many-storied, and as I hazily remember it the scene was nearly repeated on every floor—a bare, high corridor in the state of fixed dilapidation that sits like the scars of smallpox on old Istrian villas, a shuttling parade of humanity at home, women in drooping petticoats who padded with enormous saucepans, children bouncing balls against the many doors while one in his night-shirt rode up and down on a tiny tricycle.

"This way! This way! Yes, one more flight! . . . If the Signor will have the kindness to wait here, please—a quarter of a moment."

The topmost corridor was empty and austere, here the many layers of sound from below, voices monotonously arguing, the cries of a young child mingled with the whimper of radio, were alien and withdrawn like the noises of a city heard in church. Obediently waiting, breathing the persistent odours of cabbage, slops and laundry, I laboured to recall my mind to action.

"This way, if you please!"

The door to which the driver led me was newly painted and bore the name of a Zurich insurance company. We passed through an empty office strident with the emblems of efficiency and came to a second door, inscribed, 'Stefan Roloff, *Direttore*.' This was opened from inside. There, visored with tremendous spectacles, Kurt himself stood smiling like a gaoler welcoming an old inhabitant.

"Eugen, my dear friend, this is enchanting! . . . Thank you, Giuseppe, that is all. . . . Sit down, dear boy, and tell all your troubles to Papa Wenzel—alas, I know you're in trouble, since no one ever comes to see me out of love."

"If I am," I said sourly, "I should like to know who's responsible! Who asked me to attend a case on the outskirts of Trieste and then shipped me half way to Ljubljana?"

"Half way to Ljubljana?" He put a hand to his forehead. "Ah, now I remember—there was a topographical misunderstanding, I heard about it afterwards. Yes, really I feel grateful to you—that business might have led to all sorts of complications if I had not by a lucky chance entrusted it to an old and faithful friend."

"Meaning that you knew you had a simpleton at your disposal?"

"Intelligence, my dear Eugen, is not everything—in this sorry world there is room for the pure in heart as well. Now what can I find to celebrate our reunion? There's a bottle or two of Niersteiner—not too bad, as such wines go."

How easy to respond to his student amiability, to relax for an hour at least in his world of contingent purposes! I refused, however, to waste my time. I said,

"Kurt, listen—I've come on business."

"At this hour?"

"Yes, and it's urgent."

The parcel which Paula had given me was in my pocket. I put it on the table between us.

"That comes from Fräulein Kern—she wants you to sell these things to defray expenses. I think you know already what she's asking you to do—she told me she had sent you letters."

He pulled a face. "Yes, Fräulein Kern has already made her simple requirements quite clear to me. I am to wait until her brother is fit for removal, then I have to fetch him and

167

his family here, hide them as long as necessary, find a captain who doesn't worry about documents and ship the whole troupe off to Spain."

"Well, as things have turned out"—I said bluntly—"the programme has to go into operation more quickly. The Kerns have had to leave Schwarzenberg's house in a hurry, they're camping in a tumbledown shed on a hillside. One way or another, if Kern isn't moved within a day or two he's finished."

"Indeed! And does that matter?"

"You seemed to think his life mattered the last time we were together."

"Strictly, I didn't," he said. "I have really not the smallest interest in defaulting Swiss financiers. Ludwig Schwarzenberg is an old friend, he has often been kind to me, I was anxious to oblige him—that's all."

"Well, now he's a friend of mine."

"And it's Ludwig who's sent you on this errand?"

"No—actually it's Fräulein Kern. But in the end it's Ludwig's problem that has to be solved—his as much as anyone's."

He nodded, looking away from me as if the subject had ceased to interest him. "Well then, if Kern dies in the shed you speak of, that's the solution."

"And you think it's the right one? Last time we met—you may remember—you were practically accusing me of callous selfishness because I didn't want to go and attend to this same Kern."

"Was I?" He was gently smiling, as if he were dealing with a child's whimsicalities, yet I fancied he was now on the defensive, "You talk," he said, "as if it was all perfectly simple—you're as bad as the Kern woman herself! You seem to think I run a regular tourist service for criminals—you imagine there's no special difficulty or risk in getting a man over the border."

"You got *me* over."

"Yes, but it so happened that you had not got half the police in Europe looking for you at the time. And incidentally, the system's been tightened since then."

It was chiefly tiredness, I think, that provoked the fit of temper which came upon me suddenly, with the glow of spurious righteousness. I found myself speaking like a public attorney, leaning forward and drumming my fists on the arms of my chair.

"You made use of me before. You made a large claim upon our old friendship, and then you lied to me. You told me this man was a Swiss financier, knowing perfectly well he was nothing of the sort. You said I was only to go a mile or two out of Trieste and you sent me off into Slovenia. You deliberately and shamelessly abused my confidence. Well, now it's my turn to make demands on you!"

He was quite unmoved—no doubt a good deal of his time was spent with angry and impatient people.

"So you've found out who Kern is!" he said with interest. "Oddly enough, I didn't know all the facts myself at the time I was arranging for you to see him. Not that I believed a word that woman told me—obviously she was no more a Swiss than I'm a negro—but it's never intelligent to fuss over questions of identity. To tell the truth, I thought her brother would turn out to be some small-fry German officer who'd once helped himself to the regimental funds or something. Well, we know better now."

"We do!"

He pounced. "And *yet* you want to help him!"

"In a way it's a matter of duty," I said. "I've promised——"

"Oh, for God's sake!" It was his turn to be angry. "Eugen, listen! I do not—God knows—set myself up as a counsellor in ethics, or even as a man of respectable virtue. But I do not—I say I do *not*—devote myself to saving the life of one of the most repellent swine in Europe and simultaneously babble about morality. There is absolutely no reason—no excuse—for keeping that bastard alive. You know that!"

"I don't," I retorted. "As a matter of fact, I know hardly anything about the crime he's supposed to have committed."

"Then let me enlighten you. That engaging gentleman——"

"I don't want to know!"

"What?" Adjusting his spectacles, he stared at me with intense curiosity. "But this is fascinating! You know, the charm of life is all in its contradictions. You, Eugen, I have always thought of as a man of inflexible and—may I say—slightly tedious moral convictions. Not, perhaps, very subtle in mind, but logical almost to excess. And I should have said that if there was one man in the world who did not greatly care for the spiritual progeny of Heinrich Himmler——"

I stopped him. "Listen, Kurt—I'm afraid I'm too tired for a discussion of my own character. I've undertaken to see to this business of Zempelmarck's—I shan't waste your time with my reasons—and I thought you might oblige me in return for what I did earlier to please you. Well, that's that—I shall try somewhere else. There must be other unscrupulous people in Trieste."

"There are hundreds," he said, stretching back to push the receiver off his telephone, "but I am not going to have you using them." Without looking, he dialled a number. "A man like you is quite incapable of dealing with any unscrupulous body except myself."

His manner had changed as when an engine is put to work in a higher gear—he was now superlatively happy. The receiver lying on his desk began to mumble, he reached and brought it to his chest, paid out a sentence or two of rapid Italian, pitched the instrument back on the hooks and returned his attention to me.

"I shall want you to draw a little map to show me as well

as you can where the Zempelmarcks are now. Then you must leave that part of the business in my hands. Of course, things may go wrong—we must be prepared for that. But I have one or two ideas to work on—I think about these boundaries a good deal, they give everyone a lot of trouble."

He was moving too fast for me to follow. Confused, I put ingenuously the question that was all-important to me:

"What's the earliest you think you can collect them?"

"Ah, that depends on several factors. I shan't move till I hear definitely that the sea passage has been fixed—the operation has got to go straight through in one piece or else it's doomed from the start. This place nowadays is just an ants' nest of police and other nosy parkers—the idea of hiding the Zempelmarck party anywhere here for as much as twenty-four hours is merely romantic."

"But that means they might have to stay where they are now for days?"

"That depends on you, chiefly."

"On me?"

"Yes, dear boy, the maritime negotiations are going to be your part of the business. I shall be waiting till you telephone to let me know that everything's fixed." He had opened Paula's parcel, and was weighing the crucifix in his hand. "You see, the shipping people in these parts have come to know me rather well—from time to time I've arranged passages for several parties who wanted to travel just a little *incogniti*. So the prices have gone up rather."

"But I've no idea where to start. Unless I go to the Agencia Barassi in the Via del Corso."

"Yes, a shrewd suggestion! On a par, I think, with going to a Lutheran pastor and asking for the loan of his wife—'I apologize for troubling you, dear sir, but I am in urgent need of an afternoon's adultery.'" He shook his head despondently. "No, I think it would be unwise for you to work alone—I shall get a business associate of mine to act as your Vergil."

"In that case——"

"Wait! Your special contribution will be to present an appearance of unshakable respectability—no one can do that better than you. You see, the other party may want to be convinced that there's nothing fundamentally illegal in the transaction, though superficially it will not be quite according to the regulations. The money side you had better perhaps not interfere with. Ah, here we are!"

I had not heard the door opening, and was startled to find someone standing behind me.

"This," said Kurt, "is the gentleman I spoke of—he is one of the ablest of my business friends, and one in whom I have always placed the highest confidence."

"But we have met before," I said.

For it was Ricotti who came forward, luxuriously smiling.

"Indeed, yes!" Ricotti said. "Dr. Reichenbach and I were in partnership on an earlier occasion—I have the happiest memories of the time I spent in his company."

"It ended"—I said with caution—"rather abruptly."

"Indeed? My memory is not altogether clear. The important thing is that we are together again—that makes me so very happy."

It was Kurt's paternal smile that I found most difficult to bear while Ricotti, for the second time, was churning my hand.

"Dr. Reichenbach has a little shipping business to negotiate," Kurt explained. "It's for some distinguished friends of his who like to travel very unostentatiously."

"Exactly, I quite understand. And they have their passports already, these friends of Dr. Reichenbach's?"

"No, but I shall attend to that—the Doctor is going to give me all the particulars. Oh, you might ask your friend Agostino to send me up some photographs as he did before—men, women, children of all ages."

"Why, yes, a pleasure! Agostino will bring them himself for you to make a selection."

From then their conversation—mostly in Italian and running at a formidable speed—meant little more to me than the liturgy of some peculiar sect. I listened as a tired child listens to the talk of his elders, hardly believing that I myself could be concerned in such commerce as this; while from time to time the performers, pausing in their duologue, threw me the indulgent smile of parents planning a small boy's education with wisdom and forbearance. More than once my eyelids fell. By now the image of Franziska had forsaken me, and with it the will for any action. I only knew that I had totally lost my way.

4

That weariness, that sense of moving in a dimension external to the one I lived in, persisted all next day, when Ricotti, who called for me early in a hired car, led me deviously from office to office, from one dockside building to another. This tract was sprinkled lavishly with Ricotti's friends. In a room full of clerks, one—always the last I should have trusted—would nod familiarly at his appearance and come to talk to him in a corner. An old woman, heavily moustached, who emerged conspiratorially from the counting box at one end of a great warehouse, a coloured man of peculiar gentleness who came and walked beside us, speaking the strangest Italian I ever heard, these and their kind arrived with the inconsequence of dreams, voluble and oversized, to fill the foreground for a space and then to be reabsorbed in the traffic we left behind. Ricotti himself, tirelessly cheerful, his eyes and artificial teeth gleaming like those of a working model, became not more but less a human being: I could not imagine him as a man at home, husband or father, but only as an instrument designed to respond in several tongues, with a procession of gestures, winks and smiles, to the rambling pageant of obliquity which came into his range.

It seemed there was no single vessel ready to sail for Spain; or if there were, its owners had no space for the unusual cargo—'pedigree livestock of some value'—that Ricotti was offering.

"Ah, but there are many companies," he repeated re-assuringly, "many agents of foreign lines, many small people who look for a little extra business. It's a case of asking everyone, keeping one's ear to the ground."

At an early stage we had paid off the car and taken to our feet. The rain hardly slackened. The cloud that lay upon the waterfront was reinforced with the smoke of many funnels, we moved in a country that appeared to be half afloat, where a line of trucks would suddenly emerge to block our path, where gantries like siege towers strode upon us from the gloom and a stack of casks would rise into the air or a section of the landscape start to slide away. There seemed to be no boundary to this desolation, to the piled deals and drums, the stench of crude oil and of yeast and rotted fish; my shoes, twin reservoirs of rain, squelched dismally as my cold feet bore them back and forth across the concrete acres, the rain got inside my collar and up my sleeves. Night came—or so it seemed—in the early afternoon. The little colour that the cloud had left on ships and buildings faded in a uniformity of misty grey, the loading sheds turned by degrees into yellow caverns, and as a sweep of little lights took hold upon the darkness the reflections quivering on water and on rain-washed quays deleted finally the line between sea and land. There were dangers in walking now, one could run one's neck against a stretched hawser or trip on the unseen rails of a siding. I did not care; for my body was settled in weariness, and my faculties in great confusion.

"We have still some possibilities!" Ricotti said, turning inland again and marching on without a sign of discomfort.

"For the moment—a little meal, do you think, to freshen courage?"

We had stopped only once before, when he had deferentially allowed me to pay for a *spuntino*. He led me now with sciurine confidence along an alley between two concrete walls and down a flight of steps to what might have been a railroad saloon of the early Nineteen Hundreds. "This is a famous establishment, *molto bizzarro*," he said complacently. "All the sea captains of the world talk of it." I could not see why. In the hideous fluorescent light a dozen men who looked like customs officers, seated in pairs or alone at two long tables, were smoking apathetically between mouthfuls of vermicelli. The table-lamps with scarlet shades had ceased to work, the waitresses, conventionally rouged and underdressed, were thick-limbed girls with rough Venetian voices who had long surrendered to the blight of middle age. "The botargo here is something extraordinary," Ricotti said; and in this he proved to be right.

Still, I should have been quite happy to sit on the slatted chair and consume the slivers of anonymous fish submerged in onion purée which he ordered for us both, could I have done so in silence and alone. That was not Ricotti's notion. Here his social and his business sense were equally refreshed; among the dismal clerks he instantly discovered a life-long friend, I realized soon that he (or I) had become the host of half the men in the room.

"All shipping men, these fellows!" he whispered to me.

My own part, I supposed, would merely be to pay for the *rakija* which had evidently become a public issue. I smiled convivially at Ricotti's friends, and laughed when laughter seemed to be expected, letting the talk flow past me as if I were a windmill lacking sails. But when he began enlarging on my own claims to attention the force of curiosity prevailed. He had turned to Serbo-Croat, which came to him a degree less swiftly than his native tongue.

"Yes, my friend here had a large medical practice in Washington—among other things he was personal physician to the American President. He has sacrificed it all—an enormous income, immense prestige—to care for the sick and suffering in Trieste. . . . My friend's friend is a Swiss gentleman—a banker, I believe—very large interests in Geneva. A sick man. Pulmonary trouble. Yes, tuberculosis—it's an enemy which strikes at rich and poor alike. That's why my friend is trying to get him to Spain—him and his family— the climate there is the only one suitable for a case of this kind, it's the poor fellow's only chance."

The general interest, I thought, was less than tepid: his audience was staring as countrymen stare at travelling quacks. But a small man—a steward, on the evidence of his shirt and tie—who had come to sit beside me gave a glance at my face and then, looking away, asked in an undertone:

"A Swiss, this friend of yours—is that right?"

"Yes."

"And he wants to get away quickly?"

"For health reasons," I said.

He nodded, still with his eyes averted. "Yes, for some people Trieste isn't a healthy place. How old a man?"

"Oh, somewhere in the forties. Why, please?"

"A military man?"

"No no—business."

I might have been offended by the fellow's inquisitiveness, but he seemed a humble and childlike creature, a rustic Serb by his intonation, with a villager's ingenuous curiosity.

"Ah yes, a business man," he said ponderingly, "a business man with trouble in the chest. And he wants to travel privately—it's the way with business men, often enough. You haven't a photograph, by chance?"

"No—why?"

He shrugged his shoulders. "I might have met him—who can tell? My part of the country, we had all sorts of visitors —in the War, I mean. Swiss, they might have been, some of them." He smiled, as if some sudden recollection amused him. Then, gravely, he shook my hand. "It's an honour to have met you, Sir. Perhaps we shall meet again—the world becomes so small. I am called Mihovil Zhenko. I wish you good-evening, Sir, God rest with you!"

I was sorry that he left me, since Ricotti could now reclaim my attention. He was once more extolling my virtue and distinction, much as a procuress might advertise the latest beauty on her string, and I think he would have continued this nauseous performance till no one was left to listen; but a sailor who was clearly as tired of it as I took leave at last to interrupt him:

"There's old Tricoulos over there. If you want passages to Spain, why don't you ask him?"

I turned and saw at the far end of the table behind me the wizen body of what might have been a government official run to seed: there were pads of grey hair at the summit of his hollow, bluish cheeks, his blue suit was crumpled and stained, but he wore the white collar and neat black tie, the double watch-chain, of a reputable indoor man. Ricotti had turned as well.

"Tricoulos?"

"He goes everywhere," the sailor said. "Spain, Portugal, sometimes Brazil. The *Charilaos*—mangy tub."

"Independent?"

"More or less."

"Assorted freights?"

"At *his* tariff!"

The Greek seemed unaware that he was being discussed; he was intent upon the newspaper which he held in one small, feminine hand while the other mechanically rose and fell, bearing spoonfuls of curry and rice to his spinsterish mouth. A man whose name seemed to be Perpenino went over and spoke to him, first in Italian, then in Serbo-Croat. I heard the reply:

"What? Not understand."

"The *Charilaos* is for Spain now?"

"Spain? Who can tell?"

"He doesn't know!" Perpenino announced at large. "He wouldn't know if you asked him the name of his own father."

"Nor would you!" a sailor said.

The eldest of the waitresses, surveying the company with maternal indulgence, said briskly, "He's just a child—*il capitano*—poor old man! Tonight he's forgotten that little ship he steers about."

"So? But money," said Perpenino shrewdly, "he never forgets."

If I had not been so wet and tired, so desperately anxious, I might have enjoyed the sense of being back at school. A fight or a bout of bargaining, these alike return men to their boyhood. Tricoulos still looked as if he had no thought except for the day's news, but by now he must have been perfectly conscious of the business impending; while Ricotti, with his contemplative smile, the detachment mimed by his palms and chin, was so overplaying the part of nonchalance that the least perceptive would have seen in him a boxer limbering for action. There were perhaps twenty men in the room now, and every one of them was intently watching.

With his little finger Ricotti beckoned Perpenino nearer. Perpenino in his turn summoned an older man—he was, I think, a Cretan—and for a few moments the three of them were spinning between themselves a web of gesture and polyglot undertone. The Cretan then made a ceremonious approach to Tricoulos and stayed in conversation with him for some time—I had the impression that they were asking after each other's families to the third and fourth generation. He returned to Perpenino, evidently with negative results: I heard Perpenino say to Ricotti, "He has not decided—it depends on other cargoes." More talk, and the Cretan was dispatched again.

"The Captain is never clear in his mind after curry," the eldest waitress declared with authority.

"You mean," said someone, "he requires three nights with Cesca before he can think of navigation at all."

"Old men are always lonely," a younger waitress said immediately, as she stooped to examine a ladder above her knee.

"And they go to Cesca for ghostly consolation!"

The inner triangle conferred again, the Cretan was dispatched on his third diplomatic mission. There were voices now proclaiming that Tricoulos was moonstruck, others that all Greeks were thieves and liars—I have rarely seen a secret negotiation conducted before so close, so eager and vocal an audience. Ricotti and his friends went over to the other table, chair by chair they moved towards the captain, till at length the principals were opposite each other, Ricotti joyously explaining with his hands, Perpenino briefing the Cretan once again, while Tricoulos watched them all like a small boy bored with costly entertainments. On this new axis the rest of the company re-formed like spectators at roulette. The kitchen staff was now on the scene, management and customers alike were volleying advice at both contestants. Only for me there seemed to be no role in this performance.

I was sitting alone, then, slightly fuddled by the smoke and rumpus, staring at my empty plate and reflecting grimly that Franziska's relief might depend on the outcome of this harlequinade, when a hand came to rest on my shoulder. Zhenko had returned.

"Forgive me, Honourable!" he whispered, at once eager and bashful as before. "I've brought a friend of mine—Valyevitch—I think he might be some help to you."

The friend came towards me slowly, rather as one to whom some article of doubtful value is offered for sale: a tired man in the later thirties with a face of (I thought) an Albanian cast. His cheap-smart suit, with his soiled skin and poverty of flesh, suggested a working man—perhaps a motor mechanic—in his Sunday clothes; but there was in his bearing an assurance, and in his eyes and brow an appearance of intellect, which would have distinguished him in more exalted company than this. I stood to greet him. He mechanically offered me a cigarette and sat down at my side, still openly appraising me with his smoky, penetrating eyes.

"You have friends," he said in tolerable German, "who are in a hurry to get to Spain?"

I explained once more that Herr Kern's health necessitated an immediate change of climate.

"Then surely," he said, "your best course would be to go to the Agencia Barassi? They would take special pains to help you."

My answer was inevitably a lame one. Herr Kern, I told him, was exceptionally sensitive about his illness—a pulmonary infection—and if he obtained a passage in the ordinary way he was sure to find himself the object of particular attention aboard ship. That was why he wanted to travel in a cargo vessel by private arrangement.

Whether or no he believed it, Valyevitch accepted this explanation. "But there are difficulties," he said. "Independent shipowners will sometimes take certain legal risks, but they want to have their answers ready. This pulmonary trouble—it would be infectious?"

"Well, yes. But only through the sputum. If proper precautions are taken——"

"It couldn't—for the purpose of the voyage—be described as a wound? I mean, to an ordinary man the result of a wound, anything a passer-by would see, would look much the same as the disease you talk of, wouldn't it?"

"I suppose it might."

"Actually, it has come on very suddenly, this illness? That's why he needs to be moved so quickly?"

"Well, the recent severe weather has made his condition a good deal worse."

Again he nodded, still examining my face as a fortune-teller will study a customer's palm. It did not escape me that the man might well be a police agent of some kind; but if so, what could I do but go on lying to him with patience and such pitiful guile as nature had vouchsafed me? He scared me a little, with his limitless self-confidence, and yet I could not altogether dislike him. There was a certain honesty in his hard-bitten features, a faint, judicial humour that relieved the mordant structure of his mouth. Moreover, a look of his suggested that he and I were equally men who knew their world: he did not make me feel a simpleton, as Kurt had done.

"A wound," he said reflectively, "—yes, that would be much the best thing to tell people. You're sure he *looks* like a man with a wound in his chest?"

"Why, yes, I think he does."

"Perhaps we could say it's a war wound," Zhenko suggested. "That's to say, if he looks like a soldier. Is he of military appearance?"

I hesitated, and for an instant I fancied that both men were intent upon my answer. But Valyevitch, as if his friend had been guilty of an impertinence, said with decision, "Never mind—it can be called the result of an accident, if anyone wants to know. Now tell me, how many are there to be in the party, besides Herr Kern himself? Two women and a child—right! Now suppose we could secure passages at a few hours' notice, would they be ready to start immediately? I mean, are they at present in Trieste?"

"Well, no."

"But fairly close?"

Again I was uncomfortable, with the two of them waiting as a teacher waits for an awkward pupil to pull himself together. I said,

"Not too far. Not far from Ljubljana."

"Ljubljana? Ah yes," Zhenko said politely, "I think you

told me. You said, I think, that he came into Slovenia from Switzerland at some time in the autumn."

Later on it occurred to me that I had told him nothing whatever of 'Kern's' whereabouts. But I was now in some confusion, with my ears partly tuned to the rowdy debate going on behind me, and I merely answered, "Perhaps I did." Whether I saw a fleeting look of satisfaction pass between the two men, or whether I have imagined it retrospectively, I cannot be certain. I do remember Valyevitch saying with a rather overloaded tact, "Anyhow, that's nothing to do with us!"

"Well now," he continued briskly, "today's Tuesday. Suppose we could get the passages for Friday—could your friends be here, ready to sail, on Friday morning?"

I calculated quickly. "Yes, I think so." And then, distrusting his helpfulness, I said, "But there's the money question—my friend's present resources are very limited."

"I shall bargain for you," he answered shortly.

By then Zhenko had left us, to push his way into the prize-ring. I caught sight of him colloguing with Ricotti, and as he returned he made a complex sign to Valyevitch with his thumbs and little fingers—I have seen similar signals exchanged between dealers at country cattle-auctions, and in the light of what followed I conclude that Ricotti had given him some figure to work on. Tricoulos, meanwhile, had at last been baited from his lethargy. He was standing up, five feet or a little more of protesting dignity. Still clasping a spoon and fork, he raised his fists to shoulder height, waited for a lull in the hubbub and then addressed us all, a phrase at a time, in a stranger gallimaufry of Adriatic tongues than I had ever encountered.

"No! No! *No!* Your money I find ridiculous. Spain? Pssh! She goes—my ship—where I want. Under the laws—no shinky-shaky. I am honourable captain. Money? Ffeugh!"

Perhaps there was in this curious proclamation of independence some spark recovered from an ancient, Attic fire. It was effective. There came, instead of another storm of laughter, a wave of embarrassment; under cover of which the captain, kicking away his chair, cutting a passage through the crowd with his birdlike, grey and now victorious eyes, moved imperially towards the door.

Valyevitch, however, stopped him. It was done with nothing more than a beckoning movement of the head. Those two men may have had dealings before—I do not know: certainly Tricoulos behaved like a circus lion answering to the crack of the trainer's whip. They went together to a corner where they conferred for perhaps three minutes, with Zhenko standing by to guard their privacy. Then Valyevitch returned to me.

"It's fixed!" he said, with no more than a fleeting trace of self-satisfaction. "The *Charilaos*—on Friday. She sails at 6.30 in the morning—Francesco Giuseppe Wharf, Berth 86. Passages for three and one child. Your Italian friend is to settle at the last figure he proposed."

I tried to thank him, but he waved my little speech aside. "Like Zhenko here," he said, with his slightly cryptic smile, "I take an interest in people who find themselves in trouble."

5

Having little faith in Ricotti, I reported to Kurt myself by telephone.

"On Friday?" he said. "Early morning? That's not a lot of time. Well, we must see what we can do for your distinguished friends." His voice was bland and delicately derisive: as if the wire yielded vision as well as sound I could see the wickedness sparking in his eyes. "And you yourself, you will be returning now to your invaluable labours at Ljubljana?"

"Yes, immediately."

That, indeed, was the only course in reason. But it was not the one I followed. I argued in a tortuous way that my mission was unfinished—that I should not have fulfilled my promise till I saw the ship leaving with the Zempelmarcks aboard. In reality I knew that I should have no peace in spirit if I did not see and speak to Franziska once again before a long sea passage lay finally between us.

I paid for this feebleness. There were two whole days to occupy with nothing but my anxious thoughts, two days of such depression as I had never known. I could not spend the whole time in my room, for the Obrenovitch, who knew me as an active man, would have been puzzled by such behaviour; and I dared not go near the centre of the city, for fear of meeting one of my colleagues. There remained the immediate neighbourhood of my lodging, a sloping grid of residential streets which contained no single building of interest or distinction. Here, a prisoner of my own unreason, I walked as caged beasts do, and with a burden that no beast has to carry—the knowledge of another's distress and my helplessness to relieve it.

As to my own position, my special fear was that some communication from the Trieste to the Ljubljana office would reveal to Adcock that I had not been to the former at all. So, on the first of those empty, anxious days, I got through on the telephone and asked him how things were going.

He answered gently, like a poet disturbed by children, that he thought he had no troubles.

"Nothing urgent or important in?"

"Well, no, I don't think so."

"I shall be back," I said, "some time on Friday. If anything complicated turns up, just hold it for me, will you. Don't send it to the office here—I probably shan't be in for the next two days—I've been landed with a lot of private business."

"I see, yes. Yes, I quite follow."

If I had said, 'I am busy running guns into Trieste and hope to start a revolution tomorrow,' he would, I think, have answered in the same terms. Again I thanked God for creating so dull a man.

The sense of truancy continued none the less to fret me. Several times I considered going boldly to the office with some plausible story to explain my absence from duty; but then I thought, 'In a few hours this episode will be over. I can make my explanations then, if anything has occurred to demand them—most likely they will never be needed.' In a few hours—yes, and a part of me longed for that release. My father had trained me to look on every deceit as ignoble, I hated marching in the train of petty chisellers, my religion was scandalized at my being involved in what I knew already to be something far graver than illegality. And yet I dreaded the moment of escape. The evil which encompassed me had long encompassed Franziska: when I freed myself from its hold I should lose my common cause with her; and it seemed, as I went miserably up and down those dull and rainy streets, that I almost cherished the evil itself, as one cherishes the scent of clothes, the small possessions of a person who is loved and absent. They say men love a woman for her strangeness. Franziska was not strange to me. We had spent only a little time together; but her looks and voice, her moments of grace and of awkwardness, her shyness and her ease, were etched so deeply in my mind that I felt as if I had known her through her childhood. In her I saw above all the counterpart of the loneliness which had come upon me like illness to a man who has never known it before. In those hours which must have seemed to her like days, on the almost naked hillside, she had no one who could see the situation through her eyes. And this was a settled isolation. There would never be anyone to give her that comfort, to share her existence at its depth, except for me. As one starved of luxury will pore over coloured magazines, so, as

I sat in a small and flyblown restaurant smoking through a carton of cigarettes, and dawdled on to the next café along the street, to sit and smoke again, to watch with senseless eyes the tired faces passing above the muslin curtain, I lived on my little store of pictures: Franziska wet and tousled as she first came hurrying to bid me good-bye; a troubled Franziska leaning over Siegfried's bed; a moment in the dark lane when she had laughed with a schoolgirl's gaiety; the grave and wifely voice in which she had once said, 'Eugen, you look so tired!' Those riches from the past would not recur; and I could think of no future for myself when she would be finally beyond my reach. The pride and fascination of my work, the charm of my American friendships, these would be insubstantial, meaningless, in the desolation of the years that would reflect Franziska's solitude.

6

It must have been earlier than four o'clock, that Friday morning, when I turned on the light in my bedroom, knowing I should not sleep again. Had I slept at all? I had seemed merely to pass—through scenes of flight and cross-examination, of helpless losses and misunderstanding—from one stretch of wakefulness to the next. I shaved and dressed, shivering, and with a foolish sense of guilt crept out from the house to the dark, deserted street.

This felt like an extension of my dreams, the wet and naked pavements, the traffic signals turning uselessly from red to green. Once, losing all direction, I came for a second time to the little square where Aphrodite leaning from her fountain points censoriously at the Mechanics' Club. Once, when I found a man propped against a lamp-post, and stopped to ask him my way, he only stared at me in silence with eyes that plainly saw nothing. I was back in my childhood, a little boy in Schottenring, separated by four yards from his nursemaid and despairing of seeing a known face again.

Near the docks the traffic increased: from obscure byways men came in ones and twos to join a thickening stream which moved into the jungle of masts and cranes; a parade of trucks like those of an invading army lumbered over the granite setts and thundered hollowly across the bridge. But these in the almost total darkness had only the reality of nightmare. The men except for the clatter of their feet were silent. With their drivers invisible in the high cabs the lorries moved as if drawn upon a wire, scenery that would fold and be packed away somewhere behind the stage.

The *Charilaos*? None of the plodding ghosts had heard of her. But the Francesco Guiseppe Wharf was known. "It's not so far," a coloured porter said, "a hundred paces, and perhaps twice more. You turn where the light blinks at you—the light from the mole." Even then I missed my way again, confused by the curve of dockside lights and the wagons spasmodically moving on the intricacy of sidings.

To the wharf itself, when I approached it, there seemed to be no barrier or gateway. But as I went through a pool of light a sad, corpulent man with a peaked cap came out of a wooden cabin. Had I a pass, he asked. Taken aback, I simply answered, "No". But entrance to the wharf was not permitted without a pass, he said.

I followed him at his instance into the hut, where he had a table littered with forms and regulations. My passport I had with me—I was never without it—and I showed him the W.U.R.O. stamp. Elsewhere this had proved a sufficient shibboleth. But the watchman was a legalist, with the combined ignorance and pedantry of municipal clerks. W.U.R.O.—what was that? Had it an office in Trieste? Ah, then he would telephone for confirmation. I told him with restraint that the office was one of the special sort where people worked only in the daytime. In that case, he said, combing his lank moustache with his finger-nails, gazing at my face with moist, unhappy eyes, I must make a formal application for a permit.

Knowing his kind, I filled the form he gave me, reporting in both languages the colour of my eyes and my weight in kilograms. My business, I wrote, was medical attendance to a member of the *Charilaos*'s crew—in my sleepy state that was the best I could think of.

"If the man dies through this delay," I told him sternly, "there will be questions asked by the police. And I shall not be the one they'll blame."

He let me go then, but not before he had written 'W.U.R.O.' on the edge of his calendar, with the office address I recklessly gave him. "But you must attend here again before leaving the wharf," he said. "There will have to be special investigations."

The promised land, as I discovered it, seemed scarcely worth such jealous protection. The lamps slung overhead—one in three was alight—showed only dunes of cordage on a waste of granite where no living creature was visible, where nothing stirred. In the four or five vessels lying at the quay I saw no light: they looked like the carcasses of ships which had been tethered there and left to die. The *Charilaos*—I could just make out the name on her low rump—was the last of these.

It became apparent, then, as I sat on a folded tarpaulin, feebly sheltered by a dump of asphalt barrels from the inshore wind, that I had risen early to pursue a childish fantasy. Palpably the *Charilaos* existed; but so far from her sailing this morning it was hardly credible that she would ever be fit for sea again. Nor was it easier, now, to believe that the Zempelmarcks would arrive. I had no small faith in Wenzel. But as I thought again of all the obstacles, physical and legal, which had to be overcome I almost ceased to hope that the thing could be done in days rather than weeks. I was very cold. And yet, with the inertia of despondency, I went on sitting as an obedient child does, waiting patiently for someone who would not arrive, to bid her Godspeed on a voyage that would not begin.

7

In the grey, drizzling morning which slowly took the place of darkness my hopes of the *Charilaos* were not immediately encouraged. To the eye of a landsman she looked pathetically small, her gear chaotic, her grooming worthy of Vienna's slums. She was not a corpse, however. I saw, scarcely believing, that from her pygmy funnel a scroll of thin, blue smoke rose intermittently to feed the haze above; and twice, from a rusty deck-house, a man emerged in singlet and underpants to tip a pail of garbage into the harbour.

Those were slight but favourable portents; and a little later I had some oblique evidence that Kurt had not been idle. I must have been dozing—the effects of an almost sleepless night were now overtaking me—for I did not hear or see anyone coming along the quay: my first knowledge that I had company came from an assertive, too familiar voice sounding almost in my ear:

"God's groin, I've taught that fellow something! Permit, indeed! Sergeant of supplies, that's all he ever was in his Service—I pretty soon got that out of him. Beetle-spawn! I told him, 'I hold the equivalent rank of Captain-General. Retired on pension, thirty-four wounds above the navel.' Talking to me about a permit!"

He paused to stare balefully at the *Charilaos* and then again at me.

"You, Sir, are you the owner of this vessel?"

I disclaimed that distinction. "I am actually a surgeon—you may remember, Captain Babitch, that you and I were associated in a case not long ago."

"Very likely!" he answered. "I go about the world a good deal." His voice was falling to a mumble: he faintly knew, I think, that I was someone he should have recognised, and his eyes had clouded with the melancholy of self-conscious age. "I'm posted here for special duties," he said, with a rather pitiful importance. "Some Swiss, a lot of money. Something wrong with his chest—a shooting accident, I understand." And now he grew confidential. "That jack-in-office back there, do you know, he had the flaming impudence to tell me the post was filled. Said he'd let one surgeon go through already. I said, "Listen, spawn, I've got the letter here, the letter from my friend Ricotti.' Do you know Ricotti? Italian scum. Still, they have their uses, these rascally civilians."

He had started fumbling in the canvas bag at his feet, in search, as I guessed, of his indispensable cigarettes. But now, abruptly, he straightened himself and startled me again by shouting,

"Ho, there! You! Are you the shipmaster? Surgeon-Captain Babitch reporting for special employment!"

The shipmaster it was: I looked up and caught sight of Tricoulos standing on the deck, dressed as I had last seen him but crowned with a stiff cap which I took to symbolize a maritime intention. Supposing he would recall our earlier meeting, I smiled and wished him good morning. But his memory was evidently no better than Babitch's: coming slowly to the rail, he merely surveyed us with a sorrowful reserve, as if some chandler had delivered stores he could not remember ordering. I explained my business, using the simplest Italian I could find. In vigorous Serbo-Croat, Babitch stated his. Tricoulos, like a foreign prince receiving an address of welcome, gravely inclined his head and returned to the bridge.

There was one gangway in place amidships. Babitch, I think, would have resolved the situation by going aboard at once, and might easily have savaged the captain—which

for me would have been inconvenient—but for the inter-
vention of a friend. I still call Zhenko that; for although I
learnt in time that his loyalty was to no cause of mine, he
was by nature a friendly person. It was he who now
appeared from the forecastle, as if he had been born and
bred there, and greeted me with an air which reflected none
of my surprise.

"You've come," he asked politely, "to say good-bye to
the friends you spoke of?"

I told him, yes; and that the gentleman beside me had
been engaged as their medical attendant. "But I hadn't
realized that you belong to this ship!" I said.

He made a grimace peculiar to the peasantry of Serbia,
a simultaneous hoisting of the underlip and lowering of the
shoulders. "Ship? A bum-boat, I should call her. Well,
there it is"—he jerked his head towards the bridge—"he
was short of a radio man. You go where your trade takes
you."

"Can we come aboard?" I asked.

"I'll see, sir—with your pardon."

He went to the foot of the bridge ladder and called up to
Tricoulos, in what I took to be a bastard Greek in the use of
Adriatic seamen. The answer, in which I recognized the
Greek of Piraeus, he transmitted effortlessly.

"The captain wishes to know your business."

"God blast his impudence!" said Babitch. "I've told
him hours ago."

"Perhaps, Mr. Zhenko, you will explain it to the captain
for us," I said.

"Tell him," Babitch roared, "that I have been the senior
surgeon in the Serbian army. Thirty-four wounds above
the navel, five special commendations."

How accurately Zhenko forwarded these particulars I had
no means of knowing. "Captain Tricoulos," he presently
reported, "has heard nothing about a medical attendant.
He can't remember about any passengers," he added, smiling

with the curious pleasure that humble folk take in evil news. "The captain will not allow anyone except officials on board. He has ordered steam for eight o'clock, he says, and he will sail at that hour whether these passengers have come or not."

This edict put a fresh strain on Babitch's patience.

"Tell the little louse," he ordered, "that if he sails without me I shall have him sunk by the shore battery at Parano."

"Please give the captain our compliments," I amended, "and ask if he will be good enough to reconsider his decision."

"I shall tell him," Zhenko said intelligently, as one accustomed to extract essential truth from the husk of circumlocution, "that you have come from the Sanitation Department and that he must have your clearance before he sails."

Sunk in weariness and gloom, I had not the moral energy to argue against these tactics: I was once more in a world of which I had no comprehension, let alone control. The manœuvre served at least to get us aboard, where the wall of the deck-house gave us better shelter than anything on the quay. But for me that was the only gain, since at closer quarters the quadrille of which I had become a member was socially more comfortless than before. Tricoulos had descended from the bridge, but he would not recognize our presence; he walked Napoleonically up and down the deck, merely swerving a little to avoid our feet and occasionally pausing to spit, rather primly, across to the quay. This behaviour was to Babitch a source of further irritation. "You," he bawled, each time the captain passed, "will you listen, sir! I wish to be taken to my quarter, I insist on being accommodated according to my rank!" And then he would turn to me. "This man's an imbecile, I wouldn't have him in charge of a bed-pan. Tell him, you" (to Zhenko) "that he ought to be under lock and key!" "The doctor," Zhenko relayed, as far as I could follow, "says that he is used to more deferential treatment." At which Tricoulos would jerk up his chin to utter a short, contemptuous laugh and then continue his promenade, keeping his eyes on the deck and talking to himself in a rapid undertone.

The drizzle was turning back into copious rain, which a lively, veering wind caught and drove in flouncing sheets along the wharf. And soon I was given fresh cause for pessimism. I had taken Tricoulos's talk of an early start as bombast. But in the casual way no landsman understands—it resembles most a process of nature—the business of departure seemed to have begun. Like mice in winter men became visible above me and along the deck, pursuing their lone employments as children do in a progressive school, one hammering, one leisurely coiling a length of idle rope. The main cargo, I suppose, had been loaded earlier. But a railroad wagon which a single ancient man was shepherding from the rear came trundling down the track to where, opposite the *Charilaos*'s forward hold, a diesel tanker and a pair of lorries were jostling for position as puppies scramble for their mother's teats; and about this circus ring grew a corps of attendants as various and nondescript as the extras of vaudeville. No one was manifestly in command. In a makeshift shelter beside the hold a ragged fellow occasionally raised one arm and uttered a raucous cry as if he were a prophet suddenly inspired. I detected no response ashore. Tricoulos, leaning like a tourist against the rail, was surveying the theatre of operations with distant, slightly jaundiced eyes as if it conveyed no more to his intelligence than to mine.

Just before eight o'clock he did return to the bridge. By then Babitch had disappeared—I think that Zhenko, tired of his complaints, had contrived a temporary quarter for him—and I found myself virtually alone. At this stage the hope that my party would arrive had become infinitely small: since Kurt's agents had failed to get them here at the time originally fixed it was expecting too much of chance that they would make the actual hour of sailing. And now I felt curiously indifferent. In these confused and bleak surroundings, on which the rain imposed a desolate uniformity, I had lost the faculty of emotion. I wanted nothing but to be warm and dry, and to get some food inside me.

I was actually moving to go ashore when something I had not noticed before provoked my curiosity. Of two covered vans now backed towards the ship's side, one, up-to-date and freshly painted, bore the Arms of the United States. Staring, I saw below them the legend, 'W.U.R.O. Trieste'. And now I remembered that I had seen this vehicle before: Dollis had acquired it for local work just before he had posted me to Ljubljana.

As I loitered, wondering in a stupid way what business our organization could have with the *Charilaos,* a man came from behind the van, ran up the gangway and spoke to the sailor on duty by the hold. Although his hat was pulled down on his forehead, and the collar of his raincoat turned up to cover neck and ears, I recognized him easily by his gait—Ricotti. Simultaneously—or that was my impression —two uniformed men lifted a covered stretcher from the van itself and placed it on a loading tray; in a matter of seconds the arm of the ship's derrick swung over, a stevedore caught the hook and coupled it with the loading chains; the tray rose, swung nearly over my head and went down into the hold. The speed of the operation, and the dullness of my wits, were such that I did not guess what had come aboard. And now my attention was again diverted by a shout from the quay. Two men were coming towards the van at a pace as near to running as official dignity allowed—one, I think, was an officer of customs, the other a uniformed policeman. The policeman, drawing ahead, made for the man in charge of the van; who, taken by surprise, simply stared at him in bewildered silence.

That encounter took place at something under thirty yards from where I stood. I watched it, and the episode that followed, as one watches a moving picture, scarcely believing that action apparently so well rehearsed, so far removed from my daily experience, was a product of reality. A small saloon car had drawn up near the railway truck. From this, without apparent haste, three men came up and placed themselves between the policeman and the bewildered servants of W.U.R.O. The customs officer had fallen back. For a moment the policeman appeared to be maintaining his authority. Then the three men closed on him as if he were some thin but heavy object which they had to lift. I heard a scream like that of a small animal—in a peculiar way it sounded as if it were just out of synchronization. And now the assailants were returning at an easy pace to their car, watched with passive curiosity by the porters, while the policeman, doubled up and gripping his left shoulder, was crying as elsewhere I have only seen young children cry.

In this bizarre and dreadful incident, which was over in perhaps less than half a minute, there was one detail which removed it disquietingly from the realm of chimera. For an instant I had seen in profile the face of one of the interlopers; and I was almost certain it belonged to Valyevitch, the man who had negotiated the Zempelmarcks' passage. That moment of half-recognition had been at once the most actual and the hardest to believe in. It was to haunt me in the hours that followed. For I could not conceive why Valyevitch (whom I had taken for a person of essential humanity) should have resorted to such violence in aid of people with whom he had no real connection.

8

Yet those happenings have left only a superficial impression on my memory, because I had no sense of personal implication. It is otherwise with the small, dense span of time which followed. Here I ceased to be spectator; and the dead weight of my body, its coldness and lassitude, released me as gravity releases a kite caught by the wind.

My reason had then so far returned that I saw vaguely what Kurt had been doing. Doubtless using my name, he had contrived to borrow the W.U.R.O. vehicle on some imaginary pretext and taken advantage of W.U.R.O.'s quasi-diplomatic privilege: by this means Zempelmarck had been slipped through the frontier controls, and was now aboard. But because I had see no one embarking with the stretcher I jumped to the conclusion that the rest of the party had somewhere been left behind.

So it was that, when I heard a small boy's voice some-where behind me, I merely thought, 'Oh, there's a child among the crew'. It provoked, however, a whiff of curiosity which made me turn my head.

A few feet away, among a litter of deck cargo, a woman sat on an orange-box, wearing the kind of voluminous gaberdine coat one associates with English travellers. My immediate thought—before I recognized her—was 'That woman's ill—perhaps appendix'. A man in a steward's jacket—a Malay—was watching her with professional solicitude, while another woman bent over her and the boy whose voice I had heard stood at her side. It was such a group as you might come across in any season's travelling.

What did I expect, what had I pictured in the hours of waiting? Something, I suppose, less commonplace—people more dishevelled and distraught, more as I had last seen them in the shed at Tustar. I know that I stood quite still, like an actor arrived too early on the stage, while the Malay with another sailor lifted Paula with the box she sat on and carried her below.

Johannes followed them; and Franziska would have gone as well, but I shook off my paralysis in time to call to her:
"Franziska!"

She turned, and for a moment stared as if she were looking into sunlight. Then she came towards me.

My eyes recorded the physical signs of what she had been through in the last few days, the extreme pallor, inflamed and dilated pupils, an unsteadiness in her walk. But she herself appeared to have forgotten all that. Serious, collected, she greeted me as if we were meeting casually in the Volksgarten.

"It's marvellous," she said with simplicity, "the way you got everything arranged. And to come to say good-bye, that's marvellous too!"

I suppose I made some answer, but at that encounter I said nothing coherent that I remember. When you come to the awaited moment, when you have only minutes to recover the loss of wasted years, those past and those to come, the mind will not admit the discipline of language. I took her by the arm to an angle where a boat gave some shelter. I felt for her hand, which she gave and let me hold as she would have done for a nervous child, smiling to me soberly, with a tender kindness. Beside her head I saw the other world, a screen of sloping rain in which men stood with sacks round their shoulders, and carried ropes, and shouted to those on deck as they attended to chains and hawsers. That was totally unreal. All that it means to be alive, and of human status, was in the hand I held, in the small, exhausted being who let me hold it. Speechless, I prayed for time to cease, for this moment to be vested with infinity.

I heard her say, "He will be safe in Spain. I think he's safe already." And I heard myself asking recklessly,

"Then need you go as well? He'll be safe, and he'll have Paula."

"But Paula isn't his wife!" she answered patiently.

Afterwards—I don't know how long after—I spoke as perhaps all lovers do who have learnt no skill in love. "You won't forget about me altogether? You'll send me letters —just now and then? You'll let me know an address I can write to?... You see," I said, like one with impediments in speech and mind, "there's no one to look after you. There can't be, ever. No one really knows you. Not, I mean, in the way I do. At least you can write to me, you can tell me things when there's no one else you can tell."

Here was the selfishness of love, feebly disguised. I wanted her to be cared for—yes, but I found only misery in the thought of that care coming, if it were possible, from some other person. I should have been less tormented then if she had wept, confessing that for her there would be no more happiness when we were parted, only an endless famine of the heart. It was not in her to behave so, even if such thoughts had been in her mind. She was sorrowful only, I believe, for my distress. Clear-sighted, she must have foreseen a future barren of sympathy, of pride, of peaceful conscience. But that burden she had long accepted as others accept a physical infirmity. No woman was ever more in need of protection and tenderness than she, yet none was less disposed to seek it. And if, for me, she was young and frail, vulnerable as well as lovely, I could still see faintly the temper of her fortitude. She was not a small creature to whom great virtue had been added, she was one of full stature embodied at God's will in the slighter frame of women: too whole, too selfless, for the passive complexion of love.

There was a moment when she did betray some weakness; when her hand became more yielding and she shut her eyes and I thought she would let her forehead fall against my shoulder. I remember lucidly how she looked then, the darkness of a strand of her wet hair on her marble forehead, the beads of sweat beneath her lower lip: in that fraction of time life was perfected for me, for even so small a movement told me, as with the voice of trumpets, that she recognized the place lying open to her in my spirit. It passed—it had to pass—leaving me both empty and exalted. And her voice was scarcely tremulous when she said,

"But Eugen, of course I shall think of you! Often, every

day! I couldn't ever forget your kindness, you've been so good to us all—especially to me."

In the outer world there had been some shouting, a quickening of activity, which had penetrated hardly further than my senses. With the tail of my eye I was actually looking at a man unlashing the gangway when her voice abruptly changed. Stiffening, as one roused from the depths of sleep, she said almost roughly, "You must go! Eugen, you must hurry— you won't get off the boat!"

I obeyed her—or rather, I obeyed that small, prosaic voice of common sense that we are trained to answer from our childhood. With hardly a word, hardly another look, I squeezed her hand and let her go. I could only do it that way.

The man at the gangway looked up as I came automatically towards him. What he saw, I should think, was something like the most wooden of business men, the face of one incapable of emotion. For by then the mechanism which can induce normal behaviour in shellshocked and virtually unconscious men had taken me in charge. Without the use of my mind I should have found the way back to my lodging, talked politely to my hosts—had I not chanced, as I reached the gangway-head, to look over to my left. That single glance brought my intelligence back into action.

Among the men still standing on the quay there were three in lively conference. One was the policeman who had been so savagely warned to keep clear of others' business. With him, talking like a water-mill, was the watchman who had questioned me at the entrance to the wharf; and beside them, a statue of perplexity, was the large, loose figure of my colleague in Trieste, Ed Browning.

Here was the reckoning—now I should have to explain in detail a course of conduct which could make no sense to anyone alive. And that I could not face. Not that I cared about the yokels in uniform—any story would have done for them. But Ed, immense in person and in probity, with all the sunlight of Virginia in his eyes and voice, had been my friend: I could neither lie nor explain the truth to him.

He was looking the other way, but in a moment he might turn and see me. That risk I avoided. Slipping back along the deck, I pulled the first door that I came to. It opened to a shallow storeroom. I stepped inside and shut the door behind me.

There, among the brooms and buckets, I stood shivering with fear. And as the changes in vibration told me that the ship was under way, I thought—strangely—not at all of Franziska; only of myself, as of one who had thrown away his honourable status, his friends, his last hope of reputation and security.

Chapter 8

I

YET I FOUND in the hours that followed, where the past was lost and the future hopeless, at least the restfulness of having all decision taken out of my hands. The captivity of voyage admits no argument, reduces to vanity the toil of self-examination. To think of what would happen to me when we arrived in Spain was useless. Dulled by what had happened already, my mind was chiefly employed in the smaller, hourly concerns of existing with none of the apparatus I was used to.

I speak reflectively when I say that within this experience there flowed persistently a current of happiness. Happiness? So small a stream, clogged by weed, bitter with longing? I call it so. Franziska, secluded in her thoughts, opening herself to me only in rare and unexpected moments in the slight parting of her lips, the joining of her calm eyes with mine, was at least not far away. That was enough. It brought my distresses to their proper scale, to measure my lot by hers and then to see how steadily her courage burned. Weak as she was from strain and exposure, she smiled often; sometimes she even laughed at the ship's and the crew's absurdities. The laughter came, I thought, from a spring of joy in her which no temporal emotion could account for; and from that spring I drew for myself, however feebly, its warmth and sweetness. It was not a small thing to have won from such a being at least her trust, at least some part of her affection.

There was no sense of progress—one could not tell in the continuing drizzle whether it was coast line or a strip of darker cloud which kept reappearing on the port bow. My lack of confidence in the *Charilaos* was not corrected. To untaught ears the sound of her engines was always laboured and faulty, like the breathing of a man with pericarditis. She seemed to be for ever trying to ascend the sides of the great slow seas which drove towards us from the south-west, for ever slipping and falling back to roll and flounder in the valleys.

In the cramped compartment deep in her belly where I spent most of my time it was harder still to believe one was being carried from one point on the earth's surface to another. That cabin (which normally belonged, I think, to the engineer's mate) was the one where Siegfried had finally been placed. I shared it with him and with Babitch, who lay on the floor in a haze of *cannabis indica,* seldom stirring, monotonously complaining of indigestion. My own accommodation was a hammock which—at Zhenko's behest —the Malay steward had slung for me above Siegfried's berth. And for this I was grateful, having no rights aboard. I had had an interview with Tricoulos which must have meant as little to him as to me : while Zhenko translated my politic explanations he had stood in total silence with his eyes turned away, exhibiting the faint, disdainful smile of an upright man refusing to buy indecent photographs.

No—as an uninvited guest I was in no position to cavil at the ship's standard of hospitality. This I had to bear in mind as I swallowed the nauseous ragouts which the steward brought us at his occasional convenience. And I thought of it again as I tried hopelessly to open the rusty ventilator in our cabin, or to fix the door so that it did not constantly fly open, admitting from the noisome latrine along the corridor a stench so vigorous as to overcome the ruling odours of bilge and engine oil. But sometimes I permitted myself to curse aloud over the lack of light. There was but one bulkhead lamp, sealed with rust. Often, through failure of the current, it went out altogether; and at other times the aged globe gave to the cabin no more than an ochreous twilight. In this I had—besides caring for myself and a good deal for Babitch—to wait upon Siegfried, to feed and generally nurse him, while the floor lazily tilted from side to side, sometimes with an extra, screwing motion, and now and then drove up against my feet as if a charge of cordite had been fired beneath it.

It was at least fortunate that I had the case to occupy my mind. The business of getting the man downstairs at Vischak had sharpened my interest in the earlier injury to his leg, which I could now examine at greater leisure. In other circumstances I should have advised a fresh operation. As things were, I could only apply a technique in manipulative surgery which I had learnt from Oscar Cavour— Cavour's long and patient researches in this field had been bearing remarkable fruit at the time when I left New Haven. Meanwhile the chest was a continuing anxiety. The possibility of a lung abscess resulting from the continued presence of the bullet was always in my mind, and being without a single instrument I was inclined to give too much weight to every diagnostic observed by eye or ear alone: at one time I imagined that the respiration was less regular than it had been at Vischak, at another I interpreted as a serious febrile condition what was probably no more than the transient effect of living in a foul atmosphere. There was little I could do. The steward brought me what he could find in the ship's medicine chest—old-fashioned sedatives and a patented febrifuge. I made use of these as a Christian pays heed to pagan superstitions. For the rest, I made frequent journeys to the galley for drinking water which was relatively clean and cold, washed the body often, buttressed it with everything I could find against the fearful jolting, and established within the given framework some semblance of a sick-room routine.

Between bouts of nausea Franziska helped me as well as she could—Paula, who shared with her and Johannes what was called the Principal Saloon, was prostrate with seasickness—but in the space left by Siegfried's berth and the rolling person of Babitch on the floor there was room for only one at a time to manœuvre. In truth, Siegfried was his own best doctor. That he had come, apparently with little harm, through the savage ordeal of removal to Trieste was evidence of a stamina unique in my experience; and in this further trial his toughness and his fortitude did more for him than any ministrations of mine. Once he had trained soldiers to the perfect obedience he would need of them in days to come. Now, for a kindred purpose, he exercised upon his own body the same relentless command.

Occasionally we had some assistance from Zhenko as well. From the time when we came aboard he had shown all the morbid curiosity of his kind over Siegfried's case.

"The medicine chest in this boat is hopeless," he informed me, in mixed apology and contempt for the *Charilaos*, on the first day out. "As soon as we call somewhere I shall restock it entirely," he boasted, "and Tricoulos will have to pay."

I asked, "But are we likely to call anywhere before Spain?"

He became knowing, in the way of sailors with landsmen. "We may want oil," he said.

"But wasn't the ship fuelled before it left Trieste?"

"Who knows? A man like this Tricoulos, he does things his own way. And the price isn't the same everywhere."

"You think we may call at Brindisi—somewhere like that?"

He shrugged his shoulders, but the gesture was not one of total ignorance.

There was much of the child in him, I thought, and he liked to be mysterious. Yet his hint of inside knowledge left me with a new, more subtle uneasiness. My astonishment at finding him in the *Charilaos* had not worn off. Had he been of my own race I might have thought of him merely as an obliging, slightly officious fellow, but one trusts a foreigner less easily. In any case I should have preferred on this disreputable voyage to have no one aboard who had any previous acquaintance with the Zempelmarcks' or my own affairs.

3

In so far as it is possible to know someone totally antipathetic to oneself, I came to know Siegfried a little better in the hours when I was his nurse as well as his doctor. He was by now used to me, and a man will often talk to his body servant with less reserve than to his friends.

It was during the second night, I think, that I woke in the small hours to find him restless and slightly feverish. I got him some water, for which he thanked me with his usual dry politeness—"I am infinitely obliged to you!"—and while I was trying to make him more comfortable he said drowsily,

"I wonder if my wife imagines I was afraid to face the Russo-Americans. I suppose she does. In a way she has never quite grown up, she has never really understood the officer's position."

I answered that it seemed to me unlikely that his wife would ever reproach him with cowardice: it was not a failing anyone would associate with him.

"But you yourself," he persisted, "you thought I should give myself up to that *canaille*? You were in favour of the plan?"

I said, "It was not my business—I'm only concerned with your physical health. From that aspect I thought your sister's proposal to drag you over the countryside in the middle of a winter night was pure lunacy. It turned out that I was wrong, that's all."

At this he smiled gauntly. "Of course, yes, my health is what you're interested in! You were quite ready to see the Russo-Americans hang me as long as I was in first-class physical condition at the time."

"You take it for granted they'd have hanged you?"

"Why, naturally! What evidence had I except my own? And what would that have counted for with them—what do lawyers know about the necessities of war! They think you can control people by pinning up regulations on a notice-board. A beautiful notion! Unfortunately real life is not like that. We who've had the actual experience, we know there are just two instruments of control—force and fear."

"There remains," I said, "the question of who has the right to control whom."

"I can answer that for you—it's really quite simple. The people who have the right to govern are those who *can*. Always, in every circumstance! It's only when that principle's accepted that you get order and peace—which is what everyone really wants, however much the underlings may twitter and mumble. The one unforgivable thing is to use one's power timidly."

Babitch had wakened and was listening: he had just enough German to pick up a word or two when Siegfried and I were talking.

"What's the Swiss fellow saying now?" he demanded. "I wish he'd speak clearly, if he's got to yammer all night long."

I gave him in half a dozen words an account of Siegfried's views on power, and he said, "I totally agree—there's some sense in this bastard after all!" Then he rolled over and went to sleep again.

"And that," I said to Siegfried, "would have been the line of your defence?"

"Defence? I shouldn't have wasted my breath! Do you think I care twopence about a verdict brought in by a court like that! Would *you*, if you were being 'tried' by the very people you'd been fighting tooth and nail for years?"

The question caught me unprepared, and my answer (as I think of it now) was needlessly portentous: "In the end I suppose no judgement matters—for any of us—except the last one."

"What—God's, do you mean? You don't tell me you believe all that! The Last Judgement and the fires of hell—Purgatory, and all the rest of it? Well, I suppose you're in the same position as my wife—you have to believe what the priest tells you to."

Foolishly nettled, I spoke without reflection: "That, if I may say so, is just the sort of philosophic nonsense on which your Third Reich was founded—the idea that you can *make* people believe things."

"It never occurred to me," he retorted frigidly, "that a man of science could convince himself of the doctrine of fire and brimstone."

"No—because you can only think in physical terms, you can't conceive such a thing as the life of the spirit——"

"Then please explain it to me!" he said.

The challenge was only what my self-righteousness deserved. It was not an easy one to deal with, especially when the ship was pitching with some violence, forcing me to hold like a gymnast to the side of his berth. Nor was I in a state of conscience where I could comfortably review my notions of heaven and hell and preach a sermon on them. What I said, halting and fumbling, had only the virtue of coming from my own conviction.

"I believe that a human life is infinite," I told him, "because it isn't a thing of separable parts—it seems to me

207

nonsensical to think of a human being as just a focus of sensations——"

"Yes, yes!" he said impatiently, "I've heard all that before. Most ingenious, but——"

"And if I'm going to go on living through infinite time I've got to be at peace with myself—which is the same as saying I've got to be at peace with God. I can't face the purity of God as I am—it would be like going to a woman you've married with disease all over you. That's why hell is a necessity to me. A hell within me. There's a part of me that's got to be burnt away."

The moody voice of Babitch stopped me. "What's that? What are you talking about now? Did you say the ship was on fire?"

"Not yet," I told him.

Siegfried was delicately yawning. "I think," he said mildly, "you've perhaps rather over-cultivated your religious sensibilities." And presently fell asleep.

But later, more than once, he glanced at the subject again, always with a rather laborious flippancy.

"The doctor tells me he's a great believer in hell," he said to Franziska in my presence while she was re-making his bed. "He has a private one to take refuge in when he's been naughty."

She did not answer.

"I suppose that's the orthodox doctrine," he pursued, "the portable hell?"

"I don't know," she said rather wearily. "I do know what it means to have hell inside oneself."

"But is there no public hell for people like me? Somewhere you could look at me through the bars on alternate Sundays, say?"

"I'd rather not talk of such things."

"There's no need to," I interposed, "with Spain ahead of you."

"What—is Spain your idea of hell?"

"On the contrary: I mean, you're going to get well there, you're going to plan your future—as you told me some time ago."

"Yes, according to my sister that is the programme."

"But Siegfried, that's what we've all worked for!" Franziska said.

"I am infinitely grateful!" he answered dryly. "And now I think it's time for our friend here to pursue his scientific interests by pommelling the most sensitive parts of my leg."

It was nothing to wonder at, I thought, that the prospect of life and freedom should have lost some brilliance now they were nearer to his reach. This was a normal reaction after the prolonged tensions of captivity and escape. Yet there was in his present temper something I could not have foreseen—the signs of a pessimism which neither our wretched surroundings nor the problems of his future (which he must have worked at long before this) could altogether account for. Previously, I should have said that pessimism was a mood too subtle for such a mind as his, which looked for clear victories or defeats and accepted both with an athlete's tolerance. Now, for a space, I realized—almost as one discovering some intelligence in plant-life—that he was not finally incapable of mental suffering.

To Franziska as well, though surely she should long since have found her way to what depths there were in him, this indication came as something new. She said to me, in a moment when we were alone,

"He is unhappy. I've never known such a thing before— I've known him angry and disappointed and bitter, but I didn't think he could be unhappy in the way other people are."

"It will alter," I told her (and I caught the tone of my professional voice), "when he's settled down to some reasonable sort of life—when he's not a total invalid."

"I agree," she said obliquely, "that this isn't exactly a settled life."

We were standing in the narrow space on the after-deck where it was possible to breathe clean air without being shredded by the wind or soaked with rain—only an occasional burst of spray found its way to our necks and faces. Every minute or two the door beside us opened violently to release, with a raggedly bearded man carrying a bucket or a handful of tools, the ship's internal smell and noise—the hammering and long drawn râle of her engines, an incessant rattle of loose fittings, the rasp and whine which sounded like a house being torn to bits.

"But I don't know," she added, when neither of us had spoken for a time, "whether I want it to change."

"At least you want Siegfried to be contented?"

She said slowly: "I suppose so. Yes, of course I do. But not with the sort of contentment that comes from blindness."

Though I perfectly understood her meaning, that remark was hard to answer: I was always chary of talking to her about Siegfried except as an invalid for whom we were both caring. It was without premeditation—almost against my will—that I said,

"No, that sort isn't good enough for those one loves."

At this she nodded, with her serious eyes fixed on my face. "But in any case," she said, letting a fresh thought slide into the other's place, "I can't believe that we shall ever be settled and safe. I can't remember when it was ever like that with us."

4

In those words she echoed a premonition of my own. A premonition? Rather, I suppose, a general sense of disquiet, originating in my small regard for Tricoulos's capabilities and my formless misgivings about Zhenko's presence aboard.

We passengers lived in a peculiar isolation. Nearly all the

crew were Greek, and to the exclusiveness of their calling was added their native independence. They had no common tongue with us, and plainly needed none of our society, for their leisure was amply filled: at every hour, standing in odd corners, they seemed to be telling each other interminable histories, or debating the news which trickled in from Athens Radio in the manner of woodmen working a cross-cut saw. If they had any interest in us their natural politeness forbade them to reveal it: they largely ignored us as men of breeding show themselves blind to disorders in a neighbour's house. For my part, I regretted their aloofness. They appeared to be good men and able sailors, with the unpretentious dignity of those whose demand on life is satisfied by their craft. It seemed to me a little absurd, and comfortless, that we and they, sharing so small a habitation, should have to behave as if we lived on separate globes.

In practice the division did not conspicuously matter—we required nothing of them but to get us to our destination. Yet my general anxiety was sharpened when I recognized—on the third morning—a change in their mood. They were talking in larger groups, as men do at times of political crisis. Their speech and gestures were faintly excited.

I went to look for the steward, to whom I could talk in English (with the limitations imposed by our respective schools—I had learnt that language mainly in Connecticut and he in Kuala Lumpur), and found him as usual playing Sobo-Sabo with the captain's boy. Had some special news come through, I asked. He stared at me reproachfully—he never cared to have his recreation disturbed by passengers. What? News? Special news? No, he did not think so.

"The sailors seem rather excited," I explained.

The sailors? Ah, they were nothing but Greeks, they had not an idea in their heads except to get back to their piddling islands.

"You mean they don't want to go to Spain?"

"Yes, no—I think so."

"But that's the voyage they're being paid for, isn't it?"

He considered this. "The sailors," he said, "want to go to Spain dam-quick, home again dam-quick. Not to be stopping here, there, all over the place. They think the captain doesn't mind the ship any more, they think the radio-man—that Zhenko—they say that Zhenko is minding the ship."

I had realized before this that Zhenko was unpopular with his shipmates, and it scarcely surprised me. Besides being new and a foreigner, he enjoyed—I suppose—a comparatively high status derived from his trade, and with so much warrant he paraded the airs of a precocious schoolboy. The modesty he had first displayed to me was superficial: he spoke of his fellows as 'this Greek rabble', and I doubt if he took any pains to hide his contempt when in their company.

I went now to the radio cabin, but it was empty, and Zhenko nowhere to be seen. Just afterwards I met Tricoulos on his way from his quarter to the bridge. He passed without appearing to see me. That was his custom, but on this occasion I think he was actually too much engrossed in his own meditations to be aware of anything outside them. His little, feminine hands were working like a conjuror's, and the whole of his face was engaged in a kind of ballet: one could see—with the smallest knowledge of human weakness—that in his mind he was performing splendidly some scene which in reality had brought him only humiliation.

I had my duties below, and it was not till late in the afternoon that I did get hold of Zhenko.

"I hear there's some trouble," I said casually, "between the crew and the captain."

He spat in pantomime over his shoulder.

"The captain—that old wet-nurse? Why should he worry what a midden of deck-hands have to say! It's his ship, no one can tell him where he's to sail it."

I might have argued this point, but it was not worth while.

"What are the sailors complaining about?" I persisted.

He looked away, and I saw that for some reason he did not wish to tell me. But his vanity was too much for him—like every peasant who has bettered himself he loved to be in the know.

"All nonsense!" he said. "They thought the ship was to call at Corfu, that's all. Some of them have their homes there—they want to sleep with their wives before their wives get fat and old. They're just childish and sentimental."

"But why has the route been changed?"

"Because it pays Tricoulos better to go another way!"

"Pays him better? How do you mean?"

But his last answer, cryptic and smug, had evidently been more than he had meant to give me, and I could draw him no further. Had some other port of call been substituted for Corfu? Was there further cargo to be collected? Had some new direction come by radio? These questions he met with a sly and obstinate evasion. I tried to play on his conceit by suggesting that he really knew nothing. He countered this with a sickening righteousness—his position was one of trust, he said, and he could not disclose any information given him in confidence.

I said nothing to the Zempelmarcks about all this; and when Johannes came down that evening to say (with his faintly irritating wisdom) that he thought we had altered course and must now be sailing due east, I told him that he was giving way to his imagination. But I believe everyone knew, or at least suspected, that something irregular was happening—in so small a community one catches a general apprehension as easily as one contracts bacillary disease.

At some time in the night I knew, emerging slowly from heavy sleep, that my surroundings had in some way changed. The noises I had lived with for nearly four days had dwindled to silence. Presently I realized that the ship lay still.

As yet only half awake, I remembered nothing of Johannes' report. For a time I had the vague notion that we were becalmed; then an earlier one returned, and I surmised that we had arrived at Brindisi to refuel.

From that point I sleepily traced my way once more through a plan which had been shaping since I came aboard. In Italy it would be easy to break away. I should contrive to borrow money from old friends of my mother's at Potenza and fly back to Trieste. There I should go straight to Dollis Andersen and tell him what had happened, with some specious variations—Siegfried would become an aged relative, living in Trieste and suffering from tuberculosis, whom I had meant to send to an Apennine resort. . . . I became confused—the story would not fit together as I had made it fit before. And now the truth broke in and took possession of my mind: I did not want to get away, I could not bear the voyage to end. In the *Charilaos* was a kind of safety, a routine which needed no decisions. Elsewhere I should have to fix a moral bearing on which to reorientate my life; and I should be quite alone. But that was not all. For four days I had lived in revolting squalor with the archetype of all I loathed in men and a rumbling dotard for companions. Yet I was ready for that existence to continue, for its single thread of sweetness.

But while my mind was so engaged I was lowering my body from the hammock, automatically allowing for a roll which had ceased to operate, taking care as always to avoid putting a foot in Siegfried's face or on Babitch's belly. I felt about for my coat and went on deck, still hooded with sleep.

There my first impression was that the ship had somehow been lifted far inland; for we seemed to be totally surrounded by hills, a dark, serrated mass against the fainter darkness of the sky. Only when I had walked all round the deck did I see the narrow water-gate between two bluffs by which we had entered this enclosure, and the tail of an avenue of light-buoys which must have led deviously to the open sea. It remained hard to believe that the structure I stood on was waterborne. Rather, I felt as if I was on the balcony of some small inn which fronted the centre of a village. There was one light hanging from a cable between two trees. It showed the granite quay, of only a wagon's width, merging into a promiscuous floor of outcrop rock and mud on which a dozen limestone cottages, rudely made and planted in a vague half-circle, gave an appearance of whimsical theatricality. This was not Brindisi.

So operatic was the scene that when a man with a lantern came out from the darkness over on my left I almost expected to see him take position under the light and break into an aria. And the thought of Italy was still so far forward in my mind that, as he passed below me, I called to him in Italian:

"What is the name of this place, if you please?"

Evidently he understood me. But it was in Serbo-Croat that he answered, with a touch of rustic sarcasm, "This place? Why, sir, it is still called Zlot, as far as I know."

I discovered, then or shortly afterwards, that Franziska had come on deck. She was standing some feet away from me but the light from a cabin window showed her face quite clearly: I realized at once that she had heard the man's reply and that she knew as well as I on which side of the Adriatic Zlot is. 'What did I tell you!' she might have said; but she left it to me to break the silence:

"I'm afraid Zhenko has had plans of his own, right from the beginning."

She answered steadily, "Yes. Yes, I suppose the police will be with us soon. I was wrong when I thought I could run away from the truth of things. I know now that it's always wrong."

Chapter 9

I

IT MUST HAVE been still dark outside when the steward, tousled and unshaven, came to our cabin.

"All passengers," he announced without preamble, "are required to go on shore."

I had thought that nothing in the conduct of the *Charilaos* could still astonish me, but this impudence was like a blow in the stomach.

"What do you mean?" I said. "I never heard such nonsense in my life! Where does this message come from?"

"If you please, it was told me by Mr. Zhenko. He says it was the captain's order."

"Then you will go to the captain—*not* to Zhenko—and you will present my compliments and say that I do not understand his message."

He was back in a few minutes, slightly pleased with himself, as if he had matched his wits with mine and come out victorious: previously I had liked the man, but at that moment I could have slapped his face.

"The captain says it is the Regulation. All passengers to be ashore while the ship is refuelling. It is the Safety Regulation."

There seemed only one way to dispose of this nonsense, and I still do not blame myself for what proved a tactical error. I went to Tricoulos's cabin.

There I found only the Mate, a large, lugubrious man—from Leros, I believe—with whom I had had no previous dealings. He was an excellent seaman (as even Zhenko had

admitted) but no linguist, and it needed prodigies of pantomime to make him understand that I had important business
to discuss with his captain. When, at last, he had grasped my
wishes, he wiped the seat of Tricoulos's chair with the edge
of the tablecloth, motioned me to sit there and went off
murmuring something I took to mean 'Immediately!'

I had to wait for ten minutes or more, and if that was a
trial of patience it served at least to persuade me of Tricoulos's essential respectability. The cabin almost cried it
aloud. Every shelf and cupboard was draped with a velvet
curtain, majestically fringed, every square foot of the bulk-
heads was hung with tricksy gim-cracks or with photographs of pious women in the dress of 1912. The very smell
was that of the tiny parlour in Leopoldstadt where Professor
Rosinski had once taught me pianoforte; and it was
Rosinski—small, penurious, his nerve-ends all unsealed—
whom I thought of when finally Tricoulos came.

He wore the loose, fatuous smile of one who has never
the means to pay his debts. When I tried to yield him his
chair he did not appear to see that gesture, but stood with
his hands on the hinged table, scrutinizing a waybill which
to him was upside down. I said, supplementing my few
words of modern Greek with hopeful recollections from
the Tetralogies,

"Impossible the sick man to be removed on soil. This
demand impossible."

He answered in his individual German: "Regulations.
Police-law. All passengers."

"The sick man removed on soil—quickly more sick.
Death, quickly. I the physician, I so declare."

He nodded impersonally, as if that view was of some
academic interest. Then he repeated, "*Alle Reisenden!
Einrichtungen! Polizeigesetz!*"

This hobble-tongued and futile debate continued for
some time, to the credit of neither him nor me. From a
spoilt and silly woman insisting on some imagined right he

changed to a pocket-size Demosthenes; still avoiding my eyes, and addressing the females on the wall, he delivered in his own language what I took to be a lecture on law and discipline. I, in turn, losing my temper and lapsing into my native speech, rated him for his childish and baseless obstinacy—I doubt if another master of a ship was ever so harangued by a stowaway. It is hard, now, to believe that I was capable of so wasting my breath; for at the time it appeared to me that he had invented these ludicrous regulations just to parade his authority, and against such vainglory anger is the stupidest weapon. In the end, with a look of imperial righteousness which nearly changed my rage to laughter, he turned and marched out of the cabin.

Wondering what would happen next, I went out to the port deck. And there I realized the extent of my miscalculations. Ashore, a dozen villagers with a mangy dog or two were standing in a half-circle, gazing with the curiosity of cattle at something which at first one of the boats hid from me. When I had moved a pace or two I saw the object of their interest: flanked by his family, and with a folded tarpaulin for mattress, Siegfried lay there on the quay.

Not for a moment did I suppose that this *fait accompli* could be reversed. Physically, we could have carried him between us at least back to the deck. But the sailor posted at the top of the gangway, a man with the flattened face and huge fists of a pugilist, was not of a sort which yields to force or blandishments. Nor would Tricoulos in his present mood have truckled to defiance. We should re-embark only at his pleasure.

On the face of it, we were merely being put to some indignity and inconvenience. But I think I divined even then that the incident was one of greater import than a display of beadledom; for one thing, Zhenko was patently concerned with it, and I no longer doubted that he was a person of tortuous intentions. Had the issue been a small one I might have acted more boldly. It was the sense of being in conflict with larger forces than those disposed of by a trading captain which paralysed my will for action. 'I can't believe we shall ever be settled and safe': those had been the words not of a depressed and nervy woman but of one accustomed to accept realities. We were, after all, a small body, we who were trying to bring this damaged man to liberty, and there were thousands who, knowing of our purpose, would have fought to frustrate it. I thought of Gregolnitch, and then that face of fatted sophistication gave place to more homely ones: I remembered the polemics of the Vischak bus, the tingling silence which had followed Simovitch's quiet, corrosive voice. Those recollections grew into a vision of multitudes ranged against me, murmuring that it was neither their will nor God's for this man to escape. To these I had no answer. I could not explain to them—or to myself—why I should not be on their side.

2

My immediate concern, however, was professional. For the time being the rain was holding off, but at this early hour the wind was like a legion of devils, attacking us from every quarter, icy and damp; and the fact that my patient had survived one term of severe exposure was no guarantee that he was fit for a second—particularly when he had been living for four days in an almost suffocating atmosphere. The condition of Paula was a further anxiety. A very rough sea trip is not what I should prescribe for a woman already in a state of exhaustion. When I first saw her that morning she was standing bent over with her hands on her knees, shivering and almost continuously retching. Her skin was like baker's dough, the orbits of her eyes so inflamed that she must have been almost blind. I marvelled that she could stand at all.

To get the party under cover was, then, the first necessity, and the best cover that offered was the Café of Liberation, a shed of iron and timber facing the quay with a bar for longshoremen and a table or two for summer tourists. There Franziska and I settled the invalids on the floor, wrapped in blankets which I made the steward bring me from the ship. From a pump not far away Johannes got water, which a cottage woman heated for us. With that, and a small bottle of local brandy, I did for them what I could.

This was a lengthy business—the people about were not unwilling to help us, but at that time they were unused, I suppose, to foreigners, and I found them exceedingly slow in mind. The morning was far advanced before I was free to look about me and consider what was happening to the ship.

In truth, nothing was happening. The men who had been waiting on the quay in the hope of casual employment had disappeared. Of the crew, half a dozen were with us in the café, gloomily drinking rakija, while the rest had evidently decided that nothing in Zlot could amuse them and returned to their hammocks. Neither Tricoulos nor the Mate was in sight. To one familiar as I was with the *Charilaos* there was nothing remarkable in this: her life was that of the sanctified, in but not of the world. It seemed to me curious, however, that nothing was visible ashore to give a reason for our call. I had expected a cluster of oil tanks. There was none. No drums. No cargo stacked for loading. Nor, happily, any sign of a policeman. It appeared, as the cold and cloudy day wore into afternoon, that ours was just a visit of bashful courtesy.

"Why have we stopped here?" Johannes asked, as we ate the vinegary scraps which were all the café could give us for a meal.

I passed the question to Babitch, who answered, "Why, everyone comes here. Zlot is a famous place, it's chock-a-block with Roman remains."

"You think," I said, "that our captain is a zealous archaeologist?"

"What—that little louse? I should say he's here to hire himself to licentious trippers."

Though physically shaky, Babitch was greatly revived in spirits. It was he, presently, who set off to canvas opinion, by roaring from the quay at anyone he saw aboard, on the chances of our sailing again before nightfall; and returned with the news—how acquired I do not know—that we were waiting for a consignment to arrive by road. To this report I gave the value that attaches to the gossip of wardmaids. But I was not altogether right.

There is, as far as I know, only one landward approach to Zlot. It is a road of rudimentary construction which descends tortuously through a narrow defile in the cliffs to emerge in a casual, unlikely way between two derelict cottages some sixty yards from the quay. I discovered this passage when I was taking a walk after the meal, and it looked to me as if no wheeled traffic could use it. This was a false impression. Only a few minutes after Babitch had brought us his rumour, what looked like a motorized version of the American covered wagon came lurching and bouncing down this road, swung round to the quay and stopped alongside the ship's forward hold.

The event failed to disturb the repose of Zlot or of the *Charilaos*. Watching from the café window I saw at first no sign aboard the ship even of a passing curiosity. Then one man came down the gangway and went to speak to the driver and his mate. This was Zhenko. It was the first time I had seen him that day.

I was wondering just why he alone should have business with the wagon when the scene was broken by a fresh arrival—a motor-cycle and sidecar of a German military type bearing two men in the uniform of the Yugoslav State

Police. This pair, less diffident than the crew of the wagon, went immediately aboard, and I watched a sailor leading them to Tricoulos's cabin.

Convinced that their interest was in his passengers, I was not surprised when I saw them—ten minutes later—coming over to the café with Tricoulos in attendance. In truth, I waited for them to go straight to Siegfried, name and arrest him. That did not occur. The policemen, doubtless accustomed to the random ordering of village wine-shops, gave only a passing glance at the two recumbent figures beyond the café tables. Tricoulos, shy and anxious as a young bride, showed no inclination to introduce us; and Zhenko, who arrived with the two men from the wagon a few seconds afterwards, took up a position designed—as it appeared to me—to inhibit any intercourse between us and them.

Choosing my moment, I glanced towards Franziska, and on her face I saw a look as plain as a sentence: 'They are playing with us, Zhenko and those police—they find pleasure in keeping us waiting.'

3

I cannot pretend to have enjoyed the hour that followed, when I was privileged to witness Tricoulos's social life from—as it were—a seat in the stalls.

In themselves the policemen could hardly have been less sinister. They were young, good-humoured country fellows, thinly disguised by their panoply of belts and holsters—even their intermittent swagger was too coltish to be offensive. Yet their presence was enough to keep Tricoulos's nerves—as well as mine—on edge, robbing him even of his tenuous bourgeois dignity. He brought up chairs for them, paid ceremoniously for the wine he invited them to order, repeated like a phonograph the few polite phrases in Serbo-Croat at his disposal: "Greatly honoured. . . . Most welcome. . . . Your country I find choice and captivating." To Babitch—who had never, I think, been awed by uniforms—was left the grateful task of supplementing these civilities.

"Very fine you look, you piccaninnies!" he said graciously. "In my day we should hardly have dressed a general with such splendour. . . . Let me assure you, if you've come to arrest my friend the captain here, that he's the most innocent man alive—he simply hasn't the equipment for any vice worth noticing."

"Oh, but we're only here on our regular patrol," one of the policemen said hastily. "That's right, isn't it, Marko?"

"Why, yes!" the other agreed. "We certainly have no suspicions about the captain. An excellent man, I should say, and a most capable shipmaster."

"I agree with you, gentlemen—a more endearing little nancy one would go far to find."

He bestowed a kindly smile on Tricoulos, who bowed nervously and said, "Most welcome!"

"As for his seamanship, it's faultless, except for his total ignorance of navigation."

"But surely——"

"I merely ask you, my friends—would any sailor who knew the points of the compass steer his ship into a bug-trap like this?"

"But presumably he has business here."

"Business?" With his arm round Tricoulos's shoulders, head thrown back and mouth wide open, Babitch uttered two joyous barks of ridicule. "Business—in this fowl-yard! Why, my dear sirs, the only business the little runt has now —the only business he ever has had, I should imagine—is to get those German carcases you see on the floor there over to Spain."

The policeman called Marko slightly raised his eyebrows.

"Germans?"

"Indeed, yes—exported from Trieste. And I am their caretaker—with some valued assistance from my friend over there, Dr. Rosenberg. He, as you must know, is the leading authority on dise..es of the lower bowel."

"So?"

"Yes, sir, fate plays amusing tricks on wretched mortals like myself." Babitch's other arm was now round Marko's neck, he was huge and fatherly, there were tears in his handsome, honest eyes. "All my life I have been first and foremost a patriot. Thirty-seven wounds above the navel, honourable mention in nine campaigns. And all my life I have placed the Teutonic peoples in the same class as the bubonic rat: total extermination, that is what I've always preached as the only wise and humane policy. And now, in my declining years, how does an old soldier like myself earn a few morsels of bread and pottage to keep himself alive? By conducting the ruinous carcases of German rodents across the wide and lonely seas!"

By this time the darker of the two policemen—whose face suggested the keener intelligence—was gazing fixedly in our direction. I could answer his silent inquiry only with a feeble, ambiguous smile. But Zhenko, not for the first time, came to my help. I saw him look significantly at his companions, and then he winked at Marko.

"Our friend is a little confused!" he said rapidly. "This is a Swiss gentleman and his family who are on their way to Spain. They've been upset by the rough weather. He's very well known in Zurich—it's mainly a business trip."

He added something in Greek to Tricoulos. Tricoulos nodded and smiled. "Swiss!" he confirmed. "Greatly honoured."

"The Swiss," said Babitch evenly, "have special problems to meet on account of their prodigious physical dimensions. I was once called in by a young Swiss merchant on his honeymoon at Opitaja—along the coast there. He wanted me to see his wife, he was in great distress. I found the young woman in bed, the cast-iron bedstead was buckled in the middle, she must have weighed two hundred kilograms. As a matter of scientific interest I took her measurements—quite unobtrusively, you understand, during my examination. And believe it or not, the circumference of each thigh was 98 centimetres. I made a mark on the tape, which I should like to show you, but it was shot out of my hand at the battle of Dobropolye."

"Remarkable!" said the dark policeman, winking at his companion. "A pitiful story, when you come to think of it, but full of scientific interest. You will drink again, Mr. Doctor?"

"Well, perhaps a very small glass of Bakarska Vodica."

"Petar, we ought to be getting on!" said Marko.

But the dark policeman only winked again. "A motor-cycle goes that much better," he said, "if it's given time to cool. . . . So you, sir, were one of the heroes of Dobropolye? . . ."

As far as I could judge, the pair of them had quickly lost interest in Babitch's reference to his German charges, finding in Babitch himself a more piquant subject for research; with belts and tunic loosened, their caps thrown on the bar, they began to quarry his lode of reminiscence with the radiant zeal of schoolboys sidetracking their professor from a dull period. But as curiosity is the second nature of policemen— and so is the desire for promotion—I did not trust this mood to last. To cover my agitation I was trying to play dominoes with Johannes, but he must have found me a poor opponent. I kept glancing at Tricoulos, in whose paralysed politeness I saw a dreadful cartoon of my own disquiet, and then at the trio centred in Zhenko, where, in all three faces, I read a nervous impatience verging on frenzy. There were others— not excluding the man behind the bar—who were plainly ready to see the party continued into the evening. But had the young officers been sensitive they might have realized that, with a part of the company, they had outstayed their welcome.

What was Zhenko's trouble, I wondered. Tricoulos's misgivings were easy to understand: he had accepted the Zempelmarcks as passengers—at a fantastic fare—and he may well have guessed that their papers would not bear much examination. But I could not believe that Zhenko was deeply concerned about the Zempelmarcks' welfare or mine: if the police arrested us we should get no more from him than a wave and a knowing smile. . . . Then I thought again of the wagon standing close to the ship, and this brought a likely explanation. The wagon must contain some kind of contraband ready for loading—possibly weapons, for which there would be a clandestine market in Spain. I knew Zhenko already as a person likely to supplement his pay with the profits of backstairs agency; and if a man of straw like Tricoulos was being used for such business, the organizers might well have detailed one of Zhenko's kind to see it through. With caution, I began to study Zhenko's new friends more exactly. They were possibly father and son, the son the bigger man. Both had a darkness of skin and heavy nasal structure which suggested a Turkish strain, but I should not have taken them for fighters, or for adventurers of the kind one's imagination associates with the perils and excitements of smuggling. They looked, in short, like village carriers who had come with nothing more illicit than a crate of fowls or a bag of oatmeal. But if so, why—since they seemed to be bored with the Café of Liberation—could they not transfer their load to the ship and get back to their homes?

"Excuse me—I think you have placed a 'two' against a 'three'."

The gentle correction from Johannes turned my attention for a moment to him. He was playing with patient intelligence, as if he were a kindly elder and I the child, but a certain tension of his mouth showed me that he was far from blind to the precariousness of our situation. Neither, I supposed, were the rest of our party. But Paula lay with her face buried in the blanket, probably too wretched with sickness to care what happened, while Siegfried, with his eyes fixed on the ceiling, showed no emotion except his usual faint contempt. Seated against the wall, Franziska was darning a jersey of Siegfried's, and if there was fear in her mind its physical effect was absorbed by that occupation of her hands. Perhaps there was none: the capacity to be afraid is not quite infinite. Letting my eyes rest for a moment on that calm face, the lips' repose, the depth of comprehension in her eyes, I had the feeling that a spirit like hers could not be put to fear by the men of common size surrounding us.

That is how I remember them, a pattern of quiescence beside the noise and animation of Babitch's circle, through that afternoon which seemed to drag towards eternity; and they did not stir, they betrayed no feeling at all, when, with the light starting to fail, the party at last showed signs of ending. It was the policeman Marko who made the first movement—he had drunk a good deal less than his colleague. Babitch had reached the end of a turgid ballad about the seven concubines of General Kastamonu when Marko said forlornly,

"You know, Petar, we were supposed to report back before two-thirty."

"Time," said Babitch, "is the gaoler of slaves, the servant of free men. Don't you agree, Captain?"

"Greatly honoured!" Tricoulos said apathetically.

"And by my calculations it is scarcely past midday."

Automatically, the younger of the wagon men took out his watch. He said—raising his voice for the first time—"It is nearly four oclock."

Marko swung round and stared at him. His face broke into a radiant smile. "Why, its Cermak! We met at Sijulo—remember? I was with Kocevar's boys."

The wagon-driver was taken aback. He said (no doubt truthfully), "I'm sorry—I don't remember."

"But it was you who showed us where the petrol was hidden."

"Possibly, possibly."

"Why, that was a marvellous day. I shall never forget it! What are you doing here? Do you live here?"

"No. No, I don't live here."

The man's nervousness was pitiful, and I could see that Marko was now miserably embarrassed by the result of his friendliness. It was left to Cermak's companion to say sheepishly,

"He's a driver, you see—he drives for me. I'm a carrier, in just a small way."

At this, Petar, who had been smiling bibulously at some thought of his own, turned suddenly and said, "A carrier? Then that would be your vehicle, over there?"

"Yes, sir. Yes, that's mine."

"A fine one—it looks very powerful!"

"Well, yes, you need some power with roads like ours."

"I suppose you do."

The two policemen were standing side by side now, turned towards the window. I watched them candidly, fascinated. In the boyish face of Marko I saw the underlying timidity of one born to take orders, to look on regulations as the Law of God. Petar was more complex. Flushed and slightly unsteady with wine, he still knew as well as Marko that they were guilty of dilatory conduct, but the knowledge only added—I thought—to his delight in a social occasion. Back at headquarters, he would talk his way through. Certainly his intelligence was still at work; and it was he who asked Cermak, as if only to make conversation,

"You've brought a consignment for the ship?"

Cermak hesitated. His companion said,

"Yes, yes, a few small things."

Petar looked sideways at Marko—I thought the look was mischievous. He said,

"Then I think we ought to check them over. A matter of routine."

"But they're aboard the ship now."

"Oh?" Petar turned to Tricoulos. He said in the loud, clear voice that is used for the simple minded, "I think you should have shown us what you've taken aboard here. I don't remember any mention of it on your freight manifest."

In a fresh agitation, Tricoulos said hastily,

"Greatly honoured! Most welcome!"

"These 'small things', they might very well be works of art." This was addressed, with ponderous solemnity, to the carriers. "Masterpieces. You can't send those abroad—it's against the regulations."

The carriers stood like pillars of salt. Zhenko, coming at last to their rescue, said abruptly,

"It was nothing. A few bits of timber—nails and so on. The ship's carpenter wanted them for repairs."

That was a clumsy evasion, and I saw that Petar was becoming genuinely suspicious.

"But what was it that had to be repaired?" he asked.

"I don't know—I forget. Oh, it was one of the hatches."

"And the carpenter hadn't thought of supplying himself with nails and things before the trip started?"

Zhenko shrugged his shoulders. "I suppose he miscalculated his requirements. Who can tell? These Greek boats, they're just floating madhouses."

Again Marko was looking at his watch. "Does it matter!" he said crossly. "We're very late—there'll be trouble."

There was a moment—it seemed like a whole minute—when Petar stood still, gazing into space. He may have been wondering whether the situation could yield him any further amusement; or he may have seriously reasoned that to report some piece of illegal traffic would cover, in the eyes of his superiors, a deal of laxity. At length, however, he popped his lips and smiled.

"Well then," he said to Marko, "if this is an old friend of yours, an old war-comrade, I suppose we must trust him." He put his fingers saucily under Cermak's chin. "You, my friend, if you've been loading works of art into that ship there, you must take them all out again. You understand me?"

Cermak smiled feebly. "Why, yes, Mr. Constable!" His companion took up the smile, and on the sullen impatience in Zhenko's face relief dawned. By degrees, the whole party filtered out of the café; and as the door, swinging in the wind, slammed shut behind the last of them, I in my turn let out a long breath of thankfulness.

Then, through the window, I saw one man turn back.

It was Petar. Re-entering the café, he looked about him with slightly bleary eyes, and then, wrapping his official manner about him, he came deliberately to me.

"You, Sir, you are travelling with this party?"

I answered, "Yes, but independently. This lady and this gentleman have needed some medical assistance, I happen to be a doctor, and naturally——"

"Yes yes! And you came aboard at Trieste?"

"At Trieste, yes."

"Then tell me, if you please—did you happen to see an incident of any kind just before the ship sailed? A skirmish on the quay?"

"No, nothing like that. Nothing at all."

"Oh—then I apologize for troubling you. It's just a report that came through to our headquarters, originating from the Chief of Police at Trieste. It appears that one of his men got damaged in some sort of argument—it was just as the *Charilaos* was leaving. He has circulated a general request for information."

I said, "I'm extremely sorry that I can't help you."

He smiled pleasantly. "It's of no consequence! It's merely that we have to lose no opportunity of showing our cordial feelings for that little International Utopia they've started up there." This came with a sly and confidential look—he must have taken me for a Yugoslav national. "I'm afraid the policemen of Trieste must be dishearteningly fragile. . . . I would wish your honour good-evening!"

In a minute or two I heard the motor-cycle starting, and then the diminishing uproar of the engine as it shot away into the hills.

"Have the police gone?" Johannes asked me.

"Yes. Yes, thank God, they've gone!"

4

No one else spoke: the others may have been too wise to share my sense of liberation. And we had scarcely started—Franziska and I—to attend to our invalids when Zhenko returned.

In him the departure of the police seemed to have caused a curious elation. He was both trembling and smiling, and he spoke with an unprecedented officiousness:

"It's all right—I can get you back to the ship now. We'll have to hurry!"

I said brusquely, "Hurry? Why? Whose orders are those?"

"We're sailing in ten minutes," was his curt answer.

"Then you'll have to get me bearers. Herr Kern can't walk, you know."

He said, "I've got them already."

They had, in fact, been following him—not any of the sailors but the two men from the wagon and three or four others whom I took to be villagers impressed for this service. They had with them a rustic litter. On this, with no more ceremony than they would have used in handling sacks of corn, they deposited Siegfried and carried him outside.

The speed of their action gave me no chance to interfere. Fussed and impotent, I called angrily after Zhenko, who was following the bearers, "That thing will have to come back as soon as it's free—Fräulein Kern isn't fit to walk either."

But he took no notice. And I was wrong about Paula—she was already on her feet, supported by Franziska and by one of the men who had stayed behind. I should have stepped in then to take Franziska's part of the burden, but Johannes stood in my way, begging attention.

"The man," he said, "—he wants to speak to you."

'The man' was the decrepit owner of the café, who stood holding the lamp he had just lit and gazing at my face with an expression of timid avarice which brought to my mind old pictures of dealers in stolen bodies. He had made a mistake, he told me, over his charge for the brandy—there were 30 Dinars still to pay. I told him I had no money, but should borrow from my friends; at which he started a wordy explanation: it was a special brandy he had given us, at the time he had forgotten the exact price, since then he had looked it up on the merchant's list. I repeated (truthfully) that I could not pay until I had been back to the ship, but it seemed impossible to make him understand this—he himself spoke mostly in a dialect which was out of my reach. I forget how this business ended: perhaps I satisfied him with some trinket which happened to be in my pocket. I know that his importunity kept me back for three or four minutes.

When I got outside the quay appeared to be deserted. The rain which had threatened all day had begun now, in glassy curtains billowing in from the sea, hastening the fall of darkness. The hills which had leant upon the harbour were no longer visible, and the *Charilaos* looked like a dimly painted backcloth to a desolate, dismantled stage. I had no thought, just then, of taking a line of my own. In fear and sudden loneliness I ran towards the gangway.

But the gangway had already been hauled in.

The wagon was still there. From a group standing beside it, which I had not noticed as I ran, a man detached himself and came to me. I tried to ignore him, but he put a hand on my arm.

"Excuse me!"

It was Cermak.

"I'm sorry," I said tersely, "I've got to get aboard."

He gave me a sheepish smile, still holding my arm. "But your friends," he said, "aren't in the ship. They're in the wagon here."

"In the wagon? Why?"

"They have to go a little way inland. There are questions to be asked them. And we should like you, if you please, to come as well."

"What do you mean? The police want to question me?"

He smiled again. "No, not the police. The police have gone."

In a casual way—as if their movements had been perfectly rehearsed—several more men from the group had moved to form an arc behind me. One of them came close.

I said to Cermak, "If it's not a police matter I'm afraid I can't oblige you. I'm a free man——"

"No," the man behind me said, in a voice I recognized but could not place at the moment, "you're not free now— you're to do as you're told."

Feeling something pressed into my back, I thought, 'This is a practical joke—it is a thing that happens to other people, not to me.' But as I glanced right and left at the men moving in towards me, the quiet faces stony with resolution, I realized that this was reality and that no one was joking. In a voice—as I remember—strangely unaffected by the icy current between my throat and bowels, I said,

"I see!"

234

Within seconds of my tumbling over the tail-board the wagon was moving. In the near-darkness I was thrown this way and that by the violent lurching—against a man with a rifle, a body lying on the floor. I have kept, from that minute of incredulity and vortical confusion, only one distinct memory: the whispered, painful voice of Paula in a remark of which I should have thought her incapable: "You and I, Dr. Reichenbach, we make curious journeys together!"

Chapter 10

I

A PATCH OF light on the flagged roadway, stairboards deeply worn, the sound of a key turning rustily behind me: these are all I have kept of my arrival in the schoolmaster's home. I think I slept on the floor that night. I remember no discomfort, only a great thankfulness that the jolting had mysteriously ceased to be painful.

Waking in the early morning I saw a slit of paleness, formed like a half-closed eye, in the dark above my head; through this aperture, when I stood up to ease the stiffness of my hip and shoulder, there appeared a shape resembling an upturned breast, flattened at one side, which filled a great part of the milky sky. It changed as I watched it from grey to a fallow brown, grew solid and alive—a fractured cupola of limestone aproned with snow; and as, in the earliest sunlight, the snow was suffused with rose and gold, the rock itself turned golden, a thing theatrically brave and lustrous against a sky of melting green. As yet knowing nothing of this crest, or of the valley that lay beyond it, I surrendered innocently to its beauty. In the depth of humiliation there is a kind of freedom: you are brought to a passive state where you receive with simple gratitude every comfort of the senses. Heavy with ruptured sleep, alone and hopeless I found my spirit warmed by the sense of calm and permanence I saw in that strange configuration.

Against it the nearer spectacle, a vorticist design of eaves and chimneys, was at first meaningless. There was a square window which came alight at the level of my eyes, and I realized by degrees that it stood only just above the level of of the roadway; while, when I turned in the other direction, I saw the tops of houses some distance below. But this oddity of levels hardly pricked my intelligence—I had been removed too far from the channel of my life to look for normality in the things about me. As the light hardened I watched the scene taking shape in the way that primitive people look at pictures of great cities, with only a formless and fleeting curiosity.

I have learnt since that the place was in Roman times a military post, later a halt for travellers, then a home for workers in the Usitza quarries. The gorge through which the Sotta plunges on the first stage of its devious passage to the sea is mostly so narrow that there is barely room for the road beside the stream. Here, for a little way, it widens, and men have seized the chance of a rough domestication, finding room even for a mosque to crouch with its sallow dome nudging into the rock face. It wears, this pendant arabesque of human dwellings, the look of fixed dilapidation which blurs appreciation of period; so that my first impression, in that early morning, was of being reborn in a previous century. Even when my mind began to warm I saw with a vague sense of anomaly the random accretions of the age I had lived in—a rusty gasoline pump, a stave of electric cables. Above me, where the steep road turned, a faded poster was starting to peel from what might have been a Roman wall, and I remember staring at this with a childlike incredulity; the same advertisement for a motion picture had faced my window in New Haven just a year before.

A peep-show village, shabby from over-use: at bedtime the sides might be folded down, the thing put away in a nursery drawer. But soon a freshening wind brought me the smell of frying, there were lean, insolent cats scavenging a heap of rubbish in the road, somewhere the keening of a child. An old, stooping woman limped up the road and crossed an iron bridge to fill her bucket from a pipe which came out of the rock. From a house lower down a man emerged with a sack round his shoulders and gathered carefully a heap of droppings—he too was very old, and undersized. This, I thought, was a place of small people, bred to the extreme of poverty, with whom—if I had opportunity—I could live in peace.

But why was I here? Why a prisoner? In the darkness of the wagon there had been no show of force or even hostility. The men escorting us, talking laconically among themselves, had passed us bread and cigarettes; one at least had helped me in getting Siegfried better placed to escape fresh injury. So, for my part, I had not been much in fear of them. But my mind had hardly been at work: through most of those hours, enduring the vicious dance of the floorboards with no moral comfort to sustain me, I had yielded to a partial coma, conscious only of Franziska's nearness, of her whisper, "It will soon be over!" letting her courage work for mine. When the wagon stopped, when someone said, "We off-load the doctor here—the German doctor," I had done as I was told, bemused and docile as a beast brought to market. And still—standing at the roadside with my wrists held from behind, watching the rear light of the wagon as it moved on down the hill—I had failed to grasp the fact of danger or captivity: all I had thought of then was, 'She has gone, the purpose of existence is lost, there is nothing left'.

Was this, then, another life, to be traversed on a lower plane? Did I now belong to the complex pattern slowly taking shape beneath me—the fresh smoke rising, grey and crumpled women coming to their doors as a tiny donkey dragged a wheeled churn up the hill, the clanging from somewhere far down the ravine of a school-house bell?

Pravnitzar: the name—I cannot remember when I first learnt it—sounds in my ears now with no reverberation of anger. Its people, born in this cleft in the hills, inured from childhood to its cutting winds, could never move a mile from their homes without such climbing as tourists would boast about. To them the poorest meat and wine were luxuries: they looked for nothing but the means to make a daily meal, for a pannikin of goat's or sheep's milk, a townsman's cast-off coat, a little kerosene; for the warmth of each other's scrawny bodies, for liberty to breed, to scold and fondle those of their children who survived the battle of their first few weeks' existence. In their curious voices—the women's strident to my ears, the men's often barely comprehensible—they spoke of 'down the valley' as of a foreign land, and some of them I think had never been there. For in mind they were islanders, who wanted to be left to themselves. Where there is hatred in such people it belongs, I think, only to that instinct which teaches animals to fight for their young. I, at least, when the name of Pravnitzar returns and returns to me, think of them as I saw them first of all, when the light reflected from the White Lamb rock gave to the woven smoke and squalid houses a mysterious gentleness, and when they and I were strangers. I see the men going off in their sheepskin jackets and suberis, still loaded—as they looked to me—with the last day's fatigue; the morbidly thin legs and frozen faces of the children trooping down the hill; a dwarfish, man-faced woman who runs barefoot after one of them, hands clasped in front to steady her giant pregnancy, calling that he must not come home without an armful of wood.

2

Early, the sun became obscured by cloud. Clasping about my shoulders the single blanket I had been given, I walked monotonously up and down the centre of the attic room—the only part where I could stand unbent—listening abstractedly to the voices and the kitchen sounds downstairs. The flat, cold day must have come to noon before there were steps outside the door.

Some fuss ensued, with whispers and nervous giggling, before the key was turned. Then the door was opened with extreme caution and a face, stiff with vigilance, came round it.

A dismally plain face, callipered with wire-rimmed spectacles; it was that of a girl in her early twenties, who would have been nearly as tall as I but that her head with its long stalk drooped heavily towards her flat and narrow chest. Blinking anxiously, she advanced a pace or two inside the room and looked about for something on which to rest the plate she was carrying. But the only furniture was a mangle in one corner, and to reach it she would have had to pass me. This was plainly too much for her courage. To help her, I held out my hand for the plate. She drew back as if a tiger had suddenly bared its teeth, put the plate on the floor and turned to go.

I said, "Good morning—and thank you."

She did not answer. But part of another face had appeared at the door, and the voice of a child said hoarsely, "Bad man!"

"I should like you," I said to the girl, "to tell me, if you please, where I am."

She paused in her retreat and turned as if to answer, but apparently changed her mind. I persisted:

"And I wonder if by chance you've got a small oil-stove—something like that. I don't mean to grumble, but it's really hardly bearable, the cold up here."

From a little way down the stairs a woman's voice called sharply, "Sava, you're not to gossip, you're to come straight down!"

The little boy had now come boldly into the room, and from a tactical position behind his sister's skirt was staring at me with a rather self-conscious pugnacity. Inevitably I stooped and stretched a hand towards him, asking, "What's the matter, old friend—do I look like a gorilla?" But this alarmed him and his face crumpled. The girl Sava, recovering in an instant her self-command, picked him up, backed out of the room and fled down the stairs, slamming the door as she passed it.

This troubled me—I had not before been seen as a monster by children. But before I had finished the few spoonfuls of soup the girl had brought me my mood of apathy returned; and this might have lasted till nightfall if it had not been disturbed by the sound of fresh whispering and agitation from the foot of the stairs. I guessed what had happened—Sava had forgotten to lock the door. Presently I heard her creeping up again, then the noise of the stiff key being laboriously turned, followed—in my imagination if not in reality—by a sharp sigh of relief.

A breeze of curiosity now took me to the door, to see what kind of lock it was that worked with such obstreperous complaint; and so I discovered that its tongue was engaged by nothing but a slat of wood which, held by rusty screws to the wormeaten jamb, came away at the first sharp pull of my fingers. The door, hung to open inwards, swung gently towards me.

The temptation then was to march downstairs and make a vigorous complaint about the cold—at the time my ambition went no further. But I realized that my sudden appearance would probably scare the people of the house (who did not seem to have a man among them) and to risk alarming the nervy, ill-favoured creature who had brought me food was unthinkable. On a puerile impulse I did put the key in my pocket. Then I shut the door again and replaced the slat, pushing the screws loosely into their rotted holes.

It was nearly dark when I was visited again. This time the tread on the stairs was masculine, and it was a man's voice which shouted, "Mica! What have you done with the key?"

A woman answered, "Sava has it!" and then came Sava's voice: "It's in the door."

"It isn't!" the man answered.

It was time for me to assist. "If you push the door," I called, "you'll find it comes open."

It was—when he had done so—a frightened, courageous and angry man who confronted me. He was holding a candle, and no doubt its light served in some degree to caricature his features, for at that first encounter his square, grizzled head appeared to me one of simian ugliness: the face, with small eyes set too far apart by the prodigious, flattened nose, seemed all to be tightly squashed between a shallow forehead and a vast scroll of underlip, his skin was unhealthily mottled, his short neck scraggy and furred. I thought for a moment that he was going to attack me—his free hand was drawn back as if to strike an upward blow— and that might have been painful, since his lack of height was compensated by broad and powerful shoulders. But in fact he kept quite still while he said ferociously,

"You've stolen the key!"

I shook my head. "No, I've merely taken charge of it for safety." And with a little bow I handed it over.

"You had no business to take it!" he barked.

"And have you," I inquired, "any business to be keeping me locked up?"

For a moment at least this question seemed to embarrass him; and as there was nothing to be gained from a quarrel about legalities I continued:

"At any rate, if you mean to keep me here you'll have to get this door repaired."

"I can see that for myself!" he retorted.

"The first thing," I said, "will be to cut away a large portion of this jamb and replace it with fresh timber. Then you'll need a different kind of lock. This sort——"

"I am not interested in carpentry," he said acidly. "I happen to be an educated man."

"And I was educated in Vienna, where things like locks and keys have always been studied seriously. *Si parva licet componere magnis——*"

"Will you please not quote Vergil at me!"

"I thought it was Ovid."

"What nonsense! Ovid never wrote such a line in his life—that much I can prove to you."

I said, "It doesn't matter——"

"But most certainly it matters!"

Already he was off down the stairs, as if I had accused him of destroying some document of legal importance. From below he shouted back to me,

"You are not to leave the room! There are men with rifles everywhere, I warn you!"

Soon he was back with a tattered, schoolroom copy of the *Georgics*. I held the candle while he thumbed the pages, and it took him only a few seconds to bring his black fingernail on to the words I had used. I said,

"Yes, of course you're perfectly right—I apologize."

"In my bedroom," he said warmly, pursuing his victory, "I have all the works of Ovid. In a Beograd edition, I admit —no doubt you get greater accuracy in Viennese editions! However, I can bring them to you if you wish. If you can find anywhere a line of similar sense I shall be more than interested."

"No no—it was just a foolish blunder on my part."

"You don't want to satisfy yourself on the question?"

"I might," I replied, "if I were not perishing with cold."

He considered this. "My daughter told me," he said gruffly, "that you had asked for an oil-stove."

"Yes, I took that liberty."

"This is not the sort of house in which such things are kept. There's only one stove in this house. In Vienna I expect they have portable stoves to go in all the rooms. This isn't a hotel, you know."

"No, I suppose it isn't."

"I've had no instructions about providing you with a stove."

"Well, that I can't answer, because I don't know who has given you any instructions about me. Perhaps you will tell me why I've been brought here, and who is responsible for having me shut up in an ice-house."

"I am not here to answer questions."

"In that case——"

"Any information you're entitled to will come from Valyevitch when he arrives."

"Oh—so it's Valyevitch who had me brought here! I should like to know why."

"I am not here," he repeated angrily, "to be cross-examined."

Slowly as my mind was working, I had realized by now that the man's churlish and infantile behaviour was no reflection of his personality: as far as my experience goes, the Croat is not often a boor, and the lover of Vergil rarely a cantankerous fool. His obstinate ill-temper was only a cover, I thought, for his moral discomfort; and for the time it seemed better to endure the cold than to prolong an exhibition of shadow boxing which was distasteful to us both.

"That being so," I said pacifically, "I mustn't waste any more of your time."

And I held the door for his departure.

For a moment or two he stared at me as if I were a beast of some unknown species. Then he tramped off down the stairs, leaving me to shut the door behind him.

3

With nothing better to do, I stood where I was, listening. The sound that came like smoke curling up the stairs was one which has the same cadence in every language I know: a woman's voice (Mica's, I supposed) cutting through every hindrance with its edge and speed, the man's weighty and obdurate, falling at intervals like the bark of an old and sleepy dog. Occasionally I caught the softer tones of Sava, but they were always overridden by her mother, and the only words which reached me distinctly came from the older woman: "It's my kitchen, I say! And Karel was my child!" This had gone on for twenty minutes or so when my gaoler returned.

Again he searched me with a student's inquiring eyes, and then, as if to open a long address, he said, "My name is Dushan Fotez."

I responded, bowing, "I am Reichenbach—Eugen Reichenbach."

"I know!" he said; and drew fresh breath. "The question I have to ask you is this: for how long have you known Zempelmarck?"

"He has been my patient since last October."

"Oh. And you never met him before then?"

"No. For several years past I've lived in America."

"But it was you who made arrangements for him to escape from Slovenia?"

"I had a share in that."

"So you are a close friend?"

"No, not even a friend. Merely his doctor."

He seemed to review this answer as if I were an examination candidate who possibly deserved a mark or two for neatness.

"Very well!" he said at length. "We shall allow you to spend a short time in the kitchen, until you are warm—though it is quite outside my instructions."

At once, as though afraid of changing his mind, he started to lead me down the stairs. But before we reached the bottom he turned and spoke again, lowering his voice:

"My wife has made one condition—there is to be no conversation. She doesn't wish to speak with you. Do you understand?"

I said that I did.

At other times the stipulation would not have been onerous—often I need silence as others need mountain air. But in that day of solitude I had become convinced that Franziska was lost to me for always, and the double sense of exile and bereavement made me ravenous for any sort of human intercourse. It was hard, then, to sit down without a word in the chair beside his own to which Dushan motioned me, to make no audible response to Sava's glance of solicitude, bear silently the icy look that Mica gave me as she stood at the other end of the table, an egret in spectacles, fashioning the next day's meal; more painful still to feel myself a gross encumbrance, spoiling the communion of a family at evening. They spoke to each other, but only on domestic business—"Sava, see if Riko is asleep." "It needs a new wick . . . These children write so messily . . . I'll see to it tomorrow." These small flares of speech went out like paper matchsticks—I felt as if I were in a house where someone had died in the last few hours. And in the gulfs of unnatural silence that followed them my hosts returned to the condition of clockwork figures: the long, hooped body of Sava almost motionless on a chair by the stove, only her fingers moving as she turned the pages of a text-book she was pretending to read; her mother never looking up while her deft, angry hands chopped and pounded; the screwed face of Dushan rhythmically nodding as he took each exercise book from the stack on his right, fixed the open page for a minute or two in painful concentration and then turned the book over to a pile on the other side.

"Can I help at all?" I once asked him softly.

But it was Mica who answered, like an attorney pouncing, "We don't want any talk!"

So for a time I kept to the bargain. But no ordinary

mortal can stay idle when others are working. In the middle of the table, nestling among baking tins and bowls of stock, was another pile of books. I pulled it unobtrusively towards me, opened the top one and found a set of exercises in long division awaiting correction. From the pencils at Dushan's elbow I picked a reasonably sharp one. With this I began putting ticks against correct answers and writing out the sums afresh where the pupil had blundered. Mica, of course, saw what I was doing, but said nothing. Dushan was so much engrossed in his own corrections that I was half-way through the pile before he realized what was going on.

"Don't mark them!" was all he said then. "Leave that to me—you don't know the system."

A little later, reaching the end of his own work, he took the books I had done and began to go through them himself, nodding judicially at my corrections.

"I shall make them copy out the solutions you've given," he said rather officiously. "It only spoils children if too much is done for them. As a rule," he added, "I have a young woman who looks after all that—she's ill at present. To me it's unbearable, all this figure work. It has no meaning, it's not a part of life at all."

Not stopping to think, I threw him an answer: "But a good deal of life depends on it! The Cathedral of Agram could not have been raised without a knowledge of arithmetic."

"Oh, but that is beautiful," Sava broke in, "the Cathedral of Agram! They took us there once, the Sisters."

"And you know Agram?" Dushan asked me.

"Only from one visit, in my boyhood. But I remember its charm very well. My mother and I stayed——"

"Yes," said Mica, "I suppose there were always a great many German people in Agram. No doubt they had business there! No doubt they thought it would be an advantage to know the place very well!"

The vitriol in her voice was effective: we did not talk

again. I had not even the courage to deal with any more books—nor, I think, would Dushan have let me. He went on marking the exercises I had corrected, slowly and laboriously, as a man travelling in hard and dangerous country. Ostensibly, Sava returned to her reading. While I, wondering if the cold and solitude above were not more bearable than this burlesque of hospitality, sat like an image with my hands folded on the table, staring at a jungle of saucepans and fire-irons, and thought of another kitchen, and groped as if through banks of mist for one clear image of Franziska's face, a look of tender confidence she had given me on the deck of the *Charilaos*, one echo of her voice.

An hour had passed—or it may not have been so long— when Mica, after scrubbing out her stone sink, hung up her apron and turned to go upstairs. It was then, as I automatically stood up, that I first noticed a portrait, copiously garnished with crape, which hung near the door. It was a photograph, hand-coloured—a vile production. But the head it showed, of a boy in his teens, had a simple beauty which broke through the embellishment—even from where I stood I could see that the sitter was a handsome and engaging creature. In a swift upward glance Mica caught the direction of my eyes—hers missed almost nothing. And she said impulsively,

"Yes, that is Karel. He was my son."

That kind of observation is never easily answered; and I had the impression that she defied me to make any comment. It was a very small woman, compact of nerve and sinew, who was facing me with brilliant eyes and a mouth like polished stone. I began feebly,

"He's a fine looking fellow——"

But she stopped me as with the crack of a whip.

"He has gone!" she said. "He went with the others. On March the Ninth."

With that she left the room, but in a few moments she returned. Keeping her eyes away, she said to her husband,

248

"If the friend of Zempelmarck needs more covering, there's a blanket Karel used to have—it's on the shelf where the kindling is. I don't wish to have him dying of cold, not while he's still in this house."

My face, when she had left us for the second time, must have shown something of my feelings: I saw their counterpart in the face of Sava, pitiful in its embarrassment. Dushan, who had scarcely looked up, was pretending to be still at work, but in his expression too, I read distress. Twice, with apparent negligence, he let his hand slide along the table towards mine, and the third time he allowed it to rest for a moment on my sleeve.

"Sava," he said at last, "will you please go and find this blanket your mother speaks of." And when we two were alone he said, looking at his hands, "For myself, I make no judgements. Never, until all the facts are plain. It is for Valyevitch to get things in order. We shall see him, I suppose, before very long."

5

Thus he gave me the point ahead which seems to be necessary to the human being—we live by saying, 'In three weeks it will be my birthday . . . The rain must come at last . . . One day that man or woman will speak to me.' It was little enough: what good could I expect from such a man as Valyevitch! But it seemed to set some term to an existence which only the mindless could have borne indefinitely.

Meanwhile, since I had no option, I filled the dragging days with whatever came to hand. Having given Dushan my parole—with no misgivings, since escape would only have taken me farther from Franziska—I was free to move as I wished within the house; and as only the kitchen was warm enough for habitation I steeled myself to spend most of my time there, ignoring Mica's attitude, which was that of one to whom an ugly dog has been entrusted. By degrees I discovered chores—attending to the stove, cleaning utensils—which I could do without getting in her way. Admiring her as I did—for she was supremely quick and able, a merciless employer of her own mind and body—I respected her feelings. She must have hated my usefulness as much as my presence. But as Sava was out all day attending a technical school in the valley she had much on her hands, and she found it easier, for example, to do her marketing when she could leave Riko in my charge.

"You are not to touch him," she said on the first occasion, "or to speak to him. You are simply to see that he doesn't get out of the house or do himself any harm."

This was nonsense, as she must have known, but it kept our relationship in copy-book order. In practice, Riko and I soon reached an understanding—he was intelligent and easy to amuse. We played together, I cleaned him up when he got in a mess and even gave some elementary treatment to a sore on his thigh. But I was careful, when I heard Mica's hand on the latch of the street door, to occupy myself some other way and so maintain the pretence of heeding her directions. It remains a source of regret to me that we spent so many hours in such unnatural use of each other's company. In another frame I believe we should have come to friendship, she and I.

Friendship I needed. For in that strange, twilight existence I was not merely lonely. Increasingly I was frightened.

'The Ninth of March': I did not know what that meant, but I realized soon that for Pravnitzar the date had a special meaning. Once at least in every day I heard it spoken, in the way that people of one region will talk of 'The Plague Year', 'The Year of the Drought'.

"She will be nineteen in August, my Sonja," a friend of Mica's said, a woman from the bakery. "And Jovan also— he was her twin, you know—if it hadn't been for the Ninth of March."

That was spoken in a hurried undertone, as if for Mica's ear alone. But I saw the woman—a Dantesque figure in the frame of the street door—stealing a glance at me over Mica's shoulder, and the set of her face was one to which I grew direfully accustomed in the days that followed.

They came with various excuses, Mica's friends. She may have invited some of them. A few I still remember individually: an old man of such humility that he carefully wiped his boots with a piece of paper, which he then returned to his pocket, before venturing inside; a young mother with two babies—the three of them so feebly clothed that I wondered at their survival—whose sad, Levantine features Leonardo would have made immortal; the tiny, crumpled face, peering from a filthy head-shawl, of a woman called Julija who had no voice except a little whistling breeze that leaked through her furiously grimacing lips. The rest I recall only in the way that captive animals must see the people passing their cages, a procession of eyes and noses blurring into one alien and hostile face. During these visits I took my station in a corner of the room where a linen press partially screened me and where I could busy myself with filling and trimming the lamps; while Mica, as if she were used to the presence of a servant, behaved as if I were not there. Her guests could not ignore me. Shy and taciturn as children, they were for ever peeping nervously in my direction. And in those furtively appraising eyes I saw besides the corrosive resentment a look of wonder that 'the friend of Zempelmarck' could appear so commonplace a mortal. I came to realize then what kind of torture the pillory had been; so that often I could scarcely stop myself from breaking through the barrier—from facing these people boldly and begging their sympathy. 'Look at me closely—don't you see that I am like yourselves! It's only by chance that you find me connected with that man. Whatever he did I had no part in it—I am not, I have never been, a man of violence. It was only my business as a doctor, only a feeling for his family, that made me an accomplice of his flight. Judge me as you like, but at least recognize me as a being with thoughts and feelings like your own!' But they could not have understood so feeble and confused an apologia—they would hardly have listened to a foreigner's voice. These were people of great simplicity, who knew of politics and power only from the sufferer's end. Not one of them was clothed or shod as the winter of Pravnitzar demanded, not one looked forward to a meal which would not leave her hungry: through the ground-mist of poverty they watched the overhanging world where such as I belonged with incomprehension and immutable distrust. Something had happened on that Ninth of March to screw the pressure on their lives a turn beyond their bearing. And as, at night, I saw their image standing above me in the darkness, the shapeless boots and scanty shawls, the abused, arthritic hands, mourning eyes which returned to stare at me from pitifully shrunken faces, I knew that I could not stand against them: for these marched with suffering as their ensign, theirs was the inheritance of the meek and of the poor in spirit.

6

Yes, I think of Dushan as of one who saved my reason. In the evenings, when his wife had gone to bed, he would fall into talk with me—remembering as a rule to keep his voice low lest Mica should detect this treasonable correspondence; and in those hours I felt as if restored to my status as a human being.

He proved to be a zealous Catholic of a strongly Thomist complexion: his father, a small dealer in horses, had contrived to give him a few terms at the University of Agram, and I fancy he had drunk deeply from the Aristotelian stream before discovering that the Faith also could be a subject for intelligence. In the way of pedagogues he cultivated a private heresy (perhaps derived from some medieval scholiast). It concerned the nature of Atonement, and I never entirely grasped it; for his habit in disputation was to hold my face in a mesmeric stare as if I were a pupil whose tiny seam of intelligence could only be reached by laborious excavation—sometimes in his fervour he even seized me by the collar—and under this treatment I found it simpler to agree with than to understand him. Yet I experienced a contentment in those interludes; partly because men are most to be enjoyed at their highest mental temperature, but still more because the transcendental country into which he led me seemed closer to reality than the barren tract which circumscribed my senses.

"Wagner!" he would cry, stretching his hideous mouth, forgetting all discretion and letting his huckster's voice rise to a squeal, "Don't talk to me about Wagner! Who was Wagner? What great truth did he teach? What right have you to mention that mountebank in the same breath as Bach! Do you suppose that if Wagner had lived a thousand years he could have written the *Ich hab' in Gottes Herz und Sinn*?"

"I wasn't arguing about the theological importance of either. I merely said——"

"Then what else is there to argue about? What is the use of any artist who doesn't employ his talent to bring us divine truths!"

And on the back of such peculiar doctrine he would gallop away to other fields of his, to Propertius's lamentable misuse of his genius, to Roman horticulture and the light it shed for him on the Fall of Man; his voice as it gathered speed reverting more and more to the roughness and the curious cadences of peasant speech, his little eyes gleaming, his cancroid body sprung like an athlete's on the starting line. Then, suddenly exhausted, he would descend to a fresh humility.

"Forgive me!" he would say. "You are a man of the

world, you've travelled, you've lived in great cities. I am nothing but a kitchen philosopher."

On which I had to labour to restore his confidence, telling him (with sincerity) that to talk with him was all delight and illumination.

I loved the man then: who could have resisted one who journeyed so far and curiously with such unfeigned modesty! And when, with a childlike gesture, he held my hands, and quoted Horace in his own defence, I felt that no difference of opinion could ever estrange us.

So, it was like tearing a bandage from one's own wound to say—as the strain of torturing uncertainties forced me—at the end of one of those conversations,

"Mr. Fotez, I wish you'd tell me: how long am I to be kept here? What is going to happen?"

At once his other kind of shyness closed on him like a coat of mail. He took his eyes away from mine, he pushed back his chair and stood up, as if he feared some moral infection from the table on which I was leaning.

"That is not my business, Dr. Reichenbach!"

"I'm afraid I must contradict you," I said gravely. "You are keeping me a prisoner. No man has the right to do that to another unless he can show that at least the law is behind him."

As this left him silent and brooding, I pressed my advance:

"Let's leave that for a moment. I want to know about Zempelmarck's family. I'm not concerned about Zempelmarck himself—he was only my patient, I've probably done all that I can as his surgeon. But his family are in quite a different position. His sister was very ill when I last saw her. I want to know if she's being cared for. And his wife—where is she now? Is she somewhere in this village?"

"You will get all that from Valyevitch."

"Yes, you've told me that before! But Valyevitch is a long

time coming. You, Dushan Fotez, you can't for ever use the name of Valyevitch to release you from every moral obligation."

This charge touched a point of sensitivity. With a look towards the portrait of his dead son—a look he meant me to see—he said sharply,

"Morality? How can we think of morality, here in Pravnitzar! You—your people—they threw morality to the dogs, they showed us that power is the only morality that counts."

"My people? You mean Zempelmarck?"

"Him, and what he represents."

"So you think you can go on indefinitely with that excuse—saying that morality's been overthrown and so you've no more obligations? Is that what you call philosophy?"

He did not return this blow with another. He said with conviction, with infinite sadness,

"There will be nothing right in Pravnitzar—no goodness, not even a common decency—until the past has been exorcized. That may sound foolish to you. You don't know this place, you don't know the people. I've lived with them all my life, I'm one of them. I was here that Ninth of March. I'm sorry you should be involved in this. But that is how things go, you can't hold up the course of things because of one person you respect. What God thinks I do not know. I only know that I—I myself—shall have no peace in heart until that Ninth of March is paid for—paid for in full."

No, I did not know his people. But I knew my own—those who in '38 had been afraid to walk in the Vienna streets, who had sometimes cried on hearing a tap at the front door. Already, then, I partly understood his mind. There was nothing more to be said that was worth my breath.

It happened that next morning I was again in charge of Riko, while his mother was at Mass. He was fretful that day, with a cold coming on; I could comfort him only by lying on my back on the floor and setting him astride my belly, where he pulled at my ears alternately, shouting, "To the right! To the left!"—it is an occupation which keeps some children content for a long time.

After some ten minutes of the sport he abruptly fell asleep, with his drizzling nose on my chest. We were both at peace then, and when someone arrived at the street door, calling, "Can I come in?" I answered shortly, "Mica Fotez is out."

The visitor, however, walked in as a priest or landlord would, and stood looking down at Riko and me: it was a man in a coat more stylish than anything commonly worn in Pravnitzar, whom in a moment or two I recognized as Valyevitch. His mouth lay in a callow smile, as of one pleased with some performance of his own.

"Well, Doctor!" he said.

Although in a particular sense I had longed to see this man, I felt irritable now. He appeared much sleeker than when we had first met, and it angered me to think that all I had been through in the last few days could be put to the account of one with the looks and airs of a minor bureaucrat.

"I must ask you to talk quietly," I said with acerbity. "This child is poorly, I want him to stay asleep as long as he can."

"As you like!" He sat down in the chair which Sava generally used, and slackened the laces of his boots. "I shan't stay very long, anyway—I've got a lot to see to elsewhere."

"But long enough, I hope, to explain things."

"You mean——?"

"From what Fotez tells me," I said, "you're the person responsible for my being here. When I talk about an 'outrage' I'm using words very mildly. You may or may not know——"

"Listen!" he said, with weariness rather than impatience. "There's really nothing to gain by arguing over words and legalities. To begin with, you know perfectly well that you were acting without any regard for anyone's laws when you smuggled Zempelmarck out of Slovenia."

"That didn't seem to disturb you when you kindly came to my help in Trieste!"

"Why, naturally it didn't—I'm no more concerned with law than you are. Let me say that I'm grateful to you, in a way, for making things easy for us—you and that Italian chatterbox." He leant over to offer me a cigarette. "There was always the risk—from the time Zempelmarck got away at Hochfilzen—that he'd fall into police hands again. When we got wind he was somewhere near Ljubljana——"

"You mean, you thought you could deal with the matter better than all the police in Europe?"

"Why, of course!" he answered soberly. "You know what the police would have done, if they'd caught him? They'd have turned him over—after a lot of delays and bickering—to another lot of police. And then after a lot more bickering he'd have been transferred to the international set-up, the Americans and all those. Then they'd have had a showy trial lasting for months, with highly paid lawyers to say that Zempelmarck was acting according to his ideas of military duty and wasn't really responsible at all. In the end, as likely as not, they'd have said, 'Well, give the bastard ten years and let it go at that!' Do you think people here would have been satisfied? D'you think they'd have said, 'Now our husbands and our children can rest in peace!'?"

Riko had wakened and started crying. Glad to get up, I should have settled him on a chair, but Valyevitch casually took him from me, dumped him on his own knees and gave him a closed pocket-knife to play with.

"This man Babitch," he said abruptly, "I want you to tell me about him. His military record we know already—I suppose it's common property from Bitolj to Maribor. But is he any use as a doctor?"

"Why do you want to know?"

"I think you'd do best to answer my questions!"

"Babitch," I told him, "is the remains of a very able surgeon. Even now he's capable of quite good work if someone drives him—so long as he has his own brand of cigarettes."

"That's rather what I thought. We've got the cigarette situation in hand. The next thing——"

"I shoot you!" said Riko suddenly, pointing the knife at Valyevitch's face. "Bang-bang—you're dead!"

"All right, I'm dead," Valyevitch answered absently —palpably he had children of his own. "Now listen, Doctor——"

But the interruption had given me a moment or two to speculate. I said,

"One minute! What you're really asking me is whether Babitch is fit to look after Zempelmarck—I mean, as long as you want him looked after. Is that right?"

"Just so."

"Well then, if you're trying to use my professional knowledge you'd do better to put your questions in more precise terms. Zempelmarck has a bullet inside him—I don't suppose you knew that? It means that a lung abscess *might* develop at any time. If that happened, Babitch would be quite incapable of dealing with it."

He nodded, hardly looking at me. He was a tired man, and not easy to impress, since obviously he was not regarding me as a person at all. I persisted, however:

"Also, I doubt if he'd be the smallest use in dealing with Zempelmarck's sister—he's very far from being what I should call a woman's doctor. When I last saw her she was a very sick woman."

"Yes, I expect so—yes, she is now. But we're not so much interested in her."

"But you're holding her?"

"Do you think it would be safe not to?"

"And that applies to the rest of his family?"

"Naturally."

"Then you're responsible for their proper treatment."

He did not at once reply. Kneeling, he had set Riko on the floor and was engaged in a mock wrestling bout, exerting an unconscious skill and gentleness at which I wondered. When he had got the boy quiet he said,

"Dr. Reichenbach, I don't like to call you a stupid man—I believe you're very clever in your own sphere. But you seem to me remarkably slow in grasping some things. You don't seem to have realized that a person who helps a criminal to escape is himself guilty. That woman——"

"I do as a matter of fact know a little about law," I retorted. "It was you who told me five minutes ago that the law doesn't interest you."

"It doesn't. I'm interested in what I call justice, and that's something quite different. What I'm telling you is that Zempelmarck's sister was helping him escape, and that comes to the same thing as taking a share in what he did. What we have to——"

"That," I remarked, "is a travesty of law, and has nothing to do with justice or morality or common sense. His sister——"

"And the same thing," he continued, "applies to the other woman—to his wife. She——"

"His wife," I said, barely controlling my anger, "had no responsibility of any kind for his escape. In point of fact, she urged him to give himself up. She only went with him —as she had to, because she *is* his wife—when all the arrangements had been made by his sister."

"And by you."

"And by me, yes."

"So your own position is—not a very good one. That's what I wanted you to understand."

He was still partly engaged with Riko, and all this time he had spoken without once looking at my face. It was not from any bashfulness—he was a man unlikely to be troubled by that kind of sensibility. No, he simply had no interest in me except as a minor accessory to his purpose—to him I was like the man who gives two strokes of a brush to your shoulders as you leave a restaurant, whose face you never notice. That was as far as I could read his mind. No doubt he had an inward life, like other men. But if it ever involved him in hesitations, in moral uncertainties, these were safe beneath the surface of his looks and behaviour. His nature—as I saw him then—was that which one commonly associates with Englishmen: an empiricist intelligence which looks for no philosophy to live by.

"However," he went on, "you've been helpful up to now, in an accidental way. I think you may still be of some use."

"What do you mean?"

"I accept what you've told me about Babitch, and about Zempelmarck's condition. Actually his health at the moment appears to be improving, but I don't want to take any risks. If there's any deterioration between now and his trial I shall want to call you in."

"His trial?"

"He's going to be tried in the proper way. I don't mean with professional lawyers—they're not in the least necessary."

"But why a trial to decide what you've decided already?"

"Mainly for the sake of these people here. They're good people—religious most of them. Myself, I don't approve of superstition, but there it is—they're country folk, they don't change in one generation. They've got to be satisfied that everything's done in the proper way. If we'd taken Zempelmarck and shot him in the nearest field they wouldn't have been. They'd have felt just as much cheated as if the Americans had hanged him."

"So you're asking me to keep Zempelmarck alive—if my services are needed—until this 'trial'?"

"Probably a little longer. Only it's not a question of 'asking.' I've told you already, you're not in a position to refuse our orders."

"You mean that I can be 'tried' as well?"

"Exactly."

For the first time in this humiliating interview I felt a spasm of joy—the delight that comes when a self-assured opponent commits himself to some superlative folly. Till then my brain, perhaps affected by days of cold and hunger, had been working as a wasted limb does. From the shock of this fellow's puerility it seemed to gain fresh life. Just controlling my voice, I said,

"So you really believe you can get a doctor to do his work by threatening to shoot him?"

"There are other things beside shooting," he said, running his fingers through Riko's hair.

"I know. I saw what happened to the policeman on the quay at Trieste."

"That was nothing. Just a warning."

"Yes, I expect you can think of greater refinements. And you imagine that after suitable tortures a doctor will exercise the kind of skill that's needed for dealing with an infected lung?"

"Listen!" he said, "I'm making you an offer——"

"No—I'm making you one. It has been my business to attend Zempelmarck for some time past. I'm ready to go on with that, as long as my services are needed. But get it in your head, once and for all, that you're not going to get *any* sort of help from me if you mean to victimize innocent people."

"Such as——?"

"I've told you—Frau Zempelmarck is an entirely innocent party, and you have absolutely no excuse for holding her."

"We don't need to. She's set on staying with Zempelmarck. A creature of habit, I suppose."

"Then is she to be involved in this 'trial'?"

"She wants to be there, apparently."

"That's not what I asked you! I said, 'Is she to be involved?' You've threatened to bring a charge against me. Does that apply to Frau Zempelmarck too?"

His answer was evasive: "Look, I personally am not interested in these wretched women—for all I care they can go home as soon as there's no more risk of interference. But I'm not going to say that everyone will feel the same way. If Zempelmarck's wife is there at his trial they'll be interested—the village women will, if no one else. They may want to ask her questions."

"They can ask *me* questions," I said. "I shall tell them what I've told you—that Zempelmarck's wife had nothing whatever to do with his escape. I shall——"

"But who said that you were going to be there at all! We may find it more convenient to have you somewhere else at the time."

"Very well! Then you'll have to find another surgeon for Zempelmarck when he needs one."

At that Valyevitch smiled, bending over Riko as if they shared some family joke. "It looks as if we shall," he said delicately, "since any live surgeon is better than a dead one. You feel deeply about the position of Frau Zempelmarck?"

"I feel deeply about what *we* called 'justice'—we Europeans, some time ago, when there was civilization in Europe. We used to have laws, we used to have institutions built up through the centuries to protect innocent people. That seems to be over. You think that justice is a thing you can look after yourselves, you and a little squad with rifles. Your wisdom decides what's right and wrong and who's to

262

be punished. And then if a woman gets stoned for the single crime of being loyal to the man she married you say it's no concern of yours. All right! If that's what goes for justice now, I'd rather be the victim of it than anything else."

One makes so brave a speech under certain pressures, certain conditions in the supply of blood to the cells of the brain: it came with conviction, but with only a pretence of courage. On Valyevitch, as far as I could see, it made no impression at all.

He was again busy with Riko, artfully making smoke appear from the bowl of a spoon the child was sucking; and after giving me a little time to cool he said unemotionally,

"Yes, that of course is how it looks to you. The old Europe—yes, it must have been pleasant to look at, through drawing-room windows."

"As a doctor I also saw it——"

"However," he pursued, "I'm not going to waste my time with that. I'll tell you one thing. Lawyers are paid, aren't they? Judges—they get large salaries. Well, we get nothing, I and my friends, out of this business. And it has taken up some of our time."

Now, at last, he turned to look at me; and as if a light were suddenly switched on in a gloomy room I saw in his leaden, Slavic eyes, beyond the tired intelligence, a man of passion.

"It has taken five years," he said tautly, "to get where we are now. Or nearly. It was five years ago next March that this place was raped. And that was due to me, in a way—and my *komitadzi*. I said to these people here, afterwards, I told them, 'I can't give you back what you've lost—but I can see that it's paid for.' I promised them that."

He had handed Riko back to me, and he bent to re-tie the laces of his boots.

"That's what I've worked for," he said, "and that's all I care about. If others get hurt—you people who've got yourselves mixed up—well, it's unfortunate for them. These women of Zempelmarck's, I've no time to fuss over

263

their situation. Or over yours. The wife wants to be at the trial. She can. So can you. You can speak for her if you want to."

"I shall want to. I——"

"But listen!" Again he was purely a man of business, he might have been demanding a special discount on an order for canned beef. "I expect something in return for that. You may have to do some interpreting for one thing. And I want Zempelmarck kept alive, for the time being."

"Well, where is he? I shall have to make an examination at once."

"That must wait."

"Your risk!" I said.

I had not seen Mica come in, and I was taken by surprise when, as if she were rescuing Riko from a fire, she pounced and swept him away from me. Standing, then, with her thick short legs apart, fiercely holding the little boy by the shoulders, she said to Valyevitch,

"How long is this man to stay in my house?"

"A few more days," he answered. "We have still some details to organize. If you and your husband will have the goodness——"

"A few more days—and then they'll be finished off, these friends of Zempelmarck's?"

"Their position will be considered."

"Considered? And will that bring Karel back to me!"

Upon an impulse I said, hardly controlling tears, "Frau Fotez, if I myself could give Karel back to you I would give my life to do it. That is the truth, I swear it."

But she made no answer—she did not appear to hear or to see me. With Riko astride her hip, she went away upstairs.

It was an hour when, if the clouds thinned, the winter sunlight would come into that room from the high back window. That day the sun was brilliant, and I remember how, turning to Valyevitch again, I saw his face as if it had been carved at something above life-size; how every wrinkle, all the little ugly hairs on neck and chin, showed as in a portrait of Brueghel's; and how beneath them the whole fabric of muscle was taut and trembling. 'It is myself,' I thought for an instant, 'seen from another side.' I remember him speaking to me as to one in whom he had long had perfect confidence: "Yes, that's how they are, these people! You see what I've worked for, now?"—but my brain did nothing with those words except record them. For as I stood there in the channelled sunlight I felt a darkness tightening about me in which every beauty in life had withered. Once I had professed myself a healer. And here was a carcinoma so far advanced that it could not be reached, I thought, by any power of healing.

Chapter 11

I

THE ESCORT WHICH they sent for me consisted of two children—two boys, that is, of whom the elder was probably no more than seventeen. They arrived after dark on (I think) a Saturday and stood just inside the kitchen, solemn and self-conscious, each with a German rifle slung from his shoulder.

"Reichenbach? You are to come with us," the elder said.

Dushan had not come home that evening. Both Mica and Sava were out at the time, and so it happened that I was once again responsible for Riko, who had already been put to bed but who might easily have waked and called for attention.

"Valyevitch has sent you?" I asked. "Then I shall come with you, of course. But perhaps you can wait till someone gets back—there's a child upstairs who can't be left alone in the house."

"We were told to bring you as quickly as possible," the boy answered sternly.

"But five or ten minutes won't make any difference, surely? I could make you some coffee."

After some mumbling together they agreed to this; and when I had made the coffee they drank it as at Passover, still on their feet and with their spare hands nursing their trigger-guards. It was a feast lacking conviviality, and I was glad when Sava came in.

I told her that the visitors were taking me away—I did not know where or for how long. She must have known fairly well what was afoot, but she said nothing: in a seizure of her pitiful shyness she stood back against the linen press, staring at us through her ugly spectacles as if at some sport which she had no hope of understanding. This, in turn, put the boys in some confusion; and it was I—when we seemed to be fastened for ever in a tableau of embarrassment—who had to say,

"Well, I suppose we'd better be moving! Perhaps, Sava, you would be so kind as to fetch me my coat—I think my friends here want to keep an eye on me."

This she did complaisantly, and then there was a further awkwardness. It was the younger of the boys—Josi, his partner called him—who told me with a grave authority, "Our orders are that you are to be pinioned for the journey."

"What—you mean, handcuffed?"

"Well, no," said the elder, with a note of apology. "We haven't, in fact, any handcuffs."

"It means," said Josi, taking a length of cord from his ammunition pouch, "that your wrists have to be tied together."

I cautiously demurred at this discomfort, explaining that even if I were free of all encumbrance it would be impossible for me to run far from them in difficult and unknown country. Would it not suffice if the cord were tied round one of my wrists and the other end secured to Otto's (the elder's) waist? They decided at length that my proposal was sensible; and with much earnest discussion of the appropriate knots we got ourselves rigged in that fashion. Sava stood watching these manœuvres, still constrained and dumb. Only when we were on the point of departure was her nervousness swept over by the force of charity. She came close to me then, actually pushing Josi aside. She said breathlessly,

"They won't kill you! I have prayed, I keep praying. They won't hurt you!"

Those, in truth, were alarming words: they sharpened,

267

as it were, the edge of certain hints that Valyevitch had dropped in his talk with me. I was none the less grateful. "But you are kind, Sava," I said, "so very kind!" And when with tearful eyes she whispered, "God with you!" I should—but for the boys' gaze fixed on me—have put my free arm about her shoulders, drawn towards me the distressed, unlovely face and kissed her cheek.

Like the lingering warmth from wine her kindness went with me through much of the long walk I had to make. I needed such comfort, for I was not in condition or properly clothed for the open air at that altitude, and when I could not see their faces the solemnity of my escort depressed me. It appeared that most of Pravnitzar was going with us: as we descended through the village there were doors slamming everywhere, and in the panels of light thrown on the road by cottage windows I kept seeing family groups moving in the same direction as ourselves. These little parties, when we overtook them, had a sabbath air, talking if at all in undertones; and when we had left the lights behind, and were traversing a corridor between high walls of rock, the air seemed to be filled with a susurration of guarded voices, spread over the soft, purposeful rumour of a hundred feet; so that a fantasy took hold of me that I was part of a funeral procession, where none of the mourners knew that the funeral was mine. For one unused to that road the going was awkward: in parts there was loose shale on the surface, and here and there patches of ice. Twice I fell on my back—the more painfully because I had only one hand free to save myself—and the second time I nearly pulled Otto down with me. On each occasion they helped me to my feet again, not roughly but without a word. No doubt they thought me a clumsy passenger, and when I tried to make a joke of my unsteadiness there was no response.

"Is it far?" I asked.

"You will see," the child Josi said tersely.

"Are you fellows part of a special corps?"

"We have duties," was the only reply.

Further on I tried again to get them into conversation. "The last time I was marched along as a prisoner was in Wien, before the War," I told them. "It was the Black-shirts who arrested me then—it was because I didn't approve of Nazionalsozialismus. But I don't suppose you know anything about those days?"

"We know our business," Otto said.

No, of course they knew nothing; and we had no starting point for even a transient friendship, they and I. At the time it seemed to me a distortion of nature that I could win no cordiality from these decent, pleasant-faced young men to whom I was physically tethered. For I was not considering then the moral gulf there was between us. They, if stolid and humourless, were also dutiful and brave; while I had long left my virtue in disuse.

Probably we made some turn I was not aware of: the road started to go uphill, and we had climbed a fairly arduous slope for a mile or more when fresh lights appeared.

"What's this place we're coming to?" I asked; expecting no more than Otto's curt reply, "It's a farm."

But Josi—since the young cannot resist displaying knowledge—improved on this. He said, "The Bogomile farm."

"It was, once," Otto promptly corrected; and added, "It was a place for monks once."

"It wasn't!" said Josi.

"It was! But Diocletianus made it."

"He didn't. The Bogomili did. And the Germans finished it."

"They didn't. They only mended the roof."

The pair had suddenly grown human—I suppose the upward march had sufficiently re-warmed their blood. But this occurred too late to be of any use to me. We crossed an area of deeply rutted mud, and with a group of others passed through a doorway wide enough to take six men abreast. The wind followed us: at first I had no sense of being indoors. But here two giant braziers were burning, and a cluster of electric lamps slung on a cable overhead cast a pool of light which to me—emerging from an hour in darkness—seemed as intense as the illumination of an operating-table. Almost in the centre of this pool, in a space that was painfully empty, my guardians stopped. Ceremonially, Josi was holding one of my arms, the other was still linked with Otto's waist. The head of neither came much above my shoulders, but they stood very straight, these two boys, important and severe, aware of having faithfully performed an exacting mission.

From a group nearby Valyevitch detached himself. Glancing at my body—not at my face—he said to the boys, "Oh, you've brought that man—good!" and went on to speak to someone else.

2

Self-consciousness misguides the imagination—I doubt if anyone was much aware of my presence at that stage. Nobody paid me any attention.

Indeed, there came to me presently an illusion of invisibility, resembling a sensation I had known in dreams—so little did I seem to be involved in the shapeless, dawdling activity about me. There was a man of professorial appearance in earnest conversation with two or three who looked like dealers in an urban market, others who might have been the crew of a tug-boat stood in a rough line sheepishly watching them. At a trestle-table an aged peasant woman and a girl in a shabby fur were drawing some kind of beverage from a copper urn, while a man like Savonarola, with Muslim trousers leading into high top boots and a cap such as Turkish railwaymen used to wear, was wandering about with glasses which he despondently presented to everyone he found in his way. These, the figures that I best remember, earthy and substantial as they were, had been invested with an air of falsity by the ruthless light which bathed them, and this impression of distorted actuality was heightened by the muted bustle in the surrounding field of shadow. The sabbatic comportment I had noted in the people walking from the village was here intensified. By several doors they entered almost silently, and those who came into the fringe of light turned nervously away as if from a place too holy for their feet. Without direction— since no one appeared to be in control—some drifted to the wooden steps which took them to an open loft, some, turning the other way, spread themselves like lava over the rummage which filled half the building—horse-rakes, coaches resting on shafts and axles, a military litter of chests and timber. There, like worshippers, they settled in peculiar quietness, so that their stifled chatter reached me only as the sound of windswept leaves: now and then a yellow flash showed as a cigarette was lit, an old man had a fit of coughing, a baby cried, but in that phantasmic interval I did not think of them as a host of animate beings, only as a breathing rampart to the fevered area I stood in. Just then I felt no apprehension. Of the figures close to me there was none with that authority which starts the springs of fear.

Some practical authority there must have been, but I did not see how it worked. Immediately beneath the lights a space was cleared and its sides lined with schoolroom benches. As if spontaneously, the women at the urn stopped work and lifted their tackle out of sight, the table on which it had stood was shifted to one end of the arena and a high-backed chair set behind it. I had heard no word that sounded like an order.

"Reichenbach can go over there, to start with. With the witnesses—my end."

Even that was spoken casually, by Valyevitch as he strolled past us. Obediently my escort took me to the table end of the line of benches where a dozen men were settling

271

as if for a corporate photograph, while a rather larger collection of men and women were taking places on the benches opposite. At the end facing the table three chairs had been placed by themselves. These were empty.

Valyevitch himself had rejoined the group of townsmen who were still conversing as if they were alone in the building. He parted from them now, to go and sit half way between me and the table. With a leisured air the men he had left moved over to a row of chairs which faced—across the table—the one that he had taken; while a single member of the group detached himself and stood with his back to the central chair.

This was a man whose extreme shortness of stature was counterpoised by a head of particular splendour. His abundant beard, the colour of polished pewter, was of a shape one associates with the Greek priesthood. The same thick and silky hair lay in Hellenic curls upon his massive forehead, and beneath the exuberant eyebrows his deeply caved brown eyes, large and gentle, were lit (I thought) by a steadfast intelligence. Curiously, the shabby suit he wore, and the roughness of his big hands, seemed only to increase his dignity. For a little while he stood scanning an imaginary horizon, like a shepherd taking the day's tactics from the sky. Then he smiled, as if at some fleeting recollection, sat down and began to fill a Dresden pipe.

His name, I learnt afterwards, was Kastelej. He was by birth Albanian, but had spent his life as a boat-builder at Macarska.

3

Now that my eyes were used to the hard light I no longer had any sense of occasion. I saw, glancing sideways, that Valyevitch was sitting with his eyes half-closed—he looked as if he were about to fall asleep. And if he had already lost interest in the affair, who was to promote it? The tension of the audience had relaxed and they were chattering freely —manifestly they had ceased to look for excitement from a stage where the performers were only a copy of themselves. Minutes passed, no one stirred from his place. With his pipe alight, Kastelej appeared to wait contentedly for the end of the world. As the stagnant interval wore on I almost fancied I had lit on some agrarian convention which would presently spend an hour in fumbling oratory and then disperse.

The great doorway through which I had entered had been shut some minutes earlier. I was looking the other way— at the men on Kastelej's left—when it was reopened, and I did not at once realize what had brought a hush on the assembly as if a soundproof curtain had been lowered between them and me. When I turned my head the doors had been closed once more. In the empty space before them a little group was advancing; isolated not only by the fall of light but by their alien countenance and bearing.

Flanked by gaitered and belted guards, the two women were foremost. Of them, it was Paula who instantly compelled attention. She was dressed as I had last seen her, in the shapeless gaberdine coat, and her pallor was as if the sickness of the *Charilaos* still possessed her. She had changed, however. She looked, now, as if some twenty years had been added to her age; and in the anchylosed sternness of this far older face the former nerviness, the shrewish asperity, were levelled out. It happened that the man beside her was small, and this increased her apparent height. She moved—as if by calculation—very slowly; so that I had for a moment the whimsical notion that someone would presently come forward to hand her a bouquet. Perhaps it was deliberately arranged that the crowd should see her first—that a figure of such self-possession, so intractable, should be the earliest for them to fasten on. That is mere conjecture. I know that Siegfried, coming a few paces behind her, did not so powerfully command my eyes as she did.

And yet I had reason to stare at him, since for the first time I saw him on his feet. My physiotherapy, which I had regarded as amateurish, had evidently won some ground. True, a good deal of his weight was on Babitch (a dreamy, faintly exalted Babitch who had a hand in his armpit) and on the broad shoulders of the shorter man on his other side. But undoubtedly he was walking—I needed no professional discernment to see that the slow, stiff movement of his legs was under his own control.

Except for this—the only movement of his body visible to me—it might have been an effigy which was guided forward and carefully placed on the centre of the three empty chairs: a perfect, lifeless reproduction of the form and features I knew. Even the eyes were scarcely moving. In so far as they revealed emotion, it was that of a man faintly surprised by his own celebrity; while the mouth was set in that perversion of a smile which to me was its most familiar expression. Someone had taken trouble with his grooming —he was well shaved, his hair respectably cut—so that even now the head was sculpturally handsome; and to his body, so shrunk that his old coat hung loose on his chest, the blanket about his shoulders gave the dignity which belongs to an invalid. But these attributes remained pictorial, as if an actor had dressed for his part. The thought passed through my mind, 'It is all too late—they have brought for exhibition a man who has for some time been dead.'

Was his appearance a disappointment to the crowd? Had they looked for someone of more martial stature, a Samson in chains? I do not know, for at that time I had forgotten the shadowed ranks behind and above me, while the appearance of Paula and Siegfried themselves was recorded only on the surface of my intelligence. When Franziska had been led to her place on Siegfried's left she was less than a dozen yards from me. In a sense we might as well have been in separate hemispheres. But because I had lived so many days on the feeble image which is all that memory provides, she seemed to be so near that all the rest—the bucolic parade, the serried, staring palenesses—was submerged in unreality. In that light her beauty did not show. She appeared a particularly small woman, pale, severely dressed: an impoverished widow, sitting with anxious modesty at a wealthy cousin's table, would not have looked less striking or significant than she did now. It was only to the eyes of love—which are piercing and infallible—that her perfection blazed like Cristallo in morning sun.

For a time she did not see me. When I first caught her eye she started, and I thought I saw a dreadful grief there. I lifted my wrist—the cord was still round it. She made no gesture in response; but for just a moment her lips were relaxed in a smile that came to me like a phrase of music across a placid lake. This was enough. That moment, set apart from time, cancelled all the days of longing, the immediate fears and shame.

4

A darkly whiskered man on my side of the arena had risen and begun to speak, apparently on an impulse of his own. His clothes were those of a farm labourer, but the alert face and compact body were a soldier's and he spoke as soldiers do, incisively and as if he were reading from a placard thirty feet away.

"On the 19th February 1943 I was in command of No. 5 Independent Patrol. I received orders by runner to establish my patrol in the defile east of Pravnitzar. The order was to halt and destroy enemy supply vehicles proceeding by the secondary road to Usir. I therefore——"

"One minute! Who issued those orders?" This was Valyevitch, who spoke without moving.

"Why, sir, you did!"

"Yes, all right . . . Dr. Reichenbach, you will please translate into German. You can summarize some of the evidence if necessary, but the essence must be made quite clear to the prisoners. Is that right, Mr. President?"

Kastelej nodded. I did as I was told, at first awkwardly. In time the work became largely automatic—I attempted nothing more than free and abbreviated renderings—and although it was progressively tiring I found it in a sense grateful, for it gave me a certain detachment: if I had to be present, it was better to be occupied as a machine.

The soldier continued: "In accordance with these orders I established the patrol at a point in the defile approximately 800 metres to the east of the post house, which is the last building on that side of Pravnitzar. Two *fugate* were dug in at this point, and were covered by fire from a point twenty paces higher along the road. The men were posted one hour before first light. After posting the men——"

Again Valyevitch interrupted: "Were these men in uniform?"

"They had the *komitadzi* cap."

"All of them?"

"Yes. And the brassard."

"They were all actually wearing them?"

"When I posted them—yes, sir."

"You say that the ambush was established shortly before first light. But you must have reconnoitred the position before that—in daylight?"

"Why, yes. Every man was shown his position and his task in daylight."

"And after that they had some sleep?"

"Some did."

"Where?"

"In the truck."

"But some may have gone into the village—into Pravnitzar? They may have found sleeping quarters there?"

"No, sir! I should not have allowed even one of them to go so far away. They were not allowed to go out of my call."

"Not even any who had friends or relations in the village?"

"None of them knew anyone in Pravnitzar. You know that, sir! We don't come from this part, not one of us. We'd never been in this part in our lives."

"So on that night none of you went into the village? You didn't make any connections? You didn't tell people what was to happen, warn them to be careful?"

"Well, that was your orders, sir. Not to have any talk or dealings with anyone."

"All right—go on."

The soldier waited for a few minutes, as if he had lost sight of his brief. Then he continued, mechanically,

"At eight-thirty approximately I was warned by land wire signal of approach of enemy vehicles moving west. These vehicles were: motor-cycle unit with light machine-gun, half-tracked supply vehicle, small half-tracked armoured fighting vehicle. Distance between vehicles estimated forty metres. I allowed motor-cycle unit to proceed, and detonated *fugate* so as to destroy supply vehicle. Motor-cycle unit was destroyed by rifles seventy-five metres west which I had posted for this task. Crew of fighting vehicle was then engaged and destroyed. I suffered casualties—one killed, one man wounded later died, one wounded, serious, two wounded, slight."

"And all enemy personnel were killed?"

"No, sir—one got away. Remainder were destroyed."

"How many?"

"Seven. Two in motor-cycle unit. Driver and light machine-gunner on supply vehicle. Three from crew of four in fighting vehicle."

"All right. Interpreter, ask Zempelmarck if he has any questions to put to the sergeant."

I did so, but I might as well have addressed myself to a man blind and deaf.

"Ask his friends," Valyevitch ordered.

"Fräulein Zempelmarck, do you wish to ask this man any questions?"

She impatiently shook her head.

A second witness was already on his feet—or rather, on one foot and on the stump which took the other's place. This was a man whose dropsical figure I could not visualize in any military action, and his piping, sing-song voice was the least martial I ever heard. He began, however, much as the sergeant had done.

"I was a member of No. 5 Patrol. We were ordered to set an ambush on the road above Pravnitzar.... I was told by Prezihov to dig a trench for the *fugate*—and that was no light job, with the road as it was ..."

He was examined as the previous witness had been. Had he worn the cap and brassard at the time of the action? Had he slept in the village—been into the village at all—received any supplies or comforts or other assistance from the village people? To all these last suggestions he replied with an incredulous and slightly resentful "No!"

Several more witnesses—all equally civilian in their port and behaviour—were similarly treated. They covered much the same ground as the sergeant had done, each adding a few details of the action dear to himself—one had been the first to sight the enemy vehicles, one, firing at a difficult angle, had killed the motor-cycle driver with a single shot. This repetitive evidence, translated piecemeal, took up a considerable time—perhaps an hour and a half altogether. It left me with an account of the action which was fairly complete but only diagrammatic—it conveyed nothing of the chill and cramp of waiting, the dreadful tension, the seconds loaded with smoke and tearing noise and bloody violence. I should have expected the audience to lose patience with it, but they continued to sit in almost perfect silence. They had, I surmise, an instinctive confidence in Valyevitch; by which, like uninformed spectators at a Spanish *corrida*, they felt assured that these elaborate opening manoeuvres were a necessary stage in the advance upon a common objective.

And now they had some encouragement. A sheet of paper was produced; weather-soiled, with holes in the corners stained with rust. This was at once recognized. A murmur went all round the building:

'The notice ... Someone kept it, do you see!'

The man who had produced it was asked, "Where did you find this? When?"

He consulted a card from the pocket of his blouse. "On the 21st February, 1943, I saw this paper nailed on the door of the police office. I took it away the week after that. At night, that was. I kept it where my wife keeps her cheeses."

"The police office at Pravnitzar, you mean?"

"Well, of course!"

The paper was handed to Kastelej, who scrutinized it with a pair of pince-nez and passed it on to his colleagues.

One of them, with a certain deliberation, carried it down the arena and held it before Siegfried.

"Ask him," Kastelej said to me, "if the signature on that paper is his."

"*Diese ist Ihre eigenhandige Unterschrift, Herr Oberst?*"

For a moment or two, in which everyone waited with intense excitement, I thought that Siegfried would simply continue to pretend that he saw and heard nothing. But then, as if a subordinate had brought some document for his approval, he gave a little nod. A sigh of satisfaction went round the building.

The paper was brought back to Kastelej, who in turn passed it to me. I saw that the notice was typed in German and Serbo-Croat in parallel columns.

"You will be so kind as to read aloud the German version," Kastelej said.

I read: "'On the morning of the 20th February, eight German soldiers, peacefully performing their duty in the transport of food supplies, were attacked, and seven of them murdered, by a gang of civilians operating from the village of Pravnitzar. The inhabitants of Pravnitzar are held corporately responsible for this outrage, and are required to surrender the actual assailants at Military Government Headquarters, Usir, not later than Midday on the 23rd February. In the event of non-compliance with this Order, exemplary punitive action will be taken against the village of Pravnitzar.'"

"Thank you!" Kastelej said politely, and I returned the paper to him. "I shall now," he said, "read the Serbo-Croat version."

This was mere ritual: one realized that almost every adult in the building could have recited it from memory. But while he put on his spectacles again and tried them in various positions up and down his nose everyone maintained the breathless patience of a theatre audience waiting for the bravura lines of *Wilhelm Tell*. With no gift for reading, he wavered and stumbled, overran the punctuation. Yet, when he had finished, the murmur which came like an evening breeze from all the shadows sounded in my ears like an outbreak of applause.

He himself must have felt it so. I saw on his lips the modest smile of one who has achieved a personal triumph. And as if to dramatize his success he said benignly,

"We will have an interval now."

By some intuition the women in charge of the samovar seemed to have forecast this announcement—already, with a workaday expression, they were dragging their impedimenta back into the arena.

I read not long ago in a political digest published in Cambridge, Massachusetts, an account of those proceedings which emanated originally from the Kösters-Heubach agency at Zurich. I found by writing to a director of that agency (who replied to me with the greatest courtesy) that the author of the article—first published in a Swedish journal in September 1948—had been their correspondent in Sarajevo.

Presumably he had his information from someone who was present, but not from an educated or even an intelligent observer. His report contains gross inaccuracies. He says, for example, that 'Mirko Valyevitch, lawyer's clerk from Dubitza, sometime mining engineer, and former group commander of Partisans, acted as both prosecutor and judge'. This is simply false. The organization of the trial was manifestly in Valyevitch's hands and he probably arranged every detail of the procedure. But he never interfered with the essential functions of Kastelej, who, however ignorant of the finer points of magistracy, plainly knew what he was there for and was strong enough in character to brook no interference from Valyevitch or anyone else.

From so unreliable a reporter I should not accept his strong suggestion that the Yugoslav Government knew of the affair beforehand and connived at it. In all probability local police officials had some advance knowledge of what was afoot. But since—on that supposition—they decided to turn a blind eye to it, I see no reason why they should have communicated their knowledge or suspicions to higher authority.

Again, I take issue with him on his conclusion that 'the "trial" itself amounted to nothing more than a childish parody of the forms of justice'. True, it bore small resemblance to any recognized court procedure; and any rules of evidence I know of, whether of the Austrian or the American code, were not so much infringed as totally disregarded. I will not admit, however, that what took place that night was only a vacuous parade. It was honest, according to its lights: those who gave evidence were transparently truthful, and had Zempelmarck been able to produce a score of witnesses in his own cause they would all have been given an honest hearing. But the object—as I see it now—was not to prove in legal form facts which no one could seriously have disputed. Rather, it was to restore—for Zempelmarck as well as for Pravnitzar—a segment of their history so trenchantly that the facts themselves would speak with the very voice of equity.

I am convinced of that. Unlike the Kösters-Heubach reporter, I was present—I watched and listened through those grinding hours. And not as among the scribes; for, although I did not sit with the accused, I knew from the beginning that in the thoughts of every man and woman present that was where I belonged.

6

I wondered during the long intermission whether the court could ever be restored to its former state. A very small boy whose trousers constantly slipped down to his knees was seriously kicking a yellow ball up and down the floor, while a switch of rather bigger children, engaged in the sport of Wolf and Dog, ran laughing and screaming round the clumps of their elders. No one paid them any attention. A sense of holiday had supervened, men discoursed with their hands on others' shoulders, the shrill gossip of women was like the noise of a startled rookery. Right at my feet— I had been forbidden to move—a little party settled as if for a picnic on the Prater, the gay, small mother feeding two infants from a paper bag and the third from her breast. I was trying through this *fête-champêtre* to make out what was happening to Franziska, but the smoke and commotion kept her hidden. Only with Babitch did I get a word—in a burst of good nature he ploughed his way through the crowd to speak to me.

"You remember me—Surgeon-Captain Babitch? I really must offer you my compliments! Your interpretation—quite remarkable—I never knew you had such a gift. It has given everyone the keenest enjoyment."

"What about Zempelmarck?" I asked him quietly. "Is he fit to stand any more of this?"

"Zempelmarck? Bursting with health! I've been nursing the bastard like a pedigree stallion."

"Tell me, how is his wife? How is she taking all this?"

"What? Oh, I don't suppose she's followed it, you can't get women to take any interest in military matters. I remember a baggage I had just after Savobor, I gave her a description of the whole battle—first-class, I was almost fainting with excitement. Do you think she understood a word! 'It will be 20 Dinars for the extra half-hour'—that was all she said."

He drifted amiably away, and I presently caught sight of him in hearty converse with the sergeant of Partisans. Dushan Fotez—I had not realized he was there—appeared beside me.

"I've had a word with Kastelej," he said from the corner of his mouth. "I used to know him a little. I've told him that you are known to me personally as a man of the highest principles. That may be helpful."

My guards had left me for the moment to get themselves refreshment. I whispered hastily,

"I'd be still more grateful if you'd tell him something about Frau Zempelmarck. She's a woman of the noblest character. I don't see why she's here at all. She isn't involved in this—how could she be!"

"I don't know," he answered—his voice was troubled and scarcely audible. "It's the way people feel. So many of them—you understand—so many were involved."

"Conversation is not allowed!" said Otto humourlessly, returning with his mouth full and with a cup of tepid soup for me.

By then the arena was clearing again—the old man in the Turkish cap had been pushing people towards the loft with the soft insistence of countrywomen chevying oxen. Kastelej went back to his place; and it testified to his personality that while he merely stood there, smiling pacifically, the noise subsided as it does when a respected professor enters the classroom. Presently he raised his hand. There was total silence.

The mood of patience returned, the patience which is natural to those who wait through long, hard winters for the first shoots to break the ground. Wonderfully, even the children were restored to discipline. But as I looked at the reinstated pattern, the row of homely figures theatrically enlarged by the density of light, above them the heads which showed like bird's-eggs sunk in mounting folds of shadow, I was aware of some fresh quality in the quietness, a tightening of concentration as when the Mass moves deepening from the *Quam Oblationem*. The overture was finished, we were nearer what these people had come for. Somehow they knew.

And now the voices they listened to were no longer those of strangers engaged with dim technicalities: the second corps of witnesses—those who sat on the benches facing me —were of their own community.

I remember vividly one of the earliest, a bow-legged, paunchy man who had his fur cap tilted ludicrously to meet his massive eyebrows and who spoke with his eyes fixed towards the floor except when, losing his way, he gave quick and anxious glances at the friends behind him. It was strangely emotive, the diffident and almost guilty way in which he unwound his recollections:

284

"My wife was asleep, you see. She sleeps on the outside—there's more room, because of the rafters. Well, you know, she's a big woman. Not tall, but a big woman. It might have been one o'clock—I know it was gone midnight some time before, I heard the clock—it must have been one o'clock I heard all that knocking. Well, I couldn't get out, not without waking my wife, you see, and she sleeps poorly. And then I heard my son go down, and I thought, 'Well, he can see what it is, and if it's anything he can't manage he'll come and tell me. I mean, there are nights when my wife can't sleep at all, it's something in her belly. I bought some medicine—25 Dinars—they said it would settle her, but it wasn't any good. I said to my wife——"

"And in the morning," Valyevitch asked, "your son was gone?"

"Yes. Of course I thought to begin with——"

"And you never saw him again?"

"Well, no. Not unless you count the last time."

"You mean——?"

The witness was silent, struggling as a child does against the shame of tears. At last he said,

"Well, I saw him that day—March 9th."

"That will do, for the moment," Valyevitch said. "Interpreter, ask for questions."

There were none.

The woman who followed showed greater self-control. She was of gipsy appearance, with a fine physique and carriage, she wore immense gold earrings and her *jelet* shone with gold embroidery. Speaking with calm and a note of contempt she recounted how a party of soldiers had arrived late at night demanding to see her husband.

"I told them he was away, but they heard him—he was coughing, he was ill in bed. They pushed me out of the way—I kicked one of them in the groin but it was no use, there were four of them, big men. Four of them it took to drag him away."

285

"Do you suppose they had some special reason for choosing your husband?"

"Reason? What reason could they have?"

"He was not a Partisan?"

"Partisan? Bojan? With only one arm, and nearly blind!"

"He hadn't had any dealings with the Partisans? Given them information? Are you sure you never at any time let them use your cottage as a billet or a place to meet in?"

"Do you think I wouldn't remember! Do you think no one would have seen! You can ask anyone here, if you think I'm an untruthful woman."

I think that Mica Fotez came next. On the night when the soldiers arrived her husband had been away. They had lied to her—they had said that her elder son was wanted to identify one of his friends, who had met with an accident. The soldier who spoke had been a pleasant, smiling man. God forgive her!—she had trusted him.

"And did you see your son again?"

A whisper: "On March 9th I saw him."

The stories had a constant pattern: the sound of a vehicle stopping and a sharp knock on the door, a German voice, sometimes polite and sometimes peremptory; a minute of confusion, with the household in their nightclothes and only half awake; then a son or husband gone. But the telling was widely varied. There was a girl whose utterance was so submerged in tears that I gave up trying to interpret her; and another woman who talked confidentially to Valyevitch as if on her own threshold, with the corners of her mouth stitched in a faintly imbecile smile.

"Pappy thought they wanted him for a soldier—he was a soldier when he was young. But of course that was silly, Pappy was 78—he wasn't clear in his mind, you understand. He was looking for his old breeches, the ones he had for his campaigning. I said, 'Pappy, you know you haven't got them any more!' but he didn't seem to hear me. I'd cut them up, you understand—that was when he burnt a hole in his chair and I wanted something to put a new piece in. That kind of stuff, it isn't easy to come by. So he'd no proper clothes on when they took him, only his shirt and his clogs. I ran after the van with some clothes for him, but they wouldn't stop, even when I shouted. I thought that was funny of them."

Dry-mouthed, I laboured on with my paraphrase as one who would turn the purl of a stream into musical notation. The long succession of deponents, their wanderings and hesitations, were eating up the hours, but I had no sense of lapsing time. In the captured air the smoke from the braziers was stretched like a flocculous awning beneath the battery of lights, the circus of spellbound listeners receded, and as my tired vision narrowed to isolate the speakers' faces, the groping mouths, eyes which fearfully discovered the scars of memory, time seemed for me to go back upon its course. In all this effusion of witness there was no trace of art. Its very innocence, as I believe, made all the straining audience live once more through the night of sudden knockings, of paralysing mutilation. I lived it with them.

And Siegfried, did he live it too? His presence, I think, had long been ignored, as the plaster figures of a proscenium are forgotten. Translating, I had to keep my head half-turned towards him and occasionally I brought myself to look at his face. The later witnesses at least commanded his attention; the smile had gone, he watched them with the gravity of one who judges performers in a trial of skill. If, beyond that, his expression showed any feeling it was too far off for me to see. In Paula I looked for an equal self-control. But her face was invisible. She sat with her elbows on her knees, her forehead couched in her crossed hands, motionless; whether from physical exhaustion I could not determine.

For a long time I kept myself from looking directly at Franziska. Just once my eyes, escaping, bent towards her, and that moment almost overwhelmed me. She sat upright with her hands folded, her head a little tilted in the act of listening—for a casual observer it was the attitude of any conscientious woman at a public meeting. But her face was the very face I had seen at our first encounter, when she had held the torch for me; stiff and white, almost senseless in the struggle for self-command.

'At least it is nearly done,' I was thinking then. 'Ten—twenty—of these people we must have heard now. There cannot be much more for her to suffer.'

In fact there was one more to come. This was an aged woman I had seen in Mica's house; I knew her name—Julija. I thought when her friends led her forward that it was futile as well as callous to bring her there, for she seemed to have no use of language—I even doubted whether she retained her reason. She was almost hairless, small and very frail, she stood rocking her weight from one foot to the other, making contortions with her ape-like mouth, through which there came no sound that I could recognize as speech. But Valyevitch treated her with extraordinary patience.

"Don't be worried, Julija, there's no hurry! There's no need to stand. Sit down and think a little, see if there's anything you'd like to tell us."

No, she would not sit down. And as she stood continuously swaying, growing huge in my vision with her age and isolation, I could see that within the little wizened skull whatever mind she had was feverishly working. It came at length to an eerie utterance—the cracked voice was that of an entertainer's manikin, the words were just intelligible:

"It was not enough for them! My son was not enough! They had to take Zivka as well!"

"Zivka—that was your son's wife? Did she attack the soldiers who came?"

"Who would not attack them!"

With those words her powers appeared to be exhausted, but she still made no movement to retire. Instead, she slowly turned her body as a great ship turns, so that she came to confront the place where Siegfried sat. It seemed to take her a little time to get her eyes focused, but that (I have since realized) was a wrong interpretation—she retained the strong and accurate vision of mountain folk. Turning once more, and now smiling, she spoke to Valyevitch again:

"You will end him slowly. *Slowly*, so I can see."

In the vacuum which those words left a child began crying. I saw Valyevitch make a signal with his head to Kastelej, who nodded and stood up.

"Before long it will be light," he said with his peculiar dignity. "We shall have a little time for rest now, and then we shall go to the Sheepcote Valley. It will be explained to us there what happened to the people of Pravnitzar that the soldiers took away."

7

They did not all perform that pilgrimage, which, avoiding the village, meant a rough and hilly outward walk of three or four miles, partly in darkness. But between fifty and a hundred achieved it, including not a few women, and even some children. Only the Zempelmarcks themselves were transported—in a little truck with a canvas tilt—since plainly neither Siegfried nor Paula was physically capable of walking. Even Kastelej went on his feet.

That I remember, because for part of the way I found him walking beside me, and it was he who sanely ordered my escort to release me from the idiotic tether. For the rest, smoking as he walked, he talked to me most amiably, with the culture of a good tradesman. Had I known this neighbourhood before? Neither had he, but he meant at some time to explore it, he took pleasure in mountainous country. It was famous for a breed of sheep, part Merino, which was not found elsewhere in Jugoslavia.

"This little valley we're going to now is interesting—I was taken to see it yesterday. It was where they used to pen the sheep when they were brought down from the higher pastures, nature might have constructed it for the very purpose. Before the War, they say, you might have seen it completely full of sheep, perhaps 6,000 head at one time. . . . I take the liberty to say, Mr. Doctor, that you are a talented linguist. But it's a strain for you, this business?"

"I do find it a strain," I answered, "because of Zempelmarck's wife being present. I feel, all the time, with her feelings. You would not find anywhere a woman of greater gentleness or innocence."

"I understand your sentiments," he answered courteously, and said no more.

Because I was tired and cold my mind moved waywardly. The exhibition we were required to witness was simply but effectively stage-managed, and as we herded cumbrously from point to point I kept thinking of the tourist parties I had often seen in Vienna and Salzburg: the obese Dutchmen and determined Britishers, the earnest, footsore citizens of Denver and Milwaukee, united in a dogged perambulation from church to cathedral, from stuffed museum to empty dungeon, straining exhausted ears to catch a few words from the guide's recital of dates and titles as if they were drops from a holy well. Here was a more dilapidated company, but one that showed the same weary resolution, the same tortuous sense of duty, the irrational hunger for enlightenment. Gusts of wind came at our faces like the jet of a hose, bearing particles of ice; our feet were soaked and frozen by the snow, which at this height lay in drifts reaching up to a man's thighs. But I heard no complaint of these hardships, even from the smallest walkers. Slightly bemused, perhaps, by cold and the lack of sleep, the promiscuous throng advanced as it was bidden, stood patiently where it was halted, listened in religious silence to the story that almost every man or woman in it could have told for himself.

We came first to a place where, from the side of the cart road we had followed, the ground dropped almost vertically to a depth of thirty or forty feet—the edge was thickly fenced with barbed wire, though only a skilled climber would have ventured the descent. Here we had to wait a few minutes for stragglers, and I was able from this perfect point of vantage to survey the scene at leisure.

I was overlooking a narrow coomb, shaped like an elongated diamond, perhaps a hundred and fifty metres in length. At first I saw no path or opening by which the flocks that Kastelej had described could have entered: in the vaporous early light the space appeared to be totally enclosed by limestone cliffs which, low and rounded on the one long side, on the other mounted in a scale of ragged escarpments to the base of the White Lamb rock. That crest was at first invisible. When, as I watched, a shift of cloud revealed it, it looked as close as if a man standing on its crown could have pitched a stone to where I stood. In this aspect it was neither white nor lamblike; rather it resembled a mound of rusted iron which a smith had started shaping and had then abandoned with a vicious blow on one side. If it dominated Pravnitzar, here its height and mass were overwhelming; so warding the meagre light that the coomb, even with its lining of snow, looked grey and desolate, a mean hollow in the earth's crust which men would use only for their refuse. I found the spectacle a scant reward for so laborious a march.

The truck had been backed towards the wire, and when our number seemed to be complete we were gathered closely beside it. Here there was scarcely a pretence of ceremonial. Valyevitch, who was standing with his back to the wire, smoking a cigarette, may have put some question—I did not hear it. I was absorbed in trying to unfreeze my hands when I realized that a tall fellow standing at Kastelej's side—one who had given evidence before—was addressing us, gradually strengthening his voice to overcome the wind.

"They came to my house the day before—the eighth of March, that was. They said I had to be here at eight in the morning, I was to see my son then. . . . Everyone was here, everyone in Pravnitzar. . . . The soldiers wouldn't let us go any farther, we'd got to stay here by the wire. They said the people they'd taken away would come to us here."

Again I was ordered to translate, and I shouted at the truck an approximation of what the man had said. Now a young woman, another of the earlier witnesses, was questioned.

"You stood just here by the wire? Looking that way?"

"Yes. Yes, they said my husband was in the hut over there. They said he would come to me."

I looked the way she had pointed and saw, for the first time, the gable of the hut she spoke of, at the far end of the coomb.

"And did he?"

No reply.

"Did you see him?"

"I don't know. I suppose he was there. They were all together, coming out of the hut."

"Coming this way?"

"Yes."

"In a long file?"

"No. No, all together."

"And they all came straight towards where we are now? Were they running?"

"No. No, I don't think so. No, they were coming very slowly."

"And what happened then?"

The girl, who was now holding tightly to the arm of a woman beside her, parted her lips to answer, but nothing came except a suffocated cry. She let go the arm and dropped her face into her hands. Glancing at Kastelej, I saw him bite his lip.

"The hut is the next place," Valyevitch said shortly.

"We will go on there," Kastelej said.

From a little way along the road a track I had not seen before sloped down in artful twists to the valley floor and continued to the other end: at the lower level the snow had largely effaced it, but the men who led us knew its course. On this short stretch the going was formidable, and the motor had to be manhandled, yet no one—not even the girl who had broken down—refused it. As we approached the far end I saw that the rock wall was not, as it had looked before, continuous: there was a gap of about a wagon's width. The hut, standing beyond this opening, was larger than it had appeared, a rough but robust construction of timber. Here, when we had been marshalled beside it, a new witness addressed us: a wiry, quick-eyed, leather-skinned young man whom I should not have cared to quarrel with.

He and the other hostages—21 in all—had been brought here on the night of the eighth, he said, and had slept in the hut. They had been told in their own language that they would be released next day. In the morning they had been given bread and substitute-coffee; the soldiers guarding them had seemed to be in friendly humour, but rather on edge.

At eight o'clock they had all been called outside the hut. It was a fine, clear day. The sergeant had told them they were free, adding, "Your friends are waiting for you over there, on the upper road." There had been some hesitation —some of them were suspicious—and this had made the soldiers angry; one had shouted, "You stupid bumpkins, don't you want to go back to your families!" and another had clicked the bolt of his rifle. That was enough to get the party moving, all in a bunch.

All, that was, except the witness himself, who had been

still more distrustful than the rest. He had lagged behind and spoken to one of the guards, saying he was grateful for being released and hoped some time to meet him again and reward him. Then he had asked leave to stop and urinate, and—pretending to misunderstand the soldier's refusal—had dodged quickly behind the hut . . . Yes, he was a shepherd, as his father and grandfather had been. He knew every path on these hills, every rock and cave. No doubt (he said quizzically) if the brave soldiers had been on their own parade-ground they would have caught him.

"They chased you?"

"Not far. I got to a place in the rocks—they'd never have found it, not a whole army. I heard them shouting, but not for long."

"And that was all you heard?"

"Well, then there was the firing. Not at me."

"Rifle fire?"

"Rifles? Not with a din like that. Machine-guns—more than one, I'd say."

"How long did that go on?"

"Oh, a minute. Two minutes, it might have been."

"Then nothing more?"

"Well, for a bit some of them were still screaming."

Valyevitch nodded. Kastelej said, "What is the next place we have to see?"

It proved to be less than fifty paces away, a deep re-entrant in the cliff wall where at least we were sheltered from the wind. The Komitadzi sergeant who had previously given evidence was waiting for us there. He had contrived to spruce himself, and while the truck was being shoved into position he stood at attention, serenely professional.

"On instructions," he recited briskly, "I inspected this position twelve days after the shooting, that is to say, on the 21st March. Warning pickets were posted to ensure security of inspection. The earthwork you see here was then of recent construction, it is suitable for the emplacement of three machine-guns, giving ease and accuracy in handling. We found tripod marks indicating emplacement of two guns. Cases of expended rounds showed that guns were probably M.G. 34s and that two belts were probably fired from each gun . . ."

As I stood listening I suddenly saw that Franziska had got out of the truck—whether of her own will I do not know. When I caught sight of her she was standing a little way back from the crowd. By degrees I edged my way towards her and got to her side.

She did not speak, or even look at me—she was staring, as one far from her surroundings, towards the White Lamb rock—but she rested her hand on my arm. No one else had appeared to notice her except a little girl who had evidently lost sight of her grown-ups and was wandering, bored and lonely and with a streaming nose, round the edge of the assembly. It occurred to this child to go and put her head against Franziska's side; at which she, still without any movement of the eyes, placed her other arm round the small girl's shoulders. We stood like that, we three, for a minute or more. Apparently no one minded.

The sergeant was going on contentedly: "You will see that the depth of the position, which affords good concealment from the flanks, reduces the arc of fire to an angle of about 80°. Otherwise I would call it an excellent position having regard to the slope of the ground. The effective beaten zone——"

"By that you mean," said Valyevitch, interrupting for the first time, "that from this position you would be quite certain of killing anyone who tried to cross the coomb?"

"Correct, sir."

"But if he threw himself flat on the ground?"

"You'd still get him with the next burst. That's the point of the emplacement. I've been all over—there's not a foot of dead ground anywhere."

"That all seems quite clear," Kastelej said. "Does Zempelmarck want to question any point? . . . Perhaps Frau Zempelmarck will return, please, to her place in the motor."

There was one more site to be visited, at the farther side of the coomb. The truck was stopped there and we all obediently foregathered. This one required no exegesis.

The snow had been shovelled aside to disclose a shallow mound, a rectangle some fifteen feet in length. At one end had been planted—recently, from its appearance—a single slab of basalt on which I saw, beneath the inscription '9 March 1943', a list of names and ages, twenty altogether: 'Josip Ziherl, 24. Karel Fotez, 16. Janko Merin, 78. Zivka Pukl, 29. Karel Marjan, 12 . . .' I was too cold, too far from my normal command of my senses, to stand and read them all.

Kastelej, who must have seen this exhibit on his earlier visit, did not trouble to examine it again. I saw him standing some way apart with the little group who seemed to be his personal advisers and who, with their caps reverently removed, were lighting fresh cigarettes. Presently he called out, in the way of a perceptive host,

"I think we have seen enough now. I think we can go back."

I shared that view. I thought we had seen enough.

8

There was coffee of a sort and more food for everyone when we returned to the farm. This I took to be one more proof of the administrative capacity of Valyevitch—who himself, as I observed, ate nothing.

But it seemed to me—now that my mind had come to a point of stillness, of singular detachment—that he was overreaching his power of showmanship. In the great barn the electric lamps were still burning, but they scarcely held the arena against the invasion of daylight through the clerestory windows, and in this diffusion of light the solemnity of the high, pillared building, which must once have been a Christian basilica, could not survive. The iron sheets that patched the roof, tarpaulins hanging on the rood-beam, were now plainly visible; the refuse of a whole night's occupation, cigar-butts, paper, scraps of food, were stuck with fresh mud to the concrete floor, and over all the lumber in the loft and bays were draped the tousled forms of men, women and children snoring or only half awake. What more did Valyevitch mean to do with these weary people, what had he still to offer them?

For I did not know him then as I seem to now, when I have lived some time with the memory of his desiccated voice and features, the peculiar challenge in his sombre gaze. I had not realized then how passion climbs in such a man, how composedly it labours, when denied the quick relief of violence. His temper was that of the prophets, he would —at the last—have pursued his course without one observer.

Quiescent now, he sat with his chair tilted back, fingering a cocked ankle and surveying Zempelmarck with the remote complacence of a successful gardener. It was left to Kastelej and the little group who sat with him to manage the remaining business as they wished.

With some nervous fumbling, the member of that group who looked like a lawyer or professor read out (belatedly, I thought) a formal indictment: that on the 9th March 1943, in the Sheepcote Valley in the District of Pravnitzar, the prisoner Zempelmarck had caused to be murdered by machine-gun fire the following civilian inhabitants of Pravnitzar . . .

I was told to translate and then to ask Zempelmarck if he wished to call any evidence, or make a statement, or instruct anyone to speak on his behalf. Time would be given if he so required.

His response was much what I expected: when I had put

the questions a second time he looked up with a fleeting smile and spoke to me as if he and I were the only adults in the building:

"You mean, Reichenbach, these people imagine they're a court of law? I see no reason for me to encourage such a fiction."

That was all.

I reported in Serbo-Croat: "He doesn't wish to say anything."

A whispered discussion started between Kastelej and his committee, and I was looking that way, wondering how they would proceed, when a general turning of heads brought my attention back to Siegfried's end of the arena. Paula, who had been sitting with her face covered as before, had got to her feet.

She stood unsupported, not very steadily, her head bent forward, her moist eyes pointed vaguely to a place above Kastelej's head. It took some time for her to find her voice; then she began what I suppose could be called a speech. She spoke in Serbo-Croat—of which she had still no more than a tourist's knowledge—without any plan that I could recognize, and with no discernible emotion. The sentences, gauchely framed and extravagantly mispronounced, came like infants released from their first day at school, in straggling independence:

"You will not understand. You cannot understand. My brother is a soldier. Always. An officer. An officer has duties. One above all, to care for his soldiers. He lives for that. I say it is his duty, his master-duty, to waste never one life, one life of his men. That you will not understand— the duty of an officer, the responsibility."

Her alien voice, artless and unemphatic as it was, had won immediate attention: nobody was sleeping now. And as she continued, groping for words and idioms, leaving behind a trail of fractured sentences, she was accorded such patient hearing as a practised orator might have envied.

She had, as I began to see, some kind of argument to offer, starting from the ambush which the earliest witnesses had described. How, in the moment of alarm and violent fighting, in the poverty of light to which the witnesses had testified, could her brother's soldiers have seen and recognized as 'uniform' the slender insignia of the men who had fired on them? Naturally the one who escaped would have reported that the attackers were simply civilians—she knew, in fact, that he had told her brother so. Here, then, was a situation no commander in the world could tolerate—that civilians should set upon and kill his men with impunity. A lesson had to be taught, so sharply that it need not be repeated. In Pravnitzar the cost had been heavy, but the prices of war were always high. Without so stern a warning the contagion of disorder would have spread widely, demanding retaliation; the cost in lives would then have mounted to a sum beside which the loss in Pravnitzar would seem trivial. They would not understand—they who had never been in responsible positions—that relentless discipline was in the end a kind of mercy.

She got so far—I doubt if anyone had followed her reasoning—and then her tenacity with the foreign tongue gave out. She stopped. The audience waited courteously. At last she turned to me.

"Tell them," she said in her own language, "that I have been with Siegfried always, always since he was a little boy. Tell them we were not grand people, we hadn't much money. We decided he was to be a soldier—he and I, we decided that together, when we were only children. We thought it was better than getting rich and fine—to serve one's country, to give everything to that service—we thought that was the highest life for a man. That's what he has always been, a servant of his country. He has done nothing for himself, he has given himself—all his life—simply to his duty."

Those words I translated as faithfully as I could. When

I had done so she bowed to me, and also to Kastelej. Then she felt for her chair and sat down, again hiding her face.

I had the impression that at least some of the men were moved: perhaps her solitude had roused in them—if only for a moment—that chivalry which overrides all frontiers. It may have been a shock to them, as to me, when the clear, hard voice of a woman somewhere behind me was pitched into the silence:

"If she thinks the same as he does, then she's just as bad!"

At once another woman came alive, calling from the loft, "A woman was killed—Zivka was! This one ought to be!"

As if this were his signal, a man got up and pushed his way into the arena, where he stood directly opposite me: he was one I had not observed before, but whom I seemed to know, for I had met his kind in other spheres—a fellow with a womanish fatness about his body, his lickerish mouth set in a flabby jowl, the pale eyes both cowardly and impudent. I saw at once which way those eyes were moving—that the dried and sexless figure of Paula was no food for them.

His voice came like a spurt of bile: "That's his wife, isn't it, that one over there? What's *she* got to say?"

Kastelej, who did not seem perturbed by this incursion, might have given the man some pacific answer. But the high wind of my fury made me quicker than he.

"Frau Zempelmarck," I said incisively, "is not concerned in this business in any possible way!"

Franziska herself had half-risen. She hesitated and sat down again. The man's gaze lingered on her for a moment and then he turned his attention to me.

"Is that what you think! . . . Ljubo, let me have that letter."

There was a stir behind him, and a sheet of flimsy paper was passed to him through the crowd.

"This," he said at large, holding it up as if it were a winning lottery ticket, "was taken from a refuse box beside Zempelmarck's office at Usir. My friend Ljubo here, he found it. He was looking for other papers, but he thought this one interesting."

Giving neither me nor anyone else the time to interfere, he went to Franziska and held the paper before her face.

"Did you write this?"

I heard her whisper, "*Ja!*"

He returned and gave the paper to me. My instinct was to crush and throw it away, but there would have been no sense in that.

"Read it!" he demanded. "Read it aloud, and then give us a translation."

"I shall do nothing of the sort! This is a private letter."

He smiled. "Well then, I have a translation here in my pocket—it's quite reliable, it was done for me by a scholar at Agram."

It was time to appeal to the supine Kastelej. "Mr. President," I said, "I want to protest that this is quite out of order. This is a private letter, of no concern to anyone here. I have given this Court some service, and I think I have a right——"

He silenced me with a gently deprecating hand. "If the letter is quite innocent there can't be any harm in our hearing it . . . Yes, Dobuc, go on!"

Dobuc had scarcely waited for that permission. In a high voice which travestied and cheapened every sentence he read, "'In my thoughts I live with you all the time, in all the burdens and anxieties such a post must bring. How I wish I could truly share them! I think I understand what you mean when you write of the strain and danger the men live in, with hostile and resentful people all round them, and of the need for stringent measures to protect them. So long as the War lasts I suppose there must be such severity, and people must suffer hardship, and those in high positions such as yours must sometimes be the instruments of such suffering. I pray every day to God—who although we are of different faiths in your God and mine—that He will allow His will to overrule whatever duties may come to you.'"

"This letter is signed?" a man beside Kastelej asked.

Dobuc nodded. "It finishes, 'Your ever faithful and heart-loving wife, Franziska Zempelmarck'." He snapped his lips and turned dramatically to me.

"*Now* do you say this female isn't concerned?"

"*But certainly I do!* That letter's entirely in general terms, it expresses nothing at all but a wife's concern for her husband! It has nothing whatever to do with what this Court has been examining—the sheet with the date is missing—it was probably written long before the events in question. You know perfectly well——"

"In that case it would be quite an encouragement to Zempelmarck—don't you think—to know that the Will of God was helping him along with the shootings! With his wife kindly prodding from behind—'I live with you all the time, how I wish I could share in all your duties!'"

His was the kind of wit which registers with an overstrained and ignorant audience. Myself impotent and dumb with rage, I heard a crackle of schoolboy laughter, and then the hysterical voice of the woman who had interrupted before:

"Zivka was killed! *She* was a woman!"

And another: "Yes, Zivka was! Why not this tart? This one for Zivka!"

Once more I turned to Kastelej, but the fresh surge of excitement was already beyond his control. Finding my voice again, I shouted, "I tell you, Frau Zempelmarck had nothing to do with her husband's actions—she was hundreds of miles away! She didn't even know——"

"She helped him!" someone shouted back. "She tried to get him to Spain."

"She did not! She——"

"Who did, then? Who arranged all that?"

Still shaking with passion, I yelled the answer: "*I did!*"

For a few seconds that explosion abated the idiot clamour. I caught a voice which I recognized as that of Mica Fotez—"Dushan, you're not to interfere—what does he matter!" and then I saw Dushan himself pushing his way forward. Modest but determined, he stood just inside the arena and began a speech: "I wish to testify to the character of Dr. Reichenbach. I have come to know him well." But he got no further before the uproar started again. The patience of the assembly had been stretched too far, the cord had snapped: audience and witnesses became one band where every man was bellowing his opinion, the rasping voices of the women cut across the men's like fiddles out of tune, some calling wildly for Franziska's immolation, some for mine. In the space of inward calm which followed the crisis of my anger I witnessed this convulsion as if it were played before me slowly, its noises damped by some obstructions in my ears. I saw as in a narrow frame the face of Dobuc, damp and fatuous with triumph, the bored and fretful face of Siegfried, Julija's writhing countenance and the sly grimace of a youth who took the fracas as his chance to slip a hand inside a fat girl's blouse. Beyond, I scanned the wilted remnants of respectability—groups paralysed with nervous laughter, a goat-like man orating to the roof while his wife tugged at his coat-tails, a woman who simultaneously screamed for 'Justice' and pommelled the infant clinging to her knees. These simpletons, I thought, these children out of hand, why should I pay the least regard to them!

That spell of complacence was succeeded by one of sickening fear. Franziska had risen. She took a step or two away from her chair, so that she came into isolation, and there stood with her open hands raised to the height of her shoulders. I saw that she was speaking, but not a word was audible—she would have had to shout at the top of her voice to be heard above the turmoil—and soon, giving it up, she merely waited with the stilled face of Niobe for the noise to subside. This was the summit of rashness: I realized, feeling the crowd's fanatic mood, how she must look to them—the solitary figure planted before them as if in open provocation—and I knew that at any moment when a fresh wind blew on their anger it would blaze in physical violence. In a glance at Valyevitch I saw him idle and impassive, happy to let things take their course, while Kastelej, as if the disorder were nothing to do with him, was in deep discussion with his friends. Already on my feet, I started moving furtively along the edge of the arena, hoping to get within serviceable distance of where she stood, but the boys responsible for my behaviour were sharp enough to seize me from the rear and hold me with one arm twisted behind my back. Now, above the bedlam, someone was yelling with the persistent voice of mania, "Zivka! Zivka was killed! *She* killed her." Helpless, I thought, 'They will rush her now, I shall see them closing in and that will be all.'

It did not happen. Kastelej may have known his people better than I—known that the uprush of hysteria would exhaust itself in empty vociferation. Or perhaps it was Franziska herself who overruled them. For in those moments of intensified perception I came to recognize what soldiers have told me of the curious power that lies in purposed immobility. In that one face there was no excitement, neither anger nor visible fear. She made the rest seem smaller than their kind, reduced their bravery of cries and gestures to its fowl-yard scale, simply by standing calm and still.

Here was nothing that insensate rage could feed on: I felt it sinking as a storm blows itself out. When, at last, Kastelej turned and raised his hand, the final imprecations dribbled to silence as dirty water vanishes in the waste.

This I suppose was the meridian of Kastelej's functions,

but he did not make it appear so. He had been writing in a pocket-book, and now, to a distracted audience, he read a confused and pretentiously worded speech in the manner of a schoolboy rehearsing Xenophon:

"The arbiters appointed to consider this case have reached their conclusions. We are satisfied that the prisoner Zempelmarck, who has been given every opportunity to defend himself but has not done so, is responsible for the death of the twenty innocent civilians whose names have already been read out to you. Our decision is that he is to be executed by gunfire. The execution is to be in the Sheepcote Valley, on the 9th March next."

He paused, perhaps expecting some acclamation, but a sense of anticlimax prevailed. All that came, while I was delivering a toneless translation, was a charivari of female voices from somewhere behind him, with one that called in artless explanation, "It's Marija Primceva, she wants the lavatory." Against a ripple of laughter he hurried on:

"We have also decided that it is right according to universal justice that his wife Franziska Zempelmarck—who will return to her seat, please—should at that place and on that date be placed in a position to clearly witness the execution."

I heard a murmur starting, but it did not crystallize. Steeling myself to look towards Franziska, I said rapidly in German, "They have added a piece of senseless cruelty"— but I did not need to go on. She nodded, she had already understood.

And now came a clause which struck me as one of devious ingenuity:

"Regarding the part taken—on his own admission—by Reichenbach in assisting the attempted escape of Zempelmarck: we have decided in view of his service to this Court to deal leniently with his case. He will be made responsible for Zempelmarck's health up to the date of the execution. If on that date Zempelmarck is unable to stand at the place of execution, Reichenbach will be required to support him there."

With that—which I saw no reason to translate—I supposed he had finished. I caught sight of Babitch making jocose signals to me as he tossed in ribald laughter. But there was still a tailpiece. Looking up, and then re-setting his spectacles, Kastelej turned a page and read three more sentences:

"Since the woman Paula Zempelmarck has addressed the Court in a straightforward manner, we have decided that no action is to be taken against her. She is to be released at a convenient opportunity. That is all."

I doubt if, at the time, the general audience understood the whole of that oddly conceived and stilted announcement. At least some of them, I believe, would have found the total award too slender for their requirement.

But if their weariness of mind and body were equal to my own they were incapable of protesting. Most likely the very dullness of Kastelej's voice had a soporific effect which he had intended; and many can scarcely have been less thankful than I was to be done with the proceedings. The fire in the braziers had died, the air was at once cold and stale. Stiff and a little stupefied, people gathered their belongings, the little cans of milk, the drowsy children. As modestly as they had entered hours before the family groups collected, men and women holding each other's arms for steadiness, and joined the stream moving towards the doors.

8

I tried once more to get near Franziska, but the crowd in the doorway prevented this. I did for a few seconds find myself close to Paula, and seized the chance to whisper (without hypocrisy), "You spoke very well." At first I

306

thought she had not heard me, but then she half-turned her head and mumbled, "I don't know why I spoke at all. There was nothing—after what we saw—there was nothing for anyone to say."

Those words, with the frozen anguish of her eyes that attended them have continued to haunt me: they were the last I heard her speak. A few hours afterwards she got hold of a pistol belonging to one of Siegfried's gaolers, took it hidden in her clothes to an outside closet and there shot herself through the heart. She had not in the meantime spoken either to Siegfried or to Franziska, although there was nothing to prevent her. I do not like thinking of the loneliness in which she spent those final hours.

I did not hear this news at once, since I spent a few more days (lying sick with something akin to a mild encephalitis) in Dushan's house—to which, after the trial, he himself with a touching gentleness conducted me.

Chapter 12

I

IN A COPY of the *Εἰδύλλια* which Dushan gave me I have pencilled: 'To tile yard, February 25. Snow lying.'

Yes, the yard was covered with snow when I first saw it—I remember it as an enclosure not often reached by the sun. I also remember a mis-shapen juniper like a crescent moon, a lovely thing which grew in insolent solitude among the drying racks and all the litter. The rest of that scene is blurred: I have kept the dank, faintly putrescent smell of it but nothing of its colour. There were buildings on three sides, on the fourth a wall of rock. In one wing was living a Muslim family of innumerable children, creatures with dark skins and huge, soft eyes who seemed to thrive with a minimum of food and clothing. The wing opposite, then derelict, must have been the former kiln house. The block between, a long, shallow, timber and adobe building, was Siegfried's prison.

I call it that, and there was something prison-like in the blind wall it showed to the lane. But if there were locks on the doors I don't believe they were ever used, and though there was always at least one armed guard about the place I could not think of those men as gaolers. They belonged, I should say, to Valyevitch's capricious sense of correctness. The position of the building was sufficient safeguard: it was three or four miles from Pravnitzar, in a narrow *doline* accessible only by one villainous road.

I was partly glad, when I arrived, to find Johannes with his mother in the centre room.

He was sitting uncomfortably on one of the lower bunks, using a piece of paper to clean her shoes. The weeks since I had last seen him had advanced the unnatural maturity of his expression; he seemed to me now to have an old man's look, querulous and foxy; and plainly he was far from well. His manners, however, had not altered. As soon as he saw who I was—the light was poor—he rose and made his little bow.

"Good afternoon, sir! How do you do!"

Franziska, seated at a makeshift table, had scarcely looked up from her sewing; and she made several stitches more before she bit the thread and put the work down. She did then turn a little and extend her hands to me.

"Johannes has had a cold," she said. "He's still not very grand."

I said, "I must see if there's anything I can do about that," and she answered vaguely, "Yes, Doctor, yes, I shall be grateful if you will."

For a moment or two she was still troubled, looking instinctively for a chair to offer me: her mind seemed to be working like that of heavy sleepers when they wake. When I had solved the immediate problem by sitting on the bench that stood against the outer wall, she said,

"But you—we heard you were ill. You're better now?"

"Yes, thank you—except that my legs have rather forgotten their job."

She nodded gravely, and then called out, "Cvito!" At once a man came in from the next room—it was the one-legged Partisan who had given evidence at the trial. "Cvito," she said, pronouncing the foreign syllables with a gentle pedantry, "Dr. Reichenbach has come, and he looks so cold. I wonder if you would be so very kind as to make a hot drink for him."

"But certainly! A pleasure! Straight away!"

"I'm afraid," she said when he had gone, "that we haven't a great deal of comfort to offer you here. But we're improving things all the time—Johannes has been wonderful—that bench you're sitting on, it was all in pieces when we came. I've sent a message to Valyevitch that we must have another blanket—I think it will come today—he's fairly good about those things. And Hafsa—that's the woman living over there—she's fabulously kind, she lends me all sorts of odds and ends. I think you'd better have the top one of those bunks—it's rather too much for Captain Babitch to climb up there. Johannes and I have this one."

The two-tiered bunks were a relic of German occupation —at some time a Section had been quartered here, and I read later the hard-wrought verses which homesick soldiers had written on the walls. The barrack flavour remained. But the room was tidy and spotless, there were strips of sacking on the earthen floor and a piece of patterned fabric on the table. On a shelf between the bunks a sprig from the juniper had been placed with signal artistry.

"Johannes, I wonder if you'll be able to make some dominoes. I'm sure Dr. Reichenbach would have some games . . . What we lack, Johannes and I, is something to fill the evenings."

She had returned to her sewing, and so, as I drank the sage tea which Cvito brought me, I was able to watch her face without making her uneasy. It had thinned, as if from a contraction of its internal structure, and there were reflex movements about the eyes which alone would have made me anxious. But a stranger, I believe, would have seen nothing beyond the grace of her hospitality.

"Be a dear, Johannes, and stuff some paper under the door—the way you did this morning. It makes it so much warmer . . . Johannes and I want to make you as comfortable as we can. Tell me—the people you've been with, have they looked after you properly? The girl who came with a message—the rather plain one—I liked her, she spoke so nicely about you . . . There isn't much food today but Gligoric has promised to get us something for Sunday. Then we'll have a feast to celebrate your arrival—I'll cook myself, Cvito's not much use at cooking and he only has an old field cooker to work on. Or perhaps Johannes will do it, he's becoming quite a cook, aren't you, darling: I don't think Gligoric will let us down, though he's terribly stupid. He reminds me of a man Papa had once to do the pigs and poultry—Kuhan—you remember him, Johannes? Papa used to say he had a chicken face when he went to feed the hens, and then a pig face when he reached the sties. But of course he was a dear. I wonder . . . Oh, about washing—we take turns to use the kitchen—that's the room on this side. There's a tank there, Johannes will get you water when you want it, and Gligoric or someone empties it afterwards. I'm afraid it's all a little primitive . . . Do tell Johannes and me about the people you've been with."

I had not thrown off my shyness—I was like a youth in enormous boots whom an elegant hostess receives in her drawing-room. But I spoke as she bade me of Dushan and of Riko—it was luxury to be using my own language again—and while Johannes nodded with unfaltering courtesy she smiled and even laughed as my voice invited. Encouraged, I talked with growing assurance, as men do when a woman seems to be attending. In reality I doubt if she listened to one sentence; but no one else would have guessed that there was anything except my chatter to engage her mind.

Cvito returned, ostensibly to take away my cup, and stood beside me for a time, placidly watching Franziska's busy fingers while he pulled at his pipe.

"You think the ladyship looks well?" he covertly inquired of me. "Not too bad?" He smiled at her shyly.

"It will be better for you now, having someone else about, of your own kind!"

"Why, yes, Cvito!" She turned again to me and said easily, "When you feel rested, Doctor, I expect Babitch would like to discuss things with you. You go through that door, and there's another door opposite—you'll find him with Siegfried in there. Oh, and some time you must talk to Cvito, if you will be so kind. I'm so slow with his language. He's such a long way from where he lives, it's terribly dull for him here."

3

I passed through a small compartment full of lumber to the farther room as she had directed me. There, seated at a table opposite the window, his head supported on the back of his wrist, his face upturned towards the roof, Babitch was noisily asleep. His upper denture had fallen loose, to leave a huge orifice between it and the gum, and a burnt-out cigarette adhering to his lower lip moved sensitively in time with his breathing. From this display it was not hard to turn to the horsehair couch where Siegfried, reclining with his feet on the ground, was pretending to read an ancient newspaper.

For a second or two he stared at me presbyopically, then he said,

"Ah, yes, Reichenbach, I wanted to see you."

I said conventionally, "I'm sorry I've been so long in coming. How are you?"

"Oh, very well. Now look, this matter of a uniform, I want you to get moving about that. That fellow, of course"—he threw a look at Babitch—"is perfectly useless. And the women can never grasp the importance of these things."

"A uniform?"

"Yes, I've sent word to that mountebank—what's his name? Valyevitch—I've told him that he's got to find me one. But I had to send the message through Gligoric, and he's mentally deficient. I can't do anything myself, they won't let me leave this room except for my walking practice. I shall want you—I mean, I shall be greatly obliged—if you will follow it up and get things moving."

"But I don't quite understand."

"Listen!" he said, mastering some impatience. "This business of a firing party, it's all totally irregular—that comic opera we went through, and all the rest of it—you realize that, of course, as well as I do. But there it is, one has to accept the physical facts of a situation. The point is that if I've got to be shot by these buffoons I insist on being shot as a soldier. It's not just a question of my own dignity, it's something due to my nation. You, Reichenbach, I know your political position is a long way from mine—I'm really quite an intelligent person, whatever opinion you may have formed of me. But I expect you to agree with me on this—it's a matter of universal decency. Whatever the circumstances, a soldier has an absolute right to die in uniform—you must see that. It's not only his privilege, it's his last patriotic duty. Without a uniform there's no practical point in my being shot at all."

I made some temporizing reply, and then I said soberly, "But the first thing, as far as I'm concerned, is to have you fit to put a uniform on. It's time I made a fresh examination, don't you think?"

"Examination? Oh, of my legs, yes. The rest of me is all right. The legs are pretty good too. Of course that donkey's done nothing for them, but I make him walk me twice a day—we go up and down that road outside. I can do a bit by myself—look, I'll show you."

Refusing my help, he got on to his feet and made four or five steps across the room, much as a child does when walking for the first time. He reached the farther wall—this alone saved him from falling; rested, turned and walked back, finally crumpling on the sofa.

"Not bad?" he said.

"No, not bad. Let me have a look now."

I got him comfortable and took off his trousers. What I found was even more interesting than I expected—the tone of the flesh was vastly improved, the reflexes showed me at once that the vastus and semitendinosus muscles had recovered activity to an extent I should not have believed possible. I thought with fresh respect of my colleague Oscar Cavour, the unpretentious, dedicated physiologist whose teaching I had followed; but in this there was a private and absurd vanity—so little manipulation could not have achieved so much. From a source which only such a man as Cavour himself could have identified some fresh anabolic agency had been at work: for my own part I could only place that source in the will of the patient himself—and where was the physical sustentation of 'will' in such a body as this?

"Well?" he presently demanded.

I said, "There's a remarkable improvement in muscular capacity. You're acquiring quite a workable pair of legs. What I want to see now is whether the rest of your body is fit for them."

"Oh, damn the rest of my body! It's only got a fortnight to last me."

"That's irrelevant," I said quickly, "as long as you're my patient."

"What? Who's this?" Babitch suddenly demanded. He had roused himself with a snore of prodigious resonance; he came to stand beside me, fully awake and evidently in a season of exceptional lucidity. "Why, it's Reichenbach! Good day to you, my ancient friend, may all the heavenly powers wait upon your genius! What do you think of our showpiece?"

I told him that I was starting an examination. "I thought I wouldn't disturb you, as you were resting——"

"My dear sir, no apologies! Babitch is the last man on earth to indulge himself in puerile jealousies. Continue, *cher collègue,* continue! Regard me as your pupil, or as a fly crawling on the wall, whichever you please."

"Can't you get rid of this fool?" Siegfried asked.

I said, covering the legs again, "I think he only wants to be helpful."

I could indeed have done without Babitch's assistance, for it was not easy, when I had been so long without practice, to achieve the concentration needed for perceptive diagnosis. In turning over the body I had noticed immediately a considerable loss of weight. For this the general appearance and the recent history had of course prepared me: such loss could well have resulted from malnutrition alone, for it was unlikely that since I had last examined him the patient had had enough to eat, let alone food suitable in content and preparation; moreover, he admitted that he regularly left untouched a good deal of what was provided. What puzzled me was the strength of his general condition. As far as I could tell—using such elementary clinical tools as Babitch had collected—the heart was functioning satisfactorily and the lungs working better than, in the circumstances, they had any right to do. (Could this be a benefit derived from altitude—even where every other condition of life was deleterious?) To superficial tests the general nervous system responded well; and I was satisfied— mainly from the patient's intelligent answers to my questions —that the digestive system was also in fair order. He was sleeping, he told me, reasonably well, and Babitch confirmed that there was no sweating at night. These findings—in so far as they had any validity without pathological corroboration—were the opposite to what I had expected in a subject who, in succession to severe physical hardship, was now as one supposed under acute mental strain. And in fact I did not trust them at all. A certain opacity in the appearance of the eyes, a small number of minute but tactually

315

observable variations in reflex behaviour, these and other diagnostics persuaded me that here was a body which, as it were, pretended to be well—as some plants in an alien climate will appear to flourish and then incontinently wither. I thought, 'If I could have this man in my own surgery for forty-eight hours! If I had a radiographer, and Stan O'Connell, only a block away! . . .'

"I've seen carcasses in worse shape than this one," Babitch observed complacently.

I replied, "Yes, the general condition appears to me remarkable."

At this he started laughing. "And so it had better be, from your point of view! I shouldn't fancy the job myself, propping him up for a firing party. I must say, I thought it rather a witty idea of Kastelej's."

In an undertone I sharply reminded him that the patient might understand at least a word or two of what he was saying. It made no difference.

"It's curious," he continued, "I've never known a firing party yet that didn't perform like a gaggle of recruits. You get first-class marksmen, not at all squeamish, fellows who'd normally bring a man down at 500 metres, nine shots out of ten—"

"Yes, but we needn't discuss that now."

"What is he babbling about?" Siegfried asked.

"He's recollecting old campaigns."

"Can't he recollect them somewhere else!"

"Dr. Babitch," I said, "I think we ought to let the patient rest a little now." But he was too deep in the pleasures of imagination to hear me.

"Of course, if it's rifles," he persisted, "you stand just a chance. You can tip each man to aim off a fraction on the blind side. Only, that old rabbi talked about gunfire. These civilians, they never get their terms right, but if he meant M.G.s—well, I think you and I had better get this bastard standing straight up on his own tootsies."

I said angrily, "Dr. Babitch, I do not wish to discuss that question!"

"Not? Well, I see your point of view. You and your relations have Babitch's most respectful sympathy—I can guess who's doing the sweating at night!"

I had heard a knock at the door and I turned to see Franziska shyly standing there.

"I just wondered," she said, "if there's anything you want —anything I could get."

"Thank you—at the moment, nothing," I told her. "I'm going to see if Cvito can get hold of some medicine for me—there are one or two quite simple things which I think your husband would find refreshing. They might be available in the village."

"Yes," she answered, "Cvito will do that if he can."

She had come to stand beside me, quietly pushing Babitch out of her way. She took one of Siegfried's hands in hers, regarding it intently, as if it were some offered gift that she had to refuse because of its costliness.

"You think he is—is well?" she asked me.

"Yes. Yes, there's been a great improvement."

"He told you he's been walking?"

"Yes. Yes, he showed me. Yes, it's a wonderful effort."

Siegfried was watching her with an expression of strained forbearance. His look was one I have seen in the children of too affectionate parents; and some novelty in the fall of light on his features brought to my mind the thought, 'This is just Johannes with a few years added.' He said,

"I've been talking to the doctor here about the uniform. I've asked him to get on to Valyevitch—a fellow like that will never get moving unless someone's prodding him. I don't suppose Valyevitch realizes that it will have to be practically re-made when it comes—it's not in the least likely to fit me."

Franziska said, "I shall start work the moment we get it. It won't take me so very long."

317

"Well, thank you, but I think I'd rather Paula tackled it."

"But Paula isn't here now."

"What? Oh yes, you told me. That's a nuisance. Paula always had a flair for this sort of thing."

4

It was not an establishment which gave much opportunity for private conversation. Not until late that evening, when we were together in the 'kitchen', did I have a few words with Franziska alone. She asked me then what I really thought of Siegfried's physical condition, and I repeated that it seemed to me surprisingly good.

"Of course," I said, "I have none of the apparatus I need for a proper examination—I've nothing much beyond superficial evidence to go on. The only reason why that may tell me more than it tells you is that I've seen a great number of patients with many different illnesses."

"But what does it tell you?"

I answered, with some deliberation, "Well, if we were free agents—I mean, if I could get him at once into a first-class hospital—it might be possible even now to prolong his life for several years. But I'm afraid that's rather an academic postulate."

She nodded. "I know. And since we can't do that, how long—if things were normal, I mean—how long would you expect him to live?"

I said, "You're asking me a question which no doctor would answer. Not *as* a doctor—not as a scientist."

"But you have a private opinion? Wouldn't you trust me with that?"

"I should trust you with anything. I think if he were allowed to live, just as he's living now, he might last for as much as six months. I doubt if it would be longer. But then I think it's just as likely that he may die in a few days, or even hours. It may be only specialized intuition, but I feel quite certain there's a focus of sepsis in the lung. Not active at present—dormant. But it will be active, if I'm right. That might happen very quickly—it's as if the bacteria were a contained army which may suddenly break out and carry everything in a furious attack. I'm speaking in very unscientific terms, but perhaps you see what I mean?"

"Yes, I see perfectly. Thank you."

At that point someone—probably the industrious Cvito—interrupted us, and I think it was not until two nights later that we were alone again. By then I had secured some of the drugs I wanted and had begun a simple course of treatment. This happened to coincide with a fresh improvement in Siegfried's appearance—he had more colour, his appetite was increasing—and she spoke to me (as the wives of patients will) as if I had performed some feat of extraordinary skill:

"It's wonderful—he says he walked ten steps this afternoon, entirely alone. Oh, if only you'd been with us all the time he might be almost well now!"

This show of total blindness to the situation took me so much by surprise that I wondered for a moment if the truth had outstripped her understanding. I said unguardedly,

"And would that have been any use!"

She made no answer, and in a surge of candour I went on,

"Franziska, I must tell you, I have never, never in my life had a case which sickened me like this. All my working life I've been using what knowledge I have to make people well, to fit them as far as God will allow for years of living. That makes sense to me. To get a man fit for dying—it's no use, I loathe the business, whether he ought to die or not. I feel all the time it's a kind of humbug, to work with one's hands and not one's heart."

"You mean," she said, with a quietness which made my

excitement crude and foolish, "you'd rather give the work back to Babitch, for the few days that are left?"

"Does it make any difference?"

"Well, yes. Compared with you, Babitch isn't a doctor at all. You know that even better than I do. From what you've told me, Siegfried might have a bad turn at any moment. If there was no one but Babitch to deal with it, wouldn't he be sure to die?"

I answered, "Yes. Or at least it would be very likely."

This was when I realized that further evasion was only cowardly. But I still found it hard to open my mind to hers, which seemed so little in tune. Lamely, with many hesitations, I said, "No, I shouldn't hand him over to Babitch again, not in any circumstances. Even if he were to die I'd rather he was in my hands, not Babitch's. I didn't mean that I shan't do everything I can. I have to, it's what my profession demands. But suppose he did die—soon, in the next few days—isn't that the best thing that could happen?"

"You mean, for him?"

"For you, for all of us. But yes, for him."

She shook her head. "No." And then she said, "I can't explain."

I thought there was more that she wanted to say, but I could find no means to help her: I could only give her time by taking out the tank we used for washing utensils to empty it in the gully on the other side of the road. When I returned she was standing exactly as I had left her, leaning against the wall, and she spoke again—a little huskily—as if there had been no interruption:

"You see, Eugen, he wants to die the way those people decided. He wants to wear a uniform, to go out by himself and stand in front of them. I'm not sure why. It may be because of something I said—I keep hoping it's that. But you can't tell, he's changed rather—well, you've seen— there aren't even any signposts now. I only know that he's made up his mind."

To that I could have found some answer if we had been strangers—I was not without experience in talking of invalids to their friends. But as it was, the tumult in my mind would not be reduced to discipline—no words would come. I had to let another day go by.

5

That was the one in which the uniform arrived. It was characteristic of Valyevitch that he had taken trouble in this matter—somewhere he had procured an outfit which nearly fitted, and was in fair condition.

'He wants to wear a uniform': that had been an under-statement—a boy getting his first bicycle could not have been more exalted than Siegfried when it came. But this spell of sunshine was followed by cloud. The thing had belonged to a lieutenant of Engineers, the corps markings and badges of rank would all have to be changed. Then there were stains on the sleeves and lapels: these must at all costs be removed. And the pockets needed darning. He tried on the tunic and found it badly made—wartime work, he supposed, from some factory at München. The shoulders at any rate would have to be taken to pieces, some padding might be needed, the buttons must be moved. Paula—where was Paula? . . . Very well then, Franziska must do the best she could.

Before midday and again in the afternoon he had his customary walking practice, but he would not follow the rest of his routine. On previous days Cvito and I had taken turns to play chess with him, using a board and pieces which Johannes had made with paper and card. On that afternoon, when I had settled him comfortably after his walk, I set out the board as usual, but he refused to attend to the game.

"If Valyevitch won't get the right badges," he said, "then Franziska will have to make them up somehow—

321

some sort of imitation. It's all wrong, but I suppose I may as well put up with it, since all Europe's run by lunatics now. They mustn't look sloppy, that's the vital thing. I suppose the spectators will be some distance away. Quite likely they won't notice anything wrong."

Thereafter, at every call I paid on him, he came at once to the same subject. Even when I put a thermometer in his mouth he took it out almost immediately.

"Listen, Reichenbach, I'm depending on you to keep an eye on this uniform. Women simply don't understand these things. It's very important that there should be plenty of room at the armpits. I intend to stand at the salute. For an officer, I'm quite certain that is the correct thing. And you see what I mean, it would just look farcical if the tunic tore under my arm ..."

6

When I left him that night—Cvito having arrived to sleep beside him, in accordance with standing orders—I found Franziska in the centre room working on the tunic. There we could not talk confidentially, for Johannes, although in bed, might not be fast asleep; and in the kitchen Babitch was noisily gossiping with Gligoric. I told her that she was overtaxing her eyes, and needed fresh air. Would she take a short walk with me?

"But I don't think it's allowed," she said.

I went and opened the kitchen door. "Gligoric, Frau Zempelmarck and I are going out for a few minutes. That's all right?"

"What?" He was faintly vexed at being interrupted in a splendid argument. "I suppose so. Not too long."

I shut the door again. "We have the Imperial Warranty," I said, and put her into her outdoor coat.

Leaving the yard, we turned uphill. The road, with a

surface of fissured rock, slimy from the thaw, gave no easy walking, but there was light enough from the sky to reduce its dangers. The air, grown warmer in the last two days, was still, and we could move without discomfort as slowly as we pleased.

It was she who broke our silence, while I was still trying to frame what I wanted to say. "There's something I didn't understand at the trial," she began, "something that old man said. It was about you, and you didn't translate it. I thought he said that you had got to stand beside Siegfried, holding him. But that isn't possible—that can't have been right?"

This was a question I had hoped to keep away from.

"That was more or less what he said," I told her, 'but only if Siegfried couldn't stand by himself. It was just meant to warn me that I must do my job as a doctor properly."

"But if you had to stand with him you'd be killed as well!"

"Not certainly. Not unless someone decided I should be—and really I don't think anyone attaches that much importance to me."

"But Eugen, they can't have meant anything so savage as that—so utterly senseless!"

"The people were in a savage mood," I said, "—well, you understand that. They wanted something extra, something more than just a single execution. Kastelej and his friends had to pretend to give them that something. I'm inclined to think they did it rather shrewdly. And one has to accept these things."

This left us in a fresh silence, and before she could speak again I went on, keeping my voice as well controlled as I could:

"What I don't accept—what I think is the uttermost barbarity—is the order that you should witness it. At the time, I couldn't make any protest—it could easily have led to something worse. But I'm *going* to protest. I've told

Gligoric that I want an interview with Valyevitch. I think he'll see me. Up to a point he and I understand each other. I shall reason with him, and if that doesn't work I'm well enough now to fight him on it. I shall——"

"No!" she said.

"But——"

"Eugen, I want you to understand—you, if no one else. It's my part, the looking on. I'm not going to avoid it."

I had, just then, the common sensation of living through a moment for the second time. And though I knew immediately what had provoked the illusion—the darkness, the rough road, a note in her voice that was rare and private —the hold it took on me persisted. 'Since then,' I thought, 'since the night when she came to guide me down the lane at Vischak, the essence of both our lives has been in one small chamber. The rest, the separations, the accidents of mundane existence, have been insubstantial. What we discovered then has not been lost, it belongs to infinite reality.'

"They may be wrong," she said, "—they're only human —wanting to do back to him what he did. God's got to judge that, I can't—I only see it as they do. I know it has got to happen. It's a debt to be paid, there isn't another way of paying it. Nothing else will make those people start forgetting what they suffered."

"A debt to be paid, yes," I said. "But it's his, it's Siegfried's."

"It's mine as well."

"Because we are all responsible, whoever suffers?"

"No. Because Siegfried is my responsibility."

"You were far away from him when it happened."

"I was still his wife. The failure must have been partly mine—that he was totally inhuman."

No, perhaps I did not understand; not with my reason. As she went on speaking—slowly, searching for words to reflect however faintly the half-lights of her feeling—it was my heart that travelled with her, not my mind. I took as truth from her what lay outside my understanding.

"It will make it different for him, to have me watching. It's like with a child—in a way he has never grown further than boyhood—children do things better than themselves when they know you're watching them. Without me there he would only see himself as a victim. If I stand and watch he'll feel he's making a retribution."

"But does that matter, in the end?"

"In the end, yes—I think so. The way we die, it's surely something God notices."

"But to them—the others who'll be watching?"

"It's enough," she said patiently, "if it only matters for him."

We turned to go back; and soon she spoke again:

"Those people, the people who will be watching, I want them to see me there. I want them to know that I'm paying the debt as well, in a little way. After that—not until then—after that I can talk to them. You'll have to help me—I don't speak well enough in their language—you'll have to interpret for me. I don't know what I shall say. At least I can tell them I feel with them. They'll know it's true, then—they'll have seen me going through what they had to."

"You think, *liebe* Franziska, that will do some good to them?"

"It will start the healing. Later on there will be more for me to do. When I've been home, when I've got Johannes settled—perhaps earned some money—I shall come here again. There's nothing I can give them back. But I can do things for them; things, perhaps, for their children."

"Then," I said, "I shall come back as well."

"But it's not a place for you! With your knowledge, your gifts, you need to live and work in a large place."

I said, "This will be large enough."

I do not know if that turned at all the direction of her

thoughts. I do not think so. She had taken my arm for support, so that we walked together now almost as one body; she had no need to withdraw her mind from where it ranged and attend to me as to a separate person. As we were nearing home she said,

"All I long for now is to have it over. Not just because I'm so cowardly—I've been through it so many times already, in my mind, that it can't be harder to bear when it actually comes. It's because I want to feel that Siegfried and I have paid them all we can of what we owe. I want it to be over for them as well. Dear Eugen, you understand what I feel? For them it will be a kind of release, the only kind that's possible for them."

7

In the image of that time which has become a part of my being, the presence of Johannes is insistant, like that of the dwarfs in *Las Meninas*. It was perhaps a valuable presence. The order we conformed to—the routine of meals, a resolute generality and a pretended cheerfulness in conversation—were all for his benefit. Such discipline I think was good for us, if the results were small. Johannes was not a child who smiled and chattered, probably he would always have preferred to be alone; but like kindly folk exposed to amateur theatricals he accepted patiently our efforts to make a natural life for him.

For some time I was not sure if he really knew what was to happen; but that doubt was removed one morning when he and I, playing Wernicke's Patience, were alone in the centre room. Some question came up about a rule of the game and I asked him to explain it. He did so—rather with the benevolence one shows to the feeble-minded—and added, "At least, that's how my grandfather used to play."

I said without reflection, "I wonder how your grand-father's getting on."

"There's no way of knowing," he answered, in a voice as casual as mine. "But after they've shot my father I suppose they will let us go back and live with him."

That cool remark surprised me into what I now recognize as a piece of crass stupidity. I had long been anxious, chiefly for Franziska's sake, to talk to this innately lonely child as—in my imagination—a decent father would. Seizing what seemed to be my opportunity, I said, with the smile of friendship,

"You know, Johannes, I think it's tough for you. Before you're anything like grown-up you're going through the sort of thing that grown men don't go through easily. I mean, losing your father—well, I know what it was like to lose mine. But you're going to be all right—I'm certain of that—because you've got your father's bravery. As you know, he's not frightened of anything, and you won't be. I'm terribly glad of that, because, you see, it's going to make all the difference to your mother. You're going to be still more important to her than you are now. That's the main thing you've got to think of, don't you agree! Making everything as easy for her as you can."

I was trying cautiously to draw his eyes to mine, but they were intent upon his cards—he appeared to be working out his further course of play. This was natural: I had been a fool to suppose that it is a simple matter to penetrate the reserves of children.

"You know," I continued, with dwindling confidence, "that you have me as a friend. I'll do everything I can to help you."

"That is kind," he answered gravely; and added with a childish simplicity, "But I shall be living with my mother, as you say. At Vischak, I expect."

"Yes, I expect so."

"And later on my mother means to come back here. I

suppose I shall be grown up the... I shall come back with her."

"You like that idea?"

"Yes, in some ways. Will you tell me, please—do you think Mr. Valyevitch will still be alive then?"

I told him it was probable. "Why, Johannes?"

For just a moment the muscles of his face tautened, so that no childish contour remained.

"When I'm grown up," he said, "I'm going to kill him. That's decided . . . It's your turn, sir, please—I've put the Four of Diamonds against your Five and I've taken the Seven of Spades from the middle row."

Such was my cowardice that I did not try, at the time, to engage in any more confidential talk with him.

8

Yes, we all took some trouble—even Babitch, in transitory moods—to ease Johannes's state. But none of us was over-leisured. The object of our corporate existence was more demanding than Johannes.

I stayed once in a house in Gratz where a wedding was imminent, the daughter of my hosts the bride. There the news of all the world was insignificant: between breakfast and bedtime the household fretted over laggard dress-makers and wilful catering firms, history turned on whether some baroness had mislaid the invitation. Capriciously, when Siegfried's voice sounded from the farther room, as it did in every hour, I found that time returning . . . The uniform was never right. Could not Franziska see for herself that the left sleeve had to be lengthened, now that the shoulder had been altered? If that was all Cvito could do about the wine stains, then the lapel must be reversed. And now the boots Gligoric had got for him were a source of irritation. The heels would have to be made up—as they were, they made it impossible to stand correctly at attention. After that they must be stripped to the bare leather and the polish built up again.

To me he looked for more than medical attendance— indeed, his physical weakness seemed to occupy his mind scarcely at all. I was of service to him mainly as a man who spoke his own language; for, increasingly, his anxieties were of a legal nature.

"I've been trying to get some sense out of Cvito," he would say, with a sidelong questioning look at my face, "—his German's hopeless, it runs to about twelve words, I can't make out a tenth of what he's trying to say. It's a pity. This business about what they call the Komitadzi uniform, I find that interesting. Cvito seems to be quite certain they were wearing their caps and things at the time."

"Well, yes, I believe they were."

"But the question remains whether that was sufficient to give them military status. Personally I doubt it. But then it's a matter for lawyers. You can't expect an officer on active service to spend his whole time buried in legal text-books. And he can't cart a staff of lawyers about with him either."

"No, I suppose not."

"You don't think there's anyone in this district I could get hold of, some fellow with a reasonable knowledge of German who studies international questions of that sort? The matter of a fee could be arranged somehow."

"I'm afraid there's not likely to be anyone of that kind nearer than Agram."

"Well, that could be arranged, surely! In the meantime I'm going to make a memorandum setting out my own views. I've got it fairly well planned, only you'll have to do the actual writing—I can't sit up to write a great deal, it gets me coughing. Tonight, you might come along tonight, when it's quiet. Gligoric won't mind, I can always settle him. I can't concentrate in the daytime, with people barging in and out all the time. We'll get that shaped out, and then I shall leave it with you. It ought really to go before an international committee of jurists. You may be able to arrange that. I mean, after the execution."

An hour later we would go over the same ground again. He was a tired man. The walking practice, which he extended slightly each day, was really too much for him. But on this he would listen to no protest or argument. The boots were at fault: when that idiot Gligoric had got the heels right he would have no trouble at all.

Once, with a look that was strangely compounded of shrewdness and confusion, he said,

"I don't really know what's happened to Paula— Franziska doesn't seem to, either. I miss Paula—she's very clear-headed, I should have valued her opinion on all these questions."

"But your wife's opinion," I said, "is one that I myself should always value."

He did not answer this directly. But he said a few moments later, "Franziska seems to think she's got to watch this business—she thinks these village people want to have her there. Does that make any sense to you?" And before I could reply he continued, "I should have thought it would be a strain for her—someone who's never seen that sort of thing."

"I think she would face anything," I said, "that she felt to be a matter of obligation."

"What—obligation to me?"

"Yes. But also to the people of Pravnitzar."

"But that's what she was talking about last night," he said with a note of exasperation," her obligations to those people—hers and mine. It's a curious notion of hers, it strikes me as sentimental. I never understand the way women think of things."

"Don't you think that women are often more right than we are?"

"I shouldn't have thought so," he answered sombrely. "However, I should like everything to be as my wife wishes—I have always respected her sincerity. No doubt you can see to that, when the time comes. Myself, of course, I shall have no say in the arrangements. But I want things to be done in the way Franziska considers right."

9

It fills a great part of my recollection of those days, that voice of Siegfried's: stringent, often querulous, occasionally sounding with an unexpected note of self-distrust.

It was the largest element in a ragged pattern which at the time had curiously the feel of permanence. One woke each morning to a nauseous odour from the drip-stove and to the sough of Babitch's snoring, one shaved with icy water and got into chilly clothes (nothing in that place was ever dry), all day one felt a little hungry. To the vacancies in living— no letters, no prospect of a caller, scarcely anything to read —one grew totally accustomed, accepting in their place the lumbering presence of Gligoric, the incessant squawls and shouting of the Hafsa children; and since that complex of sensation seemed to have continued not for days but for half a lifetime it was natural to feel that it would last for ever. The purpose of our husbandry was soon to be extinguished: that we knew but could not wholly realize. For myself, I was used to having death as a close attendant on my offices, but as one to be as long as possible resisted: the duty laid upon me now—of working to a limit in time, preparing God's creature only for man's destruction—was so foreign to my instinct that my mind refused to take it in.

Was it only in me, this illusion of permanence? Did the other men continually recognize themselves as journeymen drovers to be paid off at the shambles? I think that in truth we shared the sense of a settled life, depending not on

Siegfried as its centre but on Franziska as its circumference. From her we heard no word, saw no expression, to suggest that we were merely in transit. Beside the routine of housewifery she continually improved a little the material framework of our existence, devising a new shelf or a patchwork curtain, making small adjustments to our time-table, imposing even on Babitch some rudiments of orderly living. To Siegfried she gave a greater part of her day than any of us: one had said that it was no strain to her to be with him. Yet she never allowed Johannes to feel neglected; and between the long spells of work on the uniform, the arduous washing of shirts and stockings, she would find some time for little jokes with Cvito, for admiring the photographs of many obese children which Gligoric would produce for her again and again. The weather improved; once at the midday meal a little sunshine found its way into the centre room. She made us move the table then, to get the sun on our faces.

"Let's stay here for a little while. Cvito, would you make a cigarette for the Doctor, a small one? Let's sit for a while and enjoy the sun."

That was her outward aspect, and it was not, I believe, simply a performance: such ministry was in her nature. But when her face was still—when she seemed to be engrossed in some handiwork and was oblivious of my presence— I had some perception of what the vigil was costing her in self-command. "Surely," she had said, in one of our fleeting times together, "it's only pagans who look on death as something vastly important. To us, us who believe, it cannot so much matter." But human instinct will not treat death so cavalierly. I knew that very early each morning and at intervals throughout the day she was engaged in agonized devotion, that she steadily prepared herself for an ordeal which must have seemed to her like an approaching wall of flame. In this I was of little use to her. She filled my own poor prayers; and I tried at moments when

I thought it would not be intrusive to tell her with a look or gesture of my understanding. But in such a passage those of her sort of courage will only walk alone.

At night, when she slept only a few feet away from me, my body's hunger for hers was torment. It was kept in restraint not by the force of my will or of circumstance but by a recognition of her transcendence. She was living far from the body's needs and satisfactions. If, for the time, I could not help or comfort her, I would allow no need of mine to distract her from her dedication.

Chapter 13

I

IT WAS SLACKNESS on my part—perhaps due to my own rather poor physical state, to weariness, a sense of futility —that I allowed the patient to go for two days without an overall examination. On the evidence of temperature and other routine indications the slight improvement in his condition was being maintained. His breathing was normal, he was eating satisfactorily; he said (as usual) that he was feeling quite well. I am not excusing myself, however.

At some time before it was light on the morning of the 7th Gligoric came and wakened me. The prisoner seemed to be ill, he said. I went at once and found him in a fit of coughing, which lasted for half a minute after I had arrived. It was not necessary to take his temperature to see that he was in fever. I examined his chest and my fears were immediately realized: the lung abscess which, in the last weeks, had seemed almost inevitable had suddenly and violently developed.

Some days earlier I had sent Babitch down to Usir to see if he could get me a supply of penicillin for such an emergency as this. He had returned with the report (whether accurate I do not know) that none was to be had from anywhere nearer than Beograd, and that particular licences would be needed. Had I had penicillin at my service now it would have given me a chance to localize the infection, with a view—which the circumstances made hypothetical—to removing later the infected lobe of the lung. As things were, the best I could do was to perform at once the simplest of operations, which needed no anaes-

334

thetic or other aids: with a razor blade which Franziska sterilized for me I opened up the track of the earlier operation to evacuate the pus.

The result was almost dramatically good. In quite a short time the patient was again breathing almost normally, the fever already abating. Next morning he was asking for his usual meal and saying that he meant to get up, be dressed and take his normal exercise. All this of course I forbade.

It was in my mind all that day that Valyevitch would probably be arriving himself to give the next instructions. He did not; but round about six o'clock a message came which Cvito brought to me. Transport would be arriving at eight o'clock to take the prisoner to Sheepcote Valley, where he was to spend the night in the shepherds' hut. In addition to the two guards, Frau Zempelmarck would accompany him, and also Babitch. I was to remain for the night at the tile yard and look after the child Johannes.

In that last instruction there was perhaps some evidence of Valyevitch's gentler side, but I am afraid I do not think so. I think he distrusted me, and imagined that in the final hours I should anticipate by euthanasia the performance he had organized. But here I may be guilty of injustice.

I asked, "Is the messenger still about?"

He was—it was my former guardian Otto, who had come on a bicycle and was being refreshed in the kitchen. I told Cvito to keep him, and after a few words with Franziska I wrote a note addressed to Valyevitch:

'Zempelmarck's condition is giving me serious anxiety. He is not fit to spend the night elsewhere than in his present quarters or without my attendance.'

That note was never answered. I do not know if it got through. Had Josi been the messenger I think it would have been delivered, for I judged him the more intelligent as well as the more biddable of those two boys. Otto may simply not have troubled.

At eight o'clock the transport came—the same truck which had been used for the earlier voyage to the coomb. I had got Siegfried ready. His temperature was hardly above normal and his appearance was such that, coming to him as a stranger, I should not have believed that a crisis had occurred only a few hours before. But I would not allow him to walk to the truck as he wanted to do. Ignoring his bitter protests, Babitch, Gligoric and I carried him there, and I wrapped him up with great care, using every blanket available.

It was only at this point that Franziska lost her equanimity. She went to and fro between the rooms, looking vaguely for trivial possessions, her mind clearly astray from reality. When I told her that the truck was ready to start she said irritably,

"Eugen, can't you see that I'm looking for Siegfried's razor! And something to cook with. There won't be anything to cook with, no one but me thinks of anything."

It was she, I must add, who did think of what I should have forgotten in the shapelessness of that oddly prosaic departure. Johannes, after quietly carrying things to the truck, had gone out of sight and—to be candid—out of my mind. Not out of Franziska's. She found him in the room where his father had been, lying face-down on the bunk the guards had used and drawing on a soap carton. From the door, where I had followed her, I heard her say gently,

"Johannes, dear, you'd like to say good night to Papa?"

He came with us silently and stood at the back of the car while his mother was getting in. She said,

"Siegfried, Johannes has come to say good night."

Johannes, at attention, said, "Good night, my father!"

Siegfried did not seem to hear him. It was necessary for Franziska to call his attention again: "Siegfried, dear, Johannes is saying good night."

"What? Oh, yes—good night, Johannes! Where's

Gligoric got to? Gligoric, are you certain you've put the boots in somewhere? And the uniform?"

The truck moved off, bouncing horribly, with Babitch shouting boisterous farewells. Johannes and I went back into the building, which felt to me like a theatre stage in daylight, empty and unreal.

I gave him his supper, which Franziska had got ready, and laboured to dissipate the silence: I talked, no doubt disjointedly, about the skills and excitements of baseball, to which he responded, "Yes, I understand . . . That must be interesting to see." We cleaned the utensils together and then, without a word from me, he swiftly put himself to bed.

In obedience to a request of Franziska's—given to me with several others—I asked him if he had remembered his prayers. "I expect you'll say a prayer for your mother and father, won't you?"

"My father doesn't want it," he replied. "He has told me so. And in any case there isn't a God to pray to. I've known that for a long time."

2

My own prayers, those which began very early next morning, were an utterance more of the mind's lips than of the thinking mind. The little sleep the night had brought me, ragged and thin, had been sickly with labyrinthine dreams; and now, as I repeated the words of familiar offices, my thoughts would only range towards Franziska as if I could sustain her not with the divine mercy but with my own enveloping love. When I had passed perhaps an hour that way I got up, went out and walked some way up the road. The last stars were giving out, the fresh day was spreading in a naked sky.

It must have been about six when the truck came again.

By then we had breakfasted. I asked the driver what was to happen to Johannes and he replied that the boy was to come with us as far as the village, where 'for the time being' the schoolmaster Fotez had undertaken to look after him. Perhaps I would have the goodness to hurry a little, there was not too much time.

"We're to bring our things?"

"I can't say, Mr. Doctor. There were no instructions."

This problem I found absurdly baffling. I had been unable to think of the future in any practical way—somehow I had vaguely imagined that we should all except Siegfried return here when the business was over. But in fact the question did not greatly matter—my own baggage consisted of nothing except a few small items of clothing and other necessaries borrowed from Dushan, and Johannes's was smaller. We did take these possessions with us, tied with bootlaces in two pieces of newspaper.

"It is growing to be a beautiful day," the driver said as we moved off.

"Yes, indeed."

Yes, a beautiful day. But to my shame and disgust I was shivering. It had come to me with sudden, freshened force that if things went wrong—if Siegfried were not strong enough to stand and if Valyevitch chose to put the harshest interpretation on what Kastelej had decreed—I was likely to miss the end of it . . . And Siegfried himself —would he have noticed that it was growing to be a lovely day?

"You're cold, Sir?" Johannes asked solicitously.

"It is rather chilly. Never mind! What about you?"

He did not answer that, but turned to look out at the back of the truck. "I hope my mother will not get cold," he said, "With my father I suppose it won't matter much longer."

At Dushan's house we both got out of the car. Mica, who was standing in the doorway, said without looking directly at either of us, "This is the boy? Very well, you can leave him with me." In a businesslike way—not roughly—she took him by the arm and I saw her putting him into Sava's chair. There was something like a small feast on the table. "There is some breakfast for you," I heard her say. "You must eat plenty."

I was getting back into the truck when she came out again.

"There's a friend of yours here," she called.

"A friend? Where? Who is it?"

"How should I know? He has come from Zlot, I think. He's talking to Trifunovic down at the police office. He has been told that no one knows where you are."

The driver was getting impatient. "There is not too much time, Mr. Doctor!"

But we were still delayed by Mica, who had her hands on the door of the truck and seemed inexplicably to be on the verge of tears. Stubbornly regarding my chest instead of my face, she said,

"You will see Dushan, he is there already. He's trusting that no harm will come to you. And I—I too."

I said, "Thank you, Frau Fotez."

"And Riko," she added, almost angrily, "he gives his love to you."

We drove on, dangerously fast, up the twisting hill. A friend of mine? What friend? He could only have sprung from some confusion in Mica's rather simple intelligence. At any rate it could not matter. By the time we had turned from the main road I had forgotten the rumour—my mind did not lack other occupation.

3

We stopped where I had previously had my first sight of the coomb. Here already a small group of spectators had arrived: there were perhaps twenty or thirty, with a number of women among them—not, I was thankful to see, any children: they were standing in patient expectation along the wire, just as the Viennese used to line the kerbs before some notability was due to pass, and their faces, which naturally turned towards me as I got out of the truck, gave me the impression of people summoned to a task demanding rare endurance. They did not stare at me for long. My nearness may have troubled them, or perhaps they simply did not recognize me as having any notable part in their business.

At intervals along the road men stood with an air of active purpose: it has occurred to me since that they were there to guard against the risk of police interruption. One of them came and spoke to me. Valyevitch, he said, was waiting for me—he was down with the gun party.

The gun party? At the moment I could not grasp that as an actuality: it was as if a child had told me, 'The demon's castle stands on yonder hill.'

In the dread of some ordeal one's mind is bound by a particular vision—the auditorium filled with sleepy or contemptuous faces, the row of bald examiners behind a table. I had gone on picturing this valley as I had seen it before; and now, in place of a dismal trough scooped from the dark hills, I saw a reservoir of sunlight, its floor brilliant with fresh grass, its sculptured walls a palette of soft greys and ochres lit with shafts of red and vaporous gold. Released from the motion of the truck I could feel the young sun's warmth on my face and hands; the little wind that blew, salt and faintly resinous, brought no more than the roughness of a child's caress; and to this assault upon the senses my mind for a time surrendered. Once again I felt the vibrant liberty which had come from the wine of early morning on my first arrival at Vischak. Within this radiance the toils and cruelties devised in artificial light would not take shape: in a cloak of sleepy exaltation I walked at my own pace down the sloping track and across the elastic turf, where flowers like tiny irises spread a yellow sash against the boulders and where the soft rustle of wind hid every sound but the cry of calandras in flight.

From this somnolence I was roused but leniently when I came to the gun party in their bay: these were men whose faces I knew already—I had seen them at the trial—and they seemed the most harmless of my fellow mortals, simple, good-natured and down-at-heel. True, the sergeant who had formerly displayed the amenities of this station was keeping himself apart, rigid and dutiful; but most of the others, lounging and smoking in a huddle, encountered my gaze as bashfully as schoolboys at the entrance to a ballroom. (For that, I thought, they could be excused. Did it really need a squad like this to take the life of a single, unarmed man?) There were just two rifles to be seen, propped casually against the rock amid a spread of satchels, coats and mugs. The gun, when a movement of one of the men disclosed it, scarcely appeared to me a serious thing—to the layman's eye it was a museum piece, crude in its construction and childishly small.

But the one woman who was there (whether by any licence but her own I do not know) may not have thought so. This was old Julija. She had placed herself a yard away from the gun and was staring at it with a solemn, faintly ludicrous expression of approval, while one of the younger men in a fatherly way was explaining its subtleties:

"Yes, Julija, the belt of cartridges goes in there—you see, it's in already. And the gun is already aimed. All the sergeant will have to do is press down this button—you see?—and a hundred bullets will have gone to the target before he can blink his eyes."

I had some sense of being an intruder on a convivial party. Valyevitch seemed to be nowhere about, but presently I saw him coming from the direction of the shepherd's hut. He walked slowly, in a proprietorial fashion, stopping to pick a flower he saw at his feet: I thought he was rather overplaying his calmness, as young surgeons do when they have to operate before an audience.

"I've been talking to Babitch," he said, coming up to me and offering a cigarette. "He thinks that Zempelmarck is capable of walking."

"Oh, he does?"

"That is, perhaps, rather fortunate for you."

I shrugged my shoulders. He took out a heavy watch, the sort of thing one's grandfather carried. I noticed with a certain pleasure—since I was vexed just then with the man's superiority—that his hand was faintly trembling.

"I want you to have him all ready by eight o'clock," he said. "At eight o'clock exactly I shall blow a whistle. You are then to bring him to where that line of hurdles begins—there, do you see? He is to walk on into that circle we've marked on the ground. That has been explained to him, but you'd better just make sure he's clear about it before you leave him. It's important—for you—that nothing goes wrong at all. You understand?"

I nodded, trying to reflect his solemnity. For some reason my normal cowardice had gone out of action: I thought, 'This is a small and unduly pompous person, he is spoiling the loveliness of the sun.'

Outside the hut I found Dushan waiting to speak to me. He was in a state of nervousness which he scarcely tried to conceal.

"I've brought Father Vladimir," he told me hurriedly. "He's in there now. It may be no use—I doubt if Zempelmarck will accept anything from the Church. But I wanted him at least to have the chance. It was the one thing I could do. Listen—I've been with Valyevitch, I've insisted that you are not to be put in any danger. I've told him that if any harm should come to you I shall make it a police matter. I've as much right to speak as anyone else in Pravnitzar. And in this country there are still some laws."

I thanked him as well as I could—my mind was drifting,

I was not in shape for making speeches. This didn't matter, as he was not listening.

"I want you to understand," he stumbled on, "this thing—this dreadful thing—I think it's a necessity." He was looking past me, along the length of the coomb to where the crowd of spectators, now much swollen, made a grey and mottled fringe to the bank of scrub behind. "These people, it's the only thing that will get them right with themselves. After that we can begin to get ourselves right with God."

He was trembling all over, and I left him in tears when I went on into the hut.

4

There, in the usual cloud of cigarette smoke, Babitch greeted me.

"I think our bastard's going to make it," he said socially, "but not with much to spare. A good thing they fixed it for today—tomorrow, I'd say, the horse wouldn't have run."

"Where is Frau Zempelmarck?" I asked him.

"Out there"—he jerked his head towards the window on the other side—"with a bum-heavy priest. Back in a minute, I expect. He's giving her a Mass or something—I don't know, I'm Orthodox, I never follow such things." He laughed in his nose. "Nor does Zempelmarck, by the look of it. One of those noxious Lutherans, I suppose—he sent the fellow off with a flea in his ear. Come and see him."

He led me through an opening hung with sacking to the larger of the hut's two compartments. Siegfried was at the farther end; and I knew at a single glance (I am speaking literally) that he would never walk to his destination.

He was sitting upright on the edge of a wooden bed-stead: he had the uniform trousers on already and Gligoric, kneeling on the floor, was fastening the boots while Cvito from behind was anxiously combing his hair. The rest of the uniform was on the bed beside him. His face was bloodless, he was breathing with difficulty and obviously with extreme pain.

I went to him quickly and said, "Look, I think you'll want a bit of a rest. There's no hurry about anything."

His only reply was a gesture of pushing me aside.

"Cvito—tunic!" he said.

Cvito looked at me with eyebrows raised. When I answered with a grimace of impotence he picked up the tunic and held it in position.

I did not think that the man gasping for breath on the bed had the strength even to get one arm in its sleeve. He had, though. He got them both in. And then, still sitting rigidly while Cvito did up the buttons, he beckoned me nearer.

"Reichenbach—you've got my memorandum?" There was so little power in his voice that I only just heard it; yet the words were perfectly formed, and it was not what I should have recognized as a sick man's voice. "You're to send it—afterwards—to international jurists, you understand? The whole of the incident needs to be reviewed."

I told him not to worry any more, that I should attend to all that; and he nodded curtly.

"Cap!" he said. And then, "Get me up."

In automatic obedience Gligoric and I lifted him on to his feet. He said,

"Thank you. Very well. I'm going now."

I still had hold of his arm, and I said persuasively, "I'm going to come with you a little way. Then we'll see how you feel. If you——"

"Alone," he said.

Why argue! I stood aside, expecting to see him fall at once. Instead, he took a short pace forward and brought his heels together; did the same again; then, very slowly

344

but with no other sign of weakness, his head erect, every muscle under fierce control, he marched across the room. That was his limit. He stood for a second or two, and it looked as if he were trying to bring his hand to the salute. Then he went over like a felled sequoia, his head striking against a jamb as he dropped to the floor.

There he lay on his back, quite still; and though I thought the last shock must have killed him instantly I went through the routine of opening his clothes and putting my ear to his heart. It was while I was doing this that I heard a voice—his voice—saying quite clearly, with a note of irritation, "Tell them I'm sorry I can't——" Instinctively I answered him as if we were having an ordinary conversation: "That's all right, leave that to me!" and then I looked at his face. He was weeping like a scolded child. "I don't understand," he said. "I don't understand."

It was over then. I remember seeing the uniform cap, which had rolled across the floor, balancing on its rim, and how for some reason that sight appeared to me intensely funny. Again, I remember thinking, when I heard the long blast of a whistle, 'It will need to be a good deal louder, my friend, before your man will hear.'

5

I met Franziska in the outer compartment. My face may have shown her what had happened, for she said immediately, "He has gone?"

"He died a few moments ago," I told her. And then, with the artlessness which afflicts one at those times, I said, "Franziska, I do think we should be intensely thankful."

She turned away; following, I suppose, the instinct to go at once and see him. But at the opening she hesitated, and then came back to me and said, almost inaudibly,

"It isn't what we wanted."

She was staring at my face but not, I thought, seeing it. "They'll be left now," she said, "all those people, they'll be left just as they were before. There's nothing we can do now, nothing we can give them."

Even if I had been perfectly collected I could not have answered that cry; and because of Siegfried's body lying just beyond the partition I did not find it possible to put my arm about her shoulders. I waited for her to ask such comfort of me; and not quite vainly, for she did then take my hands. She said—she was looking in my eyes now— "Eugen, will you go and speak to them? Now, straight away. Will you say anything you can, will you tell them we meant to give them what they asked for, that we still want their forgiveness, their love, Siegfried and I. *Lieber* Eugen, can you tell them that, can you do that for me?"

I said, "Franziska, *mein Herz,* I'll do what you ask me, now and always. Always, all my life."

She put her forehead for an instant against my shoulder; and loosed her hands and went into the other room.

6

I had been in the hut for no more, I suppose, than ten minutes, but when I went outside again the sunlight blurred my eyes as my mind was blurred already. The large and solid thing which was standing on the grass a few yards away made scarcely more than a visual impression on me: I may have thought vaguely that the truck which had brought me had come round to a new position.

A figure came towards me, larger than the common size of Pravnitzar, with the sun behind it. A voice I had once known well called, "Eugen! At last! Boy, am I glad!"

Yes, I had known this man, and loved him. But he did

not belong here, he was part of a life I had almost forgotten. I said in a distracted way, as I stood with his big hands planted on my shoulders, "Ed, I'm sorry, I'll explain about all this. Some time. I'll explain."

"Eugen, you don't have to!" His face was close to mine, immense and fatherly. "We've had it from Dragutin, he's given us the whole story."

Story? What story? What ingenious fabrication had Kurt indulged in now?

"I guess you've had a time!" he said affectionately. "Those bastards at Trieste—God, I wouldn't have thought they had that much nerve. Hell, do they not have laws, do they not have protection, in this place Europe!"

He had taken me by the arm and was leading me towards the car, which shaped itself now as an aged limousine. I recovered sense enough to plant my feet.

"Ed, wait a minute!" It was so long since I had spoken or thought at all in English that I had to grope for my phrases. "There's something I was doing. It's rather urgent. Will you—do you mind waiting?"

"Why, surely!"

You find in no other people a tact so finished, so effortless, as that of Americans. Whatever Kurt Wenzel had told him, he must have been entirely bewildered by the present scene, aching to ask me a hundred questions. But of this he betrayed nothing.

"The day's all yours!" he said simply, smiling, and let go my arm and wandered back to his car.

Ungratefully, I at once forgot him: my only thought was, 'There has been an interruption, it has taken up time.' What mattered then was to do what Franziska had asked me; and though I could see the crowd waiting up on the road with no perceptible movement I had the unreasoning fear that they would scatter before I got so far. I could not move quickly, however. A great part of my mind was tied to the fashioning of what I should say to those people; and

347

the returning lassitude which seemed to come from the sunlight, from the day's still, fresh beauty, was like a drag on all my responses. From the deepest part of my being there was rising—though I would not listen—a whispered song of delight.

I walked, then, slowly, with my face (I imagine) set in a mild and foolish smile, and instinctive timidity keeping me close to the face of the cliff. But for this instinct I should have taken the shortest way to my objective; for in that burdened interval I had ceased to think of the men and weapons stationed in the re-entrant: there was the waiting crowd, there was myself, and nothing worth my attention in between.

So I came upon the firing party with a faint surprise, and they in turn looked with surprise and curiosity at me. The sergeant was standing near the gun; the rest, a few paces behind, were lined up—as I remember—in a crude burlesque of military order; while at the farther side of the opening Valyevitch stood by himself with his hands behind his back, with a face that brought to my mind's eye the Napoleon of Delaroche. To him I nodded, still intent upon my mission.

He took a step towards me and I stopped.

"Well?" he demanded. "What's the delay?"

"Delay?"

"What have you done with him?"

I vaguely realized that this man had some claim on my attention. But chiefly I was annoyed by what I saw as a fresh and needless interruption of my task. I said perfunctorily,

"I've got to speak to those people—it's important. I'll come back later."

"What's happened—what have you done with him?" he repeated, now stiff and grey with anger.

"What, with Zempelmarck? He's dead."

"Dead! How? Why is he dead?"

Still hardly thinking what I said, I replied rather brusquely, "I'm sorry your arrangements have been interfered with. Nature sometimes has plans of her own."

All this, of course, was audible to the men behind. At the edge of my vision I saw their tension abruptly slackening. I heard, "What?" "Yes, dead, I tell you. The doctor says he's died." And now came another voice, one that would have put a mutinous mob to silence:

"*You—loafer—why don't you shoot!*"

I turned to see Julija standing in front of the sergeant, clutching the belly of his blouse and shaking with rage. Disconcerted, smiling foolishly, he was edging back a little. Suddenly she let him go, and with a quickness that astonished me in such a creature she swung round and stooped to the idle gun.

One of the men let out a laugh. One called, "No good, Julija—there's nothing to shoot at!" But that was wrong.

I looked the way Julija was looking, to the line of hurdles they had put for Siegfried's guidance, and I saw what she must have seen: someone, walking with quick and resolute steps, was coming along that line. The low, unclouded sun was right against me: the woman had reached the small, marked circle before I saw who she was, and even then my intelligence did not function—I merely thought, 'There's something she's forgotten, she wants to speak to me.' I had started moving towards her, smiling, when she turned to face us all and stood quite still, with her hands raised as if in a gesture of welcome. It was only then that I felt simultaneously the sound of my own voice screaming, "*Franziska—Achtung!*" and as if in my own head and loins a rattle that tore the sky.

I ran—she must have been in my arms within a second of the fire stopping. But when I saw the completeness of Iulija's work, the shattered breast, the face, the forehead, I could not stay with her for long. Instead, I found that I was walking the way I had first intended, along the green

349

floor of the coomb and slowly up the track to where the spectators stood.

That was almost useless, since I could not speak to them as I had meant to: for some time I sat at the roadside, watching the flag of snow which draped the peak above me and the blue, starlike flowers at my feet, while they with a curious discernment left me alone. The day's loveliness had not altered. Only for me it had become already a transient reflection of what was permanent: my first vision, my first understanding of love. For the blur of white faces about me I found at last a few short words: "She has given you what she could."

Crondall, 1955.
Blechingley, 1957.

A list of fine and classic writing,
both fiction and non-fiction,
with carefully selected reissues of
famous authors and some outstanding
new literary talent.

R.C. HUTCHINSON

'R.C. Hutchinson is one of the very few living English novelists who will be read fifty – perhaps a hundred – years hence' — C. DAY LEWIS

'The best male novelist his generation has produced in England' — COMPTON MACKENZIE

'R.C. Hutchinson is a born novelist . . . a real creative writer, and we must cherish him' — J.B. PRIESTLEY

'Genius is impossible to define . . . but I believe that R.C. Hutchinson had it' — SIR RUPERT HART-DAVIS

A Child Possessed
Johanna at Daybreak
Recollection of a Journey
Shining Scabbard
March the Ninth

ZENITH

A list of fine and classic writing,
both fiction and non-fiction,
with carefully selected reissues of
famous authors and some outstanding
new literary talent.

HENRY WILLIAMSON
author of *Tarka the Otter*

THE FLAX OF DREAM
The Beautiful Years
Dandelion Days
The Dream of Fair Women
The Pathway